W9-BZL-414

HER EVERY PLEASURE

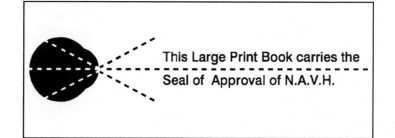

This Large Print Book carries the
Seal of Approval of N.A.V.H.

HER EVERY PLEASURE

GAELEN FOLEY

THORNDIKE PRESS
A part of Gale, Cengage Learning

Detroit • New York • San Francisco • New Haven, Conn • Waterville, Maine • London

BOCA RATON PUBLIC LIBRARY
BOCA RATON. FLORIDA

Copyright © 2008 by Gaelen Foley.
Thorndike Press, a part of Gale, Cengage Learning.

ALL RIGHTS RESERVED
Her Every Pleasure is a work of fiction. Names, characters, places, and incidents are the products of the author's imagination or are used fictitiously. Any resemblance to actual events, locales, or persons, living or dead, is entirely coincidental.

Thorndike Press® Large Print Core.
The text of this Large Print edition is unabridged.
Other aspects of the book may vary from the original edition.
Set in 16 pt. Plantin.
Printed on permanent paper.

LIBRARY OF CONGRESS CATALOGING-IN-PUBLICATION DATA

Foley, Gaelen.
   Her every pleasure / by Gaelen Foley.
      p. cm. — (Thorndike Press large print core)
    ISBN-13: 978-0-7862-9816-7 (alk. paper)
    ISBN-10: 0-7862-9816-2 (alk. paper)
    1. Princesses — Fiction. 2. Women domestics — Fiction. 3. Impostors and imposture — Fiction. 4. England — Fiction. 5. Large type books. I. Title.
   PS3556.O3913H47 2008
   813'.54—dc22   2008009452

Published in 2008 by arrangement with The Ballantine Publishing Group, a division of Random House, Inc.

Printed in the United States of America
1 2 3 4 5 6 7 12 11 10 09 08

BOCA RATON PUBLIC LIBRARY
BOCA RATON, FLORIDA

ACKNOWLEDGMENTS

To my dearest Eric, for your steadfast love and faith in me, and for making me laugh every day.

I would also like to give a special thank you to some very generous people who helped to make this book possible. Argy Darakos, for giving me an insider's view of Greek life and culture. FAM Josh Caldwell, for helping me understand more about how a real warrior thinks and fights. Charlotte Herscher, for staying on this project in spite of major new life adventures. A heap of gratitude also to Signe Pike, Shona McCarthy, Kate Collins, and Nancy Yost for helping to keep things running smoothly in the meanwhile. Last but not least, much love to my girls, Lara Adrian and Kayla Gray, for your friendship, laughter, and moral support when I needed it most.

Most of all, I would like to thank my readers, who have followed the Knight family tales since *The Duke.* Thank you for welcoming my stormy heroes and spunky heroines into your hearts. They belong to you now, and I hope they will keep you company for many years to come like faithful friends.

With love and gratitude,
Gaelen

CHAPTER ONE

England, 1818
Thick woods crowded the lonely road as the royal carriage and its phalanx of armed outriders pounded on through the black autumn night.

Inside the coach, seated across from her lady-in-waiting, the raven-haired Princess Sophia of Kavros stared out the window at the dark tangle of gnarled tree trunks and scraggly branches whizzing by. The tiny candle sconces inside the carriage cast her reflection on the window glass — a face of exotic beauty, with an expression of brooding intensity, lost in her thoughts.

Not much longer now.

In another few hours, they would reach the castle for tonight's secret meeting with the British diplomats.

The rhythmic jouncing of the coach set the beat as Sophia continued mentally rehearsing the impassioned speech she meant to give the Foreign Office lords.

On this, the very eve of her destiny, they could no longer deny her, for at the stroke of midnight, she would turn twenty-one, attaining her legal majority; then they could not brush her off anymore with their excuses and protestations that she was too young to rule.

The time had come for the British government to keep its promise and restore Sophia to her family's throne. Her people would have it no other way, and God knew, they had suffered enough.

Restlessly, she glanced at her attendant. "What is the hour, Alexa?"

The striking blonde jumped when Sophia addressed her.

Of course, they both were nervous about this night, so long in the planning.

There was so much at stake.

Alexa checked her locket-watch. "A quarter past nine, Your Highness. Ten whole minutes since the last time you asked," she added, with a taut smile.

Sophia knitted her eyebrows and flicked an impatient scowl toward the carriage window, but took no offense at her companion's irreverent tone. Alexa had been with her too long to stand on ceremony; her ancestors had been courtiers to the royal family for generations, and had even followed them into exile here in England when the kingdom had fallen to Napoleon. Alexa had been assigned as Sophia's lady-in-waiting when both girls were barely fifteen.

Besides, Alexa always made cheeky jokes when she was on edge.

"Must you look so glum?" her friend attempted again with an air of vague distress, though striving for levity. "Not every girl gets a crown and scepter for her birthday, you know."

"We're not there *yet,*" Sophia answered matter-of-factly.

When one had survived as many shocking twists of fate as she had in her brief years, one learned to take nothing for granted.

The cooperation of the English, for example.

She did not think at this point that they would refuse her outright, now that conditions on Kavros had deteriorated to such a degree. But no doubt the English government would try to keep her on a leash, and for a time, Sophia supposed, she could go along with that, at least until her power was secure.

But then, eventually, they would learn that she had bigger plans in mind than to serve their convenience as a mere royal figure-head.

Her people desperately needed true leadership. Though she had never expected to rule, now, with her father and both elder brothers dead — assassinated — the duties of the royal house fell to her.

Obviously, the task ahead was dangerous. Her family had many enemies, and her entry into public life would bring her to their attention.

But no matter. Big, burly Leon, her chief bodyguard since childhood and current head of security, had prepared her well for all eventualities.

He chose that moment to guide his horse up alongside the carriage, ducking his shaved head down to glance in the window. "How are our ladies doing?" he asked in a jaunty tone over the creaking of the carriage and the pounding of the horses' hooves.

"We're fine," Sophia assured him.

"Only a little impatient," Alexa chimed in with a pointed glance at her.

Leon's sturdy grin had a much-needed calming effect on both girls. "Happy birthday, Your Highness."

"Not *yet!*" Sophia retorted with a twinkling smile.

He'd been saying it all day.

She did not want the moment of her birthday to arrive until she had all those haughty diplomats sitting there in front of her. Then she'd take out her royal birth certificate and jam it down their throats if they dared balk at her claim.

Just then, Leon glanced ahead, his expression sobering. At the same time, Sophia felt the carriage begin to slow.

"What's happening? Have we come to a bridge?"

"There's something in the road," Leon murmured.

"What is it?"

"Not sure. Looks like a broken-down cart. Pull the blinds," he ordered, then clucked to his horse and surged ahead.

More than superstition made Sophia's heart begin to pound.

Alexa had gone ashen as Sophia gestured reassuringly to her to draw the shades on her side of the coach. The girls quickly followed Leon's order, pulling the thin leather carriage blinds over the glassed windows.

"It's p-probably nothing, I'm sure," Alexa whispered with a dread-filled stare at the carriage door, but Sophia wasn't taking any chances. She checked the locks on the door, then reached down and slid the crimson velvet skirts of her formal court gown up a

11

bit, brushing aside the gold lace trim to reach for the knife that she wore strapped around her thigh.

If they think they can take me as easily as my brothers, they're dead wrong.

Alexa's eyes widened as Sophia unsheathed her weapon and calmly opened the hidden compartment under her seat. She pulled out a loaded pistol, handing it to her friend.

Alexa shook her head rapidly, trying to refuse.

"Take it," she ordered.

"But —"

"Just in case. Calm down." Sophia took a second pistol for herself and cocked it.

Father had been poisoned. Giorgios had been drowned. Kristos had been stabbed in some dark Vienna alley. All of Europe's most powerful empires lusted to possess her tiny homeland, a small but strategically placed Greek island chain, gateway between the East and West. Napoleon himself had said that whoever ruled Kavros could control the Mediterranean and thereby dominate Western Europe — which was exactly why the victorious British had claimed it as their protectorate after Bonaparte's defeat.

But throughout those awful years of chaotic war, while Sophia had been growing up in exile in Nottinghamshire, her poor homeland had changed hands several times, first to the French under Napoleon's conquest. Then the imperial Habsburgs of Austria had seized it, only to lose it again to the Russian czar — to say nothing of the ever-present threat from fierce Ali Pasha, the so-called Terrible Turk, as well as the inscrutable sultans of the Ottoman Empire.

Any one of these great powers might still have designs on Kavros, which meant that she and Leon and all her bold Greek guards were on full alert to make sure that she, the next in line for the throne, did not meet some equally gruesome fate.

Well armed now to combat any danger, she pulled her dark woolen cloak — a very special cloak — more tightly around her, the better to conceal her royal garb. Hearing voices outside, Sophia tried to make out the words, willing herself to believe it was some English yeoman farmer whose cart had broken down, like Leon said, on the way to market.

Then she noticed Alexa's stark pallor. Taking pity on her helpless friend, she drew breath to tell her not to worry. Before she could speak, however, their carriage jolted, then rocked to a sudden halt. Gunshots pierced the night. Everything happened at once.

Horses screamed, men roared outside, Alexa shrieked, and Sophia's whole focus homed in on the sounds of the chaos outside.

There was no time to indulge her disbelief.

Her pulse roaring in her ears, Sophia seized her weapons and snapped Alexa out of her screaming hysteria with a clipped order: "Stay calm!"

Her own composure was jarred with a gasp as the butt of a rifle came crashing through the carriage window, partly tearing down the leather blind.

Sophia turned her face away from the spray of shattering glass while Alexa covered her head and dove down on the seat with another shrill scream.

When Sophia looked over again, the carriage blind was still dangling askew, but a black-gauntleted hand and forearm had hooked in through the broken window.

The hand was feeling around for the door's handle, scrabbling at the locks. Her eyes narrowed with a furious gleam. She knew enough to save her bullets.

Clenching her jaw, she brought up her dagger and slashed the intruder's hand hard, slicing through his black leather glove and cutting him all the way up to his forearm. At once, behind the leather blind, a garbled shout of pain rang out. The hand was immediately withdrawn. When the next intruder shot the locks away in the blink of an eye, Sophia was ready for him, too.

The masked man tore open the carriage door and found himself staring down the muzzle of her pistol. With the barest memory of her father and her brothers, she squeezed the trigger and killed him on the spot. Another one took his place as she reached down and picked up the pistol Alexa had dropped. She shot him, too, but her hands were shaking now; it was only a glancing blow.

Though masked like the others, with only a vertical slit for his eyes, his hatred blazed in their black depths.

He cursed at her in what she could have sworn was Turkish, then he leaned in and seized her arm, trying to haul her out of the coach.

When she came at him with her knife, he put a pistol in her face but did not shoot.

So. They want me alive.

In that brief instant as she held her attacker's stare, she saw, in her peripheral vision, Leon gliding up behind the man, but she did not move her eyes, employing all

15

her will to give no sign of his impending doom.

In the next moment, he fell with one of Leon's daggers sunk in the side of his neck.

The man had barely hit the ground and Leon was already hurrying her out of the coach, pulling one of the saddle horses over for her to ride.

"Go, go," he said, holding his side. "Red-seven, do you hear me? Red-seven. Remember, Highness?"

"Red-seven?" she breathed. "We've never had to use that code before!"

"But we need it now," he said fiercely. "Do you understand me?"

"Yes, yes, I remember it — Leon, are you hurt?" she cried.

"Never mind me, it's nothing, now go!"

She shook off her hesitation, dimly registering the thought that she had never seen that look on Leon's tough, lined face before.

It was as close to cold fear as she had ever seen him. That was when the full realization hit her: Her security had been breached. Penetrated.

The code red-seven meant her men could no longer guarantee her safety. They could only give her cover so she could flee. "Alexa —"

"It's you they're after. You're no good to

16

your people dead. Now ride!" he bellowed.

Years of obeying Leon's blunt orders launched her up into the saddle. She swung up onto her bodyguard's horse and gathered the reins. Meanwhile, Leon reached back into the coach, and then handed her the knapsack and a compass.

Sophia nodded.

"I'll see you when I can."

"Behind you!"

Leon whirled around and punched another masked man in the face, once more swallowed up in the fray while Sophia glanced at the compass and turned her horse due north.

She started to ride in that direction, but another attacker tried to grab the bay's bridle. She wheeled the animal around quickly and kicked the masked man in the chin. His head jerked up and he fell back.

Then she squeezed the horse's sides and galloped away.

Red-seven, red-seven. She knew the protocol as well as she knew her own name. They had drilled it enough. Due north, two miles — whether there was a road or not. In this case, not. She charged her horse straight at the stone fence girding some farmer's meadow. The leggy bay leaped, soaring through the air, and landed in the tall grasses, barreling on.

Sophia refused to heed the bullets chasing them. It seemed her attackers were not too particular about taking her alive, after all. She could hear them chasing her into the field. When she glanced over her shoulder, there must have been ten of those masked blackguards vaulting over the stone fence and charging after her on foot, shooting as they advanced. Her guards stayed on them, giving her cover as Sophia raced the bay gelding across the darkened countryside.

She did not slow even when she was out of the range of their guns, keeping mindful of the distance her horse was covering. Her heart still thundered even as the sounds of the battle faded into the distance behind her. She could hear her own panting breath, and her mount's.

Dear God, was Leon badly hurt? He was more like a father to her than her own regal sire had been. Her heart clenched with pain; it was too awful to think about leaving her friends behind. They had long been a tight-knit group in their exile.

Everything in her screamed to go back and help them — join the fight — but if she returned, Leon would never forgive her. That was the one great sin he had vowed she must never commit. That, he said, would be suicide.

No, she knew she had to trust her gruff old lion's advice. There was more at stake than just their lives. All of Kavros was depending on her.

Shoving her friends out of her mind for the moment, she turned her attention to her path. She could agonize with worry for them later. Right now, she needed a clear head in case some of her attackers had managed to follow her. Two miles north of the site of the ambush, she slowed her horse for a moment, glanced again at her compass, and looked at the horizon. *Northwest now for three miles.*

Always take a circuitous route in case you're being followed. All of Leon's training was indelibly imprinted on her mind. She turned her horse northwest and urged the powerful animal once more to a spirited gallop.

The darkness aided in her escape, helping to hide her from her enemies, but it did make her flight more dangerous, considering her horse could step in some rodent's hole at any time.

Thankfully, her luck held. The final leg of the red-seven protocol was a stretch of two more miles, heading due west. For this portion of her journey, she came to a lonely country lane.

It was very dark.

She slowed the horse; not only was the animal a little winded, but the narrow road was rocky, and a mount with an injured leg was not going to help her outrun whoever was trying to kill the next heir of Kavros.

Unfortunately, it was a popular sport.

For her part, her thoughts wandered back to the attacker that she had shot. She was not sorry, per se, but pulling the trigger left her a little queasy. She practiced her skills all the time, but she had never had to kill anyone before. She shuddered, thrusting off the memory.

As Leon had taught her, sometimes it simply came down to you or them. At length, Sophia looked over her shoulder again, and still there was no sign of anyone following her.

Out of immediate threat of harm, the aftertaste of fear crept in; a stark sense of vulnerability began to grow. She swallowed hard and gave her horse a frightened pat on the neck to show her gratitude for their escape.

"Good boy," she whispered. "Any idea where we are?"

All she knew was that the next step in the protocol was for her to get rid of the horse. She hated to part ways with the trusty animal after that ordeal, but the horse would keep moving, and if her attackers were following its tracks, they'd follow it instead of her.

She'd continue on foot.

She recalled the final step that Leon had included in all their drills. *Lastly, find the safest place you can near these coordinates and hide until we come and find you. Do not come out for anyone else,* he had warned. *Stay hidden until you have visual confirmation that it's really one of us. Do not allow yourself to be deceived.*

"Well, here we are," she said to the horse in a shaky whisper. She pulled the bay to a halt after they had traveled the country lane for about two miles. "It's time to hide. Let's get you out of here." Dismounting, she landed on legs that still felt wobbly.

After quickly unsaddling the bay, she took off his bridle to leave no evidence of the horse's origin.

"Thanks," she murmured, patting the strong animal's velvety neck one last time. Then reluctantly she moved back and gave the bay a slap on the rump. "Go on, boy. Move on!"

The horse just stood there, a tall, fine bay with a white star on his forehead. He tossed his head, as if a little doubtful that she'd survive without him.

"What are you, part mule? You're free to go!" Sophia exclaimed. "Shoo!" When she gave him another hearty slap on his haunches, the bay snorted and trotted off into the shadows down the road.

Sophia frowned, but when she could no longer hear the horse, she drew her dark cloak around her, feeling very much alone.

No matter. Other princesses might need a knight's rescuing, but she, by God, would never be one of those silly twits stuck, helpless, in a tower.

Glad that she still had her knife, Sophia dropped the compass into her knapsack of supplies and then tossed that over her shoulder. Concealing the horse's tack with some leaves and branches, at last she trudged off through the dark woods to search for a good hiding place — somewhere she could hunker down in safety for a few days, if need be.

Lord, in a place like this, she doubted she'd have to worry about anyone spotting her. *Leon, where have you sent me to?*

She was quite in the middle of nowhere.

Just when she was beginning to fret that she might not find a proper hiding place anywhere near these coordinates, she spotted a clearing ahead. A dilapidated old barn stood alone on the brow of a hill. *That should serve.* It looked abandoned.

Going closer, she halted at the tree line like a deer, first studying the moonlit clearing around the barn, making sure it was deserted before emerging from the woods and hurrying toward it.

A few moments later, knife in hand, she slipped stealthily inside the barn. No one was there, not even any animals. Spiders, maybe, she thought. A few sleeping swallows nesting in the eaves. She crept deeper into the old barn, glancing around for a quick survey of the place.

Well, it was no palace, she thought, but it would do.

In short order she decided that the loft was her best bet. Not only would she be safer up there if anyone wandered in, but it would also give her a better view of the surrounding countryside. That would help her get her bearings in this strange place, and more important, if anyone had followed her from the site of the attack, her perch up in the loft would give her a higher vantage point so she could see them coming.

Gripping the ladder, she climbed, moving confidently with her knapsack over her shoulder. Her thoughts were already revolving around the question of who was behind that attack.

Ali Pasha. She was sure it had to be him, damn that blackguard. Her late mother, Queen Theodora, had spit on the ground every time the Terrible Turk's name was mentioned.

The Ottoman powers had swallowed up most of Greece long ago, but what few parts had remained free, Ali Pasha had been laying claim to with his barbarous Albanian fighters over the past few decades, chasing Greek nobles like Leon from their homes. Sophia would have bet her eyeteeth that now Ali Pasha wanted Kavros, too.

Upon reaching the dusty hayloft, she continued on grimly with her final few procedures.

First, she set her knapsack aside, then took off her woolen cloak and laid it out on the ground. Carefully wielding her knife, she slit away the liner, revealing the set of plain peasant clothes hidden inside.

Stealing a nervous glance around, she quickly changed clothes, taking off her regal velvet finery in favor of simple garb befitting some rural dairymaid.

One day, she thought as she buttoned up her drab gray skirts, *I will probably laugh about this . . .*

No matter. At least she was alive.

The next step was the efficient removal from her person of all signs of her royal origins — clothes, papers, and jewelry, her signet ring, even her solid gold hair ornament with the family crest emblazoned on it. She unfastened it and shook her long black tresses free from their neat chignon.

Wrapping up all her telltale items in the discarded lining of her cloak, she looked around for a suitable place to stow them and hid the lot under a pile of musty old hay.

This left her with her knife, her knapsack of supplies, and the woolen outer layer of her cloak. The latter item she spread out over the hay, making a little place where she could rest.

Then she took the canteen out of her knapsack and helped herself to a swallow of water, but not too much. She would have to ration it in case her guards took longer than a day or so to find her. The knapsack also held several items of food and a folding telescope.

Putting her water away, she reached for the spyglass and carried it over to have a look out the little window on the east wall of the loft.

She twisted the telescope open and lifted it to her eye. She was pleased to see she had

25

a good view from here of a portion of the moonlit road by which she had come.

Beyond that, there was little to hold her interest. Trees. Sheep. No sign of a village. Just a dark, peaceful countryside slumbering under an onyx sky spangled with bright autumn stars.

After a moment, she crossed the loft to check the view out the opposite window. *Ah.* At least there was something here to see.

Her gaze homed in at once on the lonely ruins of a little Norman church just a stone's throw across the fields. She had lost her faith a long time ago, but, all things considered, it was comforting to see it there.

Carved stone angels, eerie in the moonlight, stood sentry by its crumbling entrance.

Suddenly, Sophia noticed the feeble glow of light dancing through the ancient stained glass window where a portion of the stone wall was still intact. She furrowed her brow. *Someone was moving around in those ruins — at this hour?*

Lifting her spyglass once more to her eye, she peered into the sanctuary's broken shell.

Staring for all she was worth, she suddenly caught sight of a man dressed all in black.

He was lighting candles at the altar.

She froze, studying him through her spy-glass.

With a brooding stare, seemingly lost in his thoughts, the formidable stranger lit each creamy candle on the iron rack, one by one, until their flickering glow illuminated his steely profile — stern nose, a hard, unsmiling mouth. A short scruff of a beard roughened his strong jaw, while his jet-black hair was overgrown, a rebellious tangle that curled over the back of his coat collar. Her heart pounded. Who, what, was this man?

Was he a threat?

The light was too dim and the distance too great to judge for certain. Perhaps, since he was wearing all black, he was a priest — but, no. On second thought, he looked more sinner than saint. Or rather, like a lost soul.

Watching him, Sophia did not know *what* to make of the man. He was very handsome, with the look of a gentleman, yet something in his countenance was hard and cold and fierce.

Clearly, this lonely place was not quite as deserted as she had thought.

His task completed, the stranger stood there with a downward gaze for another long moment, seemingly a million miles away, and then abruptly, she lost him from view as he moved away from the iron rack of candles.

When she found him again with her spyglass, he was stalking out of the church.

She felt a small easing of relief inside her tense body to see him heading off in the opposite direction.

There must be a house around here somewhere.

When he had disappeared past the angle of the loft's window, Sophia lowered the telescope from her eye with an uneasy frown, wondering if it was really safe to stay here.

Like her, the man appeared to have larger matters on his mind. Caught up in his own troubles, he seemed unlikely to come into the old abandoned barn.

But should she take that chance?

The alternative certainly sounded worse. She did not want to be wandering out on the road in case her attackers managed to track her this far.

Gnawing her lip, she scanned the landscape, debating with herself on which was the lesser of two evils.

After a moment, she let out a low sigh and decided to stay. The vicious creatures who had attacked her carriage clearly meant her serious harm, while the solitary stranger in the church had seemed entirely distracted by his own private demons.

He'd probably never notice she was here at all before her guards found her again — and even if he did, there was no reason to assume he'd pose a threat. True, he had a dangerous look, but if he was out at this hour visiting a church, albeit a broken-down one, lighting candles for some unknown cause, then that at least suggested that he had a conscience, which was more than she could say for her as-yet-unknown enemies.

Unknown? she corrected herself bitterly. *They're Turks. I am sure of it.* The European countries who might otherwise have been her top suspects were as tired out from the nearly twenty years of war that had just ended as England was.

Suddenly, she heard something stirring behind her.

Sophia whirled around, bringing up her knife.

Searching the shadows, her heart pounding, she saw no one. Scanning the loft, a bit of movement near the base of the haystack caught her eye.

What?

Abruptly, a small laugh escaped her. She lowered her knife and put her hand to her heart with a smile, her startled pulse beginning to slow back to normal.

Kittens.

Little puffs of fur, baby barn cats, apparently out on a grand nocturnal prowl.

The three fuzzy kittens had discovered her knapsack, she saw, shaking her head. One had crawled inside of it, leaving only his stripy tail sticking out.

The tail disappeared as the contents of her knapsack moved around. She smiled wryly as the disappearing kitten came shooting out of her knapsack again, pouncing on his brother. They tumbled.

Well. Not quite the guardian angels she could have used at the moment, but at least they would keep her amused.

With a final glance over her shoulder at the lonely church, Sophia put the intriguing stranger out of her mind and went to befriend the fuzzy trio of venturesome little clowns.

Anything to distract her from her dread over the fate of her friends. Surely they would be all right. Her Greek guards were very well trained. Still, terror had begun to creep in belatedly as the aftermath of the night's clash.

She had known, of course, that she would be a target. She just hadn't expected it to start so soon.

As she sat down on her cloak near the

tumbling, shy kittens, she couldn't help wondering who she thought she was fooling, or how she ever had dreamed this plan would work, this plan to claim the throne her father had lost. In this dark, lonely hour after what had happened back on the road, she could not seem to stop the doubts that came rushing in. Who was she to rule a country? A mere girl!

Worst of all, the secret truth was that she hardly even remembered Kavros, for she had been all of three years old when her family had been forced to flee — though she could still hear the cannons' booms on that terrifying night. Yes, she possessed the royal blood, but good heavens, she was only a young woman, barely twenty-one!

With that, Sophia abruptly remembered that it was her birthday.

She let out a low, cynical snort and lay back on her cloak, stretched out on the hay.

So much for her grand notions of shoving her demands down the diplomats' throats.

Ah, maybe the dairymaids of this world were the lucky ones, she mused while one of the kittens came over and introduced himself with a tickle of whiskers.

Such simple cares. Nobody trying to kill you . . .

As she had told Alexa a hundred times,

being a princess was so much harder than it looked. She closed her eyes, refusing with all her might to succumb to frightened tears.

All of a sudden, she laughed aloud as the lively little kitten bit her hand with its pin-prick teeth.

Well, it appeared Leon was right. *Trust no one.* Even a tiny fur-ball.

She scooped the kitten up and gave it a stern look, but it continued gnawing merrily on her knuckle.

Chapter Two

Nights were hard, for when the world was dark, his brooding thoughts churned with visions of the strange things he had glimpsed beyond the threshold of death's door, and gnawing uneasiness for the blood he had spilled in his past career.

Whether he was bound for heaven or hell, nothing was clear yet beyond his certainty that, surely, he had slipped through Death's bony fingers for a reason. There must be something more that he was meant to do — but whatever it was, he only hoped in the long, dark stretch before dawn, that it would be enough to repay his debt for all the killing.

He had been a soldier before he had come here to this lonely place. A soldier all his life. A very good one.

He was not at all sure what he was now, but somehow, the morning light always managed to restore his peace of mind.

A new day was no trifling thing to take for granted. Not when you knew that, by all rights, you should be dead.

Major Gabriel Knight stepped out onto the flagstone stoop of the old farmhouse and tasted the chilly, fresh morning air with a slow and cautious inhalation.

It felt so good to be able to breathe again without pain.

He tilted his head back, savoring the sunlight on his face. The new day brought the trace of a hard-won smile to his lips as he stretched his arms up over his head and loosened his shoulders, still a bit sore from yesterday's grueling efforts at regaining his full strength.

Dropping his arms to his sides again, he rested his hands on his waist and surveyed the picturesque scene of rustic tranquility before him.

It was so beautiful here. So peaceful.

Born and bred in British India, he had only arrived in England a couple of months ago and was slowly getting used to this tame, tidy country with its hawthorn fences and patchwork fields. Too much safety felt so odd. But it was undeniably lovely. Wisps of fog still hung in the green dips between the rolling hills, and past the ancient stone church, he spotted his white horse knee-deep in late season wildflowers, grazing in a dewy field.

His lazy smile widening, Gabriel shook his head. That horse was going to get fat.

Leaving the stoop where the faded black slab had eroded into a dip from centuries of footsteps passing over that one spot, he strode out to carry on with his morning duties.

They were very different from what they once had been, but he had left that life behind, had put away the lethal tools of his trade and all the bloodied symbols of his grand warrior pride.

His martial glory no longer signified.

He had been so driven then, as if he'd been striving for some sort of terrible godhood. But now he knew all too well he was only a man. A man whose eyes had been opened.

If a part of him sensed that fate still had more in store for the warrior in him, he shied away from that whisper of intuition. He had been given a second chance at life and did not intend to waste it. Few mortals got the chance to see what lay beyond the grave, but Gabriel had glimpsed enough to grasp that a wise man savored the simplest pleasures of everyday life — while it lasted.

Committed to doing just that, first, he

pumped water from the well, mesmerized as he watched its bright crystal flow streaming from the spigot. Things he would have taken for granted in the past sometimes astounded him now with their beauty. Water. God knew, he had led his men across enough Indian deserts to know that water was life.

As he pumped the handle, he noted that he felt no further strain in his solar plexus. He was almost healed, almost back to the state of his former power. The question was, how would he use it this time? No answers, still. *Be patient,* he told himself for the thousandth time. His answers would come.

Next he rationed out grain for his horse, inhaling the pungent smell of the sweet feed. Carrying it out to the paddock, a mere shake of the bucket was enough to bring Thunder trotting over with a hungry whicker. Gabriel set the bucket down before his kingly steed, then he noticed the deer had been at the salt lick again.

Well, the horse didn't mind sharing that. With a hearty pat on the neck, he left his trusty mount greedily crunching his grain and made his next stop at the chicken coop. While the clucking hens rioted over the handfuls of seeds he threw down, he collected a few of the eggs, so smooth to the touch. He brought them inside to Mrs. Moss, his gray-haired, ill-tempered house-keeper, who was bustling about the kitchen, just as she did every morning.

"Have you got the milk yet, sir?"

"I'm going for it now," he replied, taking the pail with him. No doubt the woman thought him very odd, a gentleman-tenant who did his own chores rather than bringing a horde of servants with him. Army life made a man supremely self-sufficient, but more than that, Gabriel had just wanted — needed — to be alone.

He strode back outside and found the farm's pair of docile cows in the meadow under the massive oak tree. When he had milked them, he brought the pail back inside, but before handing it over to Mrs. Moss, he poured some of its creamy contents into a bowl. The old woman frowned in disapproval, but Gabriel ignored her and carried the milk outside to feed the kittens.

Their mother had been killed by a fox, so he had moved the tiny orphans into the hayloft to save them from a similar fate. He'd have liked to bring them into the house, but Mrs. Moss forbade it. She said they'd get the carpets full of fleas.

As he walked into the silent, musty barn, Gabriel mused on how his old chums from the regiment would have laughed to see "the Iron Major" playing nursemaid to a troop of rowdy kittens. But no matter, he thought as he climbed the ladder, balancing the bowl of milk in one hand. He could laugh at himself more easily now, too.

Besides, though he would not have admitted it for the world, the kittens were far better company than Mrs. Moss and all her grumbling. Indeed, his only complaint about life at his rented farmhouse was that, sometimes, after these many weeks of self-imposed isolation, now and then, the loneliness grew dismal, especially with winter coming on.

His brother's house was only a couple hours' ride if he desired conversation, and London was only another hour beyond that, but Gabriel could not think of anyone he really wanted to be with. He had tried a few weeks ago to find amusement in London, but even in a crowded ballroom full of beautiful women, agreeable chaps, and all of his excellent family, he had gone through the motions, feeling more alone than ever.

So, once more, he had retreated to his rustic sanctuary. Maybe the soul took longer to heal than the body.

When he reached the top of the ladder and climbed up into the hayloft, two of his furry charges came scampering toward him, already mewling piteously for the milk, but Gabriel frowned. The orange one was missing.

Hm. He hoped the kitten hadn't got caught somewhere or hurt itself. "Kitty? Where are you?" he murmured, pacing slowly through the hayloft in search of the orange tabby.

Rounding the haystack, Gabriel suddenly stopped in his tracks. His jaw dropped as he discovered the orange kitten — snuggled up fast asleep on the shoulder of an equally sleeping girl. Gabriel forgot to breathe as he stared at her.

He had no idea what the blazes she was doing here, but her beauty sent a wave of amazement washing over him.

Smoother, rounder than the eggs, her curves entranced his eyes, her fresh skin creamier than the new-made milk he'd brought. Her sleeping innocence was sweeter than the water from the well. He wanted to wake her, to touch her, to taste her — but for a very long moment, Gabriel couldn't stop staring.

Who was she?

The girl had made a little nest for herself in the hay, a rough woolen cloak wrapped around her for a blanket. Her skirts had ridden up over one knee, exposing a stretch of shapely calf.

Gabriel crouched down slowly as he studied her, transfixed.

She was humbly dressed, a simple country girl, perhaps, but she had an exotic look, with her thick, wild tangle of dark curls. Now noting the soft tan undertones in her complexion, he wondered if she was of Gypsy blood, for she certainly wasn't the typical English rose.

She had very black eyebrows and equally black, luxurious lashes, a pronounced nose, sharp cheekbones, her jawline delicate yet crisply defined. Her big, pouty lips were slightly parted as she slept.

He swallowed hard, tamping down a surge of long-forgotten desire, but as his fascinated stare traveled over her, it slowly dawned on him why she had come.

Ah, damn that scoundrelly brother of his.

The old farm was too remote for this girl to have wandered in by accident. No, his blasted brother Derek must have sent her, devil take him.

Gabriel still remembered Derek's roguish threat some time ago. *"I shall hire some gorgeous wench with no morals to come and take care of you."* By which he meant, of course, a girl to slake his carnal drives. *"I am a kind and thoughtful brother, am I not?"*

40

Damned cruel is more like it, he thought with a mild scowl, irked by this oh-so-delectable temptation.

For God's sake, he wasn't a saint.

Of course, he knew Derek meant well. It was no mystery that his whole family was worried about him, his younger brother most of all.

Not just a brother but his closest friend and fellow officer from the regiment back in India, Derek was a worldly man of sturdy common sense and did not understand Gabriel's spiritual experiment in this place.

But as he gazed at the girl that Derek had chosen for the job of servicing him, Gabriel could say one thing for his brother: That devil certainly knew his taste in women.

This lovely wench could have him eating out of her hand if he wasn't careful.

Well, she was going to have to leave, he thought with stoic resolve, because for a man bent on redemption, she might prove more temptation than his starved male senses could endure.

He shuddered, then tamped down his lust with stringent self-discipline. Concluding that the time had come to wake her and send her on her way, he cleared his throat a bit, politely.

"Miss? Ahem, Miss. Er, good morning?"

Gingerly, he poked her dainty shoulder with one finger, trying to wake her. "I beg your pardon —" he started to say as her eyes flicked open, still unfocused with sleep.

But the second she saw him, she let out a gasp and suddenly pulled a knife on him out of nowhere.

His eyes flared. His battle-honed senses reacted to the weapon automatically. He grasped her wrist in the blink of an eye.

She flailed with a curse in some foreign tongue and a scuffle ensued.

"Let — go of me!" she shouted after a moment.

"Drop your weapon!" he roared, at which point she actually tried to cut him!

The next thing he knew, Gabriel was on top of her, holding her pinned flat on her back in the hay, his hands clamping her wrists to the floor, restraining the wild chit.

"Hold still!"

"Get off me, you devil! I *order* you to release me, this *instant!*" she yelled at him, trying to thrash her way free, to no avail.

"Oh, you order me, do you?" he countered mildly. He was breathing hard, not entirely from exertion, and yet her fiery command took him aback. As a warrior from whom countless men had fled in battle, he was rather amused by her brash readiness to try to gut him.

"I'm warning you — let me go!"

"Why, so you can try to stab me again?" he taunted in a softer tone, trying to ignore the sweetness of her luscious curves squirming beneath him.

She paused in her fight, staring up at him with big, brown eyes full of fire, and as her soft, lush chest heaved against his, it took all his steely will to remember his new ascetic creed.

Sophia swallowed hard, panting with some wild reaction more full-blooded than simple fright as she gazed up into his eyes. Deep blue eyes of piercing cobalt intensity.

The only time she had seen that brilliant shade of blue before was in the waters around her homeland. The half-forgotten memory gave her a pang. Meanwhile, the events of the previous night all came flooding back. For a moment there, she hadn't been sure where she was or why.

But now, of course, she recognized her captor as the stranger she had seen last night lighting candles in the ruined church. At least she hadn't been found by the masked men who had attacked her carriage. Under the circumstances, she supposed it could have been worse.

"Care to tell me what you're doing in my barn?" he asked in a low, cultured murmur.

"Sleeping — obviously," she retorted.

"Trespassing."

"No! I haven't done anything wrong!"

"Attempted murder?"

Well, he had a point there.

"You startled me," she conceded with regal hauteur, chagrined by her powerless position.

"Obviously," he drawled back at her.

"Humph," she answered, quite unused to being treated this way, but on the other hand, "startled" was an understatement.

He had terrified her, waking her from a deep sleep that way, and she had reacted accordingly. At least now, finally waking up, she had a clearer sense of her situation. "Would you mind getting off of me, please?" she asked through gritted teeth.

He lifted his eyebrows politely. "Are you ready to put down your knife?"

Sophia wasn't sure, but she knew when she was being mocked. "There is no need to be rude."

"Sorry, I haven't had my coffee yet, and it's been awhile since anyone's tried to kill me."

"If I had *wanted* you dead, you would *be* dead!" she informed him fiercely.

He let out a low, charming laugh, as though she had said something clever.

Sophia narrowed her eyes at him, then looked away in simmering mutiny, refusing to acknowledge the fact that up close, her captor was sinfully handsome. Especially when he laughed.

"Now, young lady, hear me well. You had better drop your weapon," he advised her, taking a no-nonsense tone. "There is no need to resort to violence, all right? I am not going to hurt you. But if you try to stab me again, I may dangle you off the hayloft by your feet till you behave."

Her gaze flew to his again as she gasped. "You wouldn't dare!"

"Meow." The tiny orange kitten chose that moment to intervene, mewling at the man and rubbing its sides back and forth affectionately against his big shoulder.

He glanced wryly at the baby cat, as though he realized with some chagrin that its adoration of him did not make him look exactly scary. But maybe he did not want her to be scared of him, after all, for he began having a conversation with the kitten. "No, I brought you your milk," he chided, as if he could understand its pitiful cries. "What else do you want? It's your own fault you missed breakfast. You were hiding here with her. Not that I blame you, understand."

Sophia pressed her lips together, determined not to smile, but when the man turned from the kitten and looked at her again, he knew perfectly well that he had charmed her. That cobalt sparkle in his eyes beguiled her; she turned her face away to hide the twitching of her lips.

"These cats," he murmured softly. She could feel his gaze traveling down the curve of her neck. "They bully me so."

She swallowed hard, striving to ignore the silken warmth of his breath against her neck and the curious sensations that his big, muscled body roused atop her. The feelings were not entirely unpleasant.

"Why don't you find these kittens new homes if they are such a bother?" she suggested tartly, still refusing to look at him.

"But they were born here. I am only a gentleman-tenant."

Gentleman? The word got her attention as it signaled his honorable intent. Slowly, cautiously, Sophia met his curious gaze from the corner of her eye.

"I will free you if you promise not to kill me," he offered in a sardonic murmur. "I give you my word as a gentleman that you will not be harmed."

What choice did she have?

Sophia said nothing, but gave him a hard look, then uncurled her fingers and let her knife plunk down onto the floorboards in a gesture of good faith.

"Ah," her handsome captor said in a husky tone of approval. "How novel. A woman of sense."

With extreme caution, Gabriel loosened his grip around her delicate wrist by degrees. Freeing her knife-hand was easy, however, compared to the self-restraint it took to ease his weight up off her warm, slim, nubile, young body. Every male atom of his being cried out to lower his head instead and claim her lovely mouth.

Of course, that might have got him stabbed. Even a harlot wanted a man to wait until he was invited.

With a heave of effort, Gabriel backed away from the raven-haired temptress; she did the same, both of them kneeling on the floor with its thin scattering of hay.

Her gaze locked with his; the girl's wary brown eyes tracked his movements as he rose slowly, moving carefully, not wishing to startle her again. He went instead to look after the kittens, giving her a moment to recover from their clash.

"You're pretty quick with that knife," he

remarked, walking over with measured paces to see if there was any milk left in the bowl.

"Practice," she answered in a low, rather defiant murmur.

Fiery, this one.

"I take it Derek sent you."

"Derek?"

"My brother." He crouched down and pushed the black kitten and the gray tabby away from the bowl so the little orange one could drink some of the milk, as well.

"Your brother," she echoed slowly, tasting his words.

"The other Major Knight, my dear. The man who hired you to come here and, ah . . . serve me, I presume." His glance flicked over her body. He couldn't seem to help it.

"Oh, right. Derek," she answered with a vague nod. "Of course."

"He does tend to think he's amusing." Gabriel lowered his head, watching the kittens to try to keep his stare off her. "Unfortunately, it isn't going to work. You are beautiful, God knows, but you can go back to London or wherever it was that he found you, for I . . ." — He faltered, then redoubled his resolve — "I do not require a bedmate at this time."

■ ■ ■ ■

A bedmate?

Sophia stared at him, her eyes wide, her whole body motionless with shock.

Was *that* what he thought she was doing here?

Zounds! He thought she was a hussy?

Her royal sire would be turning in his grave — and if Leon ever heard the cheeky blackguard imply such a thing, her old lion would pound him into the dirt!

Well, at least he would try. Even Leon might have a time of it with this one, she conceded, her gaze trailing over his formidable physique. The "gentleman-tenant" was a towering wall of muscle, six-foot-four at least, of pure iron. She could not believe she had attacked him and lived.

Still, she quickly realized that *his* explanation for her presence here was safer than the truth — especially since he claimed he did not need her "services" at this time.

Really, a girl could take insult at being so easily refused, she thought wryly.

"I see," she replied, playing her cards close to the chest. Heart pounding, she hid her astonishment, still not quite sure how to react.

He really was very mysterious. Who was he, and why would his brother send him a girl? she wondered. The most puzzling part, however, was his refusal.

Alexa said all men wanted sex constantly, and she would know. Sophia shrugged it off and supposed she should count herself lucky.

Then his gaze flicked over her peasant disguise with a mildly pitying look that stung her royal pride. "You can keep the money," he said gently, "whatever my brother has paid you. I'm sorry you've wasted your time."

Her swift indignation over his low view of her gave ground to more practical worries as he continued. "I know it must have been a very inconvenient journey for you, coming all the way out here. Come," he said, gesturing toward the ladder. "I will pay your ticket for the stagecoach back to London. We'll need to hurry to get you to the coaching inn on time —"

"Wait!" she blurted out.

"What is it?"

She stared at him, tongue-tied. According to protocol, she had to stay put at *these* coordinates until her bodyguards found her!

Good God, she could not let him kick her out now. Those vicious creatures who had attacked her carriage last night might still be out there somewhere on the hunt for her. Last night, at least she had had the cover of darkness to hide her, but now it was broad daylight, and if she came across her enemies out on the road, she doubted her peasant disguise would be enough to save her. She didn't even have a horse now on which to escape them if they spotted her. She still had her knife, but this large fellow had just reminded her afresh that, as good as she was with a blade, sheer male strength could still overpower her.

He had been watching the play of emotion on her face and now a curious frown had spread across his own. "Is something wrong?"

"Are you so eager to get rid of me?" she countered, attempting a smile. *Please don't kick me out.*

She didn't dare go wandering down that country road alone. It would be extremely stupid to try it. She had to wait for her bodyguards to come and escort her on to the castle.

She was certain it wouldn't be long. Last night, her men had been routed by the ambush, but by now, they would have regrouped.

Staving off fear, she insisted to herself that

everyone surely had come through the ambush all right. If it turned out not to be so, she would deal with it when they were all reunited and she knew the facts. God knew, if there had been casualties, she had enough practice at grieving. She ought to be an expert at that by now.

Alas, the keeper of kittens seemed all too eager to be rid of her. "I'm sorry, my dear. I'm flattered by your, er, enthusiasm, truly, but this is just one of my daft brother's practical jokes," he said in chagrin.

"You really find me that unappealing?" she exclaimed.

"No!" he vowed, sending her a searing glance. "It isn't that at all."

Sophia furrowed her brow. There had to be some way that this stubborn chap could be persuaded to let her stay for just a few hours.

Unfortunately, she couldn't tell him the truth.

Though he now seemed more trustworthy than he had at first, keeping her identity a secret was one of Leon's strictest rules. Her guards were risking too much for her sake for Sophia to repay them by ignoring the procedures she had promised to adhere to.

Oh, dear. What was she to say?

He was looking at her curiously. "Are you

that eager to . . . bloody hell, Derek told you about the Kama Sutra, didn't he?"

"The what? No — I mean — that is to say —" Her cheeks blazed crimson. Oh, for heaven's sake!

"Because I don't do that sort of thing anymore. I mean, there's more to life than mindless pleasure, isn't there?"

Sophia wanted the earth to part and swallow her like one of Greece's countless little earthquakes. She cleared her throat and cast about for her dignity. "I assure you, sir, I respect your wishes and will do my best not to molest you. But you see, I only just got here, didn't I? And it's such a long, inconvenient journey back to London, as you said. I just woke up. I scarce know where I am." Lord, this conversation was a chess game. "Would you mind terribly if I stayed here, please, just for a little while longer? To make myself ready for the day?"

"Here?" He glanced around warily. "What, in the hayloft?"

"Yes." She nodded earnestly. "I won't cause any trouble! Y-you have my word."

"Why? Why would you take a job like this out in the middle of nowhere anyway? You can't lack for customers." He suddenly narrowed his eyes. "You're on the run, aren't you?"

"What?"

He moved closer. "Have you done something naughty, my girl? Is somebody after you?"

She blanched. "Of course not, why would you think such a thing?" she evaded. Of course, she had done nothing wrong, but someone was certainly after her.

If only she had some clear idea who!

The blue-eyed man was studying her shrewdly. Then he pointed at her. "You're a Gypsy, aren't you?"

"Yes," she assented. *Whatever you say. Just don't kick me out of here yet.*

Somehow, she felt safer just being around this large and solid man. The kittens seemed to feel it, too, tumbling around at his feet.

"I get the feeling you're hiding here." He folded his arms across his chest. "Have you committed a crime?" he asked softly.

Her eyes widened. "No!"

His piercing cobalt stare seemed to probe her very soul. "I won't harbor a fugitive from the law."

"I haven't done anything wrong!" Sophia exclaimed, becoming truly rattled.

He appeared unperturbed by her vehement denials. "Your people have a certain reputation, I'm afraid. As thieves," he clarified crisply.

"I am not that sort of — Gypsy," she asserted in dismay. *Only some sort of harlot for sale, apparently, in your view.*

He scrutinized her for a long moment, his eyes narrowed. "Very well," he said guardedly. "I shall take you at your word. But you had better not be lying to me. If there is one thing I despise above all else, it is a lying female."

Oh, blast. Raking her fingers through her tousled hair, she heaved a large sigh and dropped her hands onto her lap again. "I understand. So, is it all right then if I stay here for a little while?"

If he would just leave, maybe he'd forget that she was here.

He frowned, studying her.

She held her breath as she waited for his answer, her heart pounding at the prospect of being forced out onto the road with unknown enemies after her blood.

"I won't cause any inconvenience — sir — I swear," she assured him, reminding herself to use a deferential tone like a humble country girl. She gave him a wide-eyed look of genuine desperation. "It's just that right now, I really have nowhere else to go."

Ah, damn.

Those big brown eyes could have melted hearts of stone. Gabriel looked away.

Tossing her out on her shapely arse, however, proved beyond his power.

"Very well," he mumbled. "Come inside and have some breakfast, then."

"No, that's all right, I don't wish to be a burden —"

"Have you eaten?"

"I . . . brought my own supplies."

"Really?" he asked in surprise, admittedly impressed as she nodded and reached into her knapsack, pulling out some hardtack wrapped in cheesecloth and then a bit of dried jerky.

Hm. Fancy that. Again, his brother had scored another point; Derek knew that Gabriel could not abide a helpless female. This one was as resourceful as she was plucky and independent. Devil take her, the unfortunate beauty tugged at his heartstrings.

Surely she deserved a chance at a more decent life. Was there nothing he could do to help her?

No girl ought to have to sell her body.

"What is your name, my dear?" he asked in a gentler tone.

Head down, she peered up at him from beneath her velvet lashes. "Sophia."

"Sophia, I am Gabriel Knight. But I take

it you already know that."

"Yes. Your brother told me," she said with a businesslike nod.

"I don't need a girl to warm my bed, as I, er, mentioned, but if you're willing, my housekeeper could use an extra set of hands."

"Your housekeeper?" She blinked, then stared at him. "You mean, I could work here . . . as a maid?"

"Yes. Does that sound acceptable? No one's going to harm you here. And no one is going to use you," he added meaningfully. "You can return to the life you knew or stay here and try something else. The choice is yours."

Sophia stared at him for a long moment, her curling tresses tumbling over her shoulder as she tilted her head slightly to the side, contemplating his offer.

It seemed she had never dreamed of such a position.

He lifted his eyebrow expectantly, feeling better already about giving her a new chance in life.

She nodded slowly. "Thank you. I accept."

"Good," Gabriel replied, and when she lifted her head, they stared at each other for another awkward moment.

Strange, Gabriel thought. New to England, he still wasn't used to the range of accents to be found from London's East End to the rural hamlets, but to his ear, the girl spoke with unusual refinement for one of her class.

Well, he thought briskly, tearing his gaze away, if she was to be his maid, then the matter was settled. No gentleman of any honor pestered his female domestics with his baser needs.

He cleared his throat, glad for the chance to do a good deed, though it would not be easy having her around to tempt him. "You will find Mrs. Moss in the kitchen," he clipped out. "She'll give you something fresher to eat than that hardtack, then we'll figure out where you will sleep. As for your salary — what do maids usually get these days, a shilling a week?"

She shrugged as though she hadn't the foggiest idea.

No doubt the poor young thing was used to living hand to mouth. For all her fresh-faced beauty, she had the wary look of a survivor. "Right. Well, we'll settle that later, then," he mumbled and started to turn away.

"Um, Mr. Knight?"

"Major."

"Pardon?"

"It's, er — oh, never mind," he said, abruptly remembering that he had left the military life behind. It had been his whole identity for so long, but it no longer signified. "Just call me Gabriel. What is it, Sophia?"

Her chin came up a notch. "I'm sorry you don't want to bed me," she flung out in light defiance, betraying a trace of, perhaps, stung feminine pride. Or maybe testing him.

Either way, her words caused him to lift an eyebrow.

"Yes," he answered with a sardonic half smile after a moment. "So am I, my dear, believe me. So am I."

CHAPTER THREE

"After you," her new employer said, gesturing toward the ladder.

Sophia nodded, but before leaving the hayloft, she paused and turned away from Gabriel, discreetly lifting her skirts on one side to slide her knife back into its sheath.

He watched her intently, saying nothing. She could only wonder what was going through that head of his.

This man could have taken advantage of her in ways she did not even want to think about, but instead, believing her to be a lowly trollop, he had offered her an honest living.

Now it seemed she was to be his maid.

Lord, Alexa would never let her hear the end of this — but if this was what it took to stay out of harm's way, then so be it.

Besides, the prospect of walking a mile in the shoes of a poor chambermaid filled Sophia with a gaming spirit. This was sure to be an excellent experience in her royal education. The British diplomats only meant for her to be a figurehead when she took power on Kavros, but Sophia was utterly sincere in her desire to be a good ruler. This would be a perfect chance to understand her people better, the ordinary folk she soon would be put in place to rule.

With her weapon secured, she picked up her knapsack, threw it over her shoulder, and with a resolute lift of her chin, marched across the hayloft.

Gabriel brought the kittens' empty bowl, and they climbed down from the loft one by one.

Descending first, Sophia jumped down and then turned to watch him as he followed with smooth, powerful movements. Any woman would have been impressed with that Herculean physique, she mused, wickedly eyeing the curve of his sleek derriere.

But as he stepped off the ladder, he gave her a dry look, as though he had felt her ogling his manly person. With no comment, he merely nodded toward the wide barn door.

Sophia stifled a grin and followed him outside. Together they walked toward the rambling farmhouse now visible among the trees. It had been concealed from her last night by the limited view from the hayloft windows.

Walking up the dusty drive beside him, she noted she barely came up to his shoulder. He was bigger than most of her bodyguards, all men chosen for their impressive size.

He had referred to himself as a major, and he certainly carried himself like a military man, but she was perplexed about why he was out in the middle of nowhere like this.

She kept glancing at him curiously, but he continued staring straight ahead.

"Something on your mind?" he asked at length, his tone blunt.

"Oh — nothing."

"Something," he countered, slanting her a knowing glance edged with amusement. "What?"

"Nothing, I was just wondering . . . do you live here with your wife?"

He looked askance at her. "No wife."

She surveyed the fields. "Are you a farmer?"

"Not that I know of."

"Well, what are you, then?" she exclaimed.

He laughed, a white flash of his teeth breaking through the dark scruff of his beard. He shrugged off the question with charming modesty. "Just an ordinary man."

For some reason, she had difficulty believing his answer and gave him a dubious look.

"Here," he said when he noticed her shrugging her knapsack higher onto her shoulder. His fleeting touch sent a shock through her body as he slipped the strap off her shoulder to carry it for her.

"I can do that —"

"No need."

Sophia was a bit nervous about letting him take it, for at the moment, that sack contained nearly everything she needed to survive. But he slung it over his shoulder and continued striding up the long drive to the farmhouse.

She quickened her paces to keep up with him.

"I should probably warn you that Mrs. Moss can be a curmudgeon at times," he said. "She comes in the morning and usually leaves by four."

"She doesn't live in?"

"No, she goes home to her family's cottage each night at the edge of the farm, which is a blessing," he muttered. "She came with the place, along with the rest of the furniture. She'll probably insult you, but don't take it to heart. It's part of her charm."

"I won't," she replied with a smile. Born to rule, Sophia knew she'd have no trouble handling an uppity housekeeper — but then she remembered her charade as a lowly servant. Hm, it seemed she'd have to take whatever Mrs. Moss was dishing out. But no matter. In for a penny, in for a pound.

This should be interesting, she thought, quite curious and ready to delve into her experiment.

They walked on in silence, then Sophia laughed when she saw the large white horse rolling on its back in the meadow, sans dignity, four hooves flailing in the air.

"Is that your horse? He looks happy."

Gabriel nodded, laughing along with her. "He's just glad to be alive."

"So am I," Sophia said softly. *More than he knew.* A shadow of last night's terror passed over her heart when she thought of how close she had come to being abducted, if not killed, but when she turned to Gabriel, he was staring strangely at her.

"What is it?" she murmured.

He shrugged and dropped his gaze. "You sound like you really mean that."

"I do."

He was silent for a moment as they walked on. "I guess you've had a few brushes with danger, in your sort of life."

"So I have," she answered in a grim murmur, though he did not know the truth.

He gave a taut nod, still avoiding her gaze. "So have I."

"Well," she ventured, summoning up a smile to chase away the invisible cloak of heaviness that seemed to come over him. It reminded her of his brooding last night in the church. "Today is a beautiful day," she pointed out, nodding toward the brilliant tree line and the azure sky.

It seemed to work. A faint smile eased the tension from his eyes as he watched his horse roll up onto all fours again. The animal stood and shook himself, bits of flowers flying from his creamy mane.

"Every day is beautiful," Gabriel said softly. "One need only open one's eyes."

He glanced at her at last, and Sophia laughed at him with harmless mirth. "What, are you some sort of rustic poet?"

"No, I would try, but I'm no good at spelling," he shot back with an idle grin. "So, what are *you?*" he asked at length, echoing her own question back to her, as if he could not stop himself.

She shook her head. "I'm still trying to figure that out."

"You're young," he said sagely. "It can take awhile." He opened the door for her when they reached the farmhouse, and Sophia could not help but raise an eyebrow.

This man had an extraordinary sense of chivalry if this was how he treated lowly maids.

Nodding her thanks, she walked in ahead of him, but at his show of gallantry, she found herself puzzling once more over his refusal of the "services" that he believed she'd been sent to render to him as a Gypsy harlot.

Really, why didn't he want her? He was such an interesting man — and yet quite immune to her appeal. She believed her feminine pride was a trifle miffed.

Yet, in a way, his failure to fawn on her was oddly refreshing. She had learned long ago to take flattery with one cynical grain of salt. People would say anything to butter up even exiled royalty, and while courtiers and other toadies frequently sang her praises as a "ravishing beauty," she was perfectly well aware that her Greek nose was too big and that her hair turned to a cloud of wild frizz whenever it rained — which, in England, was every other day. No, Lady Alexa with her sculpted face and smooth blond tresses was the beautiful one, but it did not signify.

The point was, Gabriel Knight did not *know* she was royalty and, thus, had no *reason* to flatter her. He was merely being honest — and he honestly found her a woman that he could resist.

You are being silly, she informed herself. *Would you prefer it if he tried to paw you?*

For her part, Sophia had dismissed from her household any number of footmen over the years who had been accused of groping her maids. Her whole staff knew she would not tolerate such nonsense.

Still, Gabriel's ambivalence toward her left her a bit confused. She was not used to being so easily denied.

In the kitchen, he introduced her to Mrs. Moss, who took an instant dislike to Sophia.

She was glad Gabriel had warned her in advance of the old woman's ill temper. She was unruffled by the housekeeper's first efforts to intimidate her.

He leaned in the open doorway off the kitchen, monitoring the housekeeper's terse, unfriendly interview of her, when suddenly, he started forward, staring toward the field where his horse was grazing.

Sophia saw his sharp movement and looked over. "Is everything all right?"

He continued staring out the door. "I think we've got a visitor."

"What?" She felt her stomach drop with fear, her first thought that her attackers from last night had tracked her down.

"Look." He pointed as she rushed over to see for herself.

As soon as she peeked out the door relief spiraled through her.

Their visitor was the bay gelding she had ridden here last night.

Oh, dear, she thought, masking her recognition of the animal. The horse must have wandered through the woods and found his way somehow onto Gabriel's property.

"I don't see a saddle on him," he murmured. "Nice-looking animal. He must have got free from one of the local farms. I'd better go and put a rope over him. His owner will probably be here soon, wanting him back."

"Do you, er, need any help capturing him?" Sophia asked uneasily.

The dazzling smile he flashed as he left the doorway took her off guard. "That's all right," he said in a confident murmur. "I've got a bit of experience when it comes to horses."

He strode off without further ado to capture the bay. Sophia gnawed her lip with a guilty wince as she watched him go. Then, behind her, Mrs. Moss demanded her attention and put her right to work.

Sophia hopped to it, determined to explore her temporary role as maid until her bodyguards arrived, but still, she was a bit surprised that no allowance was made for her to eat, as Gabriel had promised. She shrugged it off, however, not pressing the matter. A lowly maid would have to follow orders, and meals, no doubt, were sometimes skipped. Besides, she had no intention of complaining when she knew that many of her people lived with hunger like this every day.

Her duties started immediately, and it didn't take long to grasp that Mrs. Moss was eager to give her all of the most wretched jobs.

Scrubbing a large sink full of pots and pans from the previous night took her two hours, but at least it was less complicated than her next task. When Mrs. Moss ordered her to pluck a dead chicken for the master's supper, Sophia barely knew how to begin. It was a horrid job, and her ignorance of how to undertake it proved, frustratingly, to be a prevailing theme of the day.

It didn't take Mrs. Moss long to realize that the new maid couldn't cook — at all. So the old woman set her to the simpler task of peeling a mountain of potatoes and chopping another mountain of vegetables. Blazes, she thought, her hands aching after an hour of handling the blunt little knife, how much did this man eat?

Her stomach rumbled continuously, reminding her that she, meanwhile, still hadn't had her breakfast. Normally it was served to her on a silver tray while she lay abed, exotic fruits and hot chocolate and tea and whatever new delicacies of the day that her chef could dream up. Today, however, it was two in the afternoon before Mrs. Moss finally gave her fifteen minutes to herself.

Sophia gulped down a hunk of bread with a cup of cold coffee left over from Gabriel's breakfast, but her lesson in the life of a maid was not over yet.

Her next assignment involved going through all of the rooms and trimming the candlewicks and refilling the lanterns' oil. She had barely finished when Mrs. Moss hurried her outside to bring in more firewood.

With her thoughts still churning over the attack of last night and her private certainty that Ali Pasha was behind it, she looked around for Gabriel. She did not see him anywhere, but was startled to note that the autumn sun was already setting.

Good Lord, she had been working practically since sunup and there was still no end in sight. She took a moment to stretch her neck a little. Her back was sore from bending over that sink for so long.

In the next moment, she heard the housekeeper bellowing for her to hurry. She quickly bent and piled a few split logs into her arms, then sighed with exhaustion and forced herself to go back in.

The chicken and vegetables were now boiling away in a cauldron on the hearth and the lovely smell made her stomach grumble even more. Thanks to her help, Mrs. Moss now had the chaotic kitchen under control, but the old woman was not nearly done with her yet.

She put a feather duster in Sophia's hand and warned her that tomorrow was laundry day; she could change the master's bedding as soon as she had finished dusting the upstairs.

"And don't forget the hallways!"

At least the new task gave her the means to escape the old woman's unceasing bad mood. She withdrew with a mumbled "Yes, ma'am" and made her way up the creaky staircase. But as the daylight waned, the house was getting dark. How was she supposed to see what she was doing?

One thing was certain, she mused as she started with the console table in the corridor, lifting up each knickknack wearily and dusting under it, she had a whole new respect for all maids. With that, she sneezed at the cloud of dust she had stirred up.

There were several rooms on the upper floor, but most of them looked like no one had set foot in them in years, so she made only a halfhearted effort to clean them. Now and then, she glanced out of the various windows, keeping watch for friend or foe, either her bodyguards coming to find her again or any sign of the villains who had attacked her entourage last night. Neither appeared.

With daylight waning fast, she realized she had better find Gabriel's room and get on with the job of tidying it as best she could and changing his bedding. *Laundry day tomorrow. Lord.* That sounded fun.

She found the linens in the cedar chest just where Mrs. Moss had said they'd be, and took out a clean set of sheets for Gabriel's bed. First she had to locate his room.

Peeking into the various chambers that she had not yet reached in her dusting, she finally found Gabriel's quarters. He had the largest bedchamber in the house, and the only one that looked lived in — a place of dark walnut furniture and faded blues, the walls a robin's egg shade, with indigo draperies over the windows. Matching bed-hangings trailed down from the frame of the big, carved four-poster bed.

An Oriental carpet covered some of the dark hardwood floor and carried on the blue theme with a few dashes of red and gold and more browns.

Through the imposing frame of the canopied bed, she noticed an empty fireplace with a simple white mantel, a mirror above it. A large wardrobe stood by one wall, while, closer to her, a low night-chest sat beside the bed.

In all, it was a fairly sparse chamber, with none of the gilded brilliance she was used to in her opulent interiors. Sophia let herself in quietly, surveying the room. She wasn't sure where to begin, and as she walked deeper into his chamber, she could feel her pulse accelerating.

It would have helped her peace of mind if she knew where Gabriel was. She hadn't seen "the master" since this morning. And although Mrs. Moss had ordered her to do this, she couldn't help but feel she was intruding.

She halted just a few steps into the room, glancing around. Too intimidated at first to dare touch a strange man's bed, she decided to start with the dusting.

Setting aside the clean, folded sheets, she approached the night-chest with her feather duster. Feeling acutely self-conscious and all too aware of Gabriel's bed right beside her, she made a few nervous passes over the old, scuffed wood — and then suddenly stopped.

Her gaze homed in on the hilt of a sword that rested in the narrow space behind the night-chest and leaned against the wall. *Gabriel's sword?* Of course, Leon always said it was wise to keep a weapon nearby in case of an intruder in the night, but Sophia was intrigued.

With a careful glance over her shoulder, she set the feather duster down and lifted the sword and its thick leather scabbard out from behind the night-chest. To her surprise, it was a curved blade, though not the great, arched, deadly scimitar of the Turks, the traditional enemies of her people.

No, if she was not mistaken, this was a cavalry saber.

Hm. Might that be what he meant when he'd told her he had a lot of experience around horses?

Emboldened by her familiarity with all manner of weapons — Leon had been training her to defend herself ever since her eldest brother's assassination — she pulled the saber only a few inches out of its scab-bard.

Almost at once, she noticed the aged bloodstains on the blade . . . and then she saw the notches on the hilt. As if its owner had kept a tally of the foes that he had vanquished with this blade.

A chill ran down her spine as she saw the little notches all over the hilt, too many to count.

Deeper than their light scoring, beneath those wicked little lines, there were two words engraved in a flowing script, etched into the shiny steel.

No mercy.

Sophia thrust the blade back into the scabbard with a sudden shiver and quickly put the weapon back where she had found it. Her heart was pounding.

She turned around with a troubled frown, and as her questioning gaze swept the room, she noticed something she had missed before. On top of the tall walnut wardrobe sat a plumed helmet. Magnificent shiny steel like the sword, its dyed horsehair plume cresting down in the most regal fash-ion.

Just then, she heard water splashing from somewhere nearby — it sounded as though it was coming from somewhere inside the room! Rather confounded, she took a few more wary steps forward. As she started to round his bed, a flicker of light in the cheval mirror across the large, shadowy room caught her eye.

She turned and looked at the mirror and dropped her jaw at what she saw. The wide wardrobe had blocked her view of the dressing room door, which stood somewhat ajar.

The candlelight was coming from inside the dressing room, and there, in the reflection, she could see Gabriel relaxing in his bath.

His bulky arms rested along the rim of the steaming tub. His coal-black hair was wet, his chiseled face glistening with moisture. His eyes were closed and water starred his lashes.

Frozen where she stood in the deepening shadows, Sophia barely dared breathe, staring at him. The artless pleasure on his face as he dozed in the tub, the trickle of water down his throat and muscled chest.

Awe and longing filled her as she watched him, unable to tear her gaze away.

The man was simply the most seductive thing she had ever seen. Her own wild reaction shocked her, a trembling tingle that ran through her body. An image blossomed in her mind of herself touching him. *Bath-*

ing him? This was a manner of serving the "master" that she could enjoy.

Her pulse pounded, and she knew she must be very wicked, indeed, but the bold streak inside of her actually toyed with the notion and dared her to chance it.

Yesterday had been her birthday, after all, and she had not received a single present. At the moment, she had a fair idea of what she would have liked for her birthday — namely, him.

She wondered how he would react if she were to walk in there, give him a smile, and pick up the sponge and soap. Would he be shocked? Would he protest?

Or would he welcome her intrusion, invite her to explore his incredible body, and let her learn the feel of his sun-bronzed skin? She wanted to run her hands along those massive shoulders. Taste that mouth . . .

You are a fool, she told herself, putting a stern end to her dangerous fancies. She had seen that hungry look in his eyes when he had lain atop her in the stable and held her pinned beneath him. To go in there now would have been like baiting a wolf with a raw steak. On the other hand, she could think of worse fates than being consumed by Gabriel Knight.

Lord, she supposed she had all of the

usual vices of royalty. It wasn't easy to rein in one's desires when one was accustomed to having wishes granted.

Her heart racing, she forced herself to turn away. There was more to royalty than self-indulgence, after all. First and foremost, there was her duty. And being the heir to the throne of Kavros came with a very steep cost.

She knew full well that her needs as a woman would have to be thrust aside for the sake of her people. In that sense, even the lowliest maid was rich compared to her.

Perhaps when she was older, she could afford a dalliance with a handsome cavalry officer. But until she was installed in power, she had to be very careful with men. So many of her highborn would-be suitors only wanted to take over everything that was hers and steal away her power.

In time, she would probably have to wed her way into a marriage alliance that would be advantageous to her country. But until then, she intended to model herself on her idol, England's greatest queen, Elizabeth I, of Shakespeare's day. The so-called Virgin Queen.

Clever Queen Bess had managed the male rulers of neighboring countries just as a cunning belle knew how to handle a crowd of amorous suitors, playing for an offer that would suit her own best interests, and in the end, refusing all.

In this world, a woman ruler was a rarity, and with all the disadvantages she faced, Sophia knew she'd have to use whatever gifts Nature had bestowed on her.

She could not afford entanglements that would compromise her control, sway her heart, impair her judgment, and make her life any more complicated than it already was.

Ah, but she could look.

Gabriel still had no idea she was there, or if he had noticed her presence, she thought, perhaps he simply didn't care. Most wealthy people simply ignored their domestics.

Sophia indulged herself in one long, last stare to imprint his delectable image on her memory. But when she finally dragged her heated gaze away, coming back to her experiment as a maid and recalling once more her endless list of jobs, she was left rather dazed, unsure what to do now.

She still hadn't changed the sheets and frankly dared not face Mrs. Moss without carrying out her orders. There seemed no other alternative than to step to it.

Still, the mere thought of such an intimate task made her blush after seeing Gabriel that way and reveling in her glimpse of his naked splendor. Doing her best to ignore her lustful reaction to the man, along with his musky scent that clung to the sheets, she hurried to strip his bedding.

She then replaced the sheets, moving around the four-poster bed as quickly and quietly as possible, and blushing all the while at her own scandalous thoughts. Maybe Alexa was right and chastity was overrated . . .

Smoothing the clean sheets to make sure they lay neat and flat, her palm caressed the place where Gabriel slept. There was a long indentation where the feather bed had cradled his iron body.

It was her first time ever changing a bed of any sort, but eventually she muddled through it, stuffed his pillow into the pillowcase and plumped it for him, then set it where it belonged against the headboard.

Eager to get out of here before he noticed her, she gathered up the linens that she had just removed from his bed and started to exit the room. But on her way out, she realized she had failed to collect his dirty laundry.

Botheration!

Scowling, she spotted a mound of his discarded clothes on a piece of furniture in the corner. With a sigh, she set down her armful of bed linens, collected the feather duster, and then went to gather up his pile of laundry, deciding on the spot that all of her maids must receive an increase in wages for all that they went through.

She scooped up Gabriel's dirty work clothes, muddied and smelling of sweaty male, and added them to the bed linens to carry downstairs. But then, as she dusted off her hands, the piece of furniture that had been buried under his laundry caught her attention.

She had uncovered some sort of traveling trunk.

She noticed at once that it didn't fit in with the rest of the farmhouse setting. It was made of reddish teakwood and leather, and looked as though it had been through a war.

It seemed to be the only article of furniture in the room that was actually *his* rather than part of the rental property. Her heart beat faster as she tiptoed back toward the trunk. She bit her lip, fiercely tempted to see what was inside. Where was the harm in one small peek?

She glanced toward the dressing room and saw he was still dozing. This might be her best chance. If Gabriel really was a great

warrior, if every notch on that sword represented one of his kills, then might not
someone like him be a valuable asset to her
quest?

Perhaps she could recruit him. Hanging
around this farm, he didn't seem to have
anything better to do. Despite his reticence
to talk about himself, she was determined
to have answers to his mysteries — and the
clues, she suspected, lay inside that trunk.
Of course, this was prying, but she decided
to chance it. At the very least, it would tell
her more about the man she had put her
trust in when she had decided to hide here.

Wiping her hands on her skirts, Sophia
bent down, eager to investigate more closely.
Silently, she opened the lid, and her first
discovery confirmed her guess that, indeed,
he was a cavalry officer.

His uniform coat lay neatly folded on top
of his belongings inside the trunk, a dashing
dark blue jacket of one of the hussar regiments. Shiny brass buttons, gold epaulets. A
pair of white dress gloves, soft kid riding
gauntlets, were tucked under the black lapel.

Every find made her heart lift, confirming
her decision to hide here at the farmhouse
until her men found her. Why, she felt safer
already!

Quickly, she dug deeper, lifting his uniform a bit to the side. More weapons were hidden beneath it: a cavalry broadsword with its thick, straight blade, a weapon her bodyguards said a man had to have the strength of a lion to use properly. Daggers and pistols, a carbine, a disassembled rifle with a bayonet. Strange weapons, too, some she had never seen before. A round thing like a star with blades all around it and strange writings on the top.

Next, she came across a colorful regimental flag . . . and at the very bottom of the trunk, hidden away as if they were something to be ashamed of, she found medals for valor and bravery.

Gabriel opened his eyes, sensing a presence nearby. He listened sharply with battle-honed senses, then relaxed. *No. Not a threat.* He had been in a deep state of rest but not sleeping, trying to summon up a meditative mood of peace.

With night coming on, it was harder to locate, especially now. Thoughts of the girl he had found in his barn had plagued him all day, her beauty awakening a hunger within him. In an effort to ignore his body's craving, he had worked too hard and had strained his middle a bit, where the muscles of his abdomen had only just knit themselves back together again after months of careful tending. God, for as long as he lived, however short, admittedly, that might be, he would never forget the moment he had looked down and found himself impaled by a Maratha arrow.

He should be dead.

But he wasn't. No, he wasn't . . .

And he had not made love to a woman since he had made his fleeting visit to the world beyond the grave.

Which was exactly why Derek had sent Sophia to him. His body ached at the thought of her. Lovely Sophia.

Tempting Sophia.

Naughty, wayward Sophia, he mused, for it was at that moment that he saw her in the reflection of the mirror over the fireplace.

Never one to let his guard down, he had angled the tub so that even when he was doing his best to unwind, he could still see into the adjoining room by the judicious placement of mirrors. Just in case of any threat.

Old habits died hard.

Leaning forward silently in his bathing tub, careful not to stir the water, he glanced through the open doorway at the mantelpiece mirror. The reflection bounced off that of the cheval glass . . . and there was his lovely Gypsy girl.

Robbing him, it would seem.

Gabriel's face darkened; he reached for a towel.

CHAPTER FOUR

Bending over his open traveling trunk, Sophia was still marveling over her discoveries about her new employer. Dazzled, she hefted the weight of a chunky silver war medal in her palm, then traced her fingertip over the elaborate wreath that ringed it. Oh, how she could have used someone like him on her quest to take back her country.

No mercy, indeed.

With a battle-hardened warrior like this by her side, she was sure that the foes who had ambushed her carriage last night would think twice about ever attacking her again!

Shaking her head in awe at the evidence of his deeds, she started to put the medal back where she had found it, when all of a sudden, a steely hand clamped down on her arm. She let out a shriek and shot to her feet as Gabriel pulled her away from his things.

"What are you doing?" he barked as he

spun her around to face him. His hold on her shifted to the other arm, but when Sophia saw him, she blinked: He was wearing a towel and a furious glower, and loomed over her like an angry god. *"Answer me!"*

She gulped and tried to back away, but he would not let go of her, his grip on her wrist like an iron manacle.

"What the hell do you think you're doing in here?" he repeated in obvious outrage.

"N-nothing, I-I —" His nakedness and his towering size reduced her to flustered stammering. "Mrs. Moss told me to clean your room!"

Oh, God. She was perfectly mortified.

His eyes narrowed to cobalt slits in the deepening gloom of his chamber; she was caught in that blue, piercing stare. "Empty your pockets," he ordered.

"What?"

"You heard me! Empty your pockets — *now!*"

Sophia shrank from the angry warrior. Did he really have to be so scary about this?

Still holding her by one wrist, Gabriel flicked his fingers impatiently at her, then held out his palm. "Hurry up. Whatever you've taken, just hand it over and leave."

"Taken?" she breathed. *Leave?*

87

He shook his head at her in scorn. "You're really something, you know that? I try to help you, and this is how you repay me?"

Good God! she thought as the full brunt of his accusation sank in. She was guilty of prying, but the Princess Royal of Kavros was hardly a thief!

Oh, it was too lowering.

On the other hand, she could understand why he would jump to such a conclusion. Her heart sank. This did not look good at all.

She wished she could tell him her true name so he would know she had no need to steal, but protocol forbade it, and besides, if she tried to claim now that she was bona fide royalty, he would think that she was insane.

"Well?" he demanded. "Have you nothing to say for yourself?"

Tongue-tied with embarrassment, she let out a queenly huff. After all, she was hardly accustomed to having to explain herself to anyone, let alone a commoner and a soldier in a towel.

"You are mistaken," she clipped out.

"Oh, really? Then what were you doing?"

"Cleaning."

"Right."

"Very well. Snooping. I admit it, I was

88

interested in you. That's not a crime, as far as I know."

"Well, well," he murmured, moving closer. "And are you satisfied with what you learned?"

"No," she replied with a haughty toss of her chin. "I have many more questions."

"A pretty attempt at evasion," he whispered. "But I don't believe you."

"Are you calling me a liar?" she exclaimed.

"Aye," he said, "and a thief."

"You blackguard," she growled at him.

She lifted her chin; he narrowed his eyes.

"You don't want to see me angry, Sophia."

"Ha! You already are, Mr. Saint."

"No, I'm not. But I am losing patience," he warned, which only escalated her taunting.

"What are you going to do to me, Major? Reach for your saber and lop off my head?"

"Oh, you are an impertinent wench." Gabriel stared at her, amazed. Damn her, he had put the reminders of his past away for a reason and did not want anyone dragging it all out into the open again.

He needed no help in triggering the memories of how dark and violent he had been in his former career. But he was different now.

At least that's what he had to believe.

And look at her! he thought, astounded. He had never seen such audacity. How dare this little servant girl stand up to him with such cheeky defiance after he had caught her red-handed, rifling through his personal effects?

He did not believe her lies at all. She was just trying to squirm out of her obvious guilt by some quick thinking. No doubt she had been trying to decide which items would bring the best profit at some London pawnshop.

Lord, I was a fool to let this lawless hoyden into my house. The worst part was, he knew exactly why he had done it. Her dark beauty had bewitched him — and God help him, he wasn't immune to her even now. Lust pounded in his brain right along with his fury.

It made him extra wary of her.

Sophia glanced down, supremely unintimidated by his wrath, never mind that back in the regiment, he had been known to reduce grown men to quivering heaps of terror when he was displeased. "What happened to you?" she demanded, nodding at his scar.

"None of your damned business, my love — and changing the subject won't save your pretty hide. Now, are you going to turn out your pockets, or shall I do it for you?" He did not wait for an answer but yanked her to him, pulling her off balance.

She gasped as the sudden tug brought her crashing against his chest. Hooking his arm around her waist, Gabriel held her to him. He stared down into her eyes, searingly attuned to her soft body crushed against him. His heart pounded. She gazed up at him in speechless shock as he thrust his right hand down into the pocket of her plain skirts. He felt around inside of it for contraband.

The pocket was empty, but Gabriel lost his train of thought, his male senses suddenly distracted when his hand, cloaked in fabric, brushed against her shapely thigh.

The outer edges of his control had already begun to fray; boldly, he molded his hand against her leg, giving in to the blinding urge to feel her.

His rude advance infuriated her; he was glad.

"Let go of me!" she ordered, struggling against him, but Gabriel held her fast, brushing his lips against her neck with a dark laugh.

"You don't like playing by the rules, do you, my Gypsy girl? But if you're going to misbehave, you're going to have to take the consequences."

"I haven't done anything wrong!" She pushed against his chest and shoulders, trying to loosen his tight hold on her. "Unhand me now!" she roared, but the way she was squirming against his body roused a starved moan from the core of his being. Her thrashing motions had him feverishly rethinking his monkish decision not to take her.

Ah, God, he needed it so badly.

"Let me go, I say! I did not steal *anything* from you!"

"Maybe I'll steal something from you," he ground out in a ragged whisper. "You call me a saint? You are so wrong." He bent his head lower and nuzzled her throat. Unable to resist, he parted his lips and tasted the warm salt silk of her skin.

She let out a soft groan; he could feel her melting against him in spite of herself. "Is that really necessary?" she asked through gritted teeth.

"More than you know," he panted as he captured her face and tilted her head back. The lure of her lips was more than he could bear.

Holding her soft curves against him, he could feel her pulse pounding in time with his own; his whole body throbbed as he cupped her nape and captured her lips with his own. She stiffened and tried to turn away, but he followed hungrily, and when he sought her mouth again, this time, seeing, perhaps, that she could not escape, or perhaps giving way to the curiosity he knew they both felt, she gradually yielded.

Playing reticent as a virgin, she forced him to coax her lips apart by the softest stroking with the tip of his tongue. *Coy for a harlot,* he thought. No doubt still rattled about being caught trying to steal from him, but no matter. She was not going to get away with anything with him, and at the moment, he rather liked her little game.

His heart slammed behind his ribs as she finally obliged him, letting him in to taste her womanly heat.

Gabriel groaned as he kissed her more deeply, his own reservations fading into oblivion. He felt her palms molding over his shoulders. She clung to him, all unsteady with their mutual passion that was spiraling swiftly out of control. His body clamored for release.

Feasting on her mouth, Gabriel quivered as her hands inched slowly down his bare chest. Then she began exploring his arms so hesitantly, as if she had never touched a man before. God, she was driving him mad. His brother must have tipped the girl off on exactly how to seduce him; he must have warned her not to come on too strong with Gabriel after his long abstinence, and once more, Derek was right.

If she had been all over him like the sort of women he was used to, he would have found her so much easier to resist. Instead, her tentative approach made him ache. Her slow exploration had him quivering with impatience to feel those soft, sweet hands all over him.

He had sworn to himself he'd resist her, but what was the point? What was he trying to prove? He could no longer remember. There was only her beauty, her fire, her taste.

A chap was entitled to change his mind now and then, was he not?

Desperately eager to lose himself in sensuality with her, he was rock-hard, indeed, quite in danger of losing his towel, but he couldn't care less. His blood surged as he ravished her willing mouth; it was wonderful.

He felt alive again, and he wanted her.

His bed nearby seemed to beckon. Still lost in kissing her, he began moving her gently toward it.

Sophia had lost all memory of how they had

gone from fighting to this.

Her fevered trance was too deep to keep track of such petty details as Gabriel's delicious tongue swirled in her mouth. His steely arms were wrapped around her, his hands traveling up and down her back, her waist, her hair. Her duty, the danger, her quest were all forgotten in the scandalous joy of his kiss.

The feel of his skin was so beautiful under her palms, with its kid-leather texture, still slightly damp from his bath, growing warmer; she could feel his temperature rising as she stroked him. Every inch of Gabriel Knight brought her greater pleasure.

His arms were outrageous, muscled with bulging curves of smooth stone — magnificent shoulders — and, *ah, God,* his sculpted chest.

She wanted to kiss him everywhere, but for now, she contented herself with caressing him. No, she could never get bored of that, and he certainly seemed to enjoy it.

Once more, she traced her trembling fingers along the line of his thick, sturdy collarbones, and then, down, through the crisp, light furring of hair on his chest. He growled with pleasure against her mouth as her hand glided tenderly over the swell of each pectoral muscle to play with the sweet little nub of each manly nipple.

Wobbly-kneed with desire, she was aware of his raging erection throbbing against her stomach. The layers of her gown and the towel still wrapped around his waist could not disguise the mighty evidence of his want. It made her a little nervous, admittedly. At the back of her mind, she supposed she was playing with fire.

Unfortunately, her powers of reason had fled — until the moment she realized that Gabriel was shepherding her oh-so-adroitly toward his bed.

When it dawned on her what he had in mind, she planted her feet on the ground and tore her lips away from his, coming suddenly back to her senses.

Good God, what am I doing? This could not happen. Where was her brain?

"What's the matter, angel?" Gabriel murmured with a steamy half smile.

"I can't do this!" she gasped out, still panting.

He touched her cheek, his gaze full of hazy-eyed need. "Of course you can."

"No — I can't."

"Why not?" His eyes had darkened to midnight blue; his lips still shone with the wetness of her kisses.

With a low whimper of frustration, Sophia

tore her stare away from his too-delectable self. "My duty," she mumbled halfheartedly.

He let out a husky laugh. "Never mind the bloody housework. We've got better things to do. Come on, love. If it's a question of money —"

"It is *not* a question of money!" she exclaimed, reminded anew of his unflattering misapprehensions. Well, it had been her idea to let him reach his own conclusions about her supposed profession.

She dragged her hands through her hair, still muddled with passion, and cast about for a reason that he might accept. "I am not going to do — *that* with you, after you just accused me of being a thief!"

"Ah, that reminds me," he murmured with a wicked smile, "I have not finished searching you yet . . ."

"You think this is funny?" she cried.

"I think you're gorgeous. Now, come over here and let me help you get rid of that dress."

She jumped back. "Gabriel!"

"Sophia, angel, I know you want me. You practically said it flat-out in the barn." His stare smoldered, traveling over her; his whisper was gruff with desire. "Come on, now. Don't tease a starving man. You're a naughty thing, but I know you could not be so cruel. Take those clothes off and get in my bed."

When he reached for her again, she panicked and whipped out her knife. "Stay back!"

It was the wrong thing to do.

Gabriel eyed the knife sardonically, but his response was automatic; he shook his head at her and in the blink of an eye, grabbed her wrist, peeling the tight curl of her fingers away from the hilt of her blade.

She cursed as he disarmed her with ease, then he stepped back, smoothly turned away, and hurled the knife hard across the room.

The blade plunged into the wall and stuck there, shuddering, sunk deep into the old, soft plaster.

When he turned back to her with a look of cold fury, she was staring at her distant knife, her pretty mouth hanging open.

"Any more tricks you want to show me?" he drawled.

She turned to him, wide-eyed with shock.

"Now, where were we?" His voice was still gruff with desire.

When he reached for her, she jolted back with a gasp, whirled around without another word, and darted out of his room.

"Sophia!"

Gabriel strode to the open doorway of his chamber, still clutching his towel around his waist. As he listened, confounded, staring into the darkened corridor, he could hear her rushing down the creaky old stairs.

His frown turned to a glower. Damn it, what the hell sort of coy, thieving tart had his daft brother sent him?

"Sophia, come back here!" he ordered in a full battlefield roar.

But the only answer he got back was the distant muffled slam of the front door.

Sophia bolted away from the farmhouse, her hooded woolen cloak trailing out behind her. Her hastily retrieved knapsack bumped against her shoulder with every wild stride, and the drumbeat of her pulse was nearly deafening.

She could not believe he had taken her knife!

Gabriel had disarmed her as though she were as easy to vanquish as a fly. He had left her utterly defenseless, but she knew it was her own fault. She shouldn't have done that, should not have attempted to brandish a weapon at a battle-scarred warrior. Unfortunately, his mind-melting kisses had addled her wits, and she had reacted automatically from all of her self-defense training.

It had served her well last night in fighting off her would-be abductors, but she understood now that with Gabriel, it was the worst thing she could have done.

She had realized her error the second she had seen that lightning bolt of rage flash through the indigo depths of his eyes. His reaction to her weapon had been chilling, but if she had not done something drastic to push him away, then she would have given in all too willingly to his passion.

Even now, she could taste his kiss, her chin still tender, chafed from the short scruff of his beard, her hands tingling with the warm velvet texture of his skin. Running down the rocky drive as if she could flee her reaction to him along with escaping the house, it was bewildering to be aroused, insulted, scared, and angry all at the same time.

Well, she had fled her near-seducer, but now she was unarmed. And if she met her enemies out on the road, she knew she hadn't a prayer.

All the same, she was in a wholly different kind of danger if she stayed.

The autumn chill filled her lungs, and as Sophia ran down the drive, its coolness gradually helped to clear her head.

Where did she really think she was going to go?

Oh, this was a disaster.

She was stuck in the middle of nowhere with a man she could barely resist.

Gabriel Knight turned her world upside down. She had never felt such things. Her desire for him was dangerous.

Both of them had nearly lost control.

Nearing the old barn where she had slept last night, Sophia dropped back to a fast walk, her chest heaving. Her knees still felt wobbly. Twilight was deepening by the minute to a clear, cool blackness, but the white-gold moon illuminated the lonely drive before her.

She glanced around uneasily in the gathering darkness, wondering where in blazes her bodyguards were. She would have thought they'd have found her by now.

Timo particularly had an excellent sense of direction, and after all, she had only gone a few miles.

Maybe something had gone disastrously wrong.

Oh, God. Sophia stopped walking and looked up at the moon as her vision blurred with frightened tears.

All day, she had managed to ignore her gnawing worries, keeping busy with Mrs.

Moss's endless list of chores, but now, alone, defenseless, not sure where to go, and feeling all too vulnerable, her fears began to get the best of her. The tears flooded into her eyes.

Leon! Where are you?

She had never been without him for so long before. Since childhood, he had been her rock.

What if her masked enemies had wiped out her whole entourage the way that different foes had wiped out her family over the years?

What if her bodyguards *weren't* coming?

What if they all were dead?

Nothing had been taken.

At first Gabriel had thought there must be some mistake.

Moments ago, the bang of the front door had jolted him, helping to clear the fog of lust in his brain. Slamming the heel of his hand angrily on the doorframe to vent his frustration, he had stalked over to his traveling trunk with a scowl, where a quick inventory of its contents soon revealed the startling truth.

All his belongings were there, confirming Sophia's claim of innocence.

With a curse, he threw off his towel and

quickly pulled on some clothes. The realization that he had accused her unjustly was enough to turn his previous anger at her right around at himself.

Worse, he realized in hindsight that, harlot or no, he had terrified her with his randy insistence, so much so that, for all her pluck, she had seen fit to run for her bloody life.

Damn it, that was not the kind of man he was! He had never *demanded* sex from any woman — he'd never had to — and he was not about to start now. Furious at himself, he stood and hastened to button up his trousers, but winced at the denial as he pushed his long-starved cock down into its proper position to the right. What was the matter with him, anyway? A gentleman did not grope his domestics, no matter what sort of damned sultry temptresses they were. He had given Sophia his word that she would be safe here, that she would not be used, and whatever his faults, Gabriel never broke his word.

As he bent down, hurrying to pull on his boots before she vanished again as mysteriously as she had appeared, it struck him that he genuinely did not want her to go.

It was a sobering moment of self-honesty, and made him pause.

All day long, throughout his chores and

his grueling physical regimen, the truth was, he had been anticipating the chance to talk to her again, though he had not wanted to admit it to himself.

Now he had chased her away with his clumsiness, and her absence left him starkly facing the true loneliness of his situation.

It was one thing to retreat from humanity for a time, but quite another to have a beautiful girl run away from a chap for acting like a barbarian.

Maybe I have been out here too long.

Straightening up again, he quickly strode across the room to retrieve Sophia's knife from the crumbling plaster. She was more dangerous with the weapon, but the dread on her face when he had disarmed her had twisted the very heart in him.

He should have let her keep the weapon, he thought, for in hindsight, he very much doubted that she would have really stabbed him. She had merely been afraid he might actually rape her.

God.

As he yanked the knife out of the wall, his attention suddenly homed in on the feel of the weapon in his grasp.

He was stunned by the sense of pleasure that rushed into his veins, bringing back ominous echoes of the warrior he once had been.

And no longer was.

Refused to be.

Still . . . it had been months since he had held any sort of weapon. It felt so good, so natural, in his hand.

Dear God, what had that girl awakened in him, that his whole body seemed to come alive again with the feel of the knife in his hand? His mind rebounded to the last time he had grasped a dagger in this fashion. The last time he had been in India . . .

Bloodthirsty memories churning in his mind, he paused just for a moment to run his fingers down the flat of the blade; wiping it clean of the chalky plaster dust, he caught a glimpse of himself in the cheval mirror from the corner of his eye.

Yes, he thought grimly, that was the real Gabriel Knight, the man they had called the Iron Major.

The icy bastard who had quit counting his kills when they surpassed a hundred. *No mercy.* The memory of his regiment, his fellow officers, and the motto they had coined for him in all their brash esprit de corps jarred him back to the present. He was no longer that man. That cold-blooded savage.

Shrugging off the memories and the dark

uneasiness that crept over him with the return of nightfall, he marched out of the room. It was Sophia's knife, after all. He only wanted to give it back to her. For his part, he had no need for weapons anymore.

Wanting to make amends for his dishonorable behavior, he dashed downstairs and barreled out the front door, chasing after her.

"Sophia!"

His voice echoed back to him in this lonely place. Suddenly, he spotted her dark shape some distance down the moonlit drive. "Sophia, wait!"

The moment she turned and saw him coming after her, she whirled around at once and started running again.

Bloody hell.

"Sophia, come back!" He picked up his pace, striding across the courtyard.

"Stay away from me!" she yelled over her shoulder.

"I'm not going to hurt you!" He began jogging toward her down the rocky drive, even though he knew she might interpret this as threatening. He wanted to reassure her, but first he had to catch up. "Please, just stop for a moment and listen! I'm sorry!"

"I don't want to hear any more of your

accusations!"

She sounded like she was crying. *Oh, God.* He felt like such a heel. Gaining on her with his longer strides, he tried again in a more placating tone. "Sophia, I've brought you your knife. Don't you want it back?"

"Keep it!" she flung out.

"Sophia, don't go! Enough of this!" he exclaimed. "I'm not going to hurt you!" He ran faster, aware of a very slight pressure around his healing scar as he slowly closed the distance between them. "Would you just *pause* for a moment and give me a chance to apologize?"

"Ow!"

Ahead of him, he saw her twist an ankle on a large stone on the uneven drive.

He winced for her sake, but when her unladylike curse reached his ears, he couldn't help smiling ruefully. There was something so vibrant, so piquant about her, this strange, unpredictable Gypsy girl.

She could steal his very heart if he wasn't careful.

Tripped up by the rock, Sophia had not fallen, but she dropped back to a walk — or rather, a dignified limp.

"Are you all right?" he called in concern.

"I'm fine!" Ahead, she stopped — planted one hand on her waist — and slowly turned around, tilting her head to the side. She gave him a haughty look as Gabriel jogged toward her.

"That's far enough," she ordered, holding out her hand to halt him.

Still a good ten feet away, he stopped, not wishing to scare her again, but he was a little taken aback by her forcefulness. When she tossed her moonlit curls and lifted her chin, however, he saw through her show of bravado, and his heart clenched.

"Here," he mumbled awkwardly. "I thought you'd want this back." He tossed her knife, blade-down, onto the neutral turf between them.

Holding him in a guarded stare, she approached, moving stealthily despite her slight limp, and retrieved her weapon with an almost palpable satisfaction.

At least they had that much in common.

As soon as she had grasped the weapon, she hitched up her skirts and slid her knife back into its sheath, strapped to her thigh.

Gabriel's mouth watered, but he refused to ogle that beautiful stretch of sleek, feminine leg. Redoubling his will to resist temptation, he dropped his gaze and cleared his throat a bit. "I did not mean to scare you. I'm sorry. I acted like a beast. I accused you unjustly, as well. I saw that you didn't take anything."

"No, I did not!" She folded her arms across her chest, but she sounded somewhat mollified. "And yes, you did," she agreed.

Unaccustomed to making apologies for his usually impeccable behavior, let alone being scolded, however deservedly, by a mere slip of a girl, he furrowed his brow. "I don't know why you were looking at my things," he said in a slightly sterner tone. "In all fairness, you were really not at liberty to pry like that, but all the same, you did not deserve to be insulted. I apologize, and I hope you will forgive me."

She nodded, looking away and finally showing a shred of shame for her outrageous snooping. "As I told you, I was just a bit . . . curious . . . about you."

"If there was something you wanted to know, you could have just asked me."

"You wouldn't have answered!"

"Why not?"

"Because I'm just a-a lowly Gypsy girl, and you're my employer," she said, eyeing him warily. "It's not my place to ask you questions."

He gazed at her for a long moment. "Why don't you come back inside and have dinner with me, and you can ask me whatever you want?"

He suspected it was the offer of food more than his company that brought a ray of hope back into her eyes.

He could just imagine how hard Mrs. Moss had worked her today. He doubted the girl had had a decent meal since noon.

But she was still hesitant.

"What is it?" he murmured. Was she not satisfied with his apology? For God's sake, that was as close to groveling as he would ever come.

"I'm not sure I trust you," she said carefully, keeping her distance.

"Fair enough," he conceded in a low tone. "I'm not sure I trust you, either. But I'm willing to put my faith in you if you'll do the same for me." He took a step closer. "You don't have to worry about me, Sophia, all right?" he offered softly. "I'm not going to touch you. You have my word on that. I know I overstepped my bounds. It was a momentary slip and it will not happen again. You've got your knife back. If I even look at you wrong, just stab me, as you planned. I promise, this time I won't resist. I'm sure I would deserve it after that."

She returned his sardonic smile guardedly. "I wasn't really going to stab you."

"I know." He held her stare with total sincerity. "And I would not in a million years force myself on you or any woman."

"I know." Her voice was barely a whisper; she dropped her gaze. "I think I can tell that about you."

"Good."

They stared at each other for a long moment in the moonlight. He shivered a bit, for the autumn night was cold and he'd run out without a coat. She was shivering, too, holding on tight to the strap of her knapsack over one shoulder.

He looked away, frustrated by the pathetic picture of the little errant waif. Damn, she was stubborn. What more could he say to persuade her?

"Sophia, I know you're eager to get the hell out of here," he conceded, summoning up a final dose of patience. "But the nearest coaching inn is about three miles away — which you probably already know, since I assume that's how you got here. The stage-coach only passes once a day, and you've already missed it. I'll bring you over there tomorrow if you like, and I already told you I'd buy your ticket back to London. But I simply will *not* be responsible for letting a young woman wander the countryside all night by herself. Come back to the house where I'll know that you're safe. Come now, chicken stew and a proper bed — that is my offer, take it or leave it."

"A bed?"

"No, don't worry — you misunderstand me," he amended hastily "I mean I'll make sure to give you a bedchamber where the door locks, nice and sturdy. Would it make you feel better to sleep with one of my guns under your pillow?"

"Yes, it actually would."

"Well — all right then." He hadn't been quite serious on that last point, but if that's what it took to persuade her she was safe with him, then so be it, he thought in startled amusement. "If that's settled, come along, then."

Still, she balked, studying him strangely.

"Well?" he prompted.

"Why do you even care what happens to me?"

"You've got spirit. I admire that. And I guess . . . I really could do with some company," he admitted, lowering his head. "Come on," he ordered after a moment. "You're going to catch your death out here and I'm starved."

"So am I." She started toward him, but Gabriel frowned when he saw her limping.

He strode over, closing the remaining distance between them. "Let me help you."

She eyed him warily, hanging back.

"I won't bite," he murmured. "Lean on me."

Her dark eyes flickered mysteriously as she held his gaze, then she glanced down at his offered hand. "Thanks." She laid her hand in his. "I won't forget this, Gabriel," she whispered as she let him guide her carefully over the rocky ground.

"Neither will I, believe me," he answered with a dry glance.

She chuckled at his quip, and he shook his head, quite mystified by her.

"I've got to say, Sophia, you really don't seem a harlot to me."

"Well, you don't seem much like an ordinary man."

"I'm trying."

She laughed and steadied herself with a hand on his arm. And they walked back together to the house.

CHAPTER FIVE

Inside the farmhouse was dark and empty, Mrs. Moss having returned to her cottage for the night. After Gabriel locked the front door, Sophia followed him into the dimly lit warmth of the kitchen, where the low hearth-fire still glowed beneath the simmering cauldron of stew.

"Sit, please. Make yourself comfortable," he said with a gesture toward the table. "I'll serve."

"You'll serve?" she echoed in surprise.

He sent her a quick smile over his shoulder. "I invited you in as my guest, Sophia, not as my servant. Besides, you should keep the weight off that ankle for a while."

"It's not bad," she assured him as she set down her knapsack by the wall and slowly took off her cloak. "I just twisted it a little."

Still puzzled by his solicitude, she watched Gabriel cross to the hearth. Of course, she was used to people waiting on her, but they did her bidding because they had to — it was their duty — not because they wanted to. Not necessarily because they cared.

Gabriel was so different. He seemed to be concerned about her simply as a person.

Over by the large fireplace, he took a towel off the mantel and used it to protect his hand as he lifted the heated lid and peered into the simmering stew pot.

"Looks good." He glanced over his shoulder at her with a beguiling smile. "Smells even better. Hungry?"

"Starved," she admitted with a smile.

"Me, too." He set the lid aside and reached for the large serving spoon that hung from a peg driven into the thick wood mantel.

As he used the big spoon to stir the stew, she watched him with a mystified air. "You certainly seem to know what you're doing over there." When he shrugged in his modest way, she lifted her eyebrows. "A man who can cook?"

"Enough to avoid starvation," he said dryly. "Army life teaches you to become self-sufficient. Fast."

Recalling all the trouble she'd had with the simple household chores she had been assigned today, Sophia dropped her gaze with a self-conscious wince. "Well, if you can cook, I can at least set the table."

"You don't have to."

"No, no, please."

"Fair enough." He sent her a nod. "Thanks."

"Dining room?"

"I usually just eat here," he said, glancing at the rustic, old kitchen table.

Sophia nodded. "All right."

While he got the food ready, she moved around the kitchen, gathering bowls and cutlery, and carefully setting the table, but picturing Gabriel eating alone here night after night made her want to touch him, just to reach out. The truth was, she ate alone a lot of the time, as well, an army of silent, stone-faced servants arrayed around her in the lonely grandeur of her dining hall.

Maybe on this dark and lonely night, both of them were more desperate for simple human contact than either really cared to admit.

He hung the large spoon back on its peg again and then fetched a candelabra to add more light to the table for their meal. He placed it on the center of the table, but when he turned around, they nearly ran into each other, for Sophia was coming up behind him with the salt.

They exchanged a rather shy smile, avoided a collision, and circled around each other. Sophia tried not to stare, but a ripple of tingling awareness moved through her as Gabriel brushed past.

While she stepped into the old buttery, where the air was dark and damp, cooled by an underground spring, he went back to the hearth, then returned with a long match and transferred its small flame to the candelabra. Sophia collected the squat little ceramic tub of fresh butter from a shelf, then retrieved the basket of wheat rolls from the pantry, and when she had put them on the table, Gabriel smiled at her.

"I think we have everything ready now." He pulled out one of the plain wooden chairs for her, ever the gentleman.

She nodded, smiling at him, then lowered herself into the chair. He pushed her in politely, then turned away and went back to the hearth.

Her heart pounded with her awareness of him as he filled a bowl of stew and brought it to her. Sophia watched him avidly as he set it down before her, as though his simplest motions were the most gripping spectacle in all the world. She nodded her thanks, then he went back to fill a second bowl for himself.

Returning with his soup, Gabriel set it down, then paused, lifting an eyebrow.

"Hm, something's missing." He walked over to the cabinet and took a bottle of wine down from the top shelf.

Before long, he had poured it for them and, at last, sat down with her. They looked at each other for a long moment . . . cautiously, searchingly. He picked up his glass and raised it to her in a wordless toast.

She smiled, blushing a bit; somehow there was more sincerity in this hard soldier's silent offering than all the flowery eloquence of a hundred flattering courtiers.

She lifted her glass, clinked it softly against his, and whispered, "Thank you."

"Thank *you*," he replied.

"For what? Setting the table?"

"Giving an idiot male another chance."

She snorted at his wry self-deprecation. "Cheers."

He smiled sardonically, took a swallow of the white wine, and then began to eat.

Sophia lingered over her wineglass, watching Gabriel try the stew first. Ever since her father had been poisoned, her mother, Queen Theodora, had ordered her and all her brothers always to let the royal food tasters sample every dish before they partook. Without even thinking about it, Sophia waited, watching him.

"Well, go on," Gabriel urged her with a

smile, noticing her hesitation. "I thought you said you were hungry."

She blinked in surprise, realizing only then what she was doing out of mere habit. She couldn't help laughing at herself a bit, but she gave him a warm smile, then picked up her spoon and joined him in the meal. After all, no one bothered poisoning lowly Gypsy girls.

"Delicious," Gabriel remarked as he finished swallowing another mouthful.

Sophia glanced at him, pleased by his enjoyment of food that *she* had helped to cook. She had never cooked a meal for anyone before. Watching him, she was beginning to wonder if her role as princess was isolating her more than she had realized from life's simple pleasures.

When she thought of all the precautionary measures she had to take in life — food tasters, bodyguards, decoys — she could certainly understand his desire to be just an ordinary man.

Sympathy for him on that point made her reluctant to ask the questions about his military career that had been burning in her mind ever since she found his traveling trunk. Outside, he had told her that if she came back, he would let her ask whatever she wanted, but right now, it was good just to share this meal in companionable silence.

She hadn't noticed how often she was glancing at him until he pointed it out.

"Sophia," he drawled in an offhand manner. "You are staring at me again." Reaching for the butter, he eyed her with a roguish twinkle in his cobalt eyes.

She blushed. "Sorry."

"Something on your mind?"

"Not really."

"Then eat, girl! Anyone ever tell you you're too skinny?"

"I am not!"

He tossed a roll at her and she laughed as she caught it. "Very well." She took some butter and smeared it onto her supper roll. "So, what did you do today, Major? I did not see you much around the house."

"No, I was off traipsing around the countryside trying to find the owner of that bay gelding."

Her eyes widened, but she quickly chased all signs of guilt off her face — she hoped. "Any luck?"

"No," he replied nonchalantly. "It is the dashedest thing. None of the farmers around here have ever seen the animal before. A fine horse, in excellent health. Well trained, too. How he wound up here has quite mystified us all."

"He must have run away," she proposed.

"Indeed. Very careless of his owner. At any rate, I left word at the surrounding farms in case his rightful owner comes looking for him. I wouldn't want to be accused of trying to steal the animal. After all, horse stealing is a hanging offense. You do know that, don't you, Sophia?" he added softly, pausing over his meal.

"You think I had something to do with this?" she exclaimed in answer to his searching stare. "If you're accusing me again —"

"I'm not accusing you of anything. But you must admit, it does seem a bit . . . coincidental that you both showed up here at about the same time."

"I thought we've already been through this. I've never stolen anything in my life," she declared and set her spoon down.

"I'm only wondering if some — beau or brother of yours might have followed you into the area and might be responsible for, shall we say, liberating the animal."

She shook her head, her attitude cooling toward him. "I have no beaux, nor any brother within many miles of here."

He gazed into her eyes for a moment, his own so deep and ocean-blue.

He was such a solid man; Sophia felt terrible all of a sudden for lying to him about everything.

"Very well. I will say no more about it," he conceded, then he smiled cautiously. "But I do find it hard to believe that you have no beaux."

"Well, my dear Major," she said with a sigh as she picked up her spoon again. "Some women were just not meant to be tamed."

He leaned nearer and murmured, "Those are my kind of women."

Though Gabriel didn't quite trust her and didn't believe half of what she said, something about Sophia charmed him all the same. She was much more sure of herself than the women he was used to. The trait intrigued him.

He was warmed by her fire and vibrancy, drawing him back to the mortal realm. The contrast between this night — hearing Sophia's laughter, her heated exclamations; watching the lively play of emotions chase across her expressive face by candlelight — and the cold, dark night before, alone in the ruined church, fighting his demons, could not have been more marked.

The simple communal bond of sharing this meal with her, as plain as it was, felt like pure decadence. The luxury of her company made him feel like a king.

As their conversation flowed with surprising ease, he could sense her pulling him out of his isolation, yet he was hungry tonight in more ways than one.

He forced himself to banish tormenting images of brushing the plates aside and making love to her right there on the kitchen table. Everything in him longed for her, but he was *not* giving in to that impulse.

She had forgiven him once and placed her trust in him. He was not going to slip up again, especially after he had given his word not to touch her. Still, with the wayward drift of his thoughts, he couldn't help musing that it was remarkable how innocent she seemed, given her profession.

Innocent yet strong. She could not have known many men before she came here, he thought, taking another swallow of wine. A shocking thought suddenly struck him. Surely Derek was not devilish enough to have purchased a virgin for him.

Good God.

"So," Sophia said at length as their meal wound down. She sat back, slowly swirling the wine in her glass. "You are a cavalry officer."

He tensed. "Was. I've sold my commission," he said.

"Did you serve in the Peninsula?" she murmured, watching him intently.

He shook his head. "India." His mood turned a little impassive at her cautious questioning, but he knew he had promised to answer if she would agree to come back. She had, so he must, and there it was.

"India," she echoed, gently encouraging him along.

"I was born in Calcutta. My father was once highly placed in the East India Company, but he retired from his post some years ago and is now quite the gentleman of leisure." Gabriel smiled, speaking of his father. They had always been very close. "Lord Arthur Knight."

"Lord?"

"Oh, yes. Father's elder brother was a duke, now deceased. The present duke's my cousin."

She lifted her eyebrows, looking both amused and impressed. "Which one?"

"Hawkscliffe."

"Ah, the Tory who turned Whig and married his mistress."

Gabriel's lips twisted wryly. "Quite so."

"So, you're from a scandalous family," she drawled. "They are fortunate their rank protects them from the ton's censure."

"Indeed." He furrowed his brow. "You

read the Society pages or something?" He wouldn't have thought she could read at all.

"Oh, no," she amended quickly. "I eavesdrop on fine ladies' gossip."

"Aha. Well, I seem to be the only nonscandalous member of our extended family."

"So far," she replied with a mischievous twinkle in her dark eyes.

He snorted, but then got distracted, watching her as she licked her lips slowly. She paused as though gathering her courage to ask the next question in this little interview. Gabriel braced for it.

"Was it in India that you got your scar?"

He nodded.

"How did it happen?"

He stared at her for a long moment and then heaved a sigh. "My cousin the Duke of Hawkscliffe's boyhood chum and longtime friend of the family, Lord Griffith, came to India on a diplomatic mission. He's a high-ranking negotiator with the Foreign Office — what, you've heard of the Marquess of Griffith, too, in all your eavesdropping?" he asked sardonically when he saw how her eyes had flared.

She nodded, wide-eyed.

Gabriel laughed softly and shook his head. "Well, considering the long-standing family alliance between the Hawkscliffe dukes and the Griffith marquesses, Griff made a point of visiting our branch of the family when he arrived in Calcutta. Which is where he met my sister, whom he ended up marrying, but I digress. To show preferment, Griff requested that Derek and I head up his diplomatic security detail for his mission into the interior. Poor devil had been tasked with trying to keep Britain out of war with the Maratha Empire."

Sophia was staring at him as if she had seen a ghost. "You were a — diplomatic bodyguard?"

"On that occasion, yes. I can assure you my preferred location was the battlefield with my men, but my aristocratic family connections made me a favored candidate to shepherd various important personages around India when they came visiting from London. Simply put, it was my job to make sure they didn't get killed. Stupid bleeders, most of them," he muttered. "Like minding children. Tripping about as if they were still in Mayfair. Heedless of danger, insulting the locals without even realizing it." He shook his head again. "Griff was one of the few who knew what the hell he was doing."

Gabriel fell silent, staring into the candle's dancing flame as his mind revolved around all that had happened during Griff's mission, and their fateful visit to the Maharajah of Janpur. He shrugged off the past uncomfortably.

That Hindu prince had gone after his sister, Georgiana, and if he had to do it over again, he'd have killed the little bastard just the same. Nobody laid a hand on his sister.

"To make a long story short, we encountered opposition," he said abruptly.

"Someone tried to kill your diplomat?" she murmured, studying him.

"Actually, someone tried to kill my brother." Of course, Derek had instantly joined the battle to protect Georgiana. If it wasn't for Griff's quick thinking, they'd all have been dead.

He shook his head grimly. "Derek didn't see it coming. I just reacted automatically. The next thing I knew, I was down. After that, I don't remember much."

Sophia's eyes were wide, and her voice was barely a whisper. "You took a bullet for your brother?"

"Actually, it was an arrow," he said.

"Oh," she breathed, staring at him in apparent awe.

Gabriel shrugged and looked away, a bit uncomfortable with the flicker of hero-worship in her gaze. "Derek would have done the same for me."

Thankfully, she let that painful thread of their conversation fade and smiled at him after a moment. "I see now my pulling a knife on you could have been suicidal."

He scoffed. "I'd never hurt a woman."

"I know. But I do apologize for it all the same."

He smiled wryly at her. "No matter, Sophia. I've faced meaner enemies than you."

"I'm sure you have."

He stared at her, arrested by the subtle sparkle of her creamy skin in the candlelight, and once more felt the drift of his thoughts gliding off in a dangerous direction. He dropped his gaze and pushed his empty bowl away. "So, what about you?"

"What about me?" she asked guardedly.

"I think it's your turn now to answer some questions," he declared in a low tone.

She slanted him a dubious look as he rested his elbow on the table and propped his jaw on his fist, studying her with a faint smile.

"Like what?"

Gabriel took note of the nervousness behind her glance. He knew quite well she had been less than forthcoming with him, but at the same time, he sensed that pressing her for answers would only succeed in driving her farther away, and he did not want that.

After all his time alone, he was savoring the warmth of this unexpected bond between them too much to risk breaking it. The connection he felt between them was still too fragile, too new. It really was quite strange. Usually, he despised liars, and he knew she had not been honest with him, but somehow she was different. So, he opted for a gentler approach, and gave her a casual smile.

"What's it like being a Gypsy?"

She let out a small laugh and dropped her gaze with a trace of relief passing over her face that she probably did not know she betrayed. "Not very nice, sometimes, when people assume you've only come around for the old snatch-and-grab," she shot back with a pointed smile. "It's most unpleasant to have false tales circulated about one's tribe, you know."

"Well, maybe you and I can clear up a few of those mistaken notions now," he suggested.

"Let's," she agreed with a firm but playful nod.

"Babies," he said.

"What about them?"

"Is it true you Gypsies steal little children

if they misbehave for their parents?"

"Oh, yes," she averred. "We use them as our slaves."

"Horses?" He nodded toward the window through which he had seen the bay gelding first appear. "Is it true that Gypsies steal them?"

"By the herd."

"Silk handkerchiefs?" he queried with a mock frown.

"Child's play," she purred.

Gabriel laughed, dying to kiss her.

She took another sip of wine and gave him a coquettish look askance. "Come, Major, I'm sure you don't like it when Londoners assume you're some sort of colonial savage, all for having been born in India."

"Oh, but I am."

"A savage?"

"Quite. And you're ruining all my illusions! Surely some of those wonderful tales about Gypsies must be true. At least tell me you all still travel around the countryside selling trinkets and telling fortunes?"

"Well, yes, that much is true," she conceded.

"Finally! So, you can see the future, eh? Do you have a crystal ball?"

"I don't need a ball, my friend. I can do better than that."

He leaned closer and lowered his voice. "Can you read my palm?"

Holding his avid stare, Sophia reached toward him with a graceful twirl of her fingers and boldly captured his right hand, turning it, palm up, on the table. "Let's have a look," she whispered with a mysterious air. "Hmm . . . yes, I see."

Gabriel gazed at her in delighted bewilderment. Sophia lowered her head, but when she traced her fingertip over a curved line across his palm, he quivered; she looked up through her lashes and met his feverish stare.

Maybe she did have magical powers, he thought, heart pounding, for no woman had ever conjured such a storm of want in him. He would have loved to introduce her to some of India's more exotic arts.

She bit her lip, dropping her gaze to his callused hand once more. Her touch was warm and light and mesmerizing. He leaned nearer. "Can you divine my destiny, Sophia?" he asked in a husky murmur.

"I will — try."

He was pleased to hear the breathy catch in her voice. Thank God he was not the only one so powerfully affected.

"What do you see?" he whispered.

"Long life . . ."

"Now I know you are a charlatan," he teased in a low tone. "Small chance of that."

"Long life," she repeated insistently. "I see . . . courage . . . loyalty . . . strength. But wait — I see danger in your future."

"Yes, you still have your knife," he reminded her dryly.

She flicked him a chiding look and continued their flirtatious game. "There could be danger ahead for you, I'm afraid, but also much happiness. Your palm says you are destined for great things."

"Could you possibly be more specific?"

Sophia looked at him intently. Her big, brown eyes were deep and soulful, at odds with his sardonic manner of a moment ago.

"What is it?" Gabriel murmured. Had he offended her with his teasing?

"Who were the candles for?" she whispered, quite out of nowhere. "I saw you lighting them last night, from the barn."

He pulled his hand back in sudden wariness. "Why didn't you make your presence known?"

She lifted her shoulders in a delicate shrug. "You looked like you did not want to be disturbed. Besides," she admitted, "I was a little afraid of you. I thought it might be best to wait until morning to come and knock on the door. But the candles," she said again. "Do you light them for someone you loved?"

"No." He dropped his gaze, silent for a moment. "I light them for the men I've killed in battle. Glad you asked?"

When he glanced at her again, the trace of a frown wrinkled her smooth brow, but she appeared undaunted.

She picked up the bottle of wine and refilled his glass for him. Maybe he looked like he needed it. "Does that have something to do with why you're living out here in the middle of nowhere?"

He shrugged. "All I seek now is peace." Then he eyed her cautiously. "You Gypsies are said to possess occult abilities. Perhaps from your people's lore, you can explain how this can be. The strangest thing . . ." His words trailed off as he hesitated, fearing she might doubt his sanity if he revealed his secret to her.

On the other hand, God knew he had to tell someone.

"Gabriel?" she whispered, tilting her head as she studied him more closely. "What is it?"

He passed a guarded glance over her lovely face. "I saw something when I was wounded. The surgeon . . . later told me that my heart stopped." He watched her reaction with cloaked intensity.

She narrowed her eyes, then folded her arms along the edge of the table. "Do you mean to say you were . . . ?"

"Dead. Briefly. Yes."

She appeared to have been rendered speechless, then she lifted her eyebrows, taking this in stride. "I see," she said after a moment.

"The surgeon said my pulse came back approximately two minutes later. I remember that. The choking feeling. I could see him trying to revive me. I could see them all working on me — as if I were a ghost floating up above my body."

"Really?"

He nodded. "I told my brother, but not even Derek believed me. What say you? Can your Gypsy secrets tell me what this means?"

Perhaps the tone of quiet desperation in his voice had roused her sympathy. She reached out to him, laying her hand on his forearm. She gave it a firm squeeze of steadying comfort. "All it means is it wasn't your time."

"I didn't want to come back," he breathed, shaking his head. "I wanted to stay there, where it was peaceful, but they wouldn't let me."

"Who?"

"I don't know. I could not see their faces. The light was too brilliant. Angels, maybe. Ghosts? They told me I had to go back. That there was still something I had to do."

Her eyes were wide as she searched his face in amazement.

Gabriel summoned up a rueful smile. "Now you think I'm mad."

"No —"

"Believe me, Sophia, I know how absurd this all sounds. I am a commonsense man. A military man. I have never indulged in flights of fancy." He shrugged. "But I know what I saw."

She tossed back the last swallow of her wine, probably needing it at this point. She mulled over his words for a moment, then slid him a guarded look. "Do you have any idea what you're still supposed to do?"

He shook his head. "That's what I came out here to try to figure out. It's quiet here. Peaceful. If there's any place meant for contemplation . . ." His words trailed off.

"Hm," she said.

He had not told her *all* of what he had seen in those weird, suspended moments, but he had said too much already. If he told her about the fiery part of his vision, that brief, hellish tour of the smoky battlefields of his past and all the death and agony he had caused his fellow man, she would think he was a lunatic for certain.

"At least I know one thing," he declared in a confidential tone after a moment. "I know what my destiny isn't. It's not going back to the cavalry. I could not possibly kill another human being ever again. After what I saw, I'm quite sure that doing so would cost me my immortal soul."

"Gabriel." She looked a little shaken by his words, and touched his arm once more, offering him a small caress. Then, without warning, she leaned over and pressed a soft, tender kiss to his lips.

He closed his eyes, reminded achingly of that brief glimpse of heaven.

"All will be well," she whispered as she cupped his nape, her fingers threading through his overgrown hair. "Now, listen to me. I'm sure all those weapons of yours can remain put away in that box. You just stay out here where it's quiet and the air is clean," she said softly. "In time, your peace will come."

"So say your Gypsy powers?" he murmured skeptically, loving her touch.

"So says my heart." Her gentle stare caressed his face. To his amusement, she pressed an almost motherly kiss to his forehead.

Leaning back again to her own chair, she smiled uncertainly at him.

Gabriel watched her every move with riveted intensity.

"It's getting late," she mumbled. "I'd better get these dishes done."

"Leave them."

"Mrs. Moss will have an apoplectic fit."

"I'll deal with her. You've done enough work for one day. Go and choose a suitable room and we'll put some clean sheets on the bed for you."

"Clean sheets for a person who smells like a stable?" she muttered, laughing in mild embarrassment.

He shrugged. "You can reuse the bath if you want. It'd be a simple matter to add a few pails of hot water to warm it up again. It's just sitting there — or is that too Army for you?"

"No, I'll take it!" she exclaimed, lighting up. "Oh, bless you — I'm not too proud to say yes. That would be grand!"

"Right, then. We always keep a cauldron of hot water on the fire-crane. Go and choose a room to sleep in," he ordered as they both rose from the table.

"One where the door locks?" she replied

with a saucy look, recalling his words from outside.

"If that's what you prefer," he answered in a silken tone.

She blushed.

He laughed quietly and turned away. "Run along, Gypsy girl. I'll bring the water up for you."

She smiled uncertainly at him and started to go, but when she reached the doorway, she glanced back over her shoulder. "Gabriel?"

"Hm?" Heading for the hearth, he turned back to her.

"I don't think you're mad," she said softly. "I believe in destiny, too."

He smiled at her in gratitude. "Thanks." She turned to go. "Sophia?"

"Yes?" She spun around again at once with the hint of a peachy blush in her cheeks.

"I'm glad you're here," he admitted with a nod.

She gave him a tremulous smile in answer, then hurried off into the shadows, leaving him alone.

When she had gone, he let out a sigh. Well, she was certainly more interesting company than the kittens or Mrs. Moss. He reached toward the fire-crane to fetch the hot water for her bath, puzzling with some irony over how the master had become the servant.

Ah, well. Such was the power of a beautiful woman, he mused. And whatever Sophia might be, she was certainly that.

CHAPTER SIX

There was something curiously seductive about using the same water Gabriel had bathed in. She felt . . . covered in him somehow.

It was not an unpleasant feeling.

Sometime later, Sophia was luxuriating in warm water up to her shoulders and silently rejoicing to have washed the smell of the stable out of her hair. Unlike during Gabriel's bath, she had made sure to keep the door to the dressing room closed. By the light of a few candles burning here and there, she glided the small oval of soap slowly up her arm. Gabriel had gone to make a fire in her chamber so she would not catch a chill when she left the bath.

He had also said that he would make her bed. *Strangest man.* All of this was thoroughly bizarre. She leaned her head back against the edge of the tub, still in a state of lingering amazement over all that he had told her, and filled with an unnerving sense of destiny.

If Leon had shouted any other code at her in those frantic moments of her escape from the ambush, she'd have ended up elsewhere. Instead, by an unforeseeable twist of fate, she had arrived here, safely under the care of a decorated war-hero — a man not only experienced as a diplomatic bodyguard, but who also had family ties to one of the Foreign Office lords who was to have attended last night's secret meeting at the castle. She had not met Lord Griffith yet, but she had certainly heard the name.

But that was not all.

Gabriel's service in India had left him well versed in the Eastern way of warfare. Blinded as they were by chivalrous Western notions of honor, the English diplomats she had dealt with so far could not seem to grasp the kind of savagery that fought to win, by any means, at any cost. If, as Sophia suspected, she was being targeted by Ali Pasha, then the Iron Major was just the sort of seasoned ally she needed by her side.

Above all, here was a man who had defied Death itself, that black shadow that had taken so much from her. She was in awe of his mystical glimpse into the afterworld, and by his words that there was something he still had to do, some task as yet unfulfilled that he had to accomplish.

She had a fair idea she knew what it was.

No, she thought with a grim shake of her head. Enough people she cared about had already been killed. She could not ask it of him.

She did not want him involved, not after all he had been through. One thought of that cruel scar she had seen in the center of his solar plexus like a small, angry sun with little rays shooting out from all around it — that alone was enough to forbid her from asking him to join her quest.

The man had already been through hell. His courage had cost him enough of his blood. As he had said, all he wanted now was to live in peace, and he deserved that chance, the same boon she wanted to bring to her people.

Therefore, she concluded firmly, as much as she might want to tell him now who she really was, more than ever, she knew she could not. Of course he had won her trust, but her secrecy was no longer about protecting herself.

Now it was a matter of protecting *him.*

She had seen enough of Gabriel Knight to know that if she explained her situation, his honor would require him to get involved, and with all her heart, she vowed to keep him out of her family's nightmare.

Her heart ached for all he had suffered, nearly giving his life for his brother. This was one warrior who had laid down his arms, and she respected his right to do so.

Even for the sake of her people, she refused to let her own pressing goals override this man's need for peace and healing. Bad enough that she had to answer his stark honesty with deception. There was no need to drag him into this and subject him to more danger, more violence — let alone ask him to volunteer himself as a target for the faceless enemies out for her blood.

No, as much as she wanted to tell him the truth, the secret of her identity must stand.

She had already put him enough at risk just by hiding here at the farmhouse.

This was no time to lose faith in her trusty retinue of Greek guards. She had faltered outside, nearly letting her fears get the best of her, but with her flagging courage restored by food and shelter, she refused to give up hope.

It would not be long now before her men reappeared to usher her back to her mission. She merely had to give them a bit more time to locate her.

Perhaps if another twenty-four hours

143

passed and there was still no sign of them, then she might consider asking Gabriel to help her reach the castle.

But only as a last resort. She promised herself she would only involve him if she had no other choice.

She reminded herself that she was no drooping damsel in distress. With a good night's sleep, some improvements to her disguise, additional supplies pilfered into her knapsack, and a few of those unused weapons she had spotted in Gabriel's traveling trunk, she could always take the bay horse again and make her way on to the castle alone.

Just then, a hesitant knock sounded politely on the door.

Rap, tap, tap.

"Sophia?"

Gabriel.

At the sound of his deep, silken voice, she lifted her head and looked over; his trusty nearness brought the hint of a smile to her lips. Unfamiliar longings for an even greater closeness with him rippled through her.

"Yes, Major, what is it?"

"I, ah, got your bedroom ready and found you something to wear."

"How kind." He had to know that she desired him, she thought, biting her lip as she fought a girlish smile.

What was it about this man that entranced her?

At supper, she had had such trouble trying to hide her attraction to him. He must be able to feel it, to see it in her eyes.

A part of her wanted him to see it.

On the other side of the door, Gabriel cleared his throat as if he could hear her thoughts. "I have a shirt of mine for you, and a robe, as well, if you want it. I'll hang them on the door for when you're ready, all right?"

Sophia sat up straighter in the tub and answered all of a sudden: "Would you mind bringing them in?"

For a heartbeat, no sound returned.

She was motionless, having shocked herself with her scandalous invitation. It sounded like she must have shocked him, too.

But why must they go on denying their mutual attraction? Who were they fooling? He wanted her, she wanted him, and this might be the only chance she'd get before her guards returned. One precious night to shrug off the burden of her royal role and discover the pleasures other women knew.

Yes, in one impulsive moment, Sophia decided to reach out to him, to explore her first sensual experience with this man. If the old troubles of her family were back, then her days on earth were probably numbered. It was too unfair to go to her grave never knowing the sweetness of a skillful lover's touch. Gabriel Knight was beautiful in mind and body; his desire for her, his raw need had been obvious earlier when he had kissed her.

More important, she trusted him — this chivalrous, oh-so-handsome officer. She wanted her first taste of love to be with him, if he was willing.

It had to be him, for with every suitor who had ever tried to court her, she was never sure if it was she herself that each beau wanted or her throne. A tedious approach to romance, to be sure.

But Gabriel had no idea of her true status. When he looked at her, he saw a woman. That was all.

They were stuck here together anyway tonight, so why not make the best of it?

No one else need ever know.

Certainly, she'd never get away with something like this with the eagle-eyed Leon nearby — and he was *always* nearby.

The fact was, the Virgin Queen was not her only model for a female ruler.

So was Cleopatra the seductress.

The door opened slowly.

Heart pounding, Sophia leaned forward, resting her crossed arms along the edge of the tub to conceal her breasts. As she watched and waited for him to step into the little closet of a room, the first part of him to appear was one ebony riding boot, followed by a thickly muscled leg in dun-colored breeches, and then the man himself.

He glanced at her as he came in, his black eyebrows knitted in a suspicious line. As his gaze swept over her bare skin, he looked away at once, focusing his suddenly glazed stare on the clothes he had brought for her. They were draped over his arm.

"Uh, where would you like these?"

Staring at him in avid interest, Sophia gestured toward the nearby chair with an idle wave of her hand. "Over there, if it's no trouble."

He bowed his head. "As you wish."

I wonder what Mrs. Moss would have to say about this . . .

Sophia tracked him with an almost predatory stare full of wicked amusement as he walked slowly around the bathing tub. He threw the shirt and robe down on the chair, and it occurred to her that the noble major was trying very hard to keep his eyes averted.

"Well — there you are, then," he said. "Is there, ah, anything else you need?"

She giggled. "There certainly is."

He frowned at her, meeting her gaze at last as Sophia sent him a mirthful glance over one bare shoulder.

"What is it?"

She tried to think of how to put it, exactly — and suddenly lost her nerve.

"Nothing," she blurted out, turning red.

"Ahem, well, then. I shall leave you your privacy." Gabriel started back toward the door, marching past the tub with a resolute look, his gaze fixed straight ahead.

Sophia saw she was about to lose her chance. Oh, Lord, what would Cleopatra do if her stallion of a soldier, Mark Antony, were about to walk out the door?

"Um, Gabriel?" she spoke up hesitantly, scrabbling about for her nerve as best she could.

With one hand on the doorknob, he went motionless, not looking back, still staring straight ahead.

As if a part of him knew exactly what she wanted.

"Yes?" he asked hoarsely. *Why are you torturing me?* his stiff posture seemed to say.

"Could I have a towel?" she whispered.

Relief eased his tension a little. "Of course.

Sorry. I thought I gave you one."

She could not take her eyes off him. "I don't see it."

"It's right over here." His hand slipped away from the doorknob and he returned, rounding the tub toward the clean, folded towel that lay in plain view.

He reached for it. Just as he turned and started to hand her the towel, Sophia rose from the tub without warning, water coursing down her body.

Gabriel's lips parted as his gaze ran helplessly down the length of her.

Her stare was locked on his face while his gaze homed in on her jutting nipples, tautened with the chill.

Lifting his arm with a blind motion, he offered her the towel, clutching it with a white-knuckled grip.

She shook her head and commanded him in a whisper: "Dry me."

His eyes flickered, lust in their blue depths; she waited, watching his resistance crumble before her eyes.

Gabriel took a slow step closer. He dropped his gaze as he shifted the towel in his hold.

She closed her eyes and bit back a soft moan as he touched the soft cotton to her skin.

Acutely aware of his every move, she felt his hand draped in the cloth follow the curve of her shoulder, down her back, over the curve of her backside. Her chest heaved.

When she felt his lips skim along her shoulder in burning hunger, she lifted her hand and raked her damp fingers through his black hair.

Pressing her cheek with his fingertips, Gabriel turned her to him, lowered his head, and kissed her with drugging depth. She wrapped her arms around his neck and clung to him, a hot wave of desire pouring through her. Her pulse reverberated as he ravished her mouth. This kiss was more purposeful, but every bit as delicious as before. She was amazed all over again at everything — his warm, smooth lips, the tickling chafe of his scruffy jaw against her chin, the silken delight of his tongue caressing hers.

She could feel the tension thrumming through his tough, rugged frame as he slid his hand beneath her hair and drew her even closer by her nape.

When she quivered with yearning, Gabriel paused, mistaking her tremble for a chill. "Come, we mustn't let you get cold," he whispered protectively. Still holding her hand, he moved aside and steadied her as she stepped out of the tub. At once, he returned to the task of drying her, kissing her body as he went.

Sophia wove on her feet a bit, dizzy with delight. Before long, he was on his knees before her, inching the towel down her legs with his lips pressed to her stomach. She braced her hands on his broad shoulders to keep from falling, for his nibbling kisses had her simply light-headed with pleasure. She began slowly twining her fingers through his longish hair. Its texture felt silky-soft to her wondrously sensitized fingertips.

All of her nerve endings had been awakened to dazzling receptivity by his kisses and the light, feathery glide of his hands on her body.

A soft moan escaped her when his roaming lips caressed her nipple. The heat of his mouth thrilled her down to her toes as he captured the swollen peak of her breast on his tongue.

His unshaved chin tickled and chafed the tender skin of her bosom, but not for the world would she have complained. He sucked on first one breast then the other as though she were made of the most addictive confection and he could not get enough. Within a few more minutes of this delicious torment, she feared she would go mad. Her hands seemed to take on a will of their own, clutching at Gabriel's shirt, trying to undress him. She nearly tore the white linen off his back in her need to get her hands on his bare skin.

"Sit down," he ordered gruffly, pausing only long enough to peel his shirt off over his head for her.

She just stared at him, on fire, her chest heaving, too disoriented to quite absorb his words.

Flushed and panting, Gabriel cast her a devastating smile and gave her a bit of much-needed direction, guiding her down onto the chair where he had left the clothes he'd brought her.

Put in her place, she looked at him attentively, biting her lip, and barely able to think what he might do next. Alexa — who knew of such things — had told her a bit about what went on between a lover and his lady, but the wicked shine in Gabriel's deep blue eyes made her wonder if mere words could do these deeds justice.

"Are you warm now?" he murmured.

"Very. Aren't we —" She gulped at her own audacity. "Going to your bed?"

"Soon." He laid his fingertips on her knees and gently, with an almost delicate motion, parted her legs.

"Oh, dear *God*." She jerked with a violent shudder of response as his mouth began to do to her most private regions what it had just finished doing to her breasts.

At first, she did not know *what* to think. Then all thought spun away like a spool of silken thread unraveling, and all that was left was intense sensation and her sense of glorious trust in this man.

He astounded her with his attentions, though he was ruthless in making her accept what he wanted to give. Her embarrassed resistance melted away as he stoked the fires in her blood. The hot, wet, luxurious stroking of his tongue opened her senses wide, his fingers gently penetrating her in preparation for his manhood. Before long, Sophia was draped over the chair in pure abandon, her head back, her hair spilling down behind her, her legs rested on his shoulders, and Gabriel was feasting on her, absorbed in his splendid barbarity.

He had her completely mesmerized, hanging on his every whim. Her body arched in sinuous motion, begging for more in brazen hunger. Then, just when she seemed to hover at the brink of some enormous precipice, he stopped.

"*Now* we can go to my bed," he whispered as he pulled away, panting heavily.

She looked at him in astonishment, then started laughing, she wasn't sure why.

He gave her a quick but extremely rakish smile as he lifted his forearm and brushed her wetness off his chin.

Left to hunger, Sophia shook her head at his devilish cruelty. Still kneeling, Gabriel sat back on his heels and gestured toward the adjoining chamber. "After you."

"Humph." She poked him lightly in the chest with her toe. He laughed. She rose, dragging her hand through his hair as she brushed past him slowly.

He watched her pass with riveted attention. He rose to his feet and then pinched her backside lightly as he followed close behind her. When she squeaked in protest, he picked her up and tossed her onto his bed with a pirate grin and a gleam in his eyes.

She climbed under the covers while Gabriel pulled off his boots. As he joined her on the bed, she reached out and touched him in eager admiration, caressing the sleek muscled planes of his chest. He greeted her touch with a welcoming sigh. She slid her hand lower, letting her touch glide down over the chiseled muscles of his stomach. But when she noticed the scar in the center of his torso, she winced in sympathy for him. Kissing her fingertips, she pressed them lightly to the healed wound.

His hard face softened in a wistful smile.

Staring deeply into her eyes, he eased atop her.

For several quiet minutes, they just lay together, gazing at each other and kissing lightly. Sophia petted his smooth, powerful back. With his elbows planted on either side of her head, he trailed his fingertips over her cheeks and smoothed her drying hair back from her forehead.

"You're really lovely, Sophia," he whispered.

"So are you," she replied with a faint, dreamy smile. Running her hands down his back and savoring every inch of his velveteen skin, she slipped her hands inside his loosened breeches, molding her palms over the manly curves of his muscled buttocks.

He lifted an eyebrow when she squeezed both firm cheeks with a low, naughty laugh.

"Enjoying yourself, hm?"

"Immensely," she answered with another wayward giggle.

He kissed her, but Sophia went on caressing him. Gabriel moved onto his side next to her, wordlessly offering even more interesting areas for her exploration.

While he played with her breasts, she slid

her hand down the front of his body; she watched his rapt response in fascination when her wandering fingers encircled the rigid girth of his arousal. A brief wince of pleasure tightened his face. The sound of his low groan roused an eager flutter of butterflies deep in the pit of her stomach. She squeezed him, stroked him.

His skin was so blissfully warm to the touch.

He closed his eyes as she began to pleasure him in the way that Alexa had once informed her that the males of the species enjoyed being caressed.

Her brazen lady-in-waiting had demonstrated the technique on one of the fight sticks with which Leon made Sophia practice some of her self-defense techniques. But although she had collapsed in red-faced laughter at the time, the lesson came in handy now. Indeed, the solid size of Gabriel's straining phallus quite reminded her of the formidable bamboo rod with which she could break a person's kneecap when provoked.

She turned her face to his and sought his intoxicating lips once more, kissing him as she sought to give back every ounce of pleasure he had given her. His groans entranced her.

Good God, it was surely for the best that this delicious man could not belong to her, Sophia thought, for she knew she'd be horribly possessive of him with all her royal temper. If he even *looked* at another woman, she'd probably be tempted to have the girl thrown into some dungeon.

With another restless sigh full of desire, Gabriel rolled onto his back, pulling Sophia atop him. As her long hair swung down to veil them both in privacy, she smiled at him.

He did not smile back. His eyes were very serious, almost pensive.

"What is the matter?" she asked in a breathless whisper.

"I want to ask you a question, Sophia. And I want you to answer me honestly."

She paused while he wrapped his arms around her naked waist. "All right."

"My brother, Derek." He paused almost grimly. "He's sent me a virgin, hasn't he?"

Her eyes shot open wide.

"Oh, God," he groaned at her guiltily astonished look.

"Am I that bad at this that it shows?" she cried, pulling back a small space.

"Of course not," he said in a strangled tone. "I've merely done this enough to recognize someone who hasn't. This has gone far enough, Sophia. I'm not going to make love to you, no matter how much I might want to."

"Why?"

Letting out a low sound of frustration, he captured two fistfuls of her hair and hugged her to him. "What am I going to do with you? What a silly question!"

"I don't understand. Are you angry at me?"

"No. I'm angry at Derek. For torturing me." He opened his hands and let her hair sift through his fingers as she pulled back and gave him a crestfallen look.

"Don't you want me?"

He scowled at her. "Don't be a fool. You should not be doing this. You should not be for sale."

"You're lecturing me? Now?" she cried.

"Your *virginity*," he specified through gritted teeth, "should not be for sale. You can't be that desperate. Better you should keep to Gypsy ways and steal than sell yourself."

"I beg your pardon, I can do what I want with my body!" But as her craving for him cleared just a bit, of course she saw the blasted man was right.

She could not make love to a commoner. Not for her first time, anyway. Sooner or later, she'd have to wed some foppish Continental prince. After all, her maiden-

head was one of the most important resources that she had to keep in store to save
her country.

Oh, blazes.

She felt horrible for starting all this. Selfish and rotten. And insanely frustrated.

"Are you going to pout now?" he demanded.

"I don't pout!" She glowered at him, then
relented a little. "I'm just not sure I understand."

He shook his head. "It's not that difficult.
I'm not your husband."

"What would I do with a husband?" she
scoffed.

"You don't have to make this any harder
than it already is," he replied. "You know
damned well I'm going out of my mind for
you. I wanted you from that first second in
the barn."

She lowered her lashes, then bent her head
and kissed his throat. "Oh, Gabriel. I want
you, too. So much," she murmured as she
ran her hand down his side.

His skin burned as with fever to the touch
and was moist with the lightest sheen of
sweat.

"All the same, I don't deflower virgins,"
he said stoically.

His rather pompous resolve irked and

amused her simultaneously. Though she knew he was right, she still was not used to taking no for an answer.

"Very well." With a show of obedience, she slid off his body to lie beside him. But then she reached down and took his throbbing hardness in her hand once more.

He shuddered.

"So, you don't deflower virgins," she conceded in a wicked whisper, skimming her lips along his neck. She paused when she reached his earlobe. "What *do* you do to them?"

Gabriel moaned aloud. "That's it." As his passion broke loose, he flipped their positions with renewed ardor; in the blink of an eye, she was on bottom and he was back on top. His massive erection glided against her teeming wetness — but not in.

Sophia panted, thrilled down to her toes as he flirted with the possibility of taking her. *Do it,* she thought, staring into his eyes.

But he wouldn't. The silken head of his member stroked the soaked threshold of her core, only stoking her fire, tormenting her. *No mercy,* indeed. The Iron Major would not yield to temptation, would not drive it in and fulfill her crazed need the way the beating drums of instinct yearned for him to do.

"Please," she blurted out in spite of herself, unable to fight her desire.

"No." His eyes burned like blue flames in the night.

The poor man had to fight both their lust as she spread her legs wider, wanting him for all she was worth. But his control was such that he rationed out just a bit more of the dizzying pleasure — without satisfaction.

"I shall go insane," she panted.

"Mmm, be patient, Sophia."

"I can't. I want you. Why are you doing this to me?"

"You started it. Don't worry. It'll be worth it." He sent her a sly, seductive glance, then kissed her chin. "One day you'll thank me for this."

She moaned as he struck up a gentle rhythm against her body, his big rod sliding against her wetness, caressing her mound with every stroke. She arched against him, holding onto his waist.

"Touch me," he commanded.

She did. Lowering her hand down into the heated space between their bodies, she molded her fingers over his thrusting member. She shuddered to find him wet with her, but now, guided by her touch, his every stroke stimulated her pebbled center while her hand simultaneously pleasured him each time he moved his hips, back and forth.

It was perfect.

Well, it was good enough.

His moan seemed to say he thought so, too.

"Gabriel — kiss me."

He accepted the invitation with depth and ferocity, his tongue plunging deep into her mouth.

If only he would make the hunger stop.

Again, the inner precipice she had almost fallen off earlier beckoned ahead. The banked sensations she had first begun to sense in the other room came creeping back, stealing over her awareness.

She moved with Gabriel in a feverish trance. He kept on kissing her, his magnificent, fevered body still undulating rhythmically against her.

All of a sudden, she cried out, her shocked exclamation muffled under his relentless kisses. She fairly sobbed with the blinding release. Through the fiery haze of her climax, she felt Gabriel's hand cover her own, still wrapped around his steely shaft. He quit kissing her to let her breathe, and she could hear his groans, his harsh panting by her ear as he coaxed her hand to keep stroking his needy member.

Still gasping with pleasure, she gripped him harder and clenched her teeth, determined to show him she wasn't half bad for a virgin.

"Oh, God. Sophia . . ." In mere moments, her renewed efforts drove him over the edge.

He suddenly threw back his head, an enraptured grimace on his face; with a low shout, he exploded in her hand, his whole, powerful body straining in a series of massive pulsations. Racked by each wild wave of release, he covered her quivering stomach with the hot flood of his seed.

"Sophia," he groaned softly as the storm of climax finally eased from him.

She lifted her lashes and looked up dazedly into his eyes. By the candlelight, she could see they had darkened to a deep indigo shade. But it was their heart-melting sweetness that made her quiver in the aftermath of passion.

"Sophia, Sophia," he whispered. He shook his head at her with a fond but chiding half smile. Then he kissed her gently on her big Greek nose.

She was not the easiest woman in the world to figure out.

A while later, having tidied themselves up from their exertions, they lay spoon-fashion in his bed. They faced the window, and Gabriel could see the stars. Sophia nestled sweetly in his arms. They were not exactly sated, but at least now they should both be able to sleep.

Gabriel found himself in the oddest mood, all possessive. God, he had not expected any of this. He had not been with a woman since he was wounded, and after such a long abstinence, he did not mind refraining from full coition. It could wait. In a way, it was almost as if he had reverted to a state of innocence himself. The closeness he felt with Sophia, however, it had been a very long time since he had experienced anything like this.

He understood now why his brother had chosen her for him. Derek had selected her not for debauchery's sake — not because she was a virgin, but in spite of it. Gabriel had to admit she was the perfect sort of companion for him. It was rare to find a female who could hold her own with him.

He had a strong inclination to keep her around, perhaps as his mistress.

Maybe . . . if they got to know each other better, if she ever saw fit to tell him the truth about herself, and if, over time, they ended up becoming a bit more . . . attached, he thought hesitantly, then perhaps just this once he could bend his own rules against deflowering virgins. He had too many damned rules, anyway . . .

But he was getting ahead of himself.

For now, she was a question mark to him, an irresistible puzzle, with her flashing dark eyes and her strong, lithe, delicately sculpted body. Hot-blooded? She was a fireball. He savored the still-fresh memory of her eagerness, but he barely knew what to do with her.

She was a tough little fighter, but she needed someone looking after her. Keep her out of trouble. As for him, well, maybe the truth was, he needed someone, too.

They seemed to suit.

More important, ever since her arrival, a strange sense of new hope had been born in him. Perhaps the answers he sought would finally come if he stopped looking so hard for them and entertained himself for a while with this luscious young thing.

"Sophia?" he murmured in a low tone, all too aware of the soft curve of her backside against his groin.

No answer came.

He listened to the soft, even sound of her breathing and realized she already slumbered. A faint smile curved his lips as he buried his face in her rioty curls. Damn, he was already craving her again, but, ah, well. He'd let her sleep. She had worked hard today.

He still did not know how much of her Gypsy tale to believe, but at the moment, it didn't matter. The feel of her in his arms was real, and right now, that was enough.

He closed his eyes, savoring her smell and the warmth of her silky skin, and the reassuring rhythm of her breath.

Stay with me. He smiled faintly at his own errant thoughts. *I'm going to want you again tomorrow.* He dozed off with his arms around her.

The men had not slept since the target had slipped through their fingers.

Where was she? Where had the little bitch run off to?

Late that night, worn out from searching, the Tunisian took a mouthful of what passed for coffee in this cold, miserable land and spit it out again in disgust.

He was in a bad mood for he had lost his favorite dagger in the fight, but more than that had certainly not expected failure after all his precise planning. His timing had been perfect, as well, but the girl had fought back with a ferocity that none of them had been prepared for.

Though no one cared to admit it, they all felt slightly unmanned by her little victory.

But it would not last.

His men were talking quietly amongst themselves nearby, cleaning their weapons; they wanted her blood now, especially Ahmed, for the royal witch had shot his brother Abdul point-blank in the head.

Kemal stared into the darkness, musing. He had never seen anything like it. Indeed, he had never heard of a female acting in such a manner. But such was the foulness, the perversion the West brought to his people.

And to think that men like Sultan Mahmud should be blind to the danger, even learning to converse in French like an aping fool! He shook his head. Well, there would be changes in due time.

Their first attempt had failed, costing them three of their own, but no matter. Their brothers were martyrs in heaven now, but back here on earth, Kemal and his men would simply try again.

They had little choice. Having backed the wrong contender for the Ottoman throne, the rebel Janissaries were outlaws now. There was no way for them to go but forward.

Their faith in the rightness of their cause

was undimmed. God willing, the Porte Sublime would be purged of these evil influences — but first, he and his men had to prove themselves to Ali Pasha.

The Lion of Janina was their last great hope, but he would not agree to their proposal until they had persuaded him of their capabilities, showed him a little of what they could do.

Which was a great deal, indeed.

Most of them came from wealthy and important families all around the Ottoman Empire. Kemal himself was a lesser prince back in his sunny homeland on the North African coast; his elder brother was the mighty Bey of Tunis.

As boys, the Janissaries had been handed over to the emperor by their families to be trained up as warriors, consecrated to the protection of the Ottoman sultans.

Forbidden to marry, the sword and the Book were their entire lives, and as grown men, it sickened them to see the corruption that had infected the emperor's palace, the voluptuous sensuality spreading like a disease through all the Ottoman lands.

It had to be stopped. It was their duty to kill it, their jihad. The purity of sharia law had to be restored to save their dying empire.

Their fallen prince, Mustafa, would have purged their lands of this sickening Western influence if their attempt to place him on the throne had succeeded. But after one short year of rule, Sultan Mustafa had been murdered at the age of twenty-nine, and the throne had passed back once more to the so-called reformers, with all of their filthy modern ideas.

The rebel Janissaries still had hope, however. Prince Mustafa's spiritual adviser and Grand Vizier during his short reign still survived in hiding. Sheik Suleiman had advised them that Ali Pasha of Janina could be used in Mustafa's stead to bring the Empire back to the path of righteousness.

Of course, Ali Pasha was not a member of the Ottoman royal House of Osman; he was born of wild mountain brigands. Nor was he as devout as their fallen prince had been. In truth, he was a coarse, brash adventurer whose own ambitions always came first.

But he understood the dangers the West posed to their civilization — he even agreed that Europe should be brought to Allah if such an enterprise were possible. Above all, as Sheik Suleiman had correctly said, Ali Pasha alone was ruthless enough to unite all the diverse regional leaders whose lands, like so many puzzle pieces, made up the Ottoman Empire.

Kemal's brother, the Bey, had agreed in secret to support Ali Pasha if it came to it, and many others would join in, too. So many were fed up with the Porte Sublime.

But Ali Pasha was a cagey fellow, and he knew that agreeing to this adventure could cost him his head. Before he would consent to lead a revolution to overthrow Sultan Mahmud, first he wanted Kemal and his men to demonstrate their effectiveness. The task Ali Pasha had set for them was to get him the little Greek island chain of Kavros.

Ali Pasha lusted to possess it.

Kemal and his men had concurred, liking the challenge and seeing how neatly it fit into their most glorious vision of gradually converting all of Europe to Islam.

Napoleon himself had said that whoever ruled Kavros could dominate the West. It was perfect. It was a start — and a victory at Kavros would inspire more of the regional leaders to join their cause.

To that end, their fellow rebels in Mustafa's royal Order of the Scorpion had been working steadily on the goal for the past year by various techniques, making up for their lesser numbers by using their wits.

There were many more of their brethren already infiltrating the island of Kavros in secret, all of them Janissary warriors who had supported Prince Mustafa. They had agents provocateurs stirring up the people against the British troops stationed there, and causing all manner of mayhem in their steady effort to destabilize the place.

Soon, they would instigate the locals to burn a few of the Royal Navy's warships docked in Kavros Harbor, and when that happened, Kemal was confident it wouldn't be long before the British tucked their tails and fled, removing to their sturdier outpost at Malta.

The only fly in the ointment was this young Princess Sophia.

The English sought to install her in power to calm the people, which was the exact opposite of what Kemal and his comrades desired.

She had to be removed from the equation.

Now that he had seen her beauty, he thought it would be amusing to send her to his brother, the Bey of Tunis, for a concubine, but Sheik Suleiman had advised them to hand her over to Ali Pasha. The added gift of the princess would help to persuade the Lion of Janina to agree to their plot. No doubt he would teach that lawless wench proper respect for the superiority of males.

"Captain?"

Kemal glanced toward his men. Ibrahim stalked over to him, looking as strange as they all did dressed in their Western clothes, but it was necessary to try to blend in.

Ibrahim had an easier time of this; born in Belgrade, he was red-haired and fairer-complected than Kemal. His light eyes still burned with anger over the way Her Highness had sliced his arm open when he had tried to break into the carriage. It had bled for quite a long time.

Ibrahim's arm was bandaged now, but his pride was still badly bruised. "When?" he asked in grim determination.

Kemal smiled at his men's eagerness to strike again, then he glanced over and addressed his words to all of them. "Be patient," he ordered quietly. "Rest yourselves well. She's gone to ground. We can do nothing until she surfaces again."

"How will we know when that might be?" Ibrahim asked with urgent insistence.

"Don't worry," Kemal assured him with an icy smile. "Our friend inside will send us word."

CHAPTER SEVEN

Sophia awoke before sunrise, filled with a blissful sense of peace. She hadn't moved all night, still lying on her side with her head on Gabriel's pillow.

As she slowly opened her eyes, the first thing she saw was the window across from the bed. Through the glass, the world was still misty and gray. The predawn clamor of birdsong filtered into her awareness.

That must have been the sound that had awakened her. She glanced over her shoulder at Gabriel, fast asleep on his back behind her. For a long moment she just stared at him, incredulous at his proud male beauty.

The warrior in repose — defenseless in this moment.

An odd protectiveness flooded into her. How strange. Even sleeping, Gabriel Knight had the power to bring out the most unusual feelings and reactions in her.

Her gaze traveled over his hard profile, gentled with sleep, down his throat to his thickly muscled chest, rising and falling in soft, slow, steady breaths.

His sun-bronzed skin was so tempting to touch, but she refrained, not wishing to wake him. She stared at his powerful arms that had stayed wrapped around her for half of the night and had filled her with a sense of safety unlike any she had ever known.

With the stirring of renewed desire, she bit her lip and blushed to think of the scandalous things they had done together last night, both here in his bed and in the other room.

She probably should be ashamed of herself, but she could not claim to regret it. Somehow everything between the two of them felt so natural and right. She gazed at him for another long moment as a rich, private smile of remembrance played at her lips. But then suddenly she heard something outside — another noise that grabbed her attention.

Amid the morning birdsong came the startling cry of a night jar — the signal from her men!

Glancing back toward the window, she narrowed her eyes, suddenly glimpsing a dark flash of motion outside.

She drew in her breath and raised herself up higher onto her elbow.

Her men had arrived.

She tensed, her heart suddenly pounding as she spotted two, no, three of her black-clad bodyguards prowling around Gabriel's farm looking for her. At last, trusty Timo had tracked her to the red-seven coordinates. She could see he had bold Markos with him and good-natured Yannis the peacekeeper of their little band. They had found her bay horse outside in the meadow and would have realized she must be close by.

Though she was glad to see her loyal friends, that almost meant it was time for her to leave Gabriel.

Pain filled her eyes as she glanced at him again. Her heart twisted with bittersweet anguish at the realization that she had to go — now.

This country idyll was over. It was time to return to her duty and all its cares.

The prospect of never seeing him again tore a little piece off her heart. God, she had not expected it to hurt this badly. She had lost so many people in life that it seemed bitterly unfair to have to be separated from him, too. This incredible . . . friend she had found.

All she knew was that *because* she cared about him — because he'd been so kind to her — she had to protect him.

Her troubles were her own.

Pressing her eyes closed for a moment, she did her best to summon up her usual determination, ignoring the lump in her throat. She forced herself to sit up. Then she left his bed without a sound.

Tiptoeing into the dressing room, she fetched her gray peasant costume and pulled it on once more in silent haste.

There wasn't time to bother with her hair. Her curls flowed over her shoulders, wild and free, just like they had last night in her sensual adventures with the major.

She prayed he would not wake up. She did not want him getting dragged into all this. Nor did she think she could bear to admit her lies. *Let him sleep.* As she buckled the leather strap around her thigh once more, securing her knife in its sheath, she knew that the last thing she needed was a brawl between her lover . . . *her lover* . . . and her guards.

Leon would probably sense that she had been up to no good when he saw her with her rumpled hair and her flushed cheeks, but Sophia figured she would cross that bridge when she came to it. Clad in her plain disguise a moment later, she peeked out of the dressing room.

Gabriel slumbered on like Mars, the god of war, in repose.

His breathing was steady and deep. Well, he needed peace, she thought, and for the moment, he had found it.

Let him rest.

Though everything in her longed to go to him and press a gentle farewell kiss to his lips, it would be too hard to say good-bye. She crossed his chamber from the dressing room to the door.

There she paused, glancing back at him with tears in her eyes.

I'm sorry.

How she hoped he would not be too hurt by her desertion — and her cowardice. He'd probably be angry when he awoke and found her gone without a word, but she tried to remind herself that he hadn't wanted her there in the first place. She brushed a stray tear off her cheek, then blew him a silent farewell kiss.

Hearing her men coming closer to the farmhouse, she found the strength at last to tear herself away and slipped out of the room.

Gliding along the upstairs hall, she crept down the staircase, listening for any sounds from the kitchen, but there was no sign of Mrs. Moss yet.

As she stole through the house, she picked up her knapsack on her way to the front door. Escaping at last, she dashed outside, instantly signaling to her men to be silent.

Relief poured across their faces at the sight of her. She saw they had brought a fresh horse for her, a white mare with a black saddle. While Timo slipped a lead rope on the bay gelding, preparing to go, the other two followed as she ran ahead into the barn to collect her things from their hiding place.

"Are you all right?" Yannis murmured as she swiftly climbed the ladder to the hayloft.

"Fine." A moment later, she threw down the red velvet gown and other royal accoutrements that she had hidden under the moldy pile of hay.

The kittens came tumbling over to her, already mewling hungrily for their milk. With a pang, Sophia paused to stroke their tiny heads with one fingertip. "Don't worry, babies," she whispered, "he'll be back soon."

A man like Gabriel wouldn't forget.

"Your Highness, make haste!" Markos whispered from the bottom of the ladder.

Amazed at how reluctant she was to leave, Sophia glanced out the loft window at the little ruined church where she had first spotted the brooding master of this place. She closed her eyes, willing him out of her heart as best she could or she might never find the strength to go.

Her country needed her.

It was time to return to reality. This respite, this little dream, was done. Back to the world of warring factions and soulless assassins who wanted her dead.

She took a deep breath, steeling herself, then moved on, hurrying down the ladder. She jumped down onto the floor of the barn again and nodded at her men.

Striding out onto the drive, they mounted up swiftly, and in another moment were riding at top speed down the road. The dusty wind from her horse's gallop made her eyes sting with unshed tears. Sophia could not get Gabriel out of her head. His taste and touch were seared into the memory of her senses.

They rode on, keeping silence, until they had gone a mile or two down the road, where they met up with the others.

Having split up to search the area for her, the rest of her guards greeted her with exclamations of joy and relief, but when Sophia looked around, taking a welcome survey of their familiar faces, the most important one was missing.

She turned to Timo, noticed the tension around the corners of his eyes, and felt her stomach plunge with a sudden, terrible knowing.

Stark horror washed over her. She could hardly force the question past her lips. *"Where is Leon?"*

Gabriel felt like such a bloody fool.

His first reaction upon waking to find her gone had been shock, then a stunned sense of betrayal, which ultimately hardened to brooding anger.

He was furious with himself for sleeping through her departure, letting her sneak off without a word. He could only suppose it had been so long since he'd had any sort of sexual pleasure that afterward he had slept like a log. But as irked as he was at himself, it could not match his anger at Sophia.

He supposed he should be glad she hadn't robbed him while he slept, other than taking the bay gelding. Ah, but despite her protestations of innocence, he had known deep down that she had had something to do with that horse showing up when it did. They had arrived together and now they were both gone, the little liar and her stolen animal, and good riddance. He had no business engaging a mistress, anyway.

Other than the gelding, nothing had been taken, but Gabriel still considered her a thief. She had made off with a piece of him that he hadn't known he possessed.

It was the only way to explain the ache inside. He did not understand at all. *I really thought there was something between us.*

Half of him wanted to hunt her down and let her tell him to his face why she had walked out on him without a bloody word. He wanted an answer as to why she had deserted him. He deserved an explanation, and he needed a clearer-cut ending to this.

Derek would probably know where she could be found, since he had hired her, but Gabriel flatly refused to go chasing after her. He did not grovel for anyone.

He would not budge.

As the days passed, he vented his wrath by splitting several cords of firewood with his axe, but his exertions did not help him to forget her, a fact that vexed him to no end. Obviously, she didn't care about him, so why should he still give a damn about her? He barely knew the chit, and she had filled his head with lies.

Yet the realization of her indifference left him feeling more frustrated than ever, plagued by the unfulfilled lust that she had awakened in him, the pitiless hoyden.

He had come here seeking solitude, but after Sophia's brief visit, the isolation soon became intolerable.

It had been a long time since he wanted anything as much as he still wanted her.

Unable to take any more of his mental battles with himself, he gave up trying to pretend it didn't matter and saddled up his white stallion. Then he rode off to his brother's house to track Sophia down.

Only his intense annoyance with her could have dragged him back out into the world again. But maybe it was time.

He couldn't have asked for a more beautiful autumn day to venture out from the farm. The jeweled leaves were nearing their peak of vibrant changing color; a few shaken loose by the mild breeze whirled and eddied across the road ahead. Above in all directions, plump clouds, white and silver-edged, drifted across the light cerulean sky.

Cantering through the countryside, Gabriel relished the change of scenery as much as his horse enjoyed the exercise.

After an easy ride of about two hours, he turned into the rambling country drive leading up to the large white cottage that Derek had recently bought for his new bride, Lily.

Reining in at last in front of the newlyweds' quaint love nest, he leapt down from the saddle and stalked to the front door, quite ready to accept his brother's certain offer of a drink. His throat was parched after the dryness of the road. Flinging the door open, Gabriel strode inside with all the familiarity of family.

"Anyone home?" he called, glancing in the cozy rooms he passed.

No one answered. But then, through the tall, arched window, he suddenly spotted the newlyweds taking tea outside in their garden folly, Derek black-haired and sun-bronzed, Lily blond and fair, both of them visibly enchanted with each other's company.

Relieved that he had not interrupted them at any more private pursuits, Gabriel continued on through the house, heading for the door to their back garden.

"Anyone home?" he greeted them as he let himself out the door and sent a broad wave in the direction of the garden folly.

"Gabriel!"

"Why, who is this bearded stranger come to call?" his brother boomed with a grin, rising to his feet. "Lord, man, don't you have a mirror in your house?"

"Is this my greeting after coming all this way?" he answered mildly, drawing off his riding gauntlets as he sauntered toward the pair.

"Don't listen to him," Lily interjected, sending her husband a scolding smile. "You always look handsome, Gabriel. It runs in the family."

"Well, I think you look like one of the Pindari bandits. To what do we owe this honor, brother? Did you get tired of having conversations with your horse?"

"My horse happens to be excellent company," he replied with a sardonic smile.

Derek grinned as he shook his hand with a clap on the shoulder, and then pulled him in for a manly hug. Every time Derek looked at him, he seemed to be remembering the moment Gabriel had stepped in front of him to shield him from the arrow. "Welcome, brother," he said, releasing him with a meaningful look. "It's awfully good to see you out again among the living."

"Good to see you, too. Lily, you look radiant, as ever." Gabriel bent and kissed her cheek in brotherly affection. "The married life agrees with you."

"It does." She beamed at him and gestured toward the little table they had set up. "Sit, please! Have some tea with us. I am so glad you've come."

"It really is uncanny how you do that,"

Derek remarked as they all sat down.

"Do what?"

"Show up just when I'm thinking about you. You did it again just now."

"Did I?" he drawled.

"I was honestly going to saddle my horse after these refreshments and ride out to see you this very day."

Gabriel frowned at him. "Why? Is something wrong?"

"No, no —"

"Is everyone all right? Father? Georgie?"

"Yes, of course. Everyone's fine! I had a message for you, that's all."

"What sort of message?"

"From Griff. But it can wait. How have you been?"

"Ah, much better," he replied with a vague touch to his middle where he had been wounded, though he knew perfectly well that was not what his brother was asking.

Derek raised a brow at him, then sent Lily a tenderly communicative glance.

"Think I'll go inside and make us all another pot of tea," she spoke up in a delicate tone. "This one's gone cold." She smiled at Gabriel. "If you'll excuse me, gentlemen?"

Gabriel winced to think he was that transparent, but he did not intend to mention Sophia in front of Lily. He doubted Derek would have told her about his prank of hiring a fetching Gypsy harlot for his reclusive brother. Gabriel didn't want to get the rogue in trouble with his very proper young bride. Both men rose and bowed to her as the lady of the house took leave of them. They sat down again after she had gone.

"What's going on?" Derek murmured, studying him. He leaned back in his chair.

"I need to find Sophia."

"Who?"

Gabriel scoffed. "Sophia, the Gypsy girl you sent me."

"Come again?"

"I'm in no mood for more of your roguery, Derek. Just tell me where she is. I need to find her," he said tersely. "She must have been here recently to collect her payment from you. We're going to have a little chat, she and I."

"Er, my dear brother, what the devil are you talking about?"

"The wench you hired to warm my bed! Remember? Raven hair, big brown eyes like melted chocolate. Gorgeous legs."

"Sorry, but I didn't send you anything, let alone a person."

"Derek, could you please refrain from

making sport of your elder brother for once? I don't have time for this. She told me that you hired her, just the way you threatened to. I need to know where you first found the girl. Tell me where she is!"

Derek stared at him with a frown of pure perplexity. "Gabriel, I fear there's been some sort of mistake —"

"You're right about that!" he agreed. "You sent me a damned virgin. Did you know that?"

Derek's eyes widened. "You don't understand! I have no idea what you're talking about!"

"What?"

"I never hired a girl for you. I know I threatened to, but after your reaction, I didn't dare. Gabriel, I was only joking!"

Gabriel stared at his brother uncomprehendingly.

Derek shrugged. "You told me you wanted solitude and I've respected that."

Gabriel leaned closer and lowered his voice, not wanting Lily to hear. "You did not hire a girl to come out and seduce me?"

"No!"

"Are you *sure*?"

"I think I'd remember something like that," he said dryly.

Gabriel folded his arms across his chest

and frowned in utter puzzlement.

Derek looked at him matter-of-factly, then a sly grin spread across his face. "What the hell have you been up to on that farm of yours out there?"

"You don't want to know," Gabriel mumbled.

"Oh, but I do. Did you meet a lady?"

"Not a lady. No. A little thief," he muttered. But if Derek had not hired her and did not know where to find her — then it seemed Sophia was truly gone from his life.

The disappointment nearly stole his breath.

"What did she take?" his brother asked.

He avoided Derek's gaze. "Nothing of any consequence." His thoughts returned to the morning he had found Sophia asleep in the barn.

Now he saw that she had played him for an even greater fool than he had suspected. She must have simply answered yes to all his questions; letting him supply his own conclusions, she had merely played along.

But why? *And who the devil was she?*

Was Sophia even her real name?

"Are you all right?" Derek murmured, watching him with a worried look.

Gabriel sent him a guarded glance. "Never mind," he said with a vague shrug. "It doesn't matter anymore." He shook his head, trying to clear the little hellion from his mind. "What was the message you wanted to give me?"

He could sense his brother's concern for him, but thankfully Derek did not press the issue nor pester him with prying questions.

He knew him too well to do that.

"This came for you this morning." Derek reached into his waistcoat pocket and pulled out a letter from Lord Griffith, their marquess brother-in-law. "Griff didn't know where to find you, so he sent it to me and asked that I forward it to you as quickly as possible."

Gabriel accepted the letter, perplexed. "Our sister has my address at the farm."

"Apparently, he's writing to you from elsewhere. See that return address? Lily said that's one of the castles controlled by the Crown."

"As long as it's nothing to do with their child," Gabriel answered under his breath. Their sister's first baby was not due for a few more months, but the whole family had been frantically protective over her.

"No, no," Derek reassured him, "Georgiana's been in splendid health. I believe Griff's writing to you in his official capacity as diplomat."

"I wonder what he wants," Gabriel mused aloud as he cracked the wax seal on the letter.

"Probably to lure you into some plum post with the Foreign Office. He tried to sign me up, as well, and only let up on me once I got married."

"No doubt our sister's behind it."

Derek nodded. Georgie didn't want either of her brothers moving back to India. She was determined to keep the whole family together in England, and if that meant cajoling her powerful diplomat husband to find excellent posts for her brothers, she was not above such machinations.

Unfolding the letter, Gabriel discovered three pages of documents attached. "You were right," he murmured as he skimmed the letter. "He says they've got a mission for me."

"Any details?"

"No. I'm summoned to this castle — he drew me a map," he added sardonically, showing it to him. "I am to burn it and this letter once I've memorized the route."

"How mysterious," Derek replied in amusement. "What's that other page?"

"Identification papers to get me into the castle."

"Lord!" Derek let out a low whistle.

"Must have some heavy security in place, whatever's afoot."

"Griff says he'll fill me in when I get there."

"Are you going to go?"

"I am intrigued," he admitted. Indeed, his heart had begun pounding with anticipation. This could be a harbinger of the task he had been sent back from the brink of death to fulfill. If nothing else, it would at least distract him from the strange ache of knowing Sophia was gone from his life. "Do you recognize this coat of arms?" Leaning toward his brother, he showed Derek the stamped seal in the center of the official-looking document granting him passage into the castle.

Derek studied it, then shook his head. "The House of Kavros?" he read aloud, eyeing the heraldic banner above the seal. "Never heard of it."

"Neither have I."

"What are those, Cyrillic letters? Russian? Greek?"

"I have no idea." Gabriel shrugged and folded the identification paper back up to keep it safe. He turned his attention to studying the little map that Griff had drawn.

"So, are you going to go, then?" Derek prodded with a look that expressed his long-standing opinion that a new post would do Gabriel a world of good.

"I don't think I have much choice," he said. "Griff's polite to a fault, but these sound more like orders than a social invitation. Yes," Gabriel said at length with a decisive nod. "I can at least go and see what they want."

"Not looking like that!" Derek laughed, glancing at Gabriel's civilian clothes and scruffy jaw. "You can start by borrowing my razor. Papers or no, they're not going to let you into that castle looking like some sort of highwayman. Thank goodness you stored your dress kit with me before running away to the farm; it saves us a trip."

"Really, I appreciate your candor," he said dryly.

Derek flashed a cheeky grin. "What are brothers for?"

Secluded amid a thousand acres of meadows and woodlands, the ancient castle hulked atop a round hill near the south coast of England. No neo-Gothic showplace but a true medieval fortress, its stark gray stone, smoothed by centuries of wind, had been hewn in defensive lines of rugged simplicity.

After showing the papers Griff had sent

him, Gabriel was admitted through the fortified iron gates.

He rode his white stallion at an alert, rocking canter up the long drive that meandered through the property. The castle loomed nearer; he swept over a low bridge.

Again, he had to stop and hand over the papers of entry when he reached the second line of fortifications.

Whatever was going on here, clearly, the government meant business, he mused as he waited for the soldiers at the inner gates to check his papers.

"Will you dismount, please, Major? I'll show you in. We'll see to your horse. They are expecting you."

Glad that they were satisfied with his documents, he swung down off his horse and followed the brisk young officer toward the keep.

Marching under the portcullis, they crossed an inner courtyard with a massive sundial in the center and then were ushered into a vast reception hall. The young officer sent a page running to fetch Lord Griffith, and a few minutes later, his tall, patrician brother-in-law came striding into the room.

"Gabriel," he greeted him with a debonair smile, lifting up his hands by his sides. Ian Prescott, the Marquess of Griffith, had grayish-green eyes and neat, wavy brown hair.

"Griff." He accepted his kinsman's handshake heartily. "How are you?"

"Never better." The expectant father was positively beaming. "And yourself? You're looking well. How's the, er?" Griff touched his own stomach at about the same level where Gabriel had been skewered.

"Oh — better. Healed over, on the whole. Thanks."

"Excellent news." Griff shook his head. "We thought we'd nearly lost you there."

"No, you're not rid of me yet."

"Good. I want my new son or daughter to know *all* his or her uncles." Griff cast an elegant gesture toward the walkway. "Shall we?"

Gabriel nodded and fell into step beside him. "So, what's all this about?"

"How'd you like to winter in the Greek islands?"

Gabriel snorted. "Right. What's the catch?"

"We have a royal personage of considerable strategic importance to us under threat of assassination."

"Ah, lovely." Diplomatic security, then, just as his brother had surmised.

"We need a crack man in charge of these

royal bodyguards. After all, if the killers were to succeed on English soil, it would be a great embarrassment to Buckingham Palace, and a major setback to our interests in the Mediterranean."

"Plus, someone would be dead and that would be rather a pity, no?" he drawled.

"Naturally," Griff agreed with a wry look. "This way. I don't mean to sound heartless, it's just that I am married to your sister, and I would not want you getting the wrong impression."

"Wrong impression?"

"Thinking I've gone as mad for our royal idol as every other male in this place. Rest assured, I have not. Somebody's got to keep a clear head around here, after all. You're perfect for that."

"Royal idol?" Gabriel echoed.

"Mm." Passing under a high arched doorway, they came to a wing of the medieval castle that had been refurbished in the rococo style. The sudden clash of stark Norman architecture and frothy, gilded pastels had a mildly disorienting effect, as did Griff's words.

"I have heard her called a beauty on a par with Madame de Récamier," the marquess murmured as they marched across the shiny parquet floors of a mirrored ballroom. "To tell the truth, I cannot disagree."

"Madame de who?"

"Oh, right, you've been in India. Never mind. Just some dainty, dark-haired French-woman who had half of Europe at her feet a few years ago." Griff paused, halting him with a brisk tap on the shoulder. He glanced right and left, then lowered his voice. "Listen to this, there's even a rumor going around that the Regent is trying to speed up his divorce proceedings so he can pursue this blue-blooded chit for himself. If you want my advice, Major, you'd better brace yourself. Our princess is a real royal hand-ful."

"My God, man, what have you got me into?" he exclaimed.

"I didn't get you into it. That's the most intriguing part. She asked for you specifi-cally by name."

"For me? But how . . . ? I don't under-stand."

"Neither do I. But she seemed to know you or at least has heard of you, and what Her Highness wants, Her Highness gets. Better hurry, I daresay. She doesn't like be-ing kept waiting."

"Really?" he murmured, lifting an eye-brow.

"We're on rather a tight schedule, Major.

Right through there, if you will. Throne room," he said, pointing toward the esplanade. "I'll be along in a moment. I've got to sign some papers here. The lord chamberlain will do the introductions."

Gabriel nodded, mystified, while Griff walked off briskly to attend to the stack of files that an underling had brought over to him.

Well, this is all very strange. Frowning, he turned in the direction that his noble brother-in-law had indicated. He was quite sure he had never met a royal princess. A man ought to remember something like that. How could this princess have heard of him anyway, when he had lived like a recluse ever since he'd come to England? Perhaps she knew someone in Society who had spent time in India . . . *Ah, well.*

None of this made a great deal of sense to him, but Gabriel was ready for anything; bracing himself as the marquess had advised, he squared his shoulders and marched on down the esplanade, sweeping through one gilded chamber after another through a series of open doors.

The tension in him built as he approached the larger hall at the end of the row of stately apartments. He gave his name to the footman posted outside the open door to the throne room. The footman, in turn, brought him over to the lord chamberlain, a dignified little gray-haired fellow with an impressive mustache.

The chamberlain bowed to him, then Gabriel followed him into the throne room. It was the most impressive chamber yet: white walls with gilded panels, pink marble columns and pale blue pilasters. The painted ceiling full of garlands and cherubs and pastel roundels looked like it was made of candy.

With a sweeping glance of the glittering hall, Gabriel warily counted ten swarthy guards in foreign dress posted around the room. But as the chamberlain went forward to present him, his gaze homed in on the canopied throne at the far end of the long hall.

His eyes narrowed as he stared at the slim young woman seated on the intricately carved chair. He went motionless, his heart kicking into a thunderous gallop. Wonderstruck, he stared. A sparkling tiara crowned her raven curls. A magnificent brocade gown cascaded over her trim figure, those slender curves his hands knew all too well.

Staring at her in all her regal splendor, Gabriel felt time slow to a crawl, while every atom of his being overflowed with disbelief.

It was his Gypsy girl.
His sultry little . . . maid.
Sophia?

CHAPTER EIGHT

Coiffed heads turned; admiring murmurs rippled through the throne room as Gabriel came stalking toward her down the center of the glittering hall, magnificent in his scarlet dress uniform.

Sophia stared, her heart beating as if it would jump out of her chest.

He was a sight to behold. The clean shave revealed all the smooth planes and angles of his iron jaw and square chin, giving her a whole new appreciation for his fierce and oh-so-masculine beauty. He had cut his hair short, too. The messy coal-black waves of silk that she had run her fingers through that night in his bed had been neatly tamed. Her rapt gaze traveled over him.

Around his neck, no frothy cravat, but a plain black military-style stock encircled his throat. Smart brass buttons gleamed all down his chest, while gold epaulets adorned his massive shoulders.

Carrying his plumed cavalry helmet under one arm, his hands were encased in pristine white gloves. A silk sash encircled his lean waist, along with a gleaming dress sword. It was a light and gentlemanly weapon, not the stained, battered saber that he had notched with all his kills in his ferocious past. His cream-colored riding breeches met the tops of his shiny black knee-boots, and the angry rhythm of his steps striking the marble floor grew louder as he approached.

Sophia cast about for her courage when she saw the brooding glower on his face. Oh, yes, he had recognized her, all right, and she knew very well she had some explaining to do. The harsh staccato of his strides stopped as he halted, arriving before her.

"Your Highness," the lord chamberlain intoned, "Major Gabriel Knight, late of India."

Sophia held his confounded stare while the whole court waited for him to make his bow.

The consummate cavalry officer just glared at her.

She offered him a penitent smile; he narrowed his sapphire eyes and shook his head in subtle defiance.

The lord chamberlain cleared his throat

insistently.

Gabriel shot the old man a seething glance and then begrudged Her Highness the most perfunctory bow.

Satisfied, she rose from her throne and took a graceful step down from the raised dais where her chair was set, offering him her hand to kiss. "Major, how good of you to come."

The whole court watched as he frowned at her extended hand; she waited, eyebrows raised. At last, he accepted, apparently unimpressed by the great favor it signified. The moment his fingers clasped hers, however, a shock of thrilling awareness arrested Sophia.

Gabriel seemed to feel it, too. Startled, they looked at each other for a breathless second. The searing memory of their secret night together charged the air between them, like the earth's atmosphere before a storm.

Sophia feared she began blushing in front of the whole court. Her pulse clamored, but, oh, the attraction was as strong as she remembered.

Slowly, Gabriel lowered his lips to her knuckles. Trapped in his gaze, she caught her breath the second his warm, satiny lips brushed her bare knuckles. The smolder in his eyes held her spellbound. Never had a simple hand kiss felt so deliciously indecent.

From the corner of her eye, she noticed Lady Alexa studying him with obvious interest, but her flirtatious friend had better not even think about laying a finger on him. When it came to Gabriel, Sophia had no intention of sharing — but maybe Alexa would behave for once. She wasn't herself these days, badly shaken up by the attack. Alexa had been acting so clingy ever since Sophia had returned, alive and well, from her sojourn at the farm.

As Gabriel released her hand from his light hold, she dropped her gaze and cleared her throat slightly, scrambling to collect herself from his touch. Quickly regaining her poise, she bestowed a regal smile on him and gestured to the surrounding hall. "Welcome, Major, to my temporary home."

Her composure seemed to irritate him. He glared at her again. "Who are you?" he whispered fiercely.

She flicked a meaningful glance toward the lord chamberlain, who was already reciting her full name and various titles for his benefit. But Gabriel just kept staring at her in lingering incredulity.

When Alexa cleared her throat demurely, no doubt desirous of an introduction,

Sophia gathered her skirts and started down the few shallow steps from the dais. "Major, would you kindly come with me?" She did not intend to discuss this in front of the entire court.

At once, the musicians stopped playing. All the courtiers and ladies dropped in a collective bow or curtsy, which they held until she exited.

As Sophia preceded Gabriel into the adjoining chamber, her Greek guards followed right along in formation; Timo and Yannis took up their places flanking the door. Ever since their brief separation, her loyal guards had barely let her out of their sight.

Giving them a quick look of gratitude as she passed, Sophia strode into the Map Room, an ancient, wood-paneled, square box of a chamber. It was smaller and darker than the sparkling throne room, but equipped with all the tools for strategy making. Maps and charts covered the walls. Loaded bookshelves bowed under the weight of dusty atlases, while globes and diverse timepieces were arrayed amid piles of books on sturdy oak tables.

But the Map Room's most intriguing feature was the grand topographical model of the known world laid out in a large circle on the floor, complete with miniature mountain ranges and blue-painted seas, crisscrossed with the golden lines of latitude and longitude.

Toy-sized models of great landmarks appeared at the appropriate locations: miniature pyramids at Egypt, a little Blue Mosque at Constantinople, Notre Dame at Paris, the Tower of London, the great colosseum of Rome, and so on.

The world model was quite old, and though the land formations stayed the same, of course, the ownership and names of countries had changed frequently. Parts of it were still being repainted to reflect the latest reallocations of territory after Napoleon's downfall.

Sophia swept past it as she crossed the dimly lit chamber. Still scowling, Gabriel followed her in and pulled the door shut behind him with a bang.

"Can I offer you refreshments, Major?" Heading toward the liquor cabinet, she glanced over her shoulder at him. "You look like you could do with a drink."

"Hang your drink, I will have answers! Who *are* you, and what the hell is going on?" He tossed his helmet angrily onto a leather wing chair.

"Weren't you listening to the lord chamberlain?" she asked, trying to conjure a tone of conviviality as she poured him a splash of brandy. "I am the Princess Royal of Kavros. And I need your help."

"Why?" he demanded.

"Oh, because somebody's trying to kill me. That's how I ended up at your farm. Here." Lifting the hem of her long skirts up a bit to skim the floor, she brought the snifter over and offered it to him, gazing into his eyes.

In her heart, she still savored the memory of that cozy supper they had shared in his kitchen like two ordinary folk, a man and a woman enjoying simple, rustic fare.

Still glowering, the Iron Major made no move to take the drink. Sophia shrugged and tossed back a swallow of it herself. She feared she was going to need it. He was obviously furious at her. This was not going to be easy.

"I don't bloody believe this." Jaw clenched, he shook his head. "*You're* the person they want me to guard?"

"I'm afraid so. Gabriel, just give me a moment to explain —"

"Please do!"

She held up her hand soothingly.

He checked his fiery protest with a growl. Not daring to press her luck, she got straight to the point. In truth, it was a relief to be able to tell him everything at last. "That morning that you found me sleeping in your barn, I had just barely escaped with my life from a deadly attack on my entourage. We were en route to this castle when we were ambushed by masked men."

His black eyebrows drew together in an ominous line as he listened to her account.

"The members of my security detail were taken by surprise." A pang of grief made her lower her head. "It went badly for my men, and the next thing I knew, my chief bodyguard was ordering me to flee — on that bay horse you found. There were certain coordinates I had to follow so that my guards could easily find me again when the threat had passed. Those coordinates, Gabriel, led me straight to you. If that's not destiny, I don't know what is." She lifted her gaze and looked into his eyes with cautious hope.

He was frowning.

"When I took refuge in your barn, I thought the place was deserted. I thought the attackers might still be chasing me. I had to hide. When you woke me up and wanted me to leave, I didn't know what to do. I had to stay there at the proper coordinates so my men could find me again.

You've served as a bodyguard — you must know this is a common procedure and that I am telling the truth." She shook her head, willing him to believe her. "When you supplied a reason to explain my being there, all that about your brother, I just . . . went along with it."

Looking slightly dazed, he let out a short, scoffing laugh and shook his head. "So, you're not a Gypsy at all, then."

"No, Gabriel," she said with a tender smile at his understandable bewilderment, "I'm Greek. Come. Let me show you." Turning his attention to the three-dimensional map, she picked up a slender wooden pointer.

"What's all this?" he muttered, glancing down at the sprawling, permanent model on the floor.

"The world." While he folded his arms across his chest, still scowling, she pointed to the mouth of the long, narrow Adriatic. "See here? Below the heel of Italy's boot, and west of the Peloponnesus."

He nodded, taking in the layout of the region in a glance.

"This little dotting of mountainous Greek islands, here, this is my homeland — Kavros." It was little bigger than a sprinkling of bread crumbs on the map, but she lifted her gaze and sent him a tentative smile tinged with pride. "Some say Kavros is the legendary homeland of Circe, the goddess who enchanted Odysseus for seven years on his way home from the battle of Troy."

His blue eyes flickered warily.

"My family has ruled these islands for hundreds of years — until Napoleon came along and threw us out. That was in 1800. I was only three the night my family had to flee for our lives. I grew up in exile here in England, living quietly under the protection of the Crown.

"All the while, the war against Napoleon was raging. My poor country became a battleground between the great powers. First the French invaded, then the Austrians kicked them out, next the Russians took over, and finally, the British gained a foothold. They established a naval base on the main island.

"When Napoleon was defeated, England laid claim to Kavros as the spoils of war. They made it official at the Congress of Vienna; Kavros became a British protectorate.

"It is a tiny country, but as you can see, its location offers a distinct strategic advantage to whoever controls it. Your amiable kinsman, Lord Griffith, explained the importance to me of England's interests at

Kavros. Would you like to hear them?"

He nodded, still eyeing her in suspicion.

"Firstly, they wanted the base to reinforce England's holdings at Malta. Secondly, so the Royal Navy could safeguard vital trade coming out of Egypt by the overland route from India. Thirdly, the base is intended to give the British a stronger hand throughout Europe's midsection, here. All that was why Napoleon wanted it, too." She glanced warily at him. "And the others."

As she set the pointer down, Gabriel turned to her with a brooding look stamped across his chiseled face. She could see he was taking it all in, his arms folded across his chest.

"Unfortunately, your Marines can't make any headway with my people. We are a very stubborn nation," she admitted with a wry smile. "The people of Kavros are a simple folk — goatherds, winemakers, fishermen. They want to live in peace. But almost twenty years of war has reduced our land to chaos.

"Those loyal to my family have kept me apprised of conditions there." She shook her head at the disheartening realities that lay in store. "Ports and roads, bridges and aqueducts that we rely upon have been destroyed in the bombing and never repaired. The people are reduced to subsistence, and they're angry. They're not only tearing each other apart, now they've also begun lashing out at the British troops stationed there. My greatest fear is that one day, they'll go too far and provoke a retaliation from the Marines."

He snorted at this suggestion. "You are still not convinced of an Englishman's self-discipline?"

She took note of the reproachful double entendre in his murmur, but opted to ignore it.

"Because of all the unrest on Kavros, the English government has decided to restore me to my father's throne," she said. "I'm to be given full sway over domestic matters, while England will control our foreign affairs. Unfortunately, it is now clear that there are those who would prefer it if I did not come back at all. But I won't be stopped. This is my duty, Gabriel. My destiny. My people need me. And, if you're willing, I'd like for you to join me in my quest."

He stared at her for a long moment, then shook his head. "You'd better give me that," he muttered, reaching for the brandy snifter she had set aside.

He finished the rest of its contents in one

large gulp. She watched him in wary amusement as he licked his lips. Then he set the glass down, eyeing her dubiously.

"Why didn't you tell me all of this from the start?"

"I couldn't! Gabriel, those were the rules."

"You didn't think you could trust me?"

"Don't be obtuse! How would you like it if someone you were guarding back in India ignored your rules and did whatever they pleased while you were risking your life for them? Considering all my men risked for me, the least that I could do was follow the bloody protocol, and if that meant lying to you, well, I'm sorry if you feel slighted. I wanted to tell you the truth, but when you shared the story with me about how you nearly died, my mind was made up to keep you out of it. Maybe I was trying to protect you, I don't know —"

"Protect me?"

"After all you've been through, I did not want you involved. Unfortunately, that is no longer possible. For me and for my people, there is so much at stake, and you're the only one I feel that I can trust."

"What do you mean?"

"As a result of the attack, the Foreign Office is now forcing me to accept an English officer as my new head of security. They tried to appoint some fool for the post, but I told Lord Griffith that if they're going to insist on this, then at least it will be a man of my choosing."

"And that's me?" he murmured with a skeptical stare.

She tried hard not to blush. "You've been a bodyguard before, and more important, you understand the Eastern way of warfare. It is my strong feeling that Ali Pasha of Janina is behind this . . ." Her words trailed off and he slowly paced away from her.

He gave the globe an idle spin as he sauntered past it. "So, you summoned me here because I'm useful to you." He cast her a smoldering but hostile look. "Is that why you lingered at the farmhouse with me? Because I was . . . useful?" he asked with pointed innuendo.

"Of course not! What happened between us, well, you can't deny we both wanted it. I admit, the thought of being able to spend time with you again holds — a certain appeal. And if we're together again in this fashion —"

"That's not what this is about."

She stared at him, her heart pounding. "It could be."

"No, *Your Highness,*" he said in soft but pointed tone. "To be sure, I'm flattered by your interest in this lowly commoner, but you're dead wrong if you think I'm going to serve as your plaything as well as your bodyguard. You've already toyed with me enough, don't you think?"

She stiffened.

"I enjoyed it, of course, but what makes you think I'd even be willing, after the way you left me in that bed without a word?"

"What was I to say?"

"A simple good-bye would have been appreciated," he said idly while Sophia stood there, tongue-tied, to find her attempt to reestablish some sort of discreet romance with him completely rejected.

The most startling part was her realization that he was this hurt. He was trying to pretend he wasn't, of course — being a male, he had no other choice — but hurt was the most logical explanation for his rude façade of nonchalance.

Her mind was reeling. She hadn't dared hope that he cared about her enough to bother much over whether she left or stayed.

"Besides," Gabriel continued, distracting her as if he realized she had seen through him, "I don't suppose your current head of security will be very obliging about this little arrangement you're proposing. Or has he been duly sacked?"

"He is dead." Her stare sharpened, a hint of tears coming into her eyes. "Mock me as you like, but do not aim your sarcasm at him, Major. Leon gave his life so I could get away," she informed him, then drew a shaky inhalation.

Gabriel had gone motionless. He was staring at her. "I'm sorry."

She shook her head, avoiding his gaze as her tears thickened. "He was already wounded when he put me on that horse to ride away, but I didn't think . . ." Her voice failed her, her words trailing off as a tremor moved through her body. The funeral had been two days ago, but she still could not believe he was dead. The hope of having Gabriel as his replacement had been the only thing that had finally made her stop crying.

"I am sorry," he repeated, taking a step closer. "I meant no disrespect."

She wrapped her arms around herself and stared out the window. "Leon was like a father to me. That night I told you about, when I was a child and my family had to flee Napoleon's cannons, it was he who carried me as we all ran down to the ship. Now he's gone. And I must face the greatest task of my life without his counsel."

"It sounds like he prepared you well for

it." Slowly, Gabriel came over to stand before her.

"He did everything in his power to try. Any shortfalls in my abilities are my own."

Gabriel lowered his head and touched her hand with a small, tentative caress. She let him take her hand. He curled his white-gloved fingers around hers. "Is he the reason you're so good with that knife?"

She mustered up a smile and met his tender gaze at last. "He taught me every-thing I know. It was necessary," she added in a cynical tone. "People in my family have a habit of winding up dead. My father, two elder brothers. That's how I ended up next in line for the throne. I'm the last one left. I may be just a woman, but I'm all my people have got."

"Sophia," he whispered. "Come here." He drew her into his arms, sheltering her in his protective embrace. Perhaps he sensed how badly she had needed to be held. With a lump in her throat, she hugged him hard around his waist, burying her face against his chest.

"Gabriel — I'm scared."

"Of course you are." He cupped her head under his chin, standing steadfast as he held her. "It's all right, sweet," he breathed, caressing her hair for a moment. "You're not as alone as you think."

With tears tumbling from her eyes, Sophia pulled back and searched his face intensely. Her heart pounded. "Does that mean you will help me?"

"Sophia." Holding her gaze with a stormy yet gentle look, he captured her face between his white-gloved hands and wiped her tears away with his thumbs. His voice was a husky whisper. "I could never turn my back on you."

"Gabriel." She slid her arms around his neck and hugged him for all she was worth. "Thank you," she choked out, kissing his cheek as more tears spilled from her eyes. "I know what I'm asking of you is a lot. We'll do everything perfectly so you won't get hurt again and no matter what, I'm sure you won't have to kill again, but I need you —"

"Shh." He hushed her with a finger over her lips, as if he knew she was making promises she could not keep.

This was bloody dangerous. There was no way around it, and she was asking him to risk his life for her. More than his life — she was asking him to risk his soul.

After what he had seen on the edge of death, he believed he'd be damned for all eternity if he ever spilled any man's blood again. There was no certainty that it would come to that — a bodyguard protected a life more than concerning himself with trying to slay enemies. But of course the risk was there. And to her awed amazement, it was a risk that Gabriel was willing to take for her.

Still holding her in his embrace, he looked down tenderly at her; she tilted her head back, meeting his gaze.

As they stared at each other, she was aware of the exact second that a smooth subtle shift between them changed their embrace from one of comfort to desire. Her heart raced; her fingers tightened on the back of his neck with a will of their own, pulling him down to her. Her longing for his kiss shone in her eyes. She did not even try to hide it. His gaze dropped to her lips, his eyes burning like blue flame. Then he closed them.

The temptation was too great.

He lowered his head and kissed her. A soft moan escaped her as his mouth brushed hers in a silken caress. She held perfectly still, adoring him while her senses clamored and her heart rejoiced. Maybe everything would turn out all right if she had Gabriel on her side.

He curled one knuckle tenderly against

her cheek as he kissed her, and with that light touch, Sophia was on fire for him. Her body melting against him, she tightened her hold around his neck. His hands molded her waist, pressing her to him, but as she parted her lips a little to offer him her mouth, he brought their brief, relatively chaste kiss to a close.

"No," he breathed, panting slightly. "There can be no more of this between us."

He loosened his hold on her waist, but for her part, she refused to release him. The room was spinning.

"Why?"

"Oh, Sophia, do you really have to ask?" he murmured, sounding slightly short of breath from their contact. "If I had known the truth of who you were, I would never have touched you."

She leaned her forehead against his in unabated yearning. "But I wanted you to."

"Don't make me want what I can't have."

"I say you can."

"No, I can't." Gently, he pried her back from him and held her at arm's length.

Sophia gazed at him in dismay as he stared somberly into her eyes.

"It can't be like that between us anymore. As much as we both might want it. Keeping you safe needs to be my top priority now, and emotional entanglements in this line of work can get people killed."

"But you —"

"No, sweetheart. A clear head is essential." He swallowed hard. "We can only be friends."

"Friends?" she asked hoarsely, trying not to let the full brunt of her disappointment show on her face.

Gabriel nodded in regret, dropping his gaze. "You're too high above me. You know it, and certainly I do."

Sophia pulled back and took a few steps away from him, absorbing his all-too-noble rejection.

It was not easy.

"The difference in our rank didn't stop you when you thought I was the lower born one, your maid," she pointed out, perhaps churlishly, her back to him.

"It was a mistake. We both got carried away." Behind her, he fell silent. "Why did you do it?" he asked quietly after a moment. "Why did you offer yourself to me? Don't tell me you do those sorts of things with lots of men?"

She whirled around. "Of course not!"

He held up his hands. "I'm just asking. I know what goes on in these decadent palaces."

She folded her arms across her chest. "So, you still think I'm a harlot, then?"

"Sophia —"

"I'm a virgin, Gabriel." She stared at him meaningfully, until he looked away with a flicker of pained lust on his face.

She lifted her eyebrows matter-of-factly. "If you had met Leon, you would know how difficult it would have been for me ever to set foot off the straight and narrow at any time, I can assure you."

"So, what was I, then? An experiment in freedom?"

"Maybe, just a bit." She walked back to him slowly, her arms still folded across her chest. "Maybe I could also claim I was afraid of the assassins chasing me, and did not think it fair that I should die a virgin. Not that you were very compliant on that point."

"I should be sainted," he muttered under his breath, leaning his hips back against the arm of the hefty leather couch behind him. He sat there in a casual pose.

She stopped before him and gazed into his eyes. "But, truthfully, Major, those things were just a part of it. I just felt . . . drawn to you." She reached out and smoothed the lapel of his uniform coat. "I still do."

"You are making this impossible."

"Kiss me properly, Gabriel. Please. I need to taste you again —"

"This can't happen," he said tautly, grasping her wrist where her hand still rested on his chest, and stopping her caresses.

She lowered her gaze.

"Sophia, I'm an all-or-nothing kind of man. What you're offering is only part of what I would've wanted with you."

Cruel. She flinched and let out a small sound of frustration, wounded to think he'd chosen to refuse her and deny what they felt for each other based on something she could not control. Her rank, her birthright. It wasn't fair.

"Isn't part better than nothing?" she whispered.

He quivered at her insistence. "God, you are hard to say no to."

Her heart slammed behind her ribs when she saw the hunger in his eyes.

His grip on her wrist loosened and began inching down her arm, as though, any second, he would pull her to him once again. "It's only going to hurt worse if we indulge in this, you know."

"I don't care." As she wetted her lips in anticipation of his kiss, he closed his eyes, struggling for control.

"I went looking for you, you know. My Gypsy girl. I wanted you back. Back in my arms. Back in my bed."

"Oh, Gabriel."

He dragged his eyes open again. They were deep blue, hazy with desire. His hold on her arm tightened. She leaned toward him, intent on showing him just how much she had missed him, when suddenly, a rap on the door startled them apart. Sophia jumped back. Gabriel shot up, standing at attention.

"Come!" she called out, her heart pounding, her cheeks aflame.

A footman opened the door, and Gabriel's urbane kinsman, Lord Griffith, came striding into the Map Room. "Ah! There you both are. Sorry, I was detained. Your Highness. Major." The high-ranking diplomat gave Sophia an impeccable bow and then smiled suavely at his brother-in-law.

Gabriel's posture was stiff as he carefully avoided any telltale glance in Sophia's direction. "Her Highness has been filling me in on the situation with Kavros and our government's plans."

"Good. Anything I can answer for you?"

Gabriel cleared his throat. "We hadn't got round to much discussion on who might be behind the plot against her."

"Yes, that is the great question," the marquess said grimly.

"Not to me," Sophia muttered as she took a seat on the chair nearby.

Gabriel eyed her askance, then looked at his kinsman again. "From what Her Highness has told me about the way her country changed hands during the war, it sounds like several different parties might stand to gain from it. Whom do you suspect? This Ali Pasha fellow, or someone else? The Austrians? The Czar? Or perhaps the French?"

Lord Griffith shook his head. "None of the above. All of them are our allies now. Even France appears innocent in all of this. They're still trying to recover from Napoleon."

Gabriel braced his hands on his waist. "But Russia's always keen to gain a southern shipping port."

"Czar Alexander is a friend to England. And as for the Austrians, well, during the war, the Habsburgs tried to get away with staking an ancient claim on Kavros by way of their old Venetian holdings. But in peacetime, it's hard to fathom they would take the chance. To attempt such a thing would be seen as a slap in the face to England. Everyone's so damned tired of war, to be honest with you. Coffers are low, the armies are spent. Half the regiments have been disbanded across Europe and the soldiers sent home to their families. To risk another start at all that . . ." He shook his head wearily.

Gabriel frowned. "Just to be clear, there's no remote chance that this was a mere criminal act? For the sake of argument, some country roads are known for being plagued by gangs of highwaymen —"

"No." Lord Griffith was shaking his head.

Sophia stood up again. "I'll tell you who I think it was, Major. Your dear kinsman doesn't want to listen to me, but as I mentioned earlier, I would bet my bonnet it was Ali Pasha."

"And who is he, exactly?"

"Your Highness," Lord Griffith said with a long-suffering sigh.

The marquess smiled patiently at Gabriel, as though begging his pardon for her silly female notions. Sophia went and picked up the wooden pointer again.

"Ali Pasha — they call him the Terrible Turk. The Albanian tyrant rules all this territory from his capital at Janina." With an angry, sweeping motion, she indicated the Balkan Peninsula right across from the Kavros island chain, the westernmost reach of the Ottoman Empire on the Mediterranean's northern shore.

Gabriel cocked a brow at her. "Why do you suspect him?"

"Ali Pasha has long been the scourge of the Greek peoples. What few parts of Greece remained free from Ottoman rule, Ali Pasha has done his best to capture them and take them for his own. Every time he presses out his boundaries again, he chases the Greek nobles like my Leon out of their homes. He takes the land their families have held since Homer's day and gives it to his captains.

"Many of the Greek nobles have fled into the mountains, where they are forced to live as brigands, raiding the Muslim troops, and fighting as best they can for their freedom. When Ali Pasha captures any of them, he orders horrible public executions to make examples of them. The man is a monster."

"Now, now, Your Highness. We have been over this a hundred times before," Lord Griffith interjected in a smooth tone tinged with worldly male condescension. He glanced at Gabriel. "While Her Highness's theory is certainly plausible, England has just established a new treaty with Ali Pasha. The naval base at Kavros has brought us into close proximity with the unpleasant fellow. To avoid trouble, both parties have agreed to a pact of mutual nonaggression."

"You're thinking like an Englishman again, my dear marquess," Sophia informed him, growing impatient. "Ali Pasha laughs at promises he makes to infidels. He is playing games with you! He would say anything to further his own interests. Let his past deeds speak for him, not his lies. Ali Pasha has been gobbling up more territory ever since he first came to power decades ago. Why should any of us be naïve enough to hope he'd be content to stop now, just because he's reached the water's edge?"

"Your Highness, however brutal this petty chieftain might be, he's not fool enough to challenge the might of the British Navy. I agree with you — Ali Pasha is a violent cretin. But he still has to answer to his overlord, Sultan Mahmud. Trust me, the Ottoman sultans never hesitate to remove from power any of their local rulers who refuse to comply with the Empire's policies."

"What if she's right?" Gabriel asked him.

"What are we to do?" Lord Griffith countered. "Even if Ali Pasha *does* by some remote chance have designs on Kavros, Sultan Mahmud is responsible for reining him in. We cannot interfere."

Sophia let out a strangled sound of fury.

"Lord Griffith and his fellows are just afraid of stepping on the Sultan's toes!"

Gabriel nodded. "With good reason. The Ottoman Empire does not take kindly to insult," he remarked. He folded his arms across his chest and stroked his jaw in thought. "If we had proof of Ali Pasha's interference, it would be one thing, but if we were to go making unfounded accusations about one of the Sultan's most powerful vassals, then the Muslim powers all the way from Egypt could cause innumerable headaches for our overland trade route with India."

She threw up her hands. "Why must it always come down to filthy lucre?"

"I assure you, Your Highness, it isn't a matter of greed, but of England's security," the diplomat countered. "The flow of goods and gold from our trade with India is essential in keeping England strong against our much larger rivals on the Continent."

Frowning, Gabriel glanced from Sophia to Lord Griffith. "Surely something can be done?"

"I have summoned the Turkish ambassador from London," his brother-in-law informed him. "As soon as he gets here, I intend to meet with him and make our concerns known." Lord Griffith glanced at

Sophia again. "It must be handled delicately, but rest assured, I will relay to Your Highness whatever I'm able to learn. In the meantime, we can only crave your patience. We need more time to continue gathering intelligence. My colleagues in the diplomatic corps are using every channel at our disposal to find out who was behind the attack on your party. Until we have anything solid, it won't do to start jumping to hasty conclusions. In the meantime, we will do everything in our power to keep you safe."

"I take it that's where I come in," Gabriel said sardonically.

They both looked at him.

Sophia smiled in rich satisfaction. "The major has agreed to accept his new commission, my lord."

"Excellent! I will have the papers drawn up presently."

"Thank you." Gabriel nodded to his kinsman.

The marquess paused with an inquiring glance from one to the other. Discreet curiosity flicked across his patrician face. "So, it's true, then — you two were, er, previously acquainted?"

They exchanged a guarded glance, then both nodded cautiously.

"I see," he murmured with an intrigued

look. "Someday you'll have to tell me all about it."

"Oh, probably not, old boy," Gabriel answered in a cheeky drawl.

Sophia let out a nervous laugh but quickly stifled it, pressing her fingers to her lips.

Lord Griffith lifted his eyebrows. "Ah."

Gabriel sent her a wry glance, his blue eyes dancing.

Sophia grinned and shook her head at him, but the matter was decided. The story of how they had met would remain their little secret.

At least they could have that.

CHAPTER NINE

Sophia had informed him they'd be leaving for her homeland in a fortnight, but the first order of business was the grand, themed ball that the smitten Prince Regent was giving in her honor at the castle in three days' time as a charitable fund-raiser for the people of Kavros.

Four hundred of London's richest and most powerful citizens from the highest echelons of Society and government were expected to attend.

From Gabriel's perspective, it was going to be a colossal headache coordinating security for the gala affair in so little time. The castle would be overflowing with important dignitaries, ambassadors, and assorted aristocrats arriving with their retainers, to say nothing of the Regent's own troop of Royal Household Guards.

Gabriel's main priority in all this, of course, was Sophia. She was to be the guest of honor, and clearly, he would have his work cut out for him.

By the very next day, he had signed his new commission papers, receiving a large and unexpected promotion to the rank of colonel. Amused, he could hardly wait to lord it over Derek, but by midday, he was already wading knee-deep into his new duties.

He got right to work studying the layout of the castle and consulting with the captain of the garrison stationed there on how they intended to monitor all the hundreds of guests coming through the gates, as well as inspecting the army of extra kitchen workers and groundskeepers who would soon be arriving to help prepare for the fête.

As he joined the other military men in shoring up their plans for security around the grand event, he was gradually satisfied that their captain seemed to have matters well in hand. Everything appeared to be in order.

When their work was done, the practical, hardheaded officers shared a private chuckle over the "Ancient Greece" theme of the coming ball.

"Are all those nobs going to show up here dressed in togas like a lot of garden statues?" the captain asked.

"Don't know, but I sincerely hope not." Gabriel flashed a smile and clapped the captain on the back. "Gentlemen."

"Sir." They saluted him as he took leave of them.

But returning from the gatehouse to the castle, Gabriel finally had a few moments to reflect on his new situation. With all that was in motion, there wasn't much time to handle his own affairs. Last night, after being assigned to his new quarters, a spartan yet oddly cozy stone-walled room in one of the turrets, he had hurried to tie up loose ends, dashing off several letters to settle accounts with Mrs. Moss, signing off the lease of the farm, reminding her not to forget the kittens in the hayloft, and asking Derek to remove and store his belongings, and to forward his clothes and weapons as quickly as possible.

In a final note to his father and sister in London, he let his family know about his mission.

It reminded him of all the times in India that his regiment had been called up for action with very little notice in advance. He and his brother had both learned how to put their affairs in order with bracing efficiency.

For Gabriel, this was the kind of life he

knew and understood. He had to admit it felt good to be back in a position of command, and facing danger.

He was still a bit in shock to find that his "Gypsy girl" was a royal princess. For heaven's sake, the chit had dusted his furniture! He had known she was not being quite honest with him at the farm, but that was the last possibility he would have guessed.

Though he was ever so glad she had come back into his life, it was also a bitter disappointment to him privately to learn she was so far above his station. He was leery about their ability to keep their hands off each other, but there was no way in hell he could have walked away from her when she needed him. By God, if he had refused and something happened to her . . .

Well, it bloody well wouldn't now. Whoever was after her was going to have to get through him first. The thought of anyone trying to hurt Sophia affected him with dark force. Violence rumbled in his veins like distant thunder.

Maybe the lovely royal could never be his, but at least he could protect her.

He really could not explain what it was about her that turned him inside out. She made him feel like no one ever had before.

He had existed in a state of fairly unshakable equilibrium for thirty-four years on this earth and then nearly left it, but only now had he begun to taste what it meant to feel truly alive.

Yesterday in the Map Room when she had held him so hard, her sorrow, her need, had torn at his long-numbed heart; in that moment, sheltering her in his arms, he had felt as though he had been born for her. Born to protect her and to see this through, even if in the end, destiny demanded that he give his life for her.

He knew that he would, without hesitation. That was what any bodyguard gave his oath to do, if it came down to it. Besides, by escorting Sophia safely to her homeland so she could take power, he would be indirectly helping to improve the lives of many thousands of her subjects.

That had to count for something against the blood of all the men he had slain in battle.

Marching back into the castle, his next task was a meeting with her retinue of Greek bodyguards.

He knew they would be less than thrilled to find themselves placed under the command of an outsider, but they'd soon learn to like it, he thought in grim determination. Or else.

He wanted to hear from their own mouths exactly what had happened on the night of the attack. No matter what sort of heroes Sophia insisted her Greek guards were, successful penetration by the enemy clearly indicated problems of some sort. Gabriel meant to identify any flaws in their procedures and establish changes accordingly.

Considering he had three days to get his team in shape before the night of the ball, there was no time for making pretty speeches. He was sorry they had lost their captain — this Leon chap had obviously meant a great deal to them — but Gabriel did not intend to go easy on them.

First off, they needed to know who was in charge.

With Sophia's life at stake, he wanted them more afraid of *him* than they were of the enemy. It always worked on his troops back in India. His men would've charged into the mouth of hell for him. They never dared break ranks or retreat, knowing they'd have *him* to deal with.

They didn't call him the Iron Major for nothing, but his skill as a leader had kept large numbers of his men alive to fight another day. No, her royal bodyguards were not going to like him one bit.

He did not give a damn.

Before long, they were assembled in the Armory Hall for his inspection. He walked down the line of men standing at attention, scrutinizing each with a dissecting stare.

"I know you lost your leader and that you don't particularly trust me," he said as he sauntered by them. "But our lives now depend on each other, and more important, Her Highness's safety rests on our ability to function as a team. Understood?"

A surly mumble of assent was all the response the insolent bleeders would begrudge him.

"Pardon?" Gabriel quirked an eyebrow, passing a cool glance down the line of wary faces. "I did not hear you," he said mildly.

Some of the men responded with a proper "Yes, sir," but a few of the holdouts just looked at him.

Gabriel laughed softly and walked up to the largest man, who just stood there glaring at him. He looked him straight in the eyes. "Problem with your hearing? Perhaps that would explain why you were all apparently so taken off guard the night of the attack!"

Anger flared in the big fellow's face, but Gabriel held his stare. As the man read the dormant ferocity in the depths of Gabriel's eyes, he reconsidered his defiance, dropping his gaze.

"Palace guards," he mused aloud in a philosophical tone as he resumed his stroll past their ranks. "Have any of you ever even *seen* a battlefield?"

One man down the row lifted his hand. "I have."

"Yes. What is your name?"

"Demetrius, sir."

"Where did you see action?"

"I fought under Leon in the mountains of Greece for a while against Ali Pasha's troops."

"Good." He nodded and stifled a sigh. Well, it was better than nothing.

He proceeded to question them about the details of the ambush, studying each man closely. As they described the sequence of events during the attack, Gabriel listened, stunned to hear how Sophia had defended herself in the coach. She had shot one attacker and stabbed another.

No wonder she had pulled a weapon on him first thing in the morning when he'd found her in his barn.

"What about the enemy? Were any of them captured?"

"No, sir."

He looked at his list. "You are Markos?"

"Yes, sir."

"Go on."

"They took their dead with them when they finally retreated."

"It was like they just disappeared into the night without a trace," the one called Yannis added.

"Without a trace, eh?" Gabriel murmured skeptically. "These were not phantoms, they were men — a fact Her Highness proved when she made them bleed. Surely you gave chase? Which direction did they go?"

"They split up, east and south, sir."

"How far did you pursue them? How many miles?" he persisted.

They fell silent.

"Ah. Not miles, then. I see. Furlongs? Yards?" He growled when none of them supplied a solid answer. "You," he said sharply, pointing to a burly man with olive-toned skin and a thick mustache. "What is your name?"

"Timo."

"How long have you served the princess?"

"Eight years, sir."

"All right." He nodded. "Tell me what happened when the enemy went into retreat."

"Well, Colonel," he started uneasily,

"when they split up, the truth of it is, we . . . had a bit of confusion."

"Confusion."

"Yes, sir. Leon was hit. Her Highness had cleared the area. The enemies were on the run, breaking every which way. Our biggest concern was to stop them from following her, which we did. But when they broke, there were not enough of us to follow them in each direction that they ran. We argued if we should flock to the princess or chase down the enemy or what," he admitted with a look of chagrin.

"I see. So, in the moment of crisis, you fell to pieces."

They started to protest.

"Silence!" He swept them with an icy glare. "Gentlemen, this is not an acceptable performance." He counted off their failures on his fingers. "First, you were taken off guard; then, overwhelmed by superior numbers, you were unable to repulse the foes before your ranks were penetrated; lastly, when your captain was cut down, you fell into disarray. What of your chain of command?" he barked. "What of your bloody discipline? I don't want to hear any excuses. It's a miracle any of you are alive — to say nothing of Her Highness! Or maybe she should be the one protecting

you!"

Gabriel took a good long look at their contrite faces, and finally snorted. "I shall want a thorough write-up of all current security measures and protocols now in place. Get that to me by dawn. After I have had a chance to review and revise these measures as I see fit, prepare to spend the next few days in drills. Oh, and gentlemen, in closing, let me just make one thing very clear."

They looked at him again in heedful caution.

"What Princess Sophia must face in the coming months is going to be a trial for us all. But I will promise you one thing. If she is harmed, if she is touched —" He stared gravely at each man in turn as he spoke. "If she so much as breaks her little fingernail, I will personally *pulverize* any man who has not carried out his duty to perfection. Are we clear?" he bellowed in sudden fury.

Several jumped; others blanched.

"Yes, sir!"

"Good," he finished. "Carry on, then."

As the men scattered to their orders, Gabriel tugged his sleeves down neatly about his wrists, pleased that he had made his point.

With that, he strode off to find the jewel

he must safeguard and soon discovered her in the morning room in the private wing of the palace.

Sophia was curled on a satin couch, answering her correspondence, a little white poodle sleeping on her lap.

Caught up as Sophia was in answering her letters, her brow furrowed with determined concentration, her blond companion noticed Gabriel's arrival first.

The girl's gaze flicked over him from head to foot. At once, she tossed her shiny golden tresses behind her shoulders as he approached, but Gabriel ignored the familiar feminine signal, sparing the curvy young blonde naught but a polite nod, and keeping his cynicism to himself. He'd been getting that look from women all of his life, but had long since bored of idle, ornamental females.

By contrast, there was Sophia, full of fire and youthful intensity, caught up in her hundred projects, and passionate about every one. Her silk lavender gown looked so pretty on her that Gabriel could barely take his eyes off her. Striding toward the ladies, he was captivated by the soft stray curl that had escaped her loose coif and hung down to frame her face.

He longed to brush it back gently for her,

but of course he could not touch her. He was not a prince.

Perhaps she felt his stare, for she looked over and a beaming smile burst across her face when she saw him.

She quickly beckoned him over, trying not to disturb the little dog's nap. "Major, good day! Sorry — I mean *Colonel,*" she corrected herself in a jaunty tone as Gabriel joined her and offered a bow.

"Your Highness." Warmly glad to see her, he held her gaze a moment longer than he ought before abruptly recalling the purpose of his visit. "Your Highness, we shall need to take a walk-through of the palace in preparation for the ball. Would this be an inconvenient time?"

"Not at all."

"Shall we?" He offered her his hand to assist her from her seat.

The blonde cleared her throat with a delicate little cough, but again Sophia did not see fit to introduce them. Blithely ignoring the hint, she gave the little dog a cuddle, then handed it off to her friend, who sputtered in surprise. Accepting Gabriel's offered hand, the princess rose from her seat and joined him.

"What have you been doing today?" she asked with a playful sideward glance as they walked out of the morning room together.

"A thousand things. Er, Sophia," he said in a low tone as she took his arm, tucking her hand through the angle of his elbow. "Are you quite sure it's wise for you to do that?"

"Don't you like escorting me?"

"People will talk," he murmured.

"Off with their heads!" she answered lightly.

He gave her a sardonic look; she laughed.

But then she surprised him, releasing his arm with an obedient little pat. She gave him a meaningful look.

"As you wish," she whispered.

This degree of cooperation took him off guard.

Gabriel furrowed his brow. But Sophia merely clasped her hands behind her back and strolled along by his side like the model of demure propriety that he knew she most certainly was not.

She was trying.

Last night, she had lain awake, and tossed and turned in her bed trying to reconcile herself to this new arrangement with Gabriel. She should be happy.

She *was*.

She was grateful with every atom of her

being for his willingness to join her cause, and so touched by his noble unselfishness. He had forgiven her for her lies and accepted that they had been necessary. There was no doubt in Sophia's mind that he would keep her safe.

At the same time, having this handsome, charismatic man so close — but completely off limits to her — was a sweet sort of torture. She had wanted him with her, craving his solid strength at her back now that Leon was gone, but she had not foreseen how his nearness would pain her. How it would make her acutely aware that all her wealth and power could not buy her the one thing she craved.

True love.

Gabriel's gentle gaze and striking smile made her all the more sharply aware of what her duty was costing her, all the more cognizant of the womanly needs in her that would have to go unmet. What could she do? He had explained that emotional entanglements would only make his job harder. If he was putting himself on the line for her, the least she owed her new chief bodyguard was her full cooperation.

And so, friends it was.

She was used to getting her way, but not this time.

Friendship would have to be enough, and by God, she'd be grateful for that, too. Never mind the fact that every time she looked at the man, she wanted to tumble him down onto the nearest piece of furniture and have her wicked way with him. Not for the world would she make his role any more dangerous for him than it already was.

Besides, Sophia understood that these feelings were also dangerous for her. Falling in love, if that's what this was, was hazardous for any woman ruler. To be sure, it was how Cleopatra had gotten herself into trouble, losing her head over a handsome soldier.

It could lead to losing everything if she was not careful. After all, Gabriel had a commanding presence, an aura of natural leadership. As a seasoned officer, he was used to the mantle of authority and, truthfully, more accustomed to having the responsibility for people's lives on his broad shoulders than she was.

Too, she was well aware that Lord Griffith and the other Foreign Office magnates already took her less than seriously, much to her chagrin. It would be all too easy for them to start ignoring her and simply deal with Gabriel, a strong and worldly male of aristocratic descent, and one of their own.

Sooner or later, it might occur to her darling head of security that he could become the one in charge if he played his cards right.

Not that she didn't trust him. He was far more sincere with her than any other male with a romantic interest had ever been before. It was merely a matter of having studied history well as part of her royal education. Men would always be men.

For now, thankfully, there was no threat of a power struggle between them.

Friend-like, they walked through the security procedures for the night of the Grecian Gala.

Preparing for another round of possible violence during her fund-raiser ball ought to have been a grim and somber activity, but she enjoyed his company so much that the mood somehow stayed light.

Jesting and laughing together with idle banter as they went about their duties, they studiously refrained from the slightest physical contact. This was wise, especially considering all the courtiers and ladies they passed dotting the hallways and salons. Those palace parasites loved their gossip, but Gabriel and Sophia walked right past them as they bowed and curtsied.

For her part, Sophia privately rejoiced that

at last someone had arrived who treated her like a normal human being. With Gabriel's strict refusal yesterday to become her lover, she had feared she would be imprisoned once again in her royal role, thrust back into her isolation as always, but this wasn't so bad. Friendship was better than nothing.

Starting from the ballroom where the party would be held, they walked off three different exit routes she could use if trouble reared its ugly head during the festivities.

"One more," Gabriel informed her as they headed back to the ballroom so he could show the fourth and final way out that he had planned for her. "I've saved the most interesting of your escape routes for last."

"Really?"

"Come."

Once more, they were off. This time, he showed her through the vast kitchens and down a shallow flight of stairs into the castle's ancient cellars.

"Oh, my." She drew closer to him instinctively as they descended into an eerie subterranean maze dimly lit by glowing lanterns; massive storage racks loaded with barrels and crates seemed to stretch for an acre underground.

"When you come to the bottom of the steps, the first thing you'll do is grab that lantern off the peg," he said, pointing to it. "You're going to need it to be able to see down here. It's very dark."

"And nasty," she muttered. When he gestured again to the lantern, she obediently went and collected it.

"Follow me." He marched on, straight ahead.

With the lantern in one hand, she lifted the hem of her skirts off the dirty ground with the other, and grimaced as a rat scampered by through the shadows.

"Stop," Gabriel said. "Now, turn around and look back."

She did.

"Right, so when you come to the bottom of the steps, you take your lantern, go straight ahead — don't start wandering around or you'll get lost, especially if you're panicked."

"I won't panic," she assured him.

"No, I don't imagine you would," he agreed, slanting her a brisk but admiring glance. "Your guards told me how you acquitted yourself in the carriage the night of the attack. Well done. In any case — go straight ahead and count off ten of these racks, then turn right. Come." He took the lantern from her and led the way into the darkness.

She followed him down the shadowy aisle between the tall, looming storage racks, then Gabriel stopped as they approached the ancient wall. A few feet from it, a row of three barrels stood on end; he pointed at the ground behind the barrels. "Take a look."

Moving closer, she saw that the upended barrels concealed a little trapdoor with a leather strap for a handle. As he bent down to pull the trapdoor open, Sophia watched him, mystified by the change in his demeanor. All of his weighty new duties seemed to invigorate him.

"Some medieval baron must have dreamed this up six hundred years ago," he remarked. "You'll go right down the ladder." As Sophia crouched down beside him, he opened the door, revealing the entrance to a pitch-black hole that led straight down.

"Oh, dear," she murmured.

He lowered the lantern, illuminating the ladder that led down into the darkness. "The captain of the gatehouse told me this tunnel is one of the castle's original secret passageways. Only a handful of people are aware of its existence. Your Highness is asked by the Regent not to reveal it to anyone," he added.

She nodded. "Of course."

"This will be your exit of last resort. I've already been down there and checked it thoroughly. It's still structurally sound, so you don't have to worry about it collapsing on you."

"Comforting." She peered down, not liking the look of that dank, spidery hole one bit.

"The tunnel goes for a quarter mile underground and comes up inside the stable complex. If we need to go to the highest alert, this is the route you will take. We'll have men stationed by the stables with a carriage at the ready to get you out of here with all possible haste."

"Can we go now?" She brushed the trace of a cobweb off her arm and shivered. "I don't like it down here."

"We can, if you're clear on all this."

"Of course." She heaved a sigh as she straightened up again.

He closed the trapdoor and stood, dusting off his hands. He passed an assessing gaze over her face. "Something wrong?"

"Do you really think they're going to attack me at the ball? They'd have to be insane."

"I don't plan on trusting in their sanity."

"It seems to me they're more likely to set up another ambush when it's time for us to travel to the coast to board the ship that will be taking us to Kavros."

"You may be right. Perhaps I am being overcautious. But better safe than sorry. Let's get through the ball first, then we'll deal with what comes next."

"Yes," she sighed. "I suppose."

"Come." To her surprise, he touched her then, taking her elbow and shepherding her gently out of the gloom.

At the base of the wide cellar stairs, he paused to hang the lantern back on its hook, then he turned back to her with a somber stare. "I'm sorry if all this was too much at once. I didn't mean to scare you —"

"It's all right. I'm used to it, believe me." She shrugged. "I've been living this way since I was a wee girl."

"Still, it would be unpleasant for anyone."

"Thanks for caring," she murmured, offering him a fond smile.

"Everything's going to be fine," he assured her, stepping closer. "This gala is going to be your big night. You just concentrate on having fun and charming the guests into donating generously to Kavros." He slid his hands into his pockets as he gazed at her, the lantern's flickering glow sculpting his chiseled face. "Leave the worrying to me."

"All right." She lifted her eyebrows. "But

you *are* going to dance with me at the ball, aren't you?"

He stared at her for a moment, regret flickering behind his eyes. "I'm going to be on duty," he said softly.

Her hopes fell at his gentle reminder of the gap between them; Gabriel looked away.

The silence that followed was excruciating.

He cleared his throat, then swept a gentlemanly gesture toward the stairs. She lifted the hem of her lavender skirts a bit and climbed the stairs ahead of him. Behind her, she could have sworn she felt his stare on her curves. It made her body tingle with awareness. But perhaps she was only imagining it, for he seemed to possess the self-discipline of eight saints combined.

At the top of the cellar stairs, they walked back through the kitchens. Gabriel kept his gaze fixed straight ahead.

"So, what are you going to do now?" she inquired.

"I've asked your guards to ride out with me and show me the place where your party was ambushed. I want to comb the site to see if I can find any clues about who was behind this."

Her eyes widened. "I'm coming with you!"

"No, I don't think that's a good idea."

"Why not?" she exclaimed.

"There could still be danger."

"They're not going to strike twice in the same place, surely. I'll change into my riding habit and wear a net veil over my hat, will that satisfy you?"

Tenderness crept into the sapphire depths of his eyes as he held her gaze. "Another disguise?"

"When needed," she replied with a smile.

Still, he frowned. "Are you really sure you're up to this? The men told me what you went through that night. In truth, it would probably be helpful to have you there and get your perspective on how it all happened, but I would not ask you to face that place again unless you really felt you could."

Sophia moved closer to him. "If you're there, I can."

He did not move back as she had half expected. "I'll be right beside you," he whispered, holding her gaze.

She tweaked a brass button on his smart red coat and grinned. "Then let's go."

CHAPTER TEN

An eerie stillness hung over the bend in the road where her guards had led them. The sunlit canopy of the autumn trees joined overhead to form a tunnel of their boughs, like a colored-glass mosaic.

Here and there, falling leaves cascaded down to a packed earth road still scored and stained by the skirmish that had taken place there.

Gabriel glanced at Sophia, making sure she was all right. Beneath the brown net veil that draped her riding hat, her smooth, young face bore signs of quiet distress, but she kept any tears she might have wished to shed at bay. He gave her a bolstering nod; she took a deep breath.

He dismounted from his horse for a closer look around. "Stay with her," he ordered two of the men.

"I'd rather be alone," she murmured, lowering her gaze and staring blindly at her hands, still clenching the reins as she stayed in the saddle. No doubt she needed a little time to reflect on what had happened here, but Gabriel would not leave her unattended.

"Give her some room," he told the two guards in a lower tone, then he sent the others off to search the surrounding woods for anything they might find, any possible new evidence.

They proceeded to do so, dismounting and then moving slowly, studying each foot of the mossy ground. Except for the low crunch of their steps over the dry fallen leaves and the occasional snort of a horse, the whole group was very subdued. Gabriel understood why. He was not so long parted from his regiment in India that he could have forgotten this numb, tearless grief after one of their own had been killed in battle.

While the men searched the woods, Gabriel went to inspect the old cart that had been used as a barrier in the attack, forcing Sophia's entourage to halt. It had been dragged off to the side of the road, and though he examined it thoroughly, it yielded no particular information.

Next, he studied the chaotic pattern of footprints in the road — wagon tracks, hoof prints, a few dark copper stains that told a tale of pain. Blood. His gaze traveled up into the trees, from where several of the attackers not hiding in the old cart had swung down into the fray on ropes, according to Sophia's bodyguards.

The ropes the brazen bastards had used in launching their attack still dangled from the branches. Gabriel's gut tightened to see them hanging there like empty nooses.

This ambush, he thought grimly, had been carefully thought out and very well timed. Perhaps the only factor the enemy had failed to take into account was the ferocity with which their intended female target would fight back.

But now, no doubt, they would take that under advisement. Next time, they'd be ready. One look at the scene assured him that there *would* be a next time.

Whoever they were, these boys meant business.

He glanced darkly at Sophia to make sure she was still all right. She remained on horseback and was staring off into the woods. Moving on in his examination of the scene, Gabriel left the road for a closer look at the trees they had used as their hiding places before the attack.

He found a stray bullet lodged in a nearby trunk, pried it out with his knife, and studied it, but it told him little. The ordinary silver ball could have been used with a variety of guns.

He stepped back to assess the big old tree, then grasped hold of it, and began to climb. His efforts cost him a mild twinge in his middle where he had been wounded, but he persisted, wanting to see what the scene had looked like from the attackers' point of view.

Sophia watched him curiously as he reached the first main bough where two ropes were tied. Among the branches, he found broken twigs and cracked limbs where they had crouched, waiting for their moment. He inspected the knots they had tied. The ropes themselves were ordinary hempen lines available anywhere. From his perch on the thick branch, he surveyed the lay of the land. He realized the villains would have seen her party coming for at least a quarter mile through the trees.

Below, Sophia finally dismounted from her horse. With an instinctive urge to stay near her, he lowered himself from the thick bough and dropped to earth, striding over to her.

Wanting to hear her side of the story in private, he dismissed the two men guarding her and sent them off to join the others in the search for evidence. Then he asked Sophia to recount the exact order of events that night, as best she could remember them.

She did so, describing the assault on the carriage — which side the attackers had tried to come in, what they looked and sounded like, how she had fought them off, and Lady Alexa's hysterical screaming. Then she explained how Leon had brought her the bay gelding and sent her on her way. She pointed to the stone wall and meadow visible through the narrow patch of woods on the north side of the road and told him she had leapt the wall on horseback in making her escape. Gabriel nodded, easily envisioning the chaos of that night.

"Shall we go and have a look in the field?" Sophia suggested with an admirable show of bravery despite the shadows in her eyes from reliving all the details of that night.

"No."

She looked at him in question.

The men had told him that the hottest fighting had taken place in that field after she had gone galloping away. The villains had tried to chase her, but under the wounded Leon's direction, the guards had at least rallied enough to hold the bastards off so she could escape.

Sophia furrowed her brow. "Don't you think we might find something useful . . ."

she started, but her words trailed off as she read his regretful expression. "I see. That's where Leon fell?"

He nodded and reached out to give her arm a comforting stroke.

"I want to see the place."

"Sophia, you've already been through enough," he said with gentle finality. There was no need for her to see the stained patch of tall grasses and bloodied turf where someone dear to her had lost his life.

She looked away but did not argue. Though her cheeks were rosy with the brisk October afternoon, her face was a stark, emotionless mask. As she wrapped her dark cloak a bit more tightly around her slender frame, Gabriel shook his head in self-directed anger.

"I shouldn't have brought you here."

"I need you to protect me from assassins, Colonel, not from the truth." She stared off into the field where Leon had fallen. "He didn't deserve this."

Gabriel said nothing, standing with her in wooden silence. He could feel her pain as if it was his own and longed to take her into his arms. It seemed inhuman not to, but even aside from the need to maintain a professional distance, he could just imagine the sort of reaction it might get from her

Greek guards.

"Colonel!" Over by the stone wall, the men beckoned to them all of a sudden. "Your Highness, we've found something!"

As they both hurried over, Timo pointed into the brambles at the foot of the stone fence. "It looks like one of them might have dropped a weapon here! We haven't touched it yet, so you could see its exact position where it fell." Timo moved back to give them room and Gabriel leaned closer, narrowing his eyes.

A gleaming dagger with a black handle lay partly concealed inside the leaf-strewn clump of weeds.

Beside him, Sophia stared at the weapon, then she reached gingerly into the bramble-bush without waiting for their advice, and picked it up.

Turning to her to ask for it, Gabriel saw the cold anger that filled her face as she gripped the knife. She cursed under her breath in her native tongue, then swept them all with a glance. "To your horses, quickly!"

"Your Highness?" Gabriel murmured.

"I knew it," she said fiercely. "Damn him!"

"Damn who?"

"Ali Pasha!"

An angry murmur moved among her fellow Greeks at this name.

"I knew it was him all along!"

"What makes you so sure?" Gabriel asked in a low tone.

"Look!" Ashen-faced, Sophia held up the slightly curved dagger and pointed to the engravings on the black steel hilt. "You see these symbols? This is Arabic!"

"I know what it is," he replied. Thanks to his boyhood friendship in India with a local nizam's princely sons, he was quite familiar with the customs of Islam and was well aware it was a common practice amongst Mohammedan warriors to engrave one's favorite weapons with verses from the Koran. "May I see the blade?"

She handed the weapon over with a wary look. As Gabriel studied it, he noticed some strange markings on it in addition to the Koranic verses.

"Come!" she ordered, whirling away from them and striding back toward her horse.

"Where are we going?" the bulky Niko cried, hastening to follow her.

"Back to the castle!" she ordered in a tone that brooked no argument. "It's time I had a chat with the Turkish ambassador."

Gabriel wasn't so sure. He eyed her Greek guards warily. A more sinister explanation began taking shape in his mind.

How easy would it have been for one of her men to have planted the weapon there just now and only pretended to have found it? Indeed, how else might her enemies have known just where and when to find her on the road?

His heart darkened at the possibility of a traitor in their midst. Mounting up, he noted that it was Timo who had first spotted the knife and called them over to see it.

The man seemed loyal to Sophia, but that could be naught but a mask.

Gabriel stayed close to Sophia and kept his concerns to himself for the moment as they all rode back to the castle, on for miles and miles through the descending twilight.

Full night had fallen by the time they arrived. Cantering past the gatehouse, they continued up the long, winding drive.

Ahead, the castle's dark medieval hulk loomed against the stars, dim orange lights glowing in the windows. They rode over the bridge, under the portcullis, and into the central courtyard.

In short order, their princess was striding ahead of them down the stone corridors of the castle, her face flushed with the cold, her midnight curls wild from the hard gallop back. She had taken off her hat but still gripped her riding crop in her angry zeal to confront the Turkish ambassador.

Gabriel was beginning to worry a bit about what exactly she intended to do. She ordered Yannis to find out if the Ottoman representative had arrived; the answer came back quickly. Yes, he had, and he was in a meeting now with Lord Griffith in the Map Room.

Sophia nodded and headed for that unusual chamber.

Gabriel jolted into motion. "Your Highness," he clipped out, keeping pace with her brisk march.

"Yes, Colonel?" She stared straight ahead.

"What do you plan on doing in there?"

She glanced over her shoulder, apparently surprised that she was being asked to explain herself. "I'm going to show the Turkish ambassador what we found."

"And?" he challenged.

"See what he has to say for his master about it."

"Wait." Gabriel captured her forearm in a gentle but unyielding grip, halting her advance. She flicked an indignant glance down to his hand on her arm. "You can't go in there making accusations," he warned in a soft but steely tone. "Remember, we discussed the danger of offending the Ottoman Empire?"

"I know what I'm doing."

"So does Lord Griffith. Let him do his job. He's not going to want you barging in. These are delicate matters —"

"I'm not asking your permission, Colonel," she interrupted, looking him evenly in the eyes.

Her Greek guards stepped nearer, glancing from Gabriel to Sophia. His hand was still on her arm, and they appeared quite willing to intervene and remove their new commander from her path if Her Royal Loveliness desired.

Sophia eyed him warily, but Gabriel was not about to back down. He was a little surprised at her unabated tenacity, but this was in her best interest.

"As I understand it, my kinsman has been one of your greatest champions within the Foreign Office," he informed her in a low tone. "Angering him is not going to help your enterprise or your people. Overstep your bounds, and you will make him doubt your readiness for the crown."

His blunt words seemed to check the anger that had burned in her dark eyes ever since the knife had been found. She lowered her head, pausing for a moment.

"Your point is well taken, Colonel. Still, I

intend to confront the Turkish ambassador
—"

"Let Lord Griffith do it," he ordered.

"Don't tell me what to do!" She pulled her arm angrily out of his light hold. "I want to look into that blackguard's eyes and see for myself if he knows who is trying to kill me! I'm going to put this knife in front of him and see if I can call his bluff. I am not naïve — I don't expect the ambassador to be honest with me, but if I take him off guard, he may betray some telltale sign that he knows something — or not. Either way, it will be useful information."

"This is not a card game."

"You think I don't know that? I'm the one they're trying to kill! With all due respect, Colonel, I think I understand the stakes slightly better than you do."

He clenched his jaw and lifted a long-suffering gaze to the ceiling.

"If the plot against me is coming from Ali Pasha alone," she continued, "then the Turkish ambassador will let the Sultan know that his petty tyrant in Albania is up to his old tricks. Sultan Mahmud has his own interests in the region and might not appreciate Ali Pasha taking it upon himself to start making mischief again. Sultan Mahmud can crack down on Ali Pasha as nobody else can — if he chooses."

"And what if it's not Ali Pasha? Then what are you going to do?" Gabriel pressed her. "What if you go in there and find that the plot originated with Sultan Mahmud himself?"

"Don't think I haven't thought of that," she assured him defiantly. "I know full well the Sultan could be the one behind this, only using Ali Pasha to do his dirty work for him. And if that's the case, then I might as well know it, because that means I'm probably doomed."

"Well, if you're doomed, damn it, so am I," he said in a soft, fierce tone.

She looked into his eyes, taken aback; Gabriel shook his head at her, won over in spite of himself.

He gave her a reluctant little smile, and slowly, she returned it.

The reminder that he was on her side seemed to shore up her resolve. She lifted her chin, then glanced at the door to the Map Room. "Why don't we confront him together?"

Gabriel considered it, saw he could not stop her, and then decided it was better to go in there with her and at least try to rein her in a bit. "Listen." He leaned closer, lowering his voice. "Back in the army, Derek and I always had this strategy that usually worked in these kinds of situations."

"What was the strategy?"

"Whenever we had to have an unpleasant *discussion* with someone, he would be agreeable while I would scare the hell out of them. Between the two of us, it usually seemed to get results."

"I love it," she said at once. "I'll be the scary one!"

"You?" He furrowed his brow while she smiled and tweaked a button on his coat.

"I can get away with more than you can," she replied. "Let's go." She ordered her Greeks to hold their posts, then the two of them continued striding toward the Map Room.

Gabriel escorted her, somewhat beside her, but minding his place half a step behind her. "Don't overdo it, darling," he warned under his breath as both of them stared straight ahead. "If you overplay your hand, you'll look bad to Griff and I could end up sacked — not that I'd mind so much, but somebody's got to protect you."

"Trust me. I wouldn't get my favorite bodyguard sacked."

"There's something I want to talk to you about, by the way," he added grimly as they approached the door.

She glanced at him in question.

"Later," he murmured.

She nodded and stepped ahead of him. Then, without further ado, she burst into the Map Room where his kinsman was in parley with the fearsome Sultan's representative.

Gabriel prayed he wasn't making a big mistake by going along with this, but he had to give her a chance. It was time to find out what his princess was really made of.

Seated informally across from each other at one of the sturdy oak tables, Lord Griffith and the Turkish ambassador looked over in surprise.

"Sorry to interrupt," Sophia flung out, the sudden draft from the opened door making the many candles throughout the room flicker.

"Your Highness!" Lord Griffith started to rise at her entrance, but she waved off his courtesy.

"You said we needed evidence, Marquess. We found it."

Lord Griffith furrowed his brow and glanced past her at Gabriel, sending his kinsman a questioning look.

Her brawny ally muttered a convincing apology, as if he had no control over her or of this matter.

When Sophia reached the men's table, she jabbed the curved Arabic dagger down into the wooden tabletop right in front of the startled Turkish ambassador.

"What is the meaning of this?" he exclaimed. Turbaned and silken-robed, the Ottoman grandee pulled back from her a bit in puzzled alarm.

"I was hoping that you could tell me that yourself, Mr. Ambassador," she replied, bracing one hand on the table and the other on her hip as she leaned down to stare at him matter-of-factly. She did not take her eyes off him, but instead held his gaze, noting every shift and flicker of thought and emotion in his weathered countenance.

The Turk glanced from her to Lord Griffith, who, in turn, looked horrified by their intrusion.

"Your Highness, what on earth is going on?" the marquess exclaimed.

"I came to ask a favor of the ambassador," she replied in brash insolence, turning back to the Ottoman. "Sir: When you return this weapon to its rightful owner, tell him I am looking forward to our next meeting. I shall enjoy the chance to skewer him!"

The Ottoman ambassador was glaring at her with an affronted look. "I am afraid,

Your Highness," he said slowly in English, his Near East accent softened by French-trained pronunciations, "that I do not understand."

"No? Well, that is a pity. Allow me to explain."

"Perhaps it would be better if I tried —" Gabriel started in a placating tone.

"Silence!" she ordered sharply — just to keep him out of trouble with his superiors on the British side. "I can speak for myself, Colonel. I'm a woman, not a fool! And the Ottomans would do well to heed that, too," she declared. "I wish all my neighbors in the region to understand that though I am young and a female, my father's throne is ancient, and I will not be trifled with."

Gabriel gave a low cough into his fist. "Of course. I beg your pardon, Highness."

When she glanced over at him, his eyes communicated encouragement at odds with his mask of obedience. She fought back a smile, discovering that it warmed the very cockles of her heart to have an ally like him at a moment like this.

But when she turned back to the Turkish ambassador once more, she assumed her royal glower. "You see, gentlemen, Colonel Knight and I just returned from searching the spot on the road where *someone* tried to kidnap me the other night — or kill me — it's hard to say for certain which, but why split hairs? We found this dagger there and, as you can see, it comes from your corner of the world."

"If Her Highness is implying — but this is absurd!" the Turk cried, glancing from her to Lord Griffith in protest. "The Porte Sublime has no designs on Kavros!"

"Good," Sophia said coolly. "In that case, Sultan Mahmud might wish to have a word with Ali Pasha. If he has his eye on my nation, someone ought to tell him not to try it. He will fail."

The Ottoman ambassador appeared confounded. Sophia was starting to think that he knew nothing, but actions spoke louder than words. When he gave them some solid assistance in finding out who was behind this, then she'd accept his claims of innocence.

Lord Griffith, for his part, looked like he wanted to strangle her. "May I remind Her Highness that England has no quarrel with the Turks?"

"Nor do we want one," Gabriel hastened to interject. He gave the Sultan's agent a courteous smile. "If the ambassador is in a position to help us, then I am certain he will do so."

"Humph!" Sophia conceded with a haughty toss of her head, but she sensed her role in this little drama had come to an end. Time to exit left and let her able partner take center stage.

"Gentlemen," she clipped out in terse farewell. She pivoted and without a backward glance, swept from the chamber.

But unseen by the others, she sent Gabriel a wink full of cheeky satisfaction as she passed him.

Pulling the door to the Map Room shut behind her, Sophia leaned back against it for a second and let out a large exhalation. *Well, that was somewhat reassuring.*

Judging by the ambassador's reaction, she did not get the feeling that the Ottomans were the ones who were trying to kill her. And that was certainly good news.

"Your Highness?" Timo stepped toward her and searched her face in concern. "Is everything all right?"

She gazed fondly at him. "My old friend. Everything's just fine. Come." She rallied her spent strength after that nerve-racking confrontation. "I wish to retire to my chambers."

He snapped his fingers at the others. They fell into formation. Sophia's step was light as she returned to her gilded apartments with her retinue of trusty Greeks in tow.

Gabriel stepped to the fore, loosely clasping his hands as he approached the men. The placating role was wholly unfamiliar, nor did he like it much. But she was worth it, he supposed, this blow to his warrior pride. "I beg your pardon, sirs, for this intrusion by the princess. I could not stop her — Her Highness was terribly upset. I can only hope you gentlemen will understand the poor girl is distraught over the attempt on her life."

Griff eyed him warily, but the Turkish ambassador begrudged him a somewhat mollified nod.

"I am certain Her Highness would have wished me to assure you that Kavros welcomes the friendship of the great Sultan Mahmud. Which is why," he added, explaining in a delicate tone, "we thought it proper to warn the Sultan of any possible new intrigues arising from Janina. We would certainly wish to save His Serene Majesty from any embarrassment or . . . inconvenience. Just in case the Porte Sublime is not already aware of such activities, that is."

"Sultan Mahmud prides himself on knowing everything that transpires throughout his domains," the ambassador answered with an indignant lift of his chin.

"Of course, sir." Gabriel bowed modestly.

"If there is any such mischief afoot, we will certainly get to the bottom of it immediately."

"Mr. Ambassador, that is all we ask. We should be extremely grateful for whatever information you are able to provide." He paused. "By the by, sir, may I show you the markings on this blade? They are most unusual." Gabriel pulled the knife out of the table with a wrench, then presented the flat of the blade to the Turkish ambassador. "Have you ever seen these symbols before?"

Gabriel studied the Ottoman's face intensely, and saw how the ambassador paled as his stare locked on the odd little squiggle at the base of the blade, quite apart from the Koranic verses inscribed on the hilt.

"Is this symbol familiar to you?"

"No, I — I have never seen it before. May I — take this with me to show to my colleagues? Perhaps one of them may be able to identify the mark."

Gabriel nodded. "Indeed, sir. We would appreciate that."

Quickly masking his consternation, the Turkish ambassador rose from his chair and bowed to them. "Lord Griffith, Colonel. Her Highness may rest assured I will do all in my power to unearth whatever information I can to add to her protection."

"We thank you, sir. *Shukran. Masaa' alkhayr.*" Gabriel gave the Turk a bow in the Eastern fashion hand to heart.

The ambassador returned it, bid Griff a good evening, and then hurried off to start making inquiries of his own about the attempt on Sophia's life.

As Gabriel watched him leave the room, he wondered just what the man knew about the symbol on that dagger. The mysterious markings definitely seemed to worry him.

The door closed and his suave brother-in-law instantly turned to him with a rare show of anger. "What the hell was that little stunt?"

CHAPTER ELEVEN

Gabriel bristled. "Sorry?"

"You expect me to believe that young chit could run roughshod over you? You had a part in this, do not deny it! Don't you realize what a catastrophe that could have been?"

"But it wasn't," he said coolly.

Griff glared at him, but backed off a bit. "Gabriel, you *can't* let the girl go tearing about in this fashion. Good God, after growing up with a spitfire like your sister, I'd have thought you could handle the princess better than that!"

"*Handle* her?" His face darkened as he took umbrage at his kinsman's words. "I thought it was my duty to protect her, Griff."

"Yes, from herself, if need be, as well as from would-be assassins."

"Beg your pardon, old man, but considering all the girl's got on the line in this —

she's risking heart and soul and blood in this quest of hers — don't you think you're being just a little condescending toward her?"

"Condescending?"

"Do not underestimate this woman. Her Highness is more than just a pretty young thing who happens to have the right lineage for our purposes. She is young, true, but she has great courage and more brains than the average man."

"Does she, indeed?" Griff folded his arms across his chest and stared at him. "Don't tell me she's gotten to you, too?"

"Of course not! Don't be absurd," Gabriel muttered with a scowl. The blunt question confused him; his guarded response was automatic, if not entirely honest. "I just . . . think you should be fair to her, that's all."

"Well, she's not the only one risking herself here. The stakes are high for us, too. She simply can't go running about half-cocked making accusations against England's allies —"

"Ah, don't blame her, it was my idea," Gabriel admitted with a dismissive wave of his hand.

"*Your* idea?"

"Well, it worked, didn't it?"

"Gabriel!"

"You saw the ambassador's reaction to the markings on that blade! You still think there's no merit to Sophia's suspicion of the Turks?"

"I don't know, anything's possible!" Griff exclaimed with a confounded gesture. "Ali Pasha would *seem* to be the likely villain here, but why would he try it? He's the first one who'd be suspected, and besides, that brute stands more to gain by the new treaty than we do. As for Sultan Mahmud, I can't see what he'd stand to gain by harming the girl."

Gabriel furrowed his brow in thought. "What manner of man is the sultan?"

Griff shrugged. "Mahmud is widely known as a reformer. He's been surprisingly receptive to Western ways. He prefers the French to us, of course, but he has been basically peaceful. If he gives anyone problems, it's the Russians. They're still squabbling over control of the Dardanelles."

Gabriel nodded.

"Now . . . if we were dealing with his predecessor," Griff said slowly, "his half brother, Mustafa the Fourth, then I would certainly give more credence to Sophia's accusations. The previous Sultan was a dangerous and evil religious fanatic. He betrayed his half brother, Sultan Selim, another reformer, so he could gain power. Had him murdered in his harem, for God's sake.

"Mustafa surrounded himself with viziers and sheiks who wanted to expunge all Western influence and take the Ottoman Empire back to the bloody Dark Ages. But fortunately, Mustafa was only in power for a very short time. The present Sultan Mahmud's supporters destroyed him. Now Mustafa is dead, his core of supporters scattered to the winds. With a reasonable man like Mahmud in power, I cannot imagine that the Porte Sublime would undertake such an adventure as trying to take over Kavros."

"Yes, it doesn't sound like it," Gabriel agreed. "Perhaps the ambassador will be able to shed some light on all this. For what it's worth, I don't think Sophia alienated him too badly."

"Well, she went about as far up to the line as she could without crossing it."

"Somebody's trying to kill her, Griff. We still don't know yet who or why. She's scared."

"Luckily, she's got you," Griff replied wryly. "She got away with it this time, but it had better not happen again. And as your kinsman," he added delicately, "I would remind you that you, too, must be careful about stepping over any lines, my friend."

Gabriel eyed him warily. The man was too perceptive.

"I will talk to her," Gabriel assured him in a low tone. "Let me know if the ambassador learns anything of interest, will you?"

Griff nodded with a piercing look, and Gabriel took leave of him.

Striding through the castle on his way to the royal apartments, he felt a twinge of guilt for being less than forthcoming with his kinsman about his feelings for Sophia, but what was he to say? He was not even sure what he felt or what she felt, or if he'd be allowed to remain at his post if the truth were known. He could not leave her. Shrugging off the tangle of emotions, he turned his mind to practical matters and weighed Sophia's certainty of Ali Pasha's guilt against Griff's insistence that the Terrible Turk would not risk breaking his new British treaty; then he considered both sides against his own newfound suspicions that one of her Greek bodyguards might have turned traitor.

He did not want to broach the subject with Sophia after all she had been through — he knew it was going to upset her — but her safety was at stake. Besides, if he spoke to her about it, he might discover there was someone in her entourage whom she already doubted.

He made a mental note to post a few British soldiers from the castle's garrison around Sophia as an added layer of protection in case her Greeks could not be trusted. Then he reminded himself to review Leon's logbook tomorrow and any other recent notes or writings from the late head of security. If Leon had known or suspected something about the threat against Sophia, he might have kept records on any leads in the matter before he was killed.

Arriving before her suite of rooms several minutes later, Gabriel tensed when he saw four of Sophia's Greek guards posted, as usual, outside her door.

He gave no sign of his suspicions. "Is she at home?"

Niko nodded, and then Gabriel noticed with some irony that the swarthy Greeks were eyeing him as skeptically as he regarded them.

He ignored the undercurrent of resentment coming from her bodyguards and banged loudly on the door, bracing himself for what was sure to be a difficult conversation.

The door opened, but it was not Sophia who answered. He found himself face to face with the languid blonde he had seen with the princess earlier.

He bowed to her. "Ma'am. I am Colonel Knight."

The young woman smiled with a brief glance flicking over him. "I know."

Gabriel paused, taking in the speculative gleam in her eyes. "I would like a word with Her Highness, if I may."

"Of course, Colonel. She's been expecting you."

"You are . . . Lady Alexa?"

"I am," she answered, straightening up and looking pleased to have been acknowledged.

"Pleasure." He gave her a perfunctory bow, his hand resting on his gleaming sword hilt.

"The pleasure is mine, Colonel." From the corner of his eye, he noticed the two Greeks staring at Lady Alexa with panting looks.

He furrowed his brow, his manner toward her turning even more businesslike. "I understand you were there the night of the ambush."

She nodded with a pouting little frown.

"I hope you are quite recovered from your ordeal."

She peeked at him from under her lashes.

"I'm well," she said in a tremulous voice. "How gallant of you to ask."

"If it is not inconvenient, I should like to talk to you about your experience —"

One of the Greeks nearby coughed. The sound bore a striking resemblance to stifled laughter.

Raising a brow, he looked over, and the lusty mirth on the men's faces as they exchanged a glance made him wonder what exactly Lady Alexa had been doing with the bodyguards.

He turned to her again. "Your, er, experience of that night," he clarified.

"Gladly, Colonel. I am at your disposal," she murmured, curving her voluptuous body against the frame of the open door. Leaning there, her receptive pose lifted her ripe breasts for his inspection, as if she wanted to make sure he saw them.

Which he certainly did.

Gabriel faltered slightly.

Perhaps the full size of his libido had gone cramped and stifled much too long, locked up in the iron safe of his good intentions.

It occurred to him in hindsight that if his rakish brother had ever truly intended to send him a whore, Derek would have chosen someone like Lady Alexa.

A flash of memory zoomed through his

mind of his younger, wilder years, and his ardent study of India's Kama Sutra. Back then, he'd have kept a woman like Alexa very busy, indeed. Alas, his tastes had evolved from those simpler days. Complicated women were so much more trouble.

"Alexa, let the man in!" Her Highness ordered her lady-in-waiting from somewhere inside her apartments.

She sounded a little exasperated — and no wonder, that.

Sophia's friend had a body, all right, but Gabriel wasn't sure she had a brain.

Lady Alexa opened the door for him with a giggle and watched him appreciatively as he brushed past her.

"One moment, Colonel! Make yourself at home," Sophia called from an adjoining chamber that opened off the left wall of her sprawling suite, up a few, wide, shallow, marble steps.

To his right, as he sauntered in, a dainty cluster of striped satin couches and chairs were arranged around the white fireplace in elegant informality. But then, he stopped, for straight ahead at the far end of the room stood a huge canopied bed. Oh, God. He was standing in her bedroom.

He tried hard not to look at her bed, for his thoughts went instantly where they should not. Desires teased awake by her ninny-headed friend bloomed into full-blown lust by the true object of his obsession.

Especially when she emerged from her dressing room just then, clad in a long, wispy negligee of black silk with a matching robe. Gabriel's breath rushed from his lungs at the sight of her — long, soft, midnight curls flowing back over her shoulders, unbound, the black silk of her nightdress wafting over her lithe curves and trailing along the marble steps as she strode toward him.

"Leave us," Sophia ordered Lady Alexa, while Gabriel stared, transfixed.

"Good night, Colonel," Alexa squeaked.

He glanced over in dazed distraction, barely seeing the blonde before she slipped out of the room. As soon as he caught his breath, his pulse began to pound.

"Hullo, my friend!" Sophia greeted him with breezy confidence, lifting her glass of dark, ruby-red wine to her lips with an air of sophistication as she joined him. "I think our ploy went smashingly, don't you? What was your verdict? Tell me yours and then I'll tell you mine. Sit, please. Do you want some wine?"

"Uh." Not knowing where to look, he

opted for the floor, but even with his gaze downcast, he could still see her lovely feet in high-heeled mules of matching black silk. The ebony gauze of her negligee was also transparent enough to show him the trim, sleek lines of her beautiful legs. He could still feel them wrapped around his hips. The memory flooded his mind of the way she had arched beneath him that night in his bed, begging him to take her.

He swallowed hard, cursing his body for the tingling sensations rushing into his groin. No, no. Now, there would be none of that. He redirected his stare toward a safer location, namely, the painted ceiling.

Clasping his hands politely behind his back, he tried like hell to remember why he'd come before she had stunned his male brain.

"Here." She stepped closer to him. "Taste this."

"What?" he croaked.

This," she informed him, lifting her glass to him, "is a proper glass of wine."

"I am on duty," he responded stiffly.

She laughed at him. "Iron man! I *order* you to try this wine. It's Greek. Besides, we must celebrate our victory."

"What victory is that?"

"The Ottomans aren't trying to kill me!

At least I think they're not. What was your conclusion?"

"I — concur."

She frowned at him. "Is something wrong?"

"No, of course not," he replied like a very wooden soldier.

"Gabriel," she chided with the smile of a queen and the mesmerizing eyes of a sorceress.

He licked his lips and studied the ceiling again. "Your dishabille . . . distracts me."

"Oh, goodness me, I'm terribly sorry," she said in a delicious purr. Moving closer, she fingered the edge of her robe and whispered, "Would you rather I take this off?"

He quivered, looking into her eyes; the sparkle there told him she knew exactly what he was feeling, so what was the point in trying to hide it?

Succumbing to a smile, he reached out and captured her elbow. "You wicked temptress," he murmured as he drew her near. "You think you can get away with teasing me?"

"Just a bit."

"Two can play that game, love. Yes, then, take it off. I will help you." He slipped his fingers under the paper-thin layer of black silk where it draped her collarbone. He brushed it back softly, baring her shoulder.

With a soft moan, she turned her head, offering the shoulder for his kiss. He stared at the exquisite stretch of skin that she presented. His heart pounding, he could not resist. He did not even bother to try, but lowered his head and pressed his lips against the pale cream satin of her skin. He closed his eyes in tortured yearning, savoring the scent of her, the tender sweetness of her warm flesh.

He dragged his glazed eyes open again and touched her cheek, tipping her head back so that he could taste her mouth once more. But Sophia stopped him, laying her hand gently on his chest, and angling her mouth away from his.

Gabriel looked at her in question.

She stepped back, holding him at bay despite the smolder in her dark eyes.

"No, Gabriel," she whispered in regret. "We can't. I'm sorry."

"Why?" He moved closer. "I'm starving for you."

"You know why."

"I don't care." He clutched at her silken robe, trying to pull her near, but she refused him. "A bullet would be worth it."

"Oh, darling, not to me." With a slight tremble, she slipped free from his light hold, pivoted, and glided away from him.

On the other side of the room, she set her wineglass down and pulled on a loose banyan robe of dark ruby damask to cover herself. Gabriel lowered his head, trying to regret the momentary lapse of self-restraint.

But he could not.

"I'm sorry," he murmured when she returned.

"Please don't apologize," she said earnestly. "It's my fault — I shouldn't have done it." Head down, red-cheeked, she avoided his gaze and cinched the cloth belt around her slim waist. "I should've worn something proper."

"I'm not a boy, Sophia. I should hope I could control myself. Besides," he eyed her warily, "I've already seen you in less."

He noticed his words made her quiver. Then she changed the subject with a determined air. "Come, let's take a seat and you can tell me what happened after I left." As she showed him over to the furniture grouping by the fireplace, the caress she ran down his back was of the caring variety rather than seductive.

Any way she wanted to touch him was fine with Gabriel.

"I'm so glad you came up with that ruse. I thought we were splendid!"

"Of course we were," he said in amusement.

"Was Lord Griffith cross? Did the ambassador know anything about that knife?"

Gabriel dropped onto the couch and draped his arm over the back of it. Sophia perched on the cushioned arm of the sofa across from him. He proceeded to answer her questions, succinctly briefing her on what had transpired after she had made her exit.

Taking it all in, Sophia mulled it over for a second, then she let out a sigh and smiled.

"Lord, it's been a long day, hasn't it? You must be tired. You've been working since sunup. How is your scar after that long ride? Any strain?"

"I'm fine." *Other than a deepening state of sexual frustration.* He dragged his hand through his hair with a ragged sigh.

"Have you had dinner?"

"Not yet.

"Let me send down to the kitchens for you. On my orders, they'll make you whatever you like. What will you have?"

His stare traveled over her luscious body. He looked away. "Nothing, thanks. I don't intend to stay long. Here. Sit with me." He patted the sofa's cushion beside him. "I need to talk to you."

"Yes, you mentioned earlier you wanted to speak to me about something," she said as she came over and joined him on the love seat.

"I'm afraid you're not going to like it."

"Oh." She furrowed her brow and nodded, appearing to brace herself. "All right. What is it?"

Gabriel paused, glancing around at her apartments. His past diplomatic security missions had taught him that in palaces like this, the very walls had ears. "Come, sit closer to me. What I want to say to you, no one else must hear."

She eyed him with a skeptical smile. "Is it something naughty, Colonel?"

He scowled and tugged her onto his lap. She laughed rather than protesting as another adorable blush crept into her cheeks.

He wrapped his arm around her waist, electrified by the feel of her warm body on his lap, but as Gabriel bent his lips toward her dainty earlobe, he wished that all he had to whisper were sweet nothings. And not the grim possibility of treachery close by.

Demetrius captured her hand as Alexa passed by him in the hallway outside the royal apartments. He was on duty there with three of the other men. She smiled at him imperturbably as he tugged her near.

His lips dipped toward her earlobe. "Watch him for us," he ordered her in Greek.

She pulled back a small space and glanced at him in question.

"Go," he urged. "Hurry."

Alexa gave him a cool nod in answer, then she prowled down the hallway, pausing when she came to the maids' entrance.

Glancing back at her occasional lovers, she saw Demetrius urge her on with a firm nod.

With the guards watching the corridor for her, she turned the doorknob silently by degrees and then, without a sound, slipped in through the little door that the staff used to service the royal apartments.

It was an easy matter to take a position spying through the crack in the service door. To her surprise, Sophia and Colonel Knight were not in the bed, but instead, were cooing at each other like a silly pair of virgins on the couch.

She smirked.

Bad princess, she thought, spying her mistress on the colonel's lap. *You must be spending too much time with me!*

Receiving this stallion of a warrior alone

in a state of dishabille? *Tsk, tsk, very scandalous.*

Leon had always said she was a bad influence.

The thought of Leon pained Alexa.

She could not think about that. She pushed his ghost out of her mind, for the more pressing complication was his replacement, this stranger in their midst.

Colonel Knight worried them all, especially her. Alexa knew he must be handled carefully.

The men didn't trust him, and apparently their fear that Her Highness had only hired him for her own pleasure was well founded, after all. Naturally, he had a brilliant military record, but the real reason for the handsome stud's appointment as the new security chief was plainly visible from Alexa's closeted post.

No one was quite sure what he wanted out of all this. The British might have tasked him with seducing the princess as a means of achieving their own unstated ends.

But whatever the colonel's motivation, one thing was very clear as she watched them fawning on each other: Her Royal Highness was in love.

Alexa raised a brow, wondering what pretty bits of rakish naughtiness the handsome warrior had just suggested, for Sophia pulled back just then with an angry, "No! Are you out of your wits?"

"Won't you please just try to keep an open mind?"

"But what you're suggesting is impossible!"

Alexa perked up. Some positions were a challenge to one's stamina and flexibility, but nothing was impossible if one had the will, and perhaps a bit of scented oil . . .

"Shh." The colonel pulled Sophia close again, once more whispering in her ear.

Alexa watched them, musing. If Sophia lacked the adventurous spirit to indulge his wildest imaginings, she was certainly willing to volunteer herself.

Across the room, Sophia suddenly pulled out of his arms. "No more! I will not listen to you! Not another word!" Sophia clapped her hands over her ears. "I want no part of this! Do you understand me?"

He pulled her hands down gently from her ears. "Darling, I'm not trying to upset you —"

"Please, stop. That's very wrong of you." She was shaking her head at his words, looking very upset.

Alexa frowned, wondering if she should go back in and try to help. After all, some of these seemingly proper Englishmen had tastes quite beyond the pale, even by her standards.

"Just think about it," he cajoled her.

"There's nothing to think about. You're wrong on this, Gabriel. Trust me. Do you think I'm that much of a fool? You don't know what you are talking about."

Alexa shook her head in sympathy and some confusion. *Poor Sophia.* The pain her chosen lover had inflicted on her heart was written all over her face.

What bastards all men were, she mused. That was all falling in love brought a person, which was why she wanted no part of it.

"I think it's time for you to leave," the princess told her pet Englishman.

Colonel Knight clenched his square jaw, but rose obediently and heaved a sigh, holding his hands out at his sides. "I'm sorry."

Sophia just shook her head again and looked away, her arms folded tightly across her bosom. "I know you mean well, but just please — go."

He did, taking leave of her with an impeccable bow. Sophia's refusal of his proposition appeared to have upset him, as well.

When he had left the room, Her Highness buried her face in her hands and lowered herself to the couch behind her. She remained like that, motionless.

Alexa stared, unsure if she was crying.

At length, Sophia lifted her head and brushed away a tear in her determined way, then stood, and went back calmly to retrieve her glass of red wine from where she had left it. Her face was pale as she passed by Alexa's hiding place, her eyes a little red.

Alexa furrowed her brow. She was dying to go back in properly and ask her mistress some leading questions that might reveal what the colonel had been whispering to her.

But, of course, mentioning it at all would only help Sophia realize that she had been spying on her carefully for quite some time, just as she had been this morning when Colonel Knight had shown Her Highness the clandestine tunnel.

Alexa couldn't allow her royal Mistress to discover the truth. After all, Sophia's trust was the only thing standing between her and the secret, ever-present threat of the Tunisian's knife.

She shuddered with ice in her veins at the memory of that curved dagger with its evil etchings. She had been treated to a very close look at the weapon the day they had abducted her off Bond Street, where she had ambled off to buy some frippery.

The onyx-eyed Tunisian had said he would rip her throat out if she did not do exactly as they said, and she believed him. Indeed, if there had been any doubt in her mind that they meant business, they had removed it on the night of the attack.

Those moments in the coach had been so horrible, knowing it was coming, wanting desperately to warn Leon, but too cowardly to give any sign of the trap ahead.

What else could she do? It wasn't as though she could turn to the pack of body-guards to save her. She'd had them all, crude fools, and if they wanted *her,* how smart could they really be?

No, Alexa had already accepted defeat. The Order of the Scorpion had promised not to hurt Sophia — and had likewise promised to cut off *her* head if she did not cooperate.

So, she'd hand Sophia over, keep her blond head safely atop her shoulders where it belonged, and then she would finally be free of it all, free of this palace-prison life with all of its bowing and scraping. Free of the curse of living in Sophia's shadow. And free, most important, of all the bad choices she had made. Soon she would have her chance to start over again with a clean slate, become someone new . . .

She just had to get through this nightmare first, and keep on staying calm and playing stupid, just for a little while longer.

It would all be over in a fortnight.

CHAPTER TWELVE

Putting aside the confusion of her growing feelings for Gabriel, and her embarrassment over her misguided effort to attract his notice with her skimpy negligee — in hindsight, a very silly-headed notion, to be sure — his warning of a possible traitor among her bodyguards had touched a raw nerve in Sophia. Especially after growing up in a palace setting, doubtful of everyone's sincerity. With her own kin lost to her, the people in her entourage had become like family to her over the years, and for him to say that one of them might have betrayed her was a devastating proposition.

While her logical mind could easily grasp there was a chance he could be right, her heart refused to accept it. *"You don't know what you are talking about,"* she had insisted.

He hadn't liked that accusation one bit.

Pure panic had made her lash out at him, for he just kept pushing to persuade her of something that was too horrible to contemplate.

Which of her dear bodyguards would ever want her dead? They were like brothers to her.

The more she told Gabriel she was sure her people were loyal, the more he kept on saying that something just didn't add up; she could also see that at least that much was true, but in the meantime, his air of certainty terrified her. She had ordered him out of her room, and things had been tense between them ever since.

She had not meant to "shoot the messenger," as the saying went — she knew her head of security was only doing his job, and that his sole motive in saying such dreadful things all stemmed from his desire to protect her. But he just *had* to be wrong about this. She could not bear for it to be true, not after all that she and her close-knit band of Greeks had been through together. Not when a traitor among them would have cost Leon his life.

It was all just more than she could deal with as the night of the Grecian Gala drew near. She had four hundred very important guests on their way to see her, and they expected her to be charming.

She had to have her head on straight. This

was her golden opportunity to drum up support for her country's empty coffers so they could rebuild. It was too important an occasion for her to face it in an upset and distracted state.

Out of necessity, she assumed more of an emotional distance from Gabriel and let him go about his business while she concentrated on finishing her preparations for the ball.

In between memorizing the small welcome speech she would give to all her guests, as well as her toast to her royal host of the evening, the Prince Regent, she had the final fitting for her white gown, made sure her diamonds had been cleaned, handled last-minute crises from the kitchens over the menu, and oversaw the lavish decorations for the night, as well as the many, varied entertainments.

Above all, she took special care to make sure that everything was set up to discreetly receive her rich guests' donations to the people of Kavros. This money-begging mission stung her pride, but that was the point of all this effort, anyway.

She reviewed the orchestra's selection of music and made sure the dance floor had not been polished with too much beeswax to the point of becoming slippery. Lastly, she called a final meeting of the staff so that everyone knew exactly what they were supposed to be doing at all times, and when a few of the servants complained about the costumes, she reassured them that it would be fun.

While the whole castle made its final preparations for the grand affair, Gabriel poured his energies into drilling the squad of Greek bodyguards mercilessly with all his new procedures.

There was more to his ruthlessness than polishing their performance, however. He was purposely driving them to the edge of their endurance to find out who might crack, which one might show signs of weakness.

He had told Sophia he preferred not to use them at all the night of the gala, replacing them with British soldiers instead, but she refused to let him cut them out, for in her view, they would be humiliated.

Gabriel realized that the slight would indeed alert the Greeks that they were under suspicion, so he conceded with a shrug, still irked by Sophia's refusal to heed his doubts about the men. Damn it, he was only trying to protect her. The stubborn royal's insistence on having her old friends around her that night meant that Gabriel could do naught but design a second layer of security ringing the royal target and her retinue of bodyguards.

He did not communicate his suspicions of the Greek men to the dozen British soldiers he borrowed from the garrison, but the latter would be in position to watch the bodyguards *and* the princess.

At last, the long-awaited night arrived.

Gabriel, in full dress uniform, was patrolling the grand, gilded ballroom that Griff had led him through on that first day of his arrival.

On that sunny afternoon, the ballroom had been empty, its vast parquet floors agleam, but tonight, it was thronged with important guests, and full of noise — chattering voices and the clink of glasses and dessert plates, all vying with the robust rhythms of the Greek music especially procured for the occasion.

Strolling on through the sumptuous staterooms of the castle's main floor, he observed all with tense watchfulness, checking in with his men in each room, making sure there was no sign of trouble.

All was running smoothly.

The rococo reception rooms within the stark medieval castle had been dressed up to resemble a scene taken from some Hellenistic vase, a frolicking day in the life of Classical Antiquity.

The columns everywhere were decorated with vines. Tall, burning braziers reminiscent of ancient Greece warded off the autumn chill for all the poor servants who had been made to don white togas for the occasion, both males and females, with leafy wreaths around their heads. A dozen jolly Bacchuses and young Ganymedes kept the wine flowing.

Footmen in charge of directing the guests toward the various entertainments wore large, eerie, expressionless masks painted gold, like those of the ancient Greek theater, long togas flowing over their bodies like so many wandering Aristotles.

In one room, Gabriel saw the portly Regent laughing at the display of Olympian sports in the center of the large, stately chamber. Lady Alexa had also claimed a front-row seat and was watching the greased male wrestlers throw each other around for the entertainment of the highborn.

How very risqué, Gabriel thought dryly, but when it came to exalting the world of Classical Antiquity, it seemed Sophia, that Machiavellian royal, had read the ton right. It seemed the historical precedent allowed even Society's strictest matrons to overlook all sorts of immodesty this night that would normally have been forbidden. Ancient Greece and Rome were the mighty models, after all, that the Regent's England aspired to.

The English aristocracy built its homes in the columned style of the Parthenon, loaded its statuary halls with Hellenistic nudes of gleaming alabaster, painted its ceilings with Greco-Roman gods and goddesses and their adventures, and adorned its great English gardens with Greek temple follies. Every upper-class schoolboy learned Greek and Latin and, from an early age, had their heads filled with Homer's heroes and Plato's dialogues.

No wonder the ton was enchanted with her, he mused as he sauntered on, watching everything. A real, live, Greek princess, fighting for one of the last free slivers of that land that had hatched the democratic ideals the civilized world now cherished.

If only he had not upset her so badly; hurting her hadn't been his intention. He had tried to be as gentle about his suspicions as he possibly could, but he had not realized how fragile his brash little knife-girl would actually be on this point.

His heart wrenched every time he thought

of the look on her face when he told her that he suspected a traitor. He wished he had kept his mouth shut until he had gathered proof.

He had checked Leon's writings, also, but had found nothing useful. Maybe he was wrong about this. Maybe he was just being overly paranoid.

Maybe his deepening feelings for her were truly starting to cloud his better judgment, just as he had feared they would.

Restlessly, Gabriel moved on.

The next chamber was only dimly lit; a cloud of wafting steam surrounded a matronly actress representing the Delphic Oracle. She had a huge live snake draped across her shoulders and was telling the guests' fortunes, if they desired. Gabriel eyed her audience warily, then continued.

The final room he walked through before returning to the ballroom was devoted to gambling. The proceeds of the night's gaming bank would go to the people of Kavros.

His men posted in the card room confirmed that all was well. Gabriel nodded. Sweeping the glittering saloon with a vigilant gaze, he suddenly spotted a four-man whist table near the back of the room that had filled up with his highborn cousins and family friends: the twins, Lucien and

Damien Knight; their brother-in-law, William, Lord Rackford; and Devlin, Lord Strathmore, the husband of their sister's best friend, practically a family member.

They grinned when they saw him and welcomed him heartily as he went over to greet them.

"There he is! The great protector!"

"Winter in sunny Greece, indeed! You poor fellow. That is some hard duty."

"And to be plagued with the company of such an enchanting young woman all the while."

"It's harder than you can possibly imagine," Gabriel assured them.

His sardonic tone roused a laugh from his ex-spy cousin, Lord Lucien Knight. "In more ways than one, no doubt."

Gabriel ignored the rogue's sly riposte. He was grateful that his brother-in-law had made sure to invite the whole Knight clan. One of the first families of the realm, they were not out of place in such exalted company.

Besides, Griff had known how much it would mean to Georgiana to let Gabriel see all his cousins once more before he sailed off to Greece for who knew how long.

He gestured casually toward their game. "The mirror men aren't paired?"

"No, the twins are not allowed to be partnered at cards," Rackford informed him matter-of-factly. "Uncanny. They can read each other's minds."

"It wouldn't be sporting," Damien, the elder twin, agreed. As a highly decorated officer who had served in the Peninsula, Damien was a favorite with Gabriel.

Gabriel clapped his fellow warrior on the shoulder. "Set your bids high, gentlemen. The people of Kavros need roads and bridges and everything, I am told."

"We will play as deep as our wives will let us," Lucien drawled with a glance at his cards.

"Just keep Alec out of here," Strathmore mumbled. "No more gambling for him."

"Ah, no worries. He hasn't had a relapse since he quit," Lucien defended his youngest brother, Lord Alec Knight.

"Not when he knows his lady would banish him from her boudoir if he ever even looked at the dice again," Rackford murmured with a wry half smile.

"Where is our favorite rakehell, anyway?"

"There he goes!" Lucien pointed toward the doorway.

"Where?" Rackford turned around.

"You just missed him." Lucien looked down at his cards. "I'm afraid he has stolen the Sun God's chariot."

"Figures."

"Hate to tell you this, but our wives were riding in the back of the contraption."

"He is such a bad influence on them!" Damien exclaimed, turning around to look.

Strathmore scowled. "Lizzie wasn't with him, was she?"

"Relax, old boy. She's been over him for ages."

Gabriel laughed at their constant repartee. "Well, gentlemen, enjoy yourselves. Good luck to all of you. I must keep on with my duties."

"Maybe we'll come and visit you if you're still in Greece after Christmas," Strathmore said. "I haven't been traveling in ages, though God knows it was my passion in the past. Besides, my dear bluestocking tells me she would give anything to spend a whole month studying the ruins."

"Better wait until things calm down a bit," Gabriel warned. "Rather wild and woolly at the moment, I'm told. Next year might be a safer bet."

"Will you write and let us know?"

"I'll do my best," he answered with a nod, though he had his doubts he'd be alive by the time Kavros had been made safe enough for the highborn tourists who flocked to

Rome and Athens and Herculaneum.

"Ah, Lizzie will be disappointed," Strathmore said with a smile. "But I suppose if all those temples have withstood the centuries, they can last another year or so."

"Indeed." Gabriel took leave of them with a nod, returning to the task at hand. But as soon as he stepped out of the gambling hall, he heard a hearty laugh coming from farther down the wide, busy corridor.

He looked over and saw his cousin, Lord Alec Knight, jump down from the theatrical chariot that was wheeling guests around the hallways of the palace at a sedate pace.

The white horse pulling the toylike contraption wore a gold plume on its head and blinders to keep it from spooking from so many people on all sides.

Laughing, Alec returned the Chariot of the Sun to its rightful owner, but the actor hired to play Apollo was scowling under his spiky headdress of makeshift sun rays.

He looked entirely put off at the indignity of having his vehicle commandeered by a mere mortal.

Golden-haired Alec, who looked more the part of the Sun God without having to try, slipped him a fiver to make amends, still laughing. "Here's your phaeton back, old boy, no harm done! We're very sorry — it's just the Three Graces wanted to go for a jaunt and they said you were driving too slow!" Talking his way out of trouble, as usual, Alec went to help the twins' wives, Alice and Miranda, down from the back of the chariot.

The petite strawberry blonde and the tall, statuesque, raven-haired beauty were both laughing their heads off at the prank as they stepped down from the back of the chariot.

The third of the "Three Graces" turned out to be their highest-ranking kinswoman, Belinda, Duchess of Hawkscliffe. A blue-eyed blonde of quiet grace and stunning beauty, Bel smiled at Alec as she accepted his help in alighting from the chariot and shook her head at him with a fondly chiding look.

Seeing Apollo take the reins once more and return to his duties of conveying guests about — particularly the old and gouty ones — Gabriel was satisfied that order was restored, waved to his merry relatives, and moved on through the steady flow of guests passing by every which way. He kept his eyes on all of them.

It was too bad Jack couldn't be here tonight, he mused. Lord Jack Knight was the cousin he knew best — the only one who had traveled halfway around the world to visit India, for the sake of his great merchant shipping company.

Unlike all the other Knights, whom he had just met within the past year upon moving to England, Gabriel had known Jack for nearly a decade. But right now Jack was in the Caribbean, where his shipping company was headquartered. Gabriel still had not met Jack's bride, a redhead called Eden, but they were supposed to be returning to London for a visit in the spring — apparently en famille.

The thought of a little baby Jack and future terror of the seas rather amused Gabriel, but again, he found himself chasing off another doomful question about the outcome of his quest.

The vision he had experienced at death's door had left him fairly well convinced that when he fulfilled the destiny he had been sent back to finish, he would be returned to that blessed Light he had seen, this time, permanently. Until he had met Sophia, the peace that had filled him in that fleeting glimpse of heaven had been preferable to anything on earth . . .

"My son!" a deep, mellifluous voice boomed out cheerfully all of a sudden.

Gabriel looked over and saw his father, Lord Arthur Knight. He grinned. One of his favorite people on earth.

The tall, white-haired aristocrat was coming out of the refreshment room with his matronly lady-friend, Mrs. Clearwell.

As Gabriel greeted them, both elders showed him the sampling of Greek delicacies that they had collected on their small plates.

Gabriel stayed a moment longer to chat with them, for he had always been particularly close to his jolly, manly father and was delighted by his old man's budding romance with Lily's erstwhile chaperone, the adorable, plump, vivacious, little Mrs. Clearwell.

In truth, the bustling and witty widow was much nicer to his father than Gabriel could ever recall his late mother having been. At any rate, they both knew he was on duty, so they did not detain him.

He left them happily keeping each other company and continued on patrol, trying not to imagine what sort of impact news of his death would have on his old man, if it came to that.

Passing by the Delphic Oracle's room once more, he spotted his cousin, Jacinda, Lady Rackford, along with Alec's wife, Becky, both having their fortunes told, and listening to the woman's nonsense with great enthusiasm.

He smiled wryly at their girlish playfulness over the whole thing, then his watchful gaze traveled over the rest of the guests in the darkened chamber, about fifty people in all. Suddenly, he noticed a couple taking advantage of a shadowy corner to steal a kiss.

Oh, Lord, he thought, recognizing the pair as Derek and Lily. He shook his head as the couple seemed to lose themselves in their torrid embrace. *Bloody newlyweds.*

Becky spotted him in the doorway and waved, while Jacinda reveled in telling the Delphic Oracle that her husband had a tattoo a lot like that great snake of hers, all wrapped around his arm. Gabriel laughed to himself, wondering how the decidedly secretive Rackford would have felt about this revelation by his wife, but that was Jacinda for you. Never a dull moment. No wonder she got along so well with Georgiana.

Farther down the hallway, Gabriel smiled at Lord Strathmore's bluestocking bride, Lizzie, as he passed her, but he did not dare interrupt her heated discussion.

"I don't see how one can argue that Lord Elgin had any right to ship the Parthenon marbles back to London. I mean, really, they belong to the Greek people —"

"But Lady Strathmore, the statues would have been destroyed!" some pompous-looking MP was trying to convince her. "Lord Elgin saved them from the ravages of war, don't you see?"

"I'm sure Princess Sophia would agree with *my* position," she said firmly, but as Gabriel moved on, he wondered where Princess Sophia was at the moment.

First there had been the reception line, then a period of sitting at the head of the ballroom with her host, the portly Prince Regent. This done, she had been mingling and charming everyone, moving among her guests with four of the guards whom Gabriel tended to suspect the least assigned to shadow her every movement.

The English soldiers from the garrison were posted around the ballroom's perimeter, but the Greeks stayed with her. After long deliberation, Gabriel had selected Yannis, Markos, Niko, and Kosta for the honor. The others were dispersed throughout the castle.

Keeping a discreet and respectful distance, the four chosen bodyguards formed a wide, secure box around her, front and back on both sides. Whenever she took her seat at the head of the room or at table, they retreated to flank her, a pair of men behind her on each side.

All the Greek bodyguards were certainly easy to pick out of the crowd. Tonight, instead of their usual black garb, they were proudly arrayed in the traditional costume of their countrymen: a red vest, richly embroidered with gold and silver thread, worn over a white cotton shirt; a loose, skirt-like garment called a *fustanella,* also of white cotton, which was secured with a broad red sash, and worn over wool knee breeches, with stockings and odd-looking shoes called *tsaruxia.* On their heads, each man also wore a plain, circular cap of matching red felt.

Rather than also adopting the traditional dress of her country's ladies, Sophia had opted for a different strategy in her apparel. Eager to inspire her guests' generosity, the whimsical temptress had adorned herself in a modified version of the ancient fashion.

Though Gabriel and the other military men had mocked the thought of guests wearing togas — thankfully, they had been wrong about that, as formal attire had proven to be de rigeur — they had all been stunned into awed silence when they had caught their first glimpse of Sophia tonight, arrayed in gauzy white silk like some marble Aphrodite brought to life.

A wreath of bay leaves crowned her head;

a golden circlet hugged her upper arm. On her feet, sandals.

She had to be freezing.

He couldn't believe she had dressed like that, but she had caused a sensation with her daring, and that, he supposed, was exactly the sort of thing a gorgeous young royal was supposed to do.

All he knew was that he disliked intensely the overheated stares she drew from too many of the male guests. At the same time, he mocked himself for his jealousy and his useless possessiveness. She wasn't *his*. She never would be, no matter how his heart protested.

Perhaps he could at least dance with her, he thought, recalling her attempt to make him promise her a waltz when he had showed her the escape route through the wine cellar.

He had refused since he would be on duty, but did he *really* need to be quite so stand-offish? The distance that had come between them ever since he had mentioned his worries about a traitor had him now reconsidering his obstinacy.

If one dance would make her happy and bring them back into harmony with each other, then where was the harm?

Yes, he decided, he would ask her to dance.

Sauntering back toward the ballroom, Gabriel braced himself for the sight of her again, because every time he looked at her, she took his breath away.

Crown Prince Christian Frederick of Denmark had seated himself by her side and soon commenced grilling her none too subtly on all manner of topics concerning herself, from her upbringing and her education to her views on home and family. It seemed to be some sort of interview, and Sophia knew she should not be growing annoyed.

The big, strapping Norseman was perfect for her purposes: handsome, brown-haired, thirty-two, and looking for a royal bride. His country had even had the sense to try to stay neutral as best it could during all the warring between Napoleon and the rest of Europe. Greece and Denmark; fire and ice; the bottom of Europe and the top. It made perfect sense strategically and in many other ways.

The prince was undeniably attractive, too.

If the people of Kavros needed her to make a wise marriage alliance someday, she was quite certain the ideal royal husband was sitting by her side.

Unfortunately, Sophia could not stop furtively scanning the crowd for the flash of a scarlet uniform.

Where are you? she thought desperately, searching for Gabriel. She knew he was on duty somewhere nearby, overseeing all of his ironclad security measures, but she had not laid eyes on him in half an hour, and she found herself growing thirsty for lack of him, like a plant that needed water.

Perhaps it was not as her bodyguard that she needed him right now, but as the man who had already staked a claim on her heart, whether either of them had intended it or not. God, she felt so torn. She could not afford *not* to charm the Danish prince, but despite herself, she was not enjoying the reminder that she'd probably end up with someone else. She only wanted Gabriel and what on earth were they to do?

The prince noticed her distant smile and summoned a footman with an elegant wave of his jeweled hand.

But when he lifted a glass of champagne off the footman's tray and offered it to Sophia, she declined with a regretful shake of her head. "I am sorry, Your Highness," she murmured. "My chief of security has ordered that I may only accept glasses brought to me by that one fellow alone, and nobody else. See?" She pointed to one of the British soldiers from the garrison, the captain's second in command. He was in charge of the bottles served to her from private stock and every glass that was to touch her lips.

If anyone managed to poison her tonight, that tried-and-tested soldier was the one who would be hanged for dereliction of duty.

"Ah, the old threat of poison," the future king said with a world-weary smile. "Believe me, my dear, I know just how you feel. Living this way can be such a royal bore. I shall taste it for you."

"Don't!" she warned.

The Crown Prince did it anyway. He took a sip and, satisfied that he had impressed her with his gallantry, then offered her the glass.

Sophia accepted it only when she saw that he did not fall dead upon the floor.

His Highness regarded her with a speculative smile full of amusement, but she only held the glass in her hand.

She did not take a sip. To have done so would have felt disloyal to her bodyguard. After all, she told herself, if Colonel Knight was putting his life on the line for her, the least that she could do was obey the blasted protocol.

The prince eyed her Ancient Greek costume in wary amusement. "Shall we dance, my fair goddess?"

Distracted from her search for her Gabriel, she glanced over at him in surprise.

Crown Prince Christian Frederick stood and offered her his hand.

She thought of Kavros, and her people, and Gabriel's stoic refusal of her request for a waltz a few days ago — such a simple thing to ask, but he would not do it. Why was she making herself miserable over a man who was so determined to keep her at arm's length?

With that, she summoned up a brilliant smile for the Crown Prince, though inwardly she was feeling rather wretched. "I would be honored, Your Highness." She placed her hand in his and rose.

He watched her in fascination as she allowed him to escort her to the dance floor.

CHAPTER THIRTEEN

Upon walking into the thronged ballroom, Gabriel noticed at once that the music had changed, the Greek players with their rousing folk tunes replaced by the smooth elegance of the orchestra.

The dancing had begun. *Excellent,* he thought, looking around for Sophia with an air of determination. The first person he saw, however, was his sister, Georgiana.

"Brother!" She was standing right inside the entrance with her husband, Lord Griffith, and his closest friend since boyhood, their firstborn cousin, Robert, the Duke of Hawkscliffe, head of the Knight clan.

Gabriel greeted his kin with a smile. His sister hugged him with her usual doting affection, moving carefully with the now-showing curve of her pregnant belly.

Ever the protective elder brother, he had not entirely approved of her traveling over bumpy roads to the castle for the occasion, but if her husband did not see cause for alarm, then he could hardly object. Besides, a lifetime as her sibling had taught Gabriel that it was nigh impossible to stop Georgie from doing what Georgie wanted to do.

With her passion for the rights of women, he supposed that his sister was not about to be denied the chance to meet the future female ruler of a whole country, no matter how small and poor it might be.

"She's brilliant!" Georgie confided. "I love her! Ian just introduced us a little while ago."

"She's very beautiful," Robert remarked in a respectful tone. "Smart as a whip, too, from what I hear."

"She also happens to be very good with a knife," Gabriel informed them with a crooked grin.

"Egads," Robert murmured.

"I don't know how she manages to stay so strong without her family helping her through this," Georgie exclaimed. "It's tragic how so many of them have been killed. You keep her safe, Gabriel, will you?"

He put his arm around his sister. "I'm not going to let anything happen to her."

"I know you won't. Keep yourself safe, too." Georgie clung to his arm. "We're going to miss you so! You're the best brother in the whole world."

"Hey! What about me?" a voice retorted from nearby.

Gabriel laughed as their middle sibling joined them.

"Derek," Griff greeted him, laughing.

"Just because I always teased you and he was too damned noble to sink to my level?" Derek jested, giving their sister a kiss on the cheek. He nodded to the others. "Hullo, all."

"Where's Lily?"

"She got caught up trying all the Greek foods with Mrs. Clearwell and Father."

"I hope I can talk to Her Highness again later this evening," Georgie said. "I might have ideas about how to help the poorer citizens of Kavros, since that seems to be such a concern."

"My wife was very active in helping the lowliest citizens back in Calcutta," Griff told Robert with a proud gleam in his eyes.

Gabriel swept the room with a quick glance. "Where has she gone, anyway?"

"Her Highness? She is dancing."

Gabriel halted. "Oh." He turned toward the dance floor and searched the weaving crowd of whirling couples, gliding at the waltz. For a fleeting moment, he caught sight of Sophia in the arms of a tall, brown-haired man in uniform. An array of glittering medals and the red diagonal sash the haughty-looking fellow wore across his chest suggested he was some sort of dignitary.

A strange reaction moved through him in a wave when he saw them. An unpleasant pain that rather choked him. "Who is that . . . dancing with her?" he forced out.

"That," Robert informed him in a low tone, "is Crown Prince Christian Frederick of Denmark."

"Prince?" Gabriel echoed faintly, absorbing the word like a body blow.

"Yes, I understand he's looking for another wife."

"Another wife? Is he a widower?" Georgie asked blithely, only making conversation, while Gabriel stared, his mind reeling.

The strangling sensation grew. "He certainly looks like he's enjoying himself," he growled, still watching the dancers for another glimpse of the storybook pair.

"Actually, it was a bit of a scandal," Robert told them. "The prince was previously married to a young lady who I believe was his cousin. But he dissolved the marriage after learning that she was having an affair with her music teacher."

"Good heavens!" Georgie whispered.

"The prince banished his ex-wife to the

coldest reaches of Jutland, and forbade her from ever seeing their child again."

"Oh, that's terrible," Georgie murmured, while Gabriel stared at his ducal cousin with a chill arrowing down his spine. "Well, if Princess Sophia fancies him, I daresay she'd better never stray from her vows."

"Not that she would," Lord Griffith amended.

"Unless she likes the snow," Derek drawled under his breath.

"Would you all please excuse me?" Gabriel choked out abruptly. "I need to go and check on my men outside."

Derek eyed him sharply. "I'll come with you."

"That really isn't necessary —"

"I don't mind. I could use some fresh air."

Gabriel was too routed by the duke's explanation to argue. Stunned by the news about Sophia's latest suitor, he could see the writing on the wall.

He would have rather been alone at that moment, but Derek had never been one to take a hint. His younger brother had had a habit of shadowing him ever since they were small boys.

Outside, Gabriel walked to the edge of the terrace and just stood there in shock. The night's chill cut through his uniform, but he was numb; above, the stars were tiny pinpricks of silver in the onyx night, too far above his reach to illuminate his darkness.

A short distance behind him, Derek halted with a palpable air of uncertainty. "Are you all right?"

In brooding silence, Gabriel lowered his gaze to the flagstone ground.

"You know that Gypsy girl I told you about?" he responded after a moment.

"Yes."

"It was her," he whispered in agony. "It was Princess Sophia."

"What?" Derek cried. "How? But — you're joking."

Gabriel turned around slowly and denied the charge with a sardonic shake of his head.

Derek stared at him in amazement.

Gabriel gave him a brief summary of how she had wound up at his farm, then he looked away.

"Gabriel, you have to quit!"

"Quit?"

"Yes, you must resign! You can't be her bodyguard when you're in love with her!" he insisted, keeping his voice down. "You've got to keep a clear head —"

"Who says I'm in love with her?"

Derek snorted.

"I *am* keeping a clear head. I'm trying!

Derek, I can't leave her. She needs me."

"Does she know how you feel?" His eyes widened again. "Does she feel the same?"

Gabriel stared at him stoically. "I don't know."

"Damn, you are a scoundrel!" Derek let out a lusty laugh and waved his hand in his direction. "Of all the men in the world to snare a princess, of course it would be you! How do you do it, really?"

"I'm glad you find my situation amusing."

"Ah, my poor brother. Look at you. Turning yourself inside out for this woman. That is indeed how it starts."

He slung his arm around his brother's neck and shook his head with a fond, low laugh. "But don't worry, old boy. It gets much better, I swear. Love is horrible at first, it's perfectly wretched. Believe me, I speak from experience. Every little thing she does can cut your damned heart out."

"Like dancing with a prince?" Gabriel asked, then looked askance at him. "It's not going to get any better, Derek. Not for me. Lily was perfect for you from the start, but this is hopeless. Anyone can see that." He shrugged off his brother's affectionate hold and paced away a few steps. "She's a hundred miles above my station, and now she's in the arms of a man who will crush her if she stays close to me. Even as my friend."

"Listen to you! It's only a dance, man! She hasn't married him yet. For God's sake, you are the Iron Major. It is nowhere in your nature to give up without a fight. Besides, look at Robert and Belinda! The family never mentions it, but we all know Bel was only his mistress, and yet she married a duke."

"Bel's a woman!" he retorted, scowling. "It's completely different when the lowborn one's the man."

"I would hardly call you lowborn. You've got a marchioness for a sister and a duke for a cousin —"

"I'm not a prince! Derek, I'd look like a fool following her around like a dog, even if she'd have me."

"We all have to sacrifice for those we love, Gabriel. I know better than anyone that you have never shrunk from that," he added softly, with a meaningful look reminding him of the moment he had put himself in the arrow's path to shield his little brother.

Gabriel turned away and paced again, stroking his jaw restlessly in thought. "My sacrifice is staying away, then. She may need to marry this Crown Prince Bastard What's-His-Name for the good of her people. She loves her country, that's obvious. And if it matters to her, then it bloody well matters to me."

"You are so noble sometimes, you make me want to shoot you," his brother said mildly. Derek folded his arms across his chest and raised an eyebrow as he studied him with a piercing look. "But this time, I think the problem might just be your ego."

"My ego?" he retorted.

"You'd rather spill your blood than sacrifice your warrior pride." He sauntered closer and looked him in the eyes with stark honesty and a brother's loyalty. "Tell me there is not some truth to that? So, you'd walk a step behind the chit for the rest of your days. So what? If that's the only way that I could be with Lily, I would take it in a heartbeat. Hell, if I had to wheel her around in a wheelbarrow wearing a loincloth like her slave —"

"Oh, shut up." Gabriel couldn't help laughing at the image as he turned away, shaking his head. "I swear, love has made you more of a madman than you always were."

"Ah, Shakespeare had something to say about that. Lovers, poets, madmen — seething brains, whatnot? Now, go in there and get your princess back from that overblown Hamlet! Something is rotten in Denmark, I say. If you want her, go and claim her! Either find a way or make one —"

"Wait!" Gabriel suddenly came to attention, silencing Derek and staring off toward the perimeter wall. "What was that?"

"What was what?"

"Did you see that?"

"No —"

"Shh! I heard something." He pointed, his finger slowly tracking along the wall. Then he narrowed his eyes, searching the darkness. "There is someone . . . in the shadows."

Movement.

Gabriel stepped up onto the stone balustrade and jumped off the terrace into the soft grass below, instantly tearing off across the greensward toward the perimeter wall.

He pointed to the left as he ran, but Derek was already on it, charging to head off the intruder.

Ignoring the pull in his middle of newly mended muscle around his scar, Gabriel sprinted on, his gaze picking out a lone man who had spotted them coming and now was trying to flee.

"HALT!" he roared.

The slim, wiry man ignored him, leaping up to catch hold of the edge of the old medieval wall. Bearing down on him, Gabriel could see that the large pack slung over the man's shoulder added weight that impaired his ability to climb.

As he dangled there, trying to sling his leg up onto the top of the wall, Gabriel barreled into him and slammed him to the ground.

"Gun!" he yelled to warn his approaching brother, but the man did not have time to use it.

Gabriel ripped away the large pistol tucked into the front waistband of the man's trousers. The second he turned to hurl the man's weapon far over the wall, out of harm's way, the wiry fellow scrambled to his feet and went bolting off again.

Derek headed him off this time, his arms out wide; the intruder veered to the side and tore between two tall shrubberies, but when he came barreling out the other side, Gabriel was already there.

"Get him!" Derek belted out.

"Leave me be!" a Cockney voice yelped, the intruder's decidedly unhandsome English face filling with terror at the realization that he was caught between two ruthless warriors who were both inclined to break him like a toothpick.

As the weasel tried to dart past him, Gabriel tackled him to the ground.

The wiry captive began flailing and thrashing as Gabriel held him down. "Help! Help! Oppression! Tyranny!"

"What?" Derek exclaimed as he ran over to help.

"Overthrow the government! Death to Lord Liverpool! Tyrants — Tories!" the man yelped, wriggling like a worm after the rain. "The prime minister is a criminal! Burn the Home Office! Disband the corporations!"

Gabriel smacked him in the head. "Would you shut up?"

From the corner of his eye, he could see a number of men from the garrison rushing over to join them.

"Check the wall to make sure he was alone!" he ordered loudly. "Go! We have everything under control here. Then back to your posts!"

"Aye, sir!"

"Here are manacles if you want them, Colonel."

"Yes. Give them to me."

One of the soldiers gave him the shackles for their captive as the others scattered to search for any other intruders who might have snuck in with the man. Gabriel intended to find out exactly how the detestable Jacobin had breached security. But as he took a moment to catch his breath, he could not help but send up a prayer of relief to see that this lunatic had arrived with an entirely different agenda. Unless it was a ruse — and he would soon find out for sure — this man's hatred seemed to be clearly aimed at the Tory government, not at Sophia.

"Burn the Home Office!" his foaming tirade continued. "Hang the prime minister —"

"That will do," Gabriel ordered him curtly.

Derek bent down and glowered at him. "Didn't you know this party was by invitation only?"

"Look at you two! You're slaves and you don't even know it —" The intruder swallowed his words with a wide-eyed gulp when Gabriel scowled at him.

"God, I hate radicals," Derek muttered. "Don't you people ever bathe?"

"What have you got in the bag, fool?"

"Let's have a look. Ah, hand grenades," Derek said, inspecting the man's lumpy canvas pack. "Clever lad, he even remembered to bring a flint to light the matches with."

"You treasonous wretch, what were you going to do, blow up the ball?"

"Freedom!" the wiry man yelped.

"I think you mean anarchy, you ungrateful puke." He rolled him facedown into the grass and clapped the manacles on him. "Get up!" he ordered, hauling him to his feet.

The moment he had the prisoner under control, Gabriel's thoughts returned to the conversation they'd been having before the interruption. "So, what do you think I should do, then?" he persisted, ignoring the prisoner's thrashing about as they began marching him back to the castle.

"You're asking my opinion?"

"You've always been better with women than me. What would you do? Would you resign from this post?"

"Hell, no." Derek glanced at Gabriel and started to speak again, but was interrupted by the lurching dunce they had captured.

"Burn the Parliament! Burn —"

"Shut up!" Derek ordered, wrenching him a bit. At once, the man tried to make himself as limp as a noodle. "Oh, stop that. Don't be a churl. Will you walk or would you rather we drag you?"

"You were saying?" Gabriel prompted as they commenced dragging the would-be anarchist by his heels across the grass.

"I'd keep my distance," Derek replied, "but I admit, I'd have to stay until I had ripped the heads off anyone who wanted to hurt her."

"Then, we concur."

"But, now, after that job was done, mind you . . ." Derek gave him a roguish wink.

Gabriel snorted. "If I'm still alive."

"Well, in my experience," Derek said mildly as they reached the stone steps up to the terrace and hauled the prisoner to his feet, "you don't die so easily."

"True, that," Gabriel admitted with a nod, then turned to the prisoner. "On your feet again. We're taking you in."

"What are you going to do with him? Hand him over to the captain?" Derek inquired, taking hold of the man's other arm.

"In due time. First, I think I've got another use for him."

"You'll not torture me! Help!" Since his arms were pinned, he started flailing his long, skinny legs.

"Torture?" Derek exclaimed, helping Gabriel to keep him still. "Too bad we're not in India. Then we could hand you over to the chaps who do that business properly."

"Who's that?" the disheveled radical asked, his gaze darting about wildly.

The brothers exchanged a grim glance and then just started laughing.

■ ■ ■ ■

Leaving the dance floor, Sophia had beckoned Alexa over to sit with her as a buffer between her and the very interested prince. The man wouldn't let her out of his sight. But they had barely taken their seats again when the captain of the garrison came marching over to her with a curt, martial bow. "Your Highness?"

"Yes?" both she and Crown Prince Christian Frederick said at once.

Alexa giggled.

"I think he meant me," Sophia said politely.

"Ah, of course," His Highness said.

The captain cleared his throat. "Princess: The chef requires your opinion about the, er, pastries."

Alexa wrinkled her nose. "The pastries?"

Sophia stared at the captain. *Uh-oh.*

Code. Trouble.

Quickly chasing away her fearful look, she rose smoothly and smiled at her lady-in-waiting. "You know how particular I am that my guests should be treated to a proper sampling of Greek pastries, Alexa. They must be flaky, but with not too much butter. It is a point of national pride."

"Right," Alexa said abruptly.

"I must go at once to the kitchens and see my, um, very talented chef about this matter. You know how hard it is to secure the talents of Europe's finest."

"But of course."

She nodded to him. "Your Highness, if you will excuse me."

"Princess." He bowed to her.

"Ah, Alexa, come with me." She paused, turned back, and crooked a finger at her flirtatious friend. She was not about to leave Alexa with all her loose morals behind to throw herself at the Crown Prince and make him doubt *her* character by association.

The captain gestured to her. "This way, Your Highness, if you will."

Seeing her on the move, her Greek bodyguards accompanied her, holding their loose formation around her and Alexa.

"What's all this about the silly pastries?" her friend whispered. "Were you just trying to get away from him?"

"No, it's just a code Gabriel invented to let me know if there was trouble without alarming the guests."

"Trouble?" Alexa gripped her arm and paled. "What sort of trouble? You don't think —"

"Hush. We're about to find out. Don't

worry, just be calm. Colonel Knight will keep us safe."

"You trust him so much?" Alexa retorted.

Sophia paused and glanced at her. "With my life."

Then they hurried on, passing into the private service areas of the castle's main floor. The captain led them through the kitchens and down to the wine-cellar level, but they did not go the way that Gabriel had showed her that day, over by the old escape tunnel. Instead, they went down another dank, torch-lit corridor, until they came to a dead end, where a dozen British soldiers were arrayed around a thick, closed door.

Gabriel stood in the middle of all the soldiers, waiting for them.

Sophia rushed toward him. "What has happened, Colonel?"

"Everyone, stay calm," he ordered in an even tone. "Rest assured; I have everything in hand."

Sophia sent Alexa a pointed smile as if to say, *See?*

"Has there been an incident?"

"We've captured one of the attackers from the night of the ambush."

She and all her Greeks responded with a collective gasp.

Then Timo stepped forward instantly, fists clenched. "Let me at him!"

"And me!" said Yannis.

"Gentlemen," Gabriel warned, holding up his hand. "You will remain. The prisoner is bound and secured in the room behind me. I am going to question this blackguard at length, and believe me, I will make sure to tell you everything I've found out once I am through with him."

"What if he won't talk?" Demetrius challenged with a dark look, cracking his knuckles.

"Oh, believe me, there are tricks I learned in India that will make this villain sing."

Alexa gulped and took a backward step, her eyes wide.

Sophia ignored her, moving forward with ice in her veins. "I want to see him."

"Your Highness, I don't think that's a good idea —"

"He killed Leon!" she cried angrily, lurching forward. "Out of my way — you!" she ordered the British soldiers guarding the door. "I want a word with him. Now!"

"Very well," Gabriel conceded softly, coming up beside her. "But only for a moment. Men." He nodded to his British soldiers, who parted to admit them into the adjoining room.

They blocked the door again after Gabriel and she had stepped inside. The colonel went ahead of her, but the second Sophia spotted the shadowed silhouette of a man on a chair in the corner, bound and gagged, his hands tied behind him, she reached under her skirt and slid out her knife with lethal intent.

As Gabriel turned to her, she sprang at the prisoner with her knife lifted over his face.

Gabriel swore and grabbed her wrist. "What are you doing?" he shouted.

"I'm going to kill him!" she cried.

"No, you're not! Drop it, Sophia!" he ordered as she fought him. "I said drop it *now!*"

"You can't tell me what to do!" She looked at him accusingly, tears rushing into her eyes. "You're not my husband — you're just my bodyguard!"

"Put it . . . down," he ordered her through gritted teeth, his face inches from hers. "Sophia, listen to me. He's not involved," he whispered fiercely. "This is a ruse."

She blinked through her tears. "What?"

"We caught him outside, but his being here has nothing to do with you. He's a wild-eyed Jacobin with a bag of hand grenades. He wants to kill the prime minister, not you. The man's deranged."

"But — you said —"

"I lied. Sweetheart, give me the knife."

The velvet caress in his voice at the endearment made her quiver, his gentleness overpowered her more than all of his warrior strength could have done. Slowly, she released her grip on the knife and fought him no more, letting him take it.

She glanced at the prisoner and saw him staring at her, whimpering through the gag. She wrapped her arms around herself with a chill and looked away, wondering if she really could have stabbed a defenseless man.

Gabriel put the knife on the other side of the room, well out of the bound prisoner's reach, and then came over to her with a light touch on her elbow. "Are you all right?"

She nodded, avoiding his searching gaze. "What did you mean," she uttered in a shaky tone, "by a ruse?"

"When we intercepted him, I knew he was the perfect tool to use against anyone in your entourage who might want to do you harm."

She pulled away. "Oh, do not speak of that again!"

Gabriel just gave her a stoic look as he rested his hands on his waist. "Right now, all of your Greek guards think we've caught one of the attackers. If any of them are involved, this lie should force them to tip their hand. I've talked to the captain. He's got his men in place, and we're going to see what your Greeks do about this development, how they react to this information. With all eyes on you for the ball, this would be the safest time to try it."

"My men have nothing to hide," she whispered with a little less conviction than she had previously felt.

"Then they have nothing to fear," he answered. "Just let me test them."

"Very well, if that's the only way you'll be convinced."

"All that matters to me is keeping you safe."

His quiet words made her heart clench. She dropped her gaze once more. "Do what you must. I will uphold this lie."

"Sophia," he said softly as she started toward the door. "You make a wonderful Aphrodite."

She paused, glancing over her shoulder with a guarded half smile. "Thanks. But I'm actually supposed to be Artemis."

His eyebrow lifted. "The huntress virgin?" he murmured with a dubious grin.

She blushed slightly. She supposed he had cause to regard her as less than virginal, but it was only this man who had that effect on her. With a tentative smile, she turned once more to go.

"Did you enjoy your dance with the prince?" he asked from behind her.

His soft-toned question stopped her in her tracks, but she did not turn around.

"At least he asked me."

"I hear he's looking for another wife."

"I heard that, too." Her heart was pounding so loud she thought that all the guests upstairs would surely hear it through the castle's stone.

"But are you looking for a husband?"

She stared hopelessly at the formidable wall before her. "I don't know," she breathed, acutely aware of him behind her. "He dances well — though he seems a little paranoid."

"Surely you don't want him, then."

"Since when has what I want ever entered into the equation?" she uttered under her breath.

But Gabriel must have heard, for in the next instant, he was behind her, his body radiating heat as he grasped her waist and turned her around. "Sophia —"

"Don't." She tried to push him away, but it was no use.

He pulled her into his arms behind the

prisoner's line of sight and claimed her mouth in ravishing hunger. He captured her nape as he kissed her in a firestorm of what she quite believed was jealous passion, clenching her to him. His mouth slanted over hers in possessive demand, taking what she so longed to give. She parted her lips eagerly to devour his kiss, molding her hands over his broad shoulders. He tightened his arm around her waist.

Gathering her closer still while his tongue caressed hers, he drew her body against his, so warm and strong, but when she felt the tautening length of his arousal hardening against her stomach, Sophia reluctantly pulled away.

This was too scandalous, feasting on each other like this in what was nearly a dungeon. "That's enough." She backed him off; he let her go, breathing hard.

Light-headed with the pleasure that had flooded her body, she took a few dizzied paces away from him. She deemed it prudent to put a safe distance between them, for she could barely resist the still magnetic pull of his heaving passion. She could feel him burning from across the cold, dank cell. She closed her eyes.

I want you, too.

A muffled protest from the prisoner jerked

them both back to reality. Seated several feet away, his hands manacled behind the chair, the Jacobin was trying to turn around to see what they were doing.

"I, ah, I'd better tell the others what's afoot," Sophia murmured. "Your version of it, anyway."

Head down, hands on his waist, Gabriel was still panting, his glance like that of a hungry wolf as he sent her a quick nod of agreement.

She swallowed hard, her heart still racing, then she turned away, and let herself back out of the room.

Gabriel followed a moment later, after getting himself a bit better under control.

Outside the door, the members of her entourage stood waiting anxiously for her. Sophia hated lying to them, but she knew she had to let Gabriel have his way on this. Glancing around at their dear, familiar faces, she still could not bring herself to believe that any of them could be false.

At least this experiment would clear them of any taint of guilt for once and for all. And then things could go back to normal.

"It's true," she told her waiting friends with a firm nod. "We've got one of these monsters in custody. We'll know who's really after me soon."

Without daring to glance back at her head of security, she headed back to the ball. Four hundred guests were waiting, and it was nearly time to make her toast.

Alexa watched Sophia pass, her heart in her throat.

The men were murmuring amongst themselves in Greek, but she was barely paying attention, her mind reeling in pure dread.

How could this happen? How could one of the Tunisian's men have allowed himself to be captured?

Dear God, she thought in panic, what was she to do if he exposed her? To be sure, it was only a matter of time. Colonel Knight would torture it out of him. She'd be arrested. Put on trial. She would have to face Sophia, and then she'd be hanged for a traitor.

Fear spiraled out of control.

The Greek bodyguards paid her no mind, frowning at the half-dozen British soldiers who stepped in to accompany the princess now, packed in densely around her in formation. Colonel Knight gave them some instructions, but Alexa paid no heed. She had to figure out what to do or she was dead.

She nearly leapt out of her skin when

Sophia turned back and called to her. "Lex, are you coming with me?"

"Oh, yes, I — do you wish me to, Your Highness?"

Sophia shrugged. "It's your choice."

"I will come." She leapt to get near her royal guardian. Close to Sophia, no one would suspect her.

Alexa fell into step beside her mistress, taking protection from the person she meant to betray.

Oh, how she hated herself.

Alexa wanted to fall down screaming, but somehow she kept herself together and hurried along beside the princess.

"Try not to be too upset," Sophia sought to comfort her, her determined stare fixed straight ahead. "Colonel Knight has everything in order. We don't wish to upset our guests."

"Of course. I just — can't believe he caught one of them. W-what did he look like?"

"Very ugly."

That sounded accurate enough. Oh, God, with all her soul, Alexa longed to run away and forget all of this had ever happened, but as they reached the ballroom again and Sophia turned on her usual charm, giving no outward sign of her distress — damn her courage! — Alexa knew her own situation was futile.

If she dared flee without keeping up her end of the bargain, the Tunisian would only hunt her down and cut her into pieces. She had to save herself.

Slightly faint with terror, she snatched a champagne flute off the tray of a passing Bacchus-waiter and realized she had to stay calm or she would give herself away.

She gulped down a swallow to steady her nerves; it instantly gave her a throbbing headache. *Think.*

From what she recalled of her tormentors, the pure ruthlessness oozing from the Tunisian and his companions, their dead, soulless eyes, she had to believe that any one of those brutes could withstand days of torture before they would break and expose her. There was still a little time.

For now, she was still valuable to them. She dared not anger them or make any foolish mistakes. This turn of events was not her fault and they would understand that, as long as she wrote to the Tunisian right away, just like he had instructed her to do if there were any problems.

She knew how to contact him, and realized her best chances of survival lay in warning him that his plans must be changed immediately. He might not even know yet that one of his men had been captured. She must tell him they could not afford to wait another week. The timetable for Sophia's abduction must be swiftly sped up.

Oh, God, she thought. It was coming on too soon. What if she lost her nerve? But she could not, not if she liked to keep her head upon her shoulders. Whatever resentment she had toward Sophia, it would not have thrust her into this kind of treachery if her own life were not at stake.

At least she knew that outsmarting her Greek lovers would be easy because they would never suspect her. But what was she to do about Colonel Knight?

She had to get rid of him somehow . . .

But wait! she told herself as she gulped down another steadying swallow of liquid courage. This would not be as difficult as it seemed. After all, the blue-eyed cavalryman was Sophia's weakness.

Alexa saw that she would not have to try anything dangerous to get rid of him. She would not need to try to shoot him or poison him or anything nasty like that. She need only discredit him. Yes.

All she had to do was get him sacked.

And that was easy. Over the years, several tasty males in Sophia's entourage had been dismissed from service because of Alexa. Sophia always fired *them;* she never banished *her.* She was very protective that way.

Besides, the princess could not get rid of her so easily! They were stuck with each other. That was their curse, left to them by both their dead families. The courtiers served and the royals protected. That was the way it had always been, for generations.

But Alexa was tired of serving. Soon, she told herself, slowly regaining her courage, she would be free.

She'd use her wits and await her opportunity. She would write to the Tunisian. Then he could tell her what she must do next.

CHAPTER FOURTEEN

Maybe the bodyguards really were innocent.

A day and a half later, the guests were gone, and the castle was still cleaning up after the ball. Gabriel had been up for most of the night again, waiting for one of the Greek guards to act, but nothing had happened.

If anything, the men had become even more protective of Sophia. They were, or at least pretended to be, so impassioned in their anger that someone would want to do her harm that they didn't even notice they were under constant watch by British soldiers from the garrison, and by Gabriel most of all.

They were fixated on the prisoner, itching to get their hands on him. Never much of a liar, Gabriel wasn't sure how much longer he could keep up the charade.

Taking a much-needed break from his duties, he stood inside a lesser-used morning room that overlooked the soggy autumnal grounds. A gray drizzle speckled the wide span of windows where he leaned idly, watching Sophia practice her various skills and feats of arms on horseback.

At the ball, he had mistaken her for Aphrodite, but on this dreary afternoon, she was dressed all in black with her hair plaited severely behind her. Intensely focused on honing her feminine ruthlessness, she looked much more the part of the fierce virgin huntress goddess, Artemis.

He tracked her with his stare as she galloped past on the bay horse that he once had thought his Gypsy girl had stolen.

The castle offered an elaborate course with jumps and shooting targets, medieval-style quintains altered for cavalry usage, and diverse obstacles to sharpen one's skills. Smiling faintly as she passed, he made a mental note of a few pointers he could give her to polish her technique. He watched in admiration until she rounded a stand of trees and disappeared into the parkland, her horse's dark tail flying out behind him like a pennant as they continued on the course.

If only he could figure out what was going through that head of hers today.

Obviously, something was bothering her.

Maybe it was just the threat that she was

under, he thought. The strain of it all had to be getting to her.

The Grecian Gala had amassed the princely sum of three hundred thousand pounds for the people of Kavros. He would have thought she'd be happier about it, but the truth was, she had been acting strangely ever since he had kissed her in that dank cell the other night.

He did not know what had come over him, but as much as he had relished it, he was not happy with himself about it. His ironclad control had slipped, and that was not a good sign.

Sophia didn't seem too pleased about it, either. By the morning after the ball, she had turned distant, and today was even more withdrawn. He had not thought it possible for his frustration to escalate further, but that brief taste of her and the distance she had put between them ever since had put him on edge.

He shouldn't have kissed her and he was a little chagrined after the fact, especially after he had been so self-righteously insistent that nothing like that could happen between them.

At this point, she was probably equally confused about where the two of them stood with each other.

Or perhaps she was just off thinking about Monsieur Denmark, he mused with a brooding stare in the direction she had ridden. He sincerely hoped not.

But Gabriel was no fool.

A part of him felt as though he had already lost her to the Crown Prince, or rather, to her duty. But then again, he thought with a low sigh that fogged the glass before him, Her Royal Highness of Kavros had never been his to lose.

This is torture. What am I to do?

I need these men in two different ways, but I can't have them both.

Sophia was in the teeth of a crisis of faith, and it all had started with Gabriel's kiss the other night down in that dungeon. She urged the gelding on faster, as if she could outrun the choice she had to make.

The mud flew from under her horse's hooves, flecking her long coat of black leather, while the cold drizzle of the overcast day froze on her cheeks. She did not care.

She kept waiting for the crisp air to help clear her head, but it did not seem to be working. She aimed her pistol at one of the painted circular targets as she cantered by.

Crack!

She scowled at the poor shot, the powder

all but ruined by the wet. But she quickly slipped the gun back in its holster at her hip and signaled the bay to gather his stride for the upcoming fence.

They sailed over the jump, landed in a satisfying spray of mud, and pounded on over the spongy turf, the breath of both horse and rider clouding in the cold.

Sophia's forward stare was fierce, her jaw taut as she forced herself to confront the reality of her situation.

From the day Gabriel had agreed to become her bodyguard, he had told her it was necessary to keep an emotional distance, or this whole proposition would become even more dangerous for both of them.

Now the very thing he had warned of was happening, growing stronger every hour. She was falling for him, falling so desperately in love with him, and on the night of the ball, his control had slipped, too, as proven by his kiss. While her heart rejoiced to see that his feelings for her were becoming so strong that they had begun to outstrip his will, her objective, logical mind was frightened by the implications. He had warned her that he had to keep a certain distance from her in order to protect her properly.

Now that distance was vanishing, and it chilled her to her core to think that the next time they were attacked, Gabriel's feelings for her might impair his judgment, cause him to make a mistake, and get him killed. She could not bear it. If she did not end this now, they could both wind up dead.

She had to get Gabriel out of here. She had to let him go. She was already asking too much of the man; he had only just healed from a near-fatal wound. He deserved a chance to live in peace, which was all he had really wanted before she had dragged him into this.

She thought of him looking after those kittens back at the farm and couldn't believe she had been so selfish to send for him in the first place. What was wrong with her? Why couldn't she have left him alone?

And now there was Crown Prince Christian Frederick.

A stray thought came and passed of poor Cleopatra, dependent on Caesar's doting affection, while perfectly obsessed with her handsome general, Mark Antony.

Sophia didn't feel that she was behaving much better than the two-faced Egyptian queen, by comparison. She had been so desperate to have Gabriel beside her, back in her life, that she had ignored his cautions.

Selfish girl.

She could never, ever forgive herself if Gabriel was harmed. Why hadn't she stuck with her safe, old philosophy of avoiding romantic entanglements?

She had made up her mind a long time ago to give her heart only to her country, just like Queen Elizabeth of olden days. After having her family torn apart, this vow had made perfect sense to her, for a country could not die. And besides, as Alexa's many adventures had proved, men were so often false.

Like the prince . . . ?

No, he'd be the opposite, after what had happened with his first wife. He would be suspicious of her faithfulness every hour of every day, she thought. Her life would be a cage. And indeed, what if the day came when she had to marry this man for her nation's benefit? Did she intend to keep Gabriel selfishly on hand until that necessity arose, and then kick him away when it was more advantageous to her to switch loyalties? *Never.* She could not do that to him.

That would have been as cruel as what the prince had done to his first wife, banished now beyond the icy fjords of Jutland.

No, she could never take advantage of Gabriel's noble nature, nor risk his dying for her sake like Leon had.

All this was becoming just too hard.

He had captured that bumbling Radical and deceived her men with the tale that he had caught one of the attackers from the night of the ambush; this was only a ruse, but soon the danger would be real.

With every passing day, life got more dangerous for everyone around her. Just being near her could be deadly, as if she carried some sort of plague that ended not in horrid boils but in bloody murder. None of this should have ever been turned into Gabriel's problem.

The merest chance had brought her to his doorstep the night of the ambush. He had been living quietly on that farm, where she knew he still had more healing to do, perhaps not physically, but in his soul. He had been nothing but good to her, and this was how she thanked him?

She had to get him out of here, had to end this while there was still time. She simply could not bear for this man to end up dead like her father, her brothers, and now Leon. Once they sailed for Kavros, it would be too late. If she cared for him, she should let him go.

He had so much to live for.

Unlike her, Gabriel still had a family who loved him. And all of those wonderful people were going to hate her and blame her if anything happened to him, she realized.

Whack!

Morosely, she struck the quintain with the flat of her sword and sent the dummy spinning as she rode on.

Oh, what was the point of going to all these lengths to preserve her life from these silly assassins, anyway? If she had to live out the rest of her days without Gabriel's love, maybe she'd be better off if her enemies got her.

Maybe she should abandon this quest and run away with Gabriel, live as commoners on some hayseed farm in the middle of nowhere. Au revoir, duty. They could live like two happy peasant farmers, raising an army of apple-cheeked tots. That plain, lovely dinner they had shared had been the happiest night of her life.

But he would never go along with that, of course. Not him, not the soul of manly honor. Nor could she. She could never abandon her people and disgrace the royal house.

Thud!

The target rocked slightly with the impact of the knife she had just thrown.

Her own skills pleased her, restoring a little bit of her shaken faith. Those enemies hadn't managed to get her last time, so why was she overreacting so much now?

Because she was in love.

Oh, calm down, she scolded herself tersely. *Leave off with these dramatics. You are acting like some ninny-headed fool. Do you really think you need to play the mother hen to a warrior whose motto was once "No mercy"?*

She ignored the memory of his insistence that he was no longer that man. There was no need to send Gabriel packing. All would be well. *We'll just continue on the way we have been,* she assured herself.

Friends. Nobly focused on our duty.

Hypocrites.

Pretending we are not in love.

Poor Colonel Knight.

A man like that should never go deprived. Whatever Her Highness was giving him, it clearly wasn't enough.

No, Alexa knew the hungry look of a sex-starved man when she saw one. She stared at him now as she lingered in the doorway to the lower morning room, preparing to make her move.

He was staring out the bank of windows with a brooding expression, watching the princess at her unladylike pursuits. Since the magnificent brute was not yet aware of her presence, Alexa indulged in letting her gaze travel over his tall, powerful physique. God, she lusted for this man. He wore civilian clothes today, but his gentlemanly attire could not disguise his lethal aura. What it would be like to bed him made her quiver just to imagine.

The curve of his strong lower back in that snug waistcoat, down to his solidly muscled buttocks — which she had studied from a distance through his breeches on several previous occasions — all led her errant thoughts down the fascinating path of what hard thrusts he could deliver, what pleasure he could give. The bulky outline of his biceps visible through his loose white shirtsleeves made her think of how long and how tightly he could hold her if she was lucky enough to lure him to her bed.

But of course, that was not the true purpose of her visit. She wouldn't have minded a whit, but all she had to do today was get him to consider it . . .

She quite believed she was going to enjoy this.

My darling beast, you are going to waste,

pining for her, Alexa thought as she sauntered toward him.

Unfortunately, in truth, it was too late to bed him. He had lost his chance.

Yesterday she had received her instructions from Kemal, along with a small bottle of pure laudanum. Of this, she had already poured a dram into the bottle of Sophia's favorite red Greek wine, which she kept in her apartments. The rest she was saving for the bodyguards.

But she couldn't take the chance of that simple trick working on Colonel Knight. Unlike the others, he had no particular reason to trust her.

With him, her wisest move was to see him gone entirely. She had been watching for her opportunity, and she knew that it had come.

What a lucky thing Sophia was to have captivated him, Alexa mused with a jealousy that was not unfamiliar as she went toward him slowly. His hands planted on the windowsill, he was immobile, still staring outside. She admired his hard, chiseled profile, but even in this drab gray light, the sun-bronzed tone of his skin looked vibrant and warm. His hair was jet-black, and as he glanced over at her approach, his eyes were piercing cobalt blue.

Alexa was entranced. She dimpled at him with her most harmless and submissive smile. "Good afternoon, Colonel."

He turned away from the window and sketched a polite bow to her in answer. "Lady Alexa. How are you today?"

"Honestly?" She stopped before him, resting her fingertips on the window frame. "I'm so frightened," she whispered.

He frowned. "Why? Has someone threatened you?"

"No, but you caught that horrid man out in the garden, and I just know he's going to hurt Sophia. She is like a sister to me."

"You are very sweet to care about Her Highness so, but do not trouble yourself. I'm going to make sure that nothing happens to either of you ladies."

She lowered her lashes, wishing that his words were true. "You must be very brave," she murmured. It was always safest to appeal to the male ego.

He smiled wryly.

She peeked at him from beneath her lashes. "Did you still want to hear about my point of view on the night of the ambush?"

"Yes. Yes, indeed. Are you free now?"

"Yes," she answered with an eager nod. "Come, let us sit and I will tell you all that I remember." She gestured toward a couch against the opposite wall.

"Good." He stole a quick glance out the window, but Sophia was nowhere in sight, probably somewhere on the far end of the equestrian course, playing around with her guns and other nasty things.

Her heart racing, Alexa led the colonel slowly toward the couch, where they sat down side by side. "You seem like something's bothering you," she observed in a tone of cozy softness.

"Oh, it's nothing —"

"The prince," she murmured with a knowing smile.

He stopped short, lifting his eyebrows.

"I am not blind, Colonel." She reached over and gave his hand a gentle pat. "Everyone falls in love with Her Highness at some point. You're not the first to fall in love with her, and you won't be the last."

He stared at her for a second, then looked away; resting his elbow on the couch's arm, he rubbed his mouth with one hand. After a moment's restless silence, he eyed her warily. "Has she said anything to you?"

"Like what?" Alexa asked innocently.

"Like if she's going to marry him. Or why she's in this mood!"

Alexa tilted her head with a tender gaze.

"You know I cannot betray Sophia's confidence."

"Of course." He stiffened, dropping his gaze. "Forgive me. I should not have asked."

"It's all right," she whispered, daring a light, comforting touch on his arm. "I don't mind. Truly I wish there was some way that I could help. I hate to see you torture yourself for no reason."

"No reason?" he echoed with a soulful stare. This vulnerable side of him turned her inside out.

"Gabriel — may I call you Gabriel?" Alexa whispered. "The good of Kavros has always come first for Sophia."

Disappointment flickered in those dark blue eyes, then his face hardened. "Believe me, I understand."

"If it's any consolation, she said your kiss was more pleasing than the prince's."

He turned to her with sudden angry intensity. "She let him kiss her?"

Alexa feigned a startled gasp and lifted her fingers to her lips. "Oh, I should not have said that!"

"No — I'm glad you told me," he replied, pulling away. "That is very useful information." He sat forward, resting his elbows on his knees as he sat beside her. Loosely clasping his hands, he glowered at the carpet.

"Well," Alexa went on gingerly, "I did hear that the prince is making plans to come and see Her Highness again after we reach Kavros."

He looked away. "Really."

"I don't think that's a secret. Colonel." Alexa laid her hand on his arm and caressed him slowly. "He's the best that she can hope to do. You must not take it personally."

"Of course not. Why would I?" he clipped out, avoiding her gaze, seemingly oblivious to her touch traveling up his shoulder. "I'm just the bodyguard."

"Everyone falls in love with her sooner or later. The greatest beauty since de Récamier — haven't you heard it said? She doesn't mean for all of you to love her." Alexa let out a sigh as she comforted him. "Perhaps it is merely the lure of the unattainable that draws so many of you in. In my opinion," she offered in a cautious tone, "you would be wise to aim . . . a little lower."

He looked at her at last, and finally seemed to see her again as Alexa laid her hand meaningfully on his muscled thigh.

He gazed at her intently. When no objection came, she let her hand travel higher, inching toward his groin.

"I can take your mind off her, you know. Wouldn't it be nice to clear your head?"

His eyes narrowed, a speculative gleam in their depths. "You are rather bold," he observed in a husky tone.

She gave him a knowing smile. "Come, Colonel. You need this. It's written all over your face. You need to let go. I know you've noticed me. Why don't you let me help you to feel better?"

He held very still, perhaps considering her offer.

Alexa slid closer, draped her other arm around his enormous shoulders, and whispered in his ear, "You can't have her, Gabriel. She's a royal princess. But you know what? You can have me, with no strings attached. Come up to my bed right now, and let us work this fever out of you."

Gabriel shut his eyes, severely tempted.

It had been so long, and every word that she had said felt all too true. He might have doubted her sincerity, but he could not persuade himself to think that this sweet little cream puff offering herself to him on a silver platter had either the nerve or the intellect to try to lie to him.

Certainly, her silken words made perfect sense to his needy cock, which had not had the proper care and nursing in more months than he desired to count.

But while his body responded to Alexa's attentions in a raw, physical sense, his heart and mind were reeling with the news that Sophia had seen fit to kiss the prince. Especially as Gabriel recalled how she had pushed *him* away the night of the ball.

Now he understood why she had been in this distant mood ever since the night of the Grecian Gala.

Damn it, he had told Derek that it was hopeless between him and Sophia, and now her best friend's words bore out his grim assessment.

Why should he be surprised, let alone at all hurt? *Fool.* He was the one who had insisted that they keep a cool, safe distance, remain no more than friends. The writing, it seemed, was on the wall. Princess and prince belonged together. Bodyguard was better off in the sack with the nymphomaniac lady-in-waiting.

What real choice did either of them have?

So, his Gypsy girl had kissed the prince. So what?

Gabriel did not own her.

The average royal did not "befriend" her bodyguards, anyway. He was here for duty's sake. For England's benefit, helping to place the figurehead princess on that strategic Greek throne.

What the hell had she kissed the prince for? And how dare she compare them? Reviewing each man's performance with her friend?

She damned well *better* have found Gabriel to be the superior lover. The prince, he was quite sure, had never studied the Kama Sutra. Now *that* was a skill he could share with Alexa. Gabriel still hadn't bothered to push her away. He wasn't sure if he wanted to.

If Sophia was never going to be his, then why should he persist in this agony of self-denial? Every man had needs, and this randy lass was certainly game. For all he knew, maybe Sophia had put her up to this. Maybe Her Highness had encouraged Alexa's move on him as a way of redirecting his affections. It was possible, since it seemed she did not want them for herself.

Bloody hell.

He was torn, and Alexa's touch felt like just what he needed. He had half a mind to let himself be seduced, if that would work Sophia out of his system.

Maybe if he spent a day or two in this willing woman's bed, he'd be able to think again, for his want of the princess was driving him mad, the tantalizing knowledge of all he could not have . . .

Bloody prince of Denmark! Who did that

blackguard think he was? Gabriel could have thrashed him with one arm tied behind his back —

"Let it go," Alexa whispered, climbing astride his lap with a smooth move. He did not fight it. The next thing he knew, her mouth was on his, and somehow his hands were resting tentatively on her thighs as she straddled him.

She was moving against him, offering firm, succulent breasts for his enjoyment. He pulled his lips away from hers with a groan and found himself staring down into the milky valley between her lush globes, breathing heavily as he struggled to make up his mind.

Sophia stood in the doorway, stunned by what she saw. She had just come in, still dripping mud and rain, her grip tightening on her riding crop as she stared at them in shock.

She could not believe her eyes.

Well — no. Nothing Alexa did ever surprised her anymore, but seeing Gabriel indulging himself this way rocked her to the foundations and made her a little ill. Especially when he had been so virtuous about keeping his hands off *her*.

She had not been expecting this, though

perhaps she should've. She had never expected him to be false like all the courtiers. She knew he had been jealous of Crown Prince Christian Frederick ever since the ball, but she had not foreseen that he would vent his sexual frustration with Alexa.

She forced herself to watch them for a moment longer. Well, then, she thought, steeling herself at length. This would make it easier to do what she had to do.

Until she had walked in from her practice and found them together, she had been undecided about letting Gabriel go. But seeing him with his nose buried in her friend's cleavage made her decision considerably more clear.

Yes, she understood that the two of them could not be together for a myriad of reasons. She also understood that Gabriel had certain physical needs. But by God, she was not going to stand back and watch the man she was in love with fall into her troubled friend's snare.

In all fairness, she doubted Alexa was Gabriel's first choice, but that was meager consolation. She could not share him. She was not that generous.

When she saw his strong, tanned fingers digging into Alexa's pale skirts as he pulled her closer on his lap, Sophia looked away, her heart pounding. *Oh, this is intolerable. Why couldn't it be her?*

But that desire alone could get both of them killed, and if she'd eventually have to marry Christian Frederick, she might as well let Gabriel go now. Her course was clear.

He was going to be outraged — the proud, impeccable officer with his unmarred, sterling record — but the time had come to send him away.

Then at least she could avoid getting him killed. It hurt terribly to see him with Alexa, but she knew this was the perfect chance to send him out of harm's way.

She leaned her shoulder against the door frame while the raindrops trickling off her black leather coat pooled on the floor by her black riding boots. She braced herself for the confrontation and summoned up all of her most regal iron.

She lifted her chin, set her hand on her hip, and announced herself with a polite, "Ahem."

The pair froze.

Alexa glanced over her shoulder with a look of chagrin, while Gabriel closed his eyes, cursed under his breath, took his hands off Alexa, and then stared fiercely at Sophia from across the room, his face turning ashen.

"Oh, don't let me interrupt, children," she drawled in a tone of insolence. "I just wanted to deliver a message to the colonel."

"What's that?" he forced out.

She smiled blandly. "You're fired."

CHAPTER FIFTEEN

Gabriel nudged Alexa impatiently off his lap, shot up off the couch, and rushed out of the morning room after Sophia, who had already walked away. Cursing himself with a mental tirade of pure brimstone, he glanced left and right, then spotted her ahead, walking down the stone corridor.

His heart thudded as he ran after her. Did he have the worst luck in the world or did she just have excellent timing? He did not know. His brain was still clouded with too much sexual frustration and the most tangled confusion over what was happening between the two of them.

If she preferred the prince to him, then why had she resorted to that bravado he remembered so well from the night at the farm, when he had followed her out into the darkness, trying to lure her back to safety?

He knew how vulnerable she had been

that night, standing there trying to act tough. It had touched his heart then, and she had had the same tough-little-miss scowl on her face a moment ago in the doorway.

He wasn't buying it. He had hurt her. He despised himself for it — even if she'd rather have the prince.

"Soph— Your Highness, wait!" he corrected himself as several vapid courtiers and ladies standing around looked on.

"Thank you, Colonel. That will be all," Her Royal Highness said, striding on, staring forward. "You are relieved from your post, and We thank you for your service."

Bloody hell. She had resorted to the royal "We." Not a good sign. "Don't walk away," he demanded in a low tone, keeping pace with her. "Sophia, I'm sorry. I didn't mean for that to happen. It wasn't as bad as it looked."

"Bad enough." She shook her head, refusing to soften toward him. "Alexa is what she is, but you? I had expected better from you."

"Nothing happened!" he exclaimed as his cheeks flushed with anger. "It was only a minute or two before you came in! I swear to you, it was totally insignificant. She means nothing to me!"

"That doesn't speak much in your favor, actually."

He cringed at this good point. "Your Highness, be reasonable. For your own safety! You have people out to kill you, and you'd dismiss me all because of this one idiotic kiss?"

"It's not the kiss itself, Colonel. I scarcely care what you do, or with whom. The problem is that it reflects a worrisome lack of judgment on your part. I'm not sure it's wise for me to trust you."

"Oh, what rubbish!" he retorted. "I don't believe you. You're trying to put a fine face on it, but I daresay this is all typical female jealousy, plain and simple. You don't own me, you know."

"Nor you me." She stopped and turned to him with a withering look. "Sorry, Colonel. I think you were not the right man for the job, after all."

"Who is? The prince of Denmark?" he spat.

"Maybe." She tossed her head in defiance. "I hadn't thought of it, really."

"Sophia," Gabriel said flatly, "I am not letting you fire me."

"Sorry, my dear, but the one with the shiny tiara gets to make the rules. Good-bye."

"Don't be a fool! You need me!"

"You can be replaced."

Her words cut like a knife. "I'd like to see you get along without me," he shot back.

"I'll do fine. Again, I thank you for your service, Colonel. I'll see that Lord Griffith settles what you're owed."

"Don't bother," he snarled. "I was never in this for the money." He almost walked away at that point, cut by how nonchalantly she would banish him from her life.

Devil take the haughty wench, her life was in danger. How the hell was he going to protect her if he was fired?

He clenched his jaw in a state of pure exasperation as she walked on. He shook his head, torn between disappointment in himself and a vague desire to wring her neck. So he had faltered, sampling Alexa's offerings — but come, was Sophia any better than him, kissing the prince?

Well, he thought stubbornly, he was not about to mention that little tidbit. Just as blaming Alexa for pouncing on him would have been beneath his dignity, he'd be hanged before he'd let Sophia know how insanely jealous he felt at the thought of that Norseman's hands on her.

No, he did not like that thought one bit. Nor did he like being scolded. He did not take it well.

Maybe he had erred, but after all that he had done for her from the first moment they had met, did he not deserve just an inkling of forgiveness?

His boot heels struck the cold flagstones in a terse staccato as he caught up to her again, staving off a wild impulse to shove her up against the stone wall and kiss her senseless in front of all the petty clusters of eavesdropping courtiers lingering here and there.

"Did you expect me to swear off women for your sake, Highness?" he inquired, not about to let her get away so easily. "Because if this was an unspoken rule of my post, I think I should've been informed of this requirement when I was given the commission papers to sign."

She sent him a warning look askance. "Do not be clever."

They pounded up a shallow flight of stone stairs.

"Please go without making a fuss," she said. "You will not change my mind."

"Sophia! I always deemed you a woman of sense, but you're being foolish, taking petty revenge."

She stopped and turned to him at the top of the stairs, her chest heaving, her dark eyes huge. "This has nothing to do with vengeance or my sex. It has to do with judgment, Colonel! I'm sorry, but you have given me too much cause to doubt you. First, you take liberties with my person. Then you make ludicrous accusations against my loyal guards. Now I find you dallying with my lady-in-waiting. What am I to think? None of it bodes well. If you're not going to take this mission seriously, you might as well go home."

"That's nonsense —"

"That is my royal will!" she thundered, taking a step closer, completely unintimidated by his size or all the ways that he knew how to neutralize a person.

God, he loved her.

"Who are you to naysay me? A common soldier?" she shouted as she poked him in his chest.

Gabriel fell silent, glowering at her for a moment. "You didn't find me so common that night at the farm, as I recall," he murmured.

"That night," she answered through clenched teeth, "never happened." She pivoted and marched away again, but not before he glimpsed her pained expression beneath the regal bravado.

What on earth was going on in her head?

He felt like he was making progress, but she would not hear his apology and would not let him break through to find the truth. Still, he suspected grimly he knew what it was.

"Why don't you just admit what's really going on?" he demanded in a low tone as he caught up, matching strides with her again as they traversed the castle corridors — going where, he did not know. "You just want to get rid of me because you've decided you prefer the prince."

She lifted her eyebrows. "Now *you're* acting like a typical jealous male. And like all your breed, you understand nothing."

"Really?"

"This has become too dangerous for both of us, and you know it. I cannot work with you! It's just too hard. Gabriel, I don't want to do this, but being a leader means making the hard decisions. Can you honestly look me in the eyes and say that you're detached enough from all of this to keep me safe?"

She paused and waited for his answer; he could not find his voice.

"My people are counting on me!" she said, impassioned. "You were right from the start. This was not a good idea."

He stared at her, feeling as though the rug had been pulled out from under him. He could argue with her over the prince and his right to grope Alexa if he bloody well chose.

But she had him there.

For a long moment, he was silent, trying to find some basis to object. He could not.

She was right. It wasn't working. He wanted her too much, and it was only putting her at risk.

Good God, he could not believe he had found his destiny only to lose it.

Lose her.

He was the one who felt lost.

He did not want to accept this. He would try harder, kill his own needs just to stay near her. He would steer clear of Alexa and every other woman on the planet if only he could stay near her.

His heart pounding, he could not bear to look at her. He did not know how she'd react to the complete devotion that he feared showed in his eyes.

"What are you going to do about your men?" he muttered, studying the seams between the hard gray flagstones.

"I am perfectly confident in their loyalty," she said. "I always have been. I only went along with that ruse to humor you."

He glanced angrily at her.

"I'll promote one of them to security

chief, and if Lord Griffith still insists on my having an Englishman in my company, then I'll take the captain from the garrison. You trust him to look after me, don't you? Gabriel — I'm not your problem anymore."

"You were never my problem. You were my hope." He gazed at her, wanting to take her hand, but forcing himself not to. "Sophia, I'm sorry," he whispered with his heart in his eyes. "I know I was an idiot. Can't you give me another chance?"

"No. Gabriel. I'm sorry, too." Tears filled her eyes. "I'm sorry I ever involved you. Go back to your family. Go back to your farm. I've got a job to do. If you'll excuse me."

Just like that, she walked away.

"Sophia —"

"Go home, Gabriel," she said with a dismissive wave of her hand, not looking back.

"Damn it, don't you walk away from me!" he roared, his rebuke of Her Royal Highness reverberating down the old stone corridors.

She snapped her fingers, and her Greek bodyguards were there, all too happy to defend her from him. "Remove him."

"With pleasure, Highness."

With that, they grabbed his arms and piled

on until they had wrestled him into submission.

It was only Sophia's withering look over her shoulder that convinced him to stop fighting. He plainly saw that this was not helping his cause. His chest heaving, he reined in his rage and stopped trying to pound his way through the mass of eight men. At last, they hauled him up to his feet again.

And then they threw him out.

Sophia walked into her royal apartments, shut the door behind her, and burst into tears. She dropped her riding crop and buried her face in her hands.

How was she going to cope with all that lay ahead without him? But now at least he would be safe.

That must have been the hardest conversation of her life. She was glad it was over. But God help her, she missed him already.

Trembling, she lifted her head again after a moment and rested it back against the closed door.

Be happy, Gabriel. Live a long, peaceful life.

As for Alexa — who was still hiding from her at the moment — maybe it was time to start making new arrangements for her reckless friend, she thought with an empty, brooding stare. She had done her best to keep Alexa out of trouble ever since they were girls. But she had just had about all that she could take.

No doubt Alexa would come soon and apologize, and simper and sob and do all of her familiar routine until Sophia took pity on her and told her that she was forgiven. But Alexa had to have known how much Gabriel meant to her.

She shook her head. Sometimes she thought Alexa was no friend to her at all.

By that evening, Alexa was giddy with triumph and nerves and hope that this would soon be over.

When she brought the pitchers of beer to Sophia's retinue of Greek bodyguards, who were celebrating having gotten rid of Colonel Knight, she almost couldn't believe how good doing wrong could make a person feel.

It was a powerful feeling unlike any she had ever known, outsmarting everyone this way. What an intoxicant!

She did not consider herself anything near a bad person — after all, she had been coerced into this. It wasn't her fault, but she was beginning to see how *some* people could be seduced by the sensation.

Especially when wrongdoing involved

such pleasurable activities as kissing the likes of Gabriel Knight, and this sweet taste of revenge on all the men who had used her and tossed her aside, and taking down a peg her ungrateful mistress who always acted so superior.

All the men were congratulating her, cheering her.

"There she is! Our heroine!"

"Well done, Lexie!"

She nodded with a feline smile from ear to ear.

But then she remembered to frown. It would not do to let them know her real emotions.

"I know Her Highness is going to hate me now," she said with a little pout. "I didn't mean any harm."

"Of course you didn't, poppet." Timo pinched her cheek. "She'll get over him. Don't you fret."

She pulled away. "You say it as if you think I did it on purpose!"

"Of course you didn't, sweet pea!"

"You were just doing what comes naturally," Niko said, as if he thought she was too stupid to know she was being insulted.

The men guffawed and clinked their tankards together, sloshing splashes of beer onto the table like a lot of slobs.

She watched them furtively, secretly relieved as they gulped it down without showing any signs that they might taste the dosage of laudanum in it.

Alexa did not think it prudent to stay too long. She wasn't sure how much time must pass for the drug to start to work. But she didn't want to be anywhere near here when they started passing out.

She stood near the doorway, hands on hips, letting them take their last admiring looks at her wonderful bosom. "Well, I'm glad you all are pleased that Colonel Knight is gone, but for my part, I feel just *awful.* I had no idea that Her Highness would have such a fit over it."

"Lex, you've never had an idea of any kind," someone said with teasing affection under his breath.

She pretended not to hear it as the men she had so often pleasured made sport of her.

We'll see who gets the last laugh.

"I'm going to check on Her Highness," she announced, but nobody even noticed when she walked out.

To hell with them. Soon she'd be on to new pastures.

Before long, she arrived at Sophia's apartments. Her heart was pounding as she tapped with her knuckles.

No answer.

Slowly she opened the door.

The sprawling room was dark except for one candle left burning. Alexa closed the door behind her and tiptoed into the room.

Crossing it silently, she came to stand by Her Highness's bed. The never-to-be-queen of Kavros was fast asleep. The laudanum had already done its work.

The bottle of Sophia's favorite Greek red wine lay empty on its side on the nightstand, only a few drops left.

Ah, love.

She really must have fancied her English stud if she would go to such lengths as to drown her sorrows in wine over him. What man was worth it?

"Your Highness?" Alexa murmured carefully, making sure.

There was no response.

Her heart thumping, Alexa reached down and gently brushed back some of Her Highness's wild raven curls, revealing her tear-stained face.

The princess was in dreamland, just like her guards soon would be.

Alexa's pretty face hardened. *Perfect.* Now all she had to do was smuggle the princess out of the palace. Thanks to Colonel

Knight's revelation of the secret tunnel leading out of the wine cellar, Alexa knew the route to take. She had investigated it earlier on her own, making sure her plan would work.

It was not going to be easy tugging her friend along through that dark, rocky tunnel, but once they reached the stable, she could easily spirit Sophia away in the back of her curricle. The drugged royal was in no shape to fight her.

"First things first," she said to herself under her breath. Obviously Sophia could not go out in her dressing gown.

Alexa shook Sophia by her shoulder, rousing her from the depths of her slumber. She knew she would have to help dress her mistress for their excursion, just as she had assisted her so many times before — only more so this time, thanks to the laudanum.

If anyone saw them making their way down to the wine cellar, Alexa planned to insinuate that Her Highness was drunk. No one would have any trouble believing that, given the fireworks display between Sophia and Colonel Knight earlier today. Most of the courtiers had witnessed their passionate lovers' quarrel, and tonight the palace still buzzed with the gossip; Alexa did not think anyone would find it all that strange that the outrageous princess had spent the evening trying to forget the lover she had banished with a bottle or two of expensive champagne.

That, indeed, would be Alexa's explanation for anyone who saw them heading for the wine cellar, with herself acting the part of the dutiful companion, watching out for her distraught highborn friend in her state of intoxication.

Some of the kitchen staff might still be on duty tonight when the ladies passed through on their way to the wine cellar, but Alexa trusted that, like good servants, they would see nothing.

By morning, it would be too late for them to report the ladies' visit to the wine cellar, for, by then, the two of them would be long gone. Alexa supposed that the truth of her guilt would be known as soon as the bodyguards woke up, but she could not think about that right now.

Her new life in France would be worth it.

She shook Sophia's shoulder again, determined to get this unnerving night over with. "Your Highness, wake up!"

The dose of laudanum she had poured into the wine was too strong to restore Sophia to a state of clarity, but Alexa's efforts to rouse her finally succeeded in bringing the princess to a groggy state of semi-consciousness.

"What's the matter?" Sophia slurred. Her eyes focused enough to make out Alexa. "What do you want with me? I'm not speakin' to you."

"I know you're angry," Alexa said with an angelic look. "But I've come to make it up to you! You must get up, get dressed! Lord, how much did you drink?"

Sophia growled at her and started to roll over to go back to sleep. "Leave me alone."

"You don't understand — Colonel Knight is waiting to see you!"

"Gabriel?" she breathed, dragging one glazed eye open in question.

"Yes, he sent me to fetch you! He wants to see you, Your Highness. He's waiting to apologize."

"Oh . . . Gabriel," she uttered in a plaintive moan.

"You won't disappoint him, will you? We must go to him."

"Where is he?" Sophia mumbled in confusion.

"He's waiting for you just outside the castle grounds. The soldiers won't let him through the gates now that you've dismissed him. He is distraught over you, the poor man!"

"Oh, Gabriel."

"Will you let him speak his piece? Your Highness, he said if you do not come to him at once, then he will know you do not love him —"

"But I do!" she whispered with a bleary stare full of misery.

"I know you do. I realize that now. That's why I want to help the two of you, to make it right. Sophia, he said if you do not go to him tonight and give him some shred of hope that you care, he will know he means nothing to you and will never seek you out again."

"Never?"

"That's not what you really want, is it?"

"Oh, . . . no." Sophia struggled to sit up, rubbing her head with one hand as she wove unsteadily. She looked so helpless and uncertain, in all, so un-Sophia-like in her drugged state, that Alexa was nearly overcome with guilt. "I love him," the princess uttered barely audibly.

"And he loves you." Alexa chased off her momentary faltering, reminded anew of how unfair her own life was.

It wasn't enough that Sophia got a crown and half the world bowing and scraping to her; she also got the devotion of a man like Gabriel Knight. Alexa did not feel at all sorry for her royal mistress in that moment.

Instead, she reserved her pity for herself alone. "Come. We have to get you dressed so you can see him."

"Yes. Let us go. Oh, Lord — I'm drunk, I fear. The wine gave me such a headache tonight! I feel so strange . . ."

"You didn't eat any supper," Alexa reminded her. "You were too upset."

"I s'pose you're right. Help me, Alexa. The room is spinning."

"Of course," Alexa murmured, helping her wobbly friend to rise from her bed. "I've already got your clothes ready."

She dreamed she was in Gabriel's arms and he was rocking her slowly like that night in his bed . . .

She could almost taste the salt of his skin, or perhaps it was the flavor of the tears that streamed down her face as he made love to her, whispering that he'd never leave her again.

The dream changed.

She was locked in an icy castle, banished alone beyond the sea, screaming his name from the highest tower. She paced the battlements with a sword in her hand like a warrior queen, heedless of the piercing cold, but she was frantic with the fear that she would never see her mate again.

The urgency that invaded her sleep tightened her body, her head jerked against the unfamiliar-smelling pillow, and all of a sudden, the distant but still piercing cry of a bird awoke her decisively.

At once she winced and brought one leaden hand up to her head. She was thoroughly groggy, her skull throbbing as though someone had clubbed her. Her mouth was painfully dry.

The salty smell from her dream still lingered.

As she dragged her eyes open, it took a moment for her fuzzy gaze to focus. God, how much wine had she ended up drinking?

She did not remember giving way to quite so much intemperance. But as her vision cleared, she stared without recognition at the cramped wooden space in which she found herself. Another bird's cry pierced the stillness and made her flinch from her headache.

Was that . . . a seagull? She furrowed her brow and suddenly realized the whole world was rocking.

Oh, my God. Where am I?

She sat up suddenly, ignoring a wave of nausea from the pain in her head.

What's happened? What's going on? She quickly pressed her fingers to her skull and felt around for any sign of dried blood, but there was no sign of a bruise or a wound of any kind.

She shoved herself to an upright position and saw that she was in a kind of cot built into a small, cramped space.

The rocking . . . she heard the rhythm of waves slapping against a wooden hull. With pure horrified confusion choking her, she forced herself up from the berth and steadied herself against the ship's motion.

Someone must have drugged me.

The last thing she remembered with any clarity was weeping in her pillow over Gabriel. She seemed to remember Alexa talking to her, but looking down at herself, she did not know how she had come to be wearing her dark blue pelisse.

With fingers turned to ice, she felt for her knife by her thigh, but it was gone. There were scrapes and bruises on her knees, but she could not remember how she had got them. Panic rose. She closed her eyes and fought with every ounce of her will to steady herself as she realized what had occurred.

She had been kidnapped. Her enemies, whoever they were, had succeeded. *God, please help me.*

She had to find out what was going on.

Taking a deep breath, she squared her shoulders and crossed the narrow, grubby cabin to the low door. To her relief, it was unlocked. She opened it and stepped out into a slim passageway. Though the boat's slow rocking made her bump into first one side and then the other, she made her way down the passage until she came to a ladder.

She looked up at harsh, gray daylight. She heard voices up there, but she had no idea of who or what she might find. Her heart pounding, she forced herself to climb the ladder with a white-knuckled grip, moving up each rung.

Coming up on deck, she saw seagulls fluttering around the masts and dingy sails. She looked toward the bow at the same time a dark-skinned man with black eyes like polished coal noticed her from across the decks.

He flashed an arrogant, mocking smile.

She wanted to scream but refused to cower. Instead, she kept her chin high and scanned the decks, discovering a whole variety of lethal-looking, swarthy fellows like Barbary corsairs, armed to the teeth. The nearest one had a curved dagger tucked into the broad length of cloth tied around his waist.

Suddenly, her scan of the decks stopped when she spotted Alexa. Sophia let out a low gasp and started forward instinctively. Dear God, they had captured Alexa, too! Her poor friend had a bad case of the mal de mer, puking her guts out over the rails.

"Alexa!" she called anxiously.

"Well, well, look who's awake," someone said nearer to her in French, grasping her arm.

Sophia shrieked and tried to pull away, cowering from a red-haired man with pale, hate-filled eyes.

He clutched her arm in his left hand and yanked her off balance. "Remember me, madam royal? I hope so, for it was you who left me with this parting gift." He nodded toward his bandaged right arm. "I almost lost my hand because of you, you little bitch."

A small whimper escaped her as she tried to back away.

"Ah, what's wrong? Not so bold now?" He smiled at her while across the decks, Alexa finally managed to gather herself enough to pull her blond head back over the side of the boat.

"Alexa! To me!" she called protectively,

but when her green-faced friend glanced over at Sophia, her eyes instantly filled with tears.

Alexa started bawling and turned away, as if she could not bear to look at her.

Standing there, even now, it took Sophia a long moment to comprehend the truth.

Alexa had betrayed her.

"That's right, ma petite," the red-haired man said in mocking satisfaction. Her mind was reeling with heartbreak, terror, and disbelief, but his grip on her arm jerked her back to attention. "You're ours now."

Her gaze homed in on the necklace he wore. The metal was worked into the same squiggle shape she had seen on the blade of that curved dagger they had found, the one they had given to the Turkish ambassador to investigate.

She fought for all her worth to stay calm and keep her wits about her. "Who are you and where are you taking me?" she demanded.

"In due time, Your Highness. You will see. But if I were you, I wouldn't be in too great a hurry to find out."

She recoiled from his cold laughter, but when she glanced toward the stern of their fast frigate, she saw England fading in the distance.

CHAPTER SIXTEEN

Gabriel hadn't gone far.

It had been quite a battle between the two of them, but after being ousted from the castle, he had swung up onto his white horse and retreated only a few miles down the road to regroup and decide on his next move.

He had taken lodgings for the night at the first travelers' inn he had come to, but he was awake again before dawn, hurriedly readying himself to return to the castle. As he dressed in plain civilian clothes with swift efficiency, his mood was one of stoic resolve.

Today he would go back and make it right.

He had any number of reasons to be angry at himself, but Sophia's opinion of him was what mattered. Perhaps having had some time to cool off, she would be ready this morning to hear him out.

His message was simple: She was not getting rid of him that easily. The night he'd spent tossing and turning had helped to make up his mind.

It didn't matter if she didn't love him. It didn't matter if she did not want to be his friend. He didn't need the official post as her head of security; he would still protect her.

Tender words and romantic gestures had never been his forte, but if he had to station himself outside the castle gates like her damned guard dog, he would do it.

The bottom line was that he could not live with himself if anything happened to her.

As he finished strapping his sword and pistols around his waist, ignoring the lumpy bed behind him where he had barely slept and the breakfast he had ordered but could not force himself to eat, he heard a commotion of clattering hoofbeats and shouts outside.

He frowned toward the window.

"Colonel!"

"Colonel Knight!"

"Are you there?"

He edged over to the window of his room and peered out warily. Oh, bloody hell. Her Greek bodyguards. Obviously, these men bore him no great love, but he had hardly expected them to come after him afresh in their spare time.

They flooded the quiet courtyard below, dismounting, running about, one banging open the inn's front door while others checked the stable to see if his horse was there.

He decided to save them the trouble and opened the shutters, leaning out the window. "Morning, boys," he drawled.

"Oh, thank God you're here! Is she with you?" Timo asked frantically.

Gabriel's eyes narrowed. *"What?"*

"Her Highness! Did she ride out to spend the night with you?" he cried.

"I beg your pardon," he retorted, his face darkening.

"Sophia! Is she there?"

"Never mind your pride, we all know what's going on between the two of you! Is Her Highness with you or not?" Yannis shouted, running over to stare up at him.

"No, she's not with me. Isn't she with you?"

"No!" they shouted in wild unison.

"They've taken her!" Niko yelped.

Horror flooded Gabriel. He gripped the frosted windowsill.

"Alexa drugged us and now Sophia's gone!" Timo yelled. "We thought Sophia might've put Alexa up to it so she could slip past us to go to you, but now there's no sign of either girl!"

"I'll be right down." Gabriel grabbed his coat and the rest of his weapons and rushed out of his room, pounding down the steps, tossing several guineas at the landlord as he ran out.

Alexa! She had been the traitor all along. By God, how could he not have seen that?

He could not believe he had been deceived by that insipid blonde. Was it chivalry that had blinded him to her treachery, or had she merely distracted him with her curves and her hand on his groin? If he were not so caught up in Sophia, so tied up in knots with want of her, the truth should have been plain.

All this time, he had known in his bones that there was a traitor among them, but so far, he had only suspected the men. He had shrugged off the notion that Sophia's girlhood friend and confidante could have possibly betrayed her.

Damn it, he should have suspected it the second Alexa had come on to him — caressing him and covering him with flattery. It had all been a ruse. She had needed him out of the way, that little simpering wench.

But it was himself he blamed above all. Indeed, he had made the same mistake as

Griff, underestimating Alexa's calculating intelligence as much as his brother-in-law had underestimated Sophia's leadership abilities.

Fool! God, he did not deserve Sophia. He could not believe how he had let her down. He sincerely hoped the prince of Denmark was more worthy of her than he, but at the moment all that mattered was getting her back.

He joined the men outside as a groom brought his horse out of the stable, freshly saddled for him.

"Tell me what happened," he ordered the men.

"When we came to, both women were nowhere to be found."

"Are all the men accounted for?"

"Of course we are!" Markos retorted. "Why would you ask that?"

Demetrius stepped closer, scowling. "You think one of us might've something to do with this?"

"Did you?" he asked coolly.

"No!" they all said variously.

"You need to let us talk to the prisoner," Timo insisted. "He'll know where they've taken her!"

"No, he won't," Gabriel muttered. "Trust me."

"Why?"

"Because I lied," he said grimly. "He wasn't one of them."

"What?"

"You tell us to trust you and then say you *lied?*" Niko demanded, moving toward him in angry shock. "What game have you been playing, Knight?"

Now it was his turn to be the suspect, Gabriel thought, glancing around at them. "I knew we had a traitor in our midst, but it was one of you that I suspected, not Alexa. That fool I caught at the ball that night had nothing to do with Sophia. I thought I could trick whoever the traitor was into showing their hand. Apparently, it worked. Come on," he muttered. "It's time to get her back."

He swung up onto his horse while they exchanged a few surly, skeptical looks, but they must have realized he would not be deterred.

They flew back to the castle complex at an all-out gallop, thundering under the massive gate-towers. In short order, they were marching through the stone corridors of the palace.

The men told him on the way that Lord Griffith had already been alerted to what was afoot, but Gabriel's chief concern was to find out for once and for all what the

Turkish ambassador knew.

He had not forgotten the look of recognition that had crossed the man's guarded face when he had seen that curved dagger with the strange markings on the blade. The man knew more than he was saying, and Gabriel intended to find out what the ambassador was hiding.

Meanwhile, the men were cursing Alexa in the foulest possible terms.

"How could she do this to us?"

"The little whore!"

"After all we've done for her!"

Every male ego among them was dented, for that mere *girl* had led them all into a trap.

She must have had outside help, he thought. Somebody pulling the strings, telling her what to do. But who?

The Turkish ambassador ought to be able to tell him that, if anyone could.

A short while later, Gabriel had the turbaned dignitary pinned against the wall in a most undiplomatic fashion. "Now, you are going to tell me what I want to know."

Down the corridor, Griff saw what was happening, but casually turned a blind eye and ambled out of sight with his hands clasped politely behind his back, leaving Gabriel to gather answers the old-fashioned way.

The marquess might not like his approach, but Gabriel was no longer employed by the British government and no longer in uniform, and no longer had much of anything to lose. Until he had Sophia back safely, the whole damned world had better stand clear.

"Who has her? Answer me!" He slammed the man against the wall again to persuade him.

"I — don't — know!" The Turk kicked his dangling feet in his curl-toed shoes.

"Don't lie to me," Gabriel warned through gritted teeth. "Sophia's life is at stake, do you understand? I know you recognized that symbol on that knife. Tell me what it means, you blackguard, or I will choke the life out of you!"

"Wait! Very well! Put me down, put me down, and I will tell you!"

Gabriel narrowed his eyes, but slowly lowered the offended but cowering dignitary until his feet touched the floor again. The ambassador rubbed his neck, blanching and puffing for breath.

"Quickly."

"The symbol on the blade signifies the Order of the Scorpion."

"What's that?"

"A secret religious sect that sprang up around Prince Mustafa, Sultan Mahmud's half brother. Mustafa staged a coup and tried to hold on to power, but we put an end to that. He had many followers among our elite Janissary troops. Once we were victorious over this rebellion, Sultan Mahmud offered a pardon to all those who renounced Mustafa's backward views and swore an oath of loyalty to His Majesty, but not all of Mustafa's warriors took the offer. The core of true believers scattered under the guidance of Prince Mustafa's spiritual adviser, a man known as Sheik Suleiman.

"We have never managed to capture the sheik, and as for the other Janissaries, we have heard the faintest whispers that they've been making overtures to Ali Pasha."

Gabriel remembered vividly how Sophia kept saying that Ali Pasha wanted Kavros. Well, maybe it was time to lend more credence to her views. She had been right, after all, about her bodyguards' loyalty.

"How many are there, these Janissaries who've turned outlaw?"

The ambassador shook his head. "Hundreds."

Gabriel's stomach clenched. "Where are they taking her?"

"I do not know."

"If you could guess?" he hissed in warning.

The man just looked at him; Gabriel drew his own conclusions. "Janina."

The ambassador nodded grimly.

Gabriel released him and walked away.

When he went to confer briefly with his brother-in-law, he found the captain of the garrison with Griff, and the three of them combined what they each had learned.

Griff relayed a report from the lord chamberlain that some kitchen servants had seen Alexa and Sophia going down into the wine cellar last night. Alexa had told the curious kitchen staff that Her Highness wanted to pick out a fresh bottle of champagne.

This morning, the servants had been loathe to mention having seen the girls last night because the princess had been in an embarrassing state of intoxication — or so it had appeared. In fact, this told Gabriel that Alexa had drugged Sophia as well as the bodyguards.

The captain of the garrison then filled in more of the picture with news that his men had opened the castle gates to let Alexa drive out last night in her curricle.

When the soldiers on duty at the gatehouse had asked her where she was going, the saucy wench had slyly told them she was slipping out to spend the night with Gabriel!

Given Alexa's reputation and Gabriel's all-too-public spat with Sophia yesterday, the men had accepted her story with lewd laughter and sent her on her way. They had not searched her vehicle for they had had no reason to suspect that she was smuggling the princess out in the back of her closed carriage.

"So, what's our next move?" the captain asked grimly.

"They're probably taking her to Janina." Gabriel related what the Turkish ambassador had told him about the Order of the Scorpion.

Griff paled as he listened.

"How far is the nearest port?" Gabriel asked urgently. "They'll have to get her out to sea as soon as possible."

"We're only an hour's ride from the coast," the captain answered.

"I'll send word for some Navy vessels to start the search and when we find them —"

"Easy," Gabriel cautioned him. "We don't know what these men are capable of. If we come at them with a whole flotilla of British warships, there's no telling how they might react. It's not as if we can subject them to a cannonade with her onboard."

"He's right," the captain of the garrison concurred.

"I'll take her bodyguards and pursue them toward the Mediterranean in a civilian vessel. That should let us get closer than sailing under the Union Jack. We can do naught but find them and follow at a safe distance until we see our opportunity to move in and get her back."

Griff nodded. "Right. If there's anything you need —"

"Supplies. Armaments —"

"Men?" the captain offered in an urgent tone.

"No," Gabriel clipped out. "A smaller team will be more mobile. God only knows where this chase will lead us before we reach Albania. God willing, we will take her back before we set foot on Ali Pasha's territory."

"I will send word to Sultan Mahmud of what's occurred," Griff said. "He may be able to help from his end."

"I can get you and your team supplied," the captain chimed in.

Gabriel nodded. "I'll keep you informed as opportunity permits."

"Do what you must," Griff murmured. "Just get her back safe."

Gabriel gave him a steely-eyed look.

"You're damned right I will."

No more than eight hours behind the kidnappers, he and the men rushed to the port to procure the fastest vessel they could hire. Gabriel dispatched some of the men to quickly interview sea captains and sailors, scouring the docks for any witnesses who might have noticed suspicious activity pertaining to Sophia.

Before long, Timo and Yannis found them a swift sloop whose captain said she was ready to make sail whenever they were. Gabriel was overjoyed when Markos and Demetrius located an old salt on the docks who confirmed seeing some suspicious-looking foreigners last night. They had arrived on horseback, he said, and had left at once on a frigate called *The May,* embarking in the middle of the night when most boats stayed safely harbored.

Within the hour, they were out to sea.

Gabriel stood with one foot braced on the bow with the sea foam flying around him and a spyglass to his eye, angrily searching the rolling waves. The long ends of his black wool greatcoat billowed in the cold wind as he held onto the rail to balance himself.

Somewhere out there, she was waiting for him. He could feel her. But his thoughts focused darkly on her captors.

If you harm one hair on her head . . .
No mercy.

Alexa had taken to her cabin with the wretched seasickness, but a hard rap on the cabin door roused her from her sickened slumber.

"On your feet, woman! Hurry up! It's almost time to go ashore!"

Ashore? *Finally.* Alexa was eager to part ways with them. As she dragged herself up to a seated position, she found herself feeling much recovered. She still felt nauseated both in body and soul, but the severity had lessened.

The frigate's rocking was not so violent now. They must have left the sea for the Garonne River. Britain ruled the waves, which was why the Tunisian preferred to take the overland route through France.

It was an intelligent decision, for if any of Sophia's English allies sought to follow them, they'd find little help from the people here. The war had ended, but the traditional hostility between the French and the English was alive and well.

Alexa could hardly wait to reach land and be rid of these brutes, as they had agreed to part ways at the town of Bordeaux. But for now, she concentrated on one task at a time to keep her nerves in check, and slowly went about putting herself in order. She was not sure how long she had slept, but it was very dark.

She freshened up, then donned the veil that they required of her. With her identity concealed, she picked up her small valise stuffed with her things and some jewels to sell so she could begin her new life in France.

When she finally went topside, her cloak wrapped around her, still tightly clutching the handle of her valise, she saw lights in the distance.

Her excitement grew. The men were hard at work, angling the sails to counteract the current.

"How long till we reach Bordeaux?" she asked, but everyone ignored her.

She frowned, sensing something strange in the air. A new tension that had not been there before.

It made her uneasy. With a sudden bad feeling taking shape inside her, she tried to ask a few of the men what was happening, but they told her to shut up and wait.

She frowned, glancing around the decks. Then she spotted Her Highness, veiled like her.

Sophia was standing at the taffrail, staring

back toward the distant sea. Alexa did not want to face her, but she was probably the only one who'd tell her what was going on.

Sophia did not look at her, treating her to frigid silence as Alexa crept closer. "H-how long before we reach land?" she inquired.

"Go to hell," Sophia replied in a low cutting tone after a moment.

"Your Highness, please —"

"How dare you speak to me?" she uttered dully, turning her back on her.

Alexa stared imploringly. "They said they'd kill me if I didn't help them."

"Now they will kill both of us."

"No! That was part of the bargain, you see?" Alexa whispered, wheedling and cajoling her old friend with all her skill. "I did it to protect you. They promised they won't kill you — as long as you cooperate."

"Oh, Alexa, you little fool." Sophia turned at last and stared at her in scorn. "Don't you know that promises to infidels don't count?"

"You two, come away from there!" Kemal ordered, waving them aft with his gun. "Go sit down until we tell you it's time to disembark."

Sophia knew why the men were nervous: They were being followed. It was no accident, but she was not about to admit that to Alexa and give the girl a whole new chance to stab her in the back.

In the late afternoon, while Alexa had been sleeping, Kemal had spotted the smaller, faster sloop behind them, still many miles out on the horizon, but tracking their path, and gaining on them.

Sophia knew it was Gabriel, as surely as she knew the sound of her own heartbeat. Never mind that she had fired him yesterday. She knew that he would come.

But she had to show him where to go.

To that end, she had found a little mirror in her cabin and had hidden it beneath the long, covering veil her captors made her wear. Coming back up on deck, she had stood at the taffrail and had flashed the mirror furtively in the bold light of sunset, praying that it would send a signal that her men could see even from this distance.

More of Leon's tricks had surfaced in her mind. She might not be able to fight these barbarians, but she could do her best to keep her allies apprised of her location.

By now, they would already be on the hunt for her. They would have brought Gabriel back, she surmised, and, of course, they all would have realized that Alexa was a traitor and that her overtures to Gabriel yesterday had been a deliberate ruse.

Sophia felt like a fool for having walked into the trap so trustingly. Then again, she was still in a state of disbelief over her friend's betrayal. How many years had they spent together? She wanted Alexa to tell her why, but the reason scarcely mattered now. The results were still the same. God, she could not even dwell on it or she'd break down in tears, but she needed her wits about her for whatever was to come.

Reaching the harbor, they went ashore, the women cloaked. Through her veil, Sophia read signs identifying the town as Bordeaux. Beneath the capacious sleeves of her covering robes, Sophia's hands were tied.

Kemal hurried them toward a waiting carriage, but there, Alexa balked.

"No, it's time for us to part ways. You said when we came to Bordeaux that I could go free."

She could hear them arguing, though the Tunisian's words were too low to make out.

"But you promised!" Alexa cried, backing away from him and bumping into two of the other men behind her. They took her arms.

Sophia watched in mounting concern as Alexa fought them as best she could.

"Let me go!"

"Settle down, you whore! The plan's changed! You're coming with us."

"You said I wouldn't have to!"

"Alexa!" Sophia ordered her. "Don't fight with them."

"You can't tell me what to do anymore!" she shot back.

"Get in the carriage before I break your neck," Ibrahim snarled at her.

Alexa cowered. "You don't mean that, surely."

Sophia watched grimly as Alexa tried out her simpering routine on these heartless assassins. Maybe it would work. They were males, after all.

"Please," she said sweetly, trying to squirm free of them with a gingerly motion. "I don't see why you need me anymore. I won't tell anyone about this. Just let me go —"

"You're not going anywhere!"

"I beg you —"

Kemal slapped her hard and sent her reeling. "No more questions!"

She fell to the ground with a shriek while Sophia started forward. "Alexa!"

A pair of passing Frenchmen saw what was happening and cried out when Alexa went falling.

"Monsieur! What are you doing?"

"Leave that lady alone!"

Kemal turned and stared at them in bristling stillness. With his back to her, Sophia could not see Kemal's face, but she saw the two Frenchmen blanch. Whatever they read in her captors' eyes, it frightened them away from interfering. They looked down and hurried on about their business.

Kemal laughed softly.

"Oh, God," Alexa sobbed. Still in a heap on the ground, she glanced at Sophia with terror in her eyes, perhaps understanding at last that she had made a fatal miscalculation.

Sophia grimly hoped that those two sensible Frenchmen at least had had the wits to remember her friend's name, for she had shouted it deliberately.

Somehow Kemal hadn't noticed, but she knew she had better be careful. When she met his black empty stare, she doubted that the man possessed a soul.

Then Ibrahim hauled Alexa to her feet and thrust the sobbing girl into the waiting carriage.

Her turncoat friend might have been confused, but Sophia understood perfectly well why they would not let Alexa go as planned. They must have realized they could use the girl as leverage to make Sophia comply, never mind the fact that Alexa had betrayed her. Her royal duty was the same, and Alexa had always been her responsibility.

When Kemal gestured Sophia toward the large black coach, she stood there for a moment longer in simmering rage, thinking of all the ways she would've liked to kill them; but, knowing it was futile to try it, she kept her fury tightly in check and stepped up into the carriage.

A moment later, they were under way.

CHAPTER SEVENTEEN

Hold on, love, Gabriel thought. *I'm coming.*

From the moment they had spotted the kidnapper's vessel ahead, Gabriel did not let the ship out of his sight. His hope had soared when he had seen the glint of Sophia's signal with the mirror, confirming their discovery.

The men had cheered, knowing it meant that she was awake and on her toes. Their brave girl had her wits about her and was ready to be rescued.

At Gabriel's command the hearty captain of the sloop had told his crew to let out more sail than was probably wise in the cold, choppy seas of autumn. But they would not be deterred.

All day, they had been steadily gaining on their quarry. But then, with the telescope pressed almost constantly to his eye, Gabriel had felt his hope harden to a fresh wave of anger when he saw the frigate changing course to head toward France.

About twenty-four hours since the Greeks had found him at the coaching inn, they were slowly making their way up the Garonne River. The wide waterway was busy with boat traffic coming and going from Bordeaux Harbor.

When they finally disembarked at the quaint, bustling harbor town, Gabriel gave Markos and Demetrius a large sum of gold to buy horses and supplies, and sent the rest to search the town for any word of the visitors.

Unfortunately for him, the harbormaster saw his English passport and decided to give his Gallic prejudice free rein, detaining him with needless questions, pretending not to understand his answers and forcing him to repeat them numerous times.

Gabriel longed to throw him overboard, but instead, he finally bribed the man into cooperating. The harbormaster's manner turned somewhat more cordial, but it took an additional sum to unlock a bit of information from him about a scuffle that had taken place last night by the docks.

The harbormaster said that two of the town's citizens, brothers who owned a dry goods shop, had seen a strange party of several Eastern-looking men and two cloaked women come ashore. The brothers had tried to intervene when they witnessed one of the men strike one of the ladies. They had backed down from the fight, vowing that the strangers had a murderous look about them, but had reported what they had seen.

Gabriel prevailed upon the harbormaster to tell him where these two brothers could be found. The harbormaster pointed to a shop on the quay, where, even now, Gabriel could see his comrades going in to buy supplies.

Excellent.

He thanked the harbormaster, then had a few lads from the sloop's crew row him ashore. Joining Markos and Demetrius at the dry goods store, he spoke to one of the brothers personally, and heard it from the man himself that one woman had called the other by the name Alexa. Then they got into a coach and drove away.

"The question now is which way did they go," Markos said as they left the store.

They met the others outside and convened briefly to discuss their course, studying the detailed local maps that the men had purchased in a bookstore on the boulevard.

"Eventually, they'll have to decide whether to go south to the Mediterranean and try to lose us at sea again or press on due east, cut across Italy, and head straight for the Adriatic."

"That overland journey is hard. Mountains."

"But no danger of meeting with English warships. The Mediterranean's crawling with them."

"It's a direct shot across the Adriatic to Ali Pasha's territory," Kosta remarked.

Gabriel nodded. "We need to catch up to them before they have to choose between these two routes. Above all, I want to avoid having to split up into two parties to pursue them. These are Janissary warriors. No trifling foe. We're all going to have to be on hand to get her back."

"The fact that they're in a carriage also helps us," Yannis chimed in. "With all the battles throughout France, they say the roads are not in as good shape as those in England. It should slow them down a bit."

"Then let's see what these French mounts can do."

The others nodded, and swinging up onto their horses, soon they were off.

The main road heading east out of Bordeaux took them through southwest France, into the tranquil but dramatic beauty of the Dordogne Valley, with the snowcapped Midi

Pyrenees outlined against the sky many miles to the south.

After a grueling ride of about three hours, their mounts were nearly spent. Since keeping up their hard pace was paramount, Gabriel called for a change of horses at the next posting inn with a livery stable.

But then, another glance through the telescope revealed a small splash of bright color against the dusty earth. "There's something in the road ahead."

"What is it?"

"Another signal from Her Highness?"

"Hard to say. Let's go find out." He spurred his horse's flagging canter back into a strained gallop and went to investigate the dash of color in the road.

Because she had made it clear that she did not intend to give them any trouble, her captors had finally agreed to untie Sophia's hands. Now she could only pray that Gabriel and her bodyguards would find the clue that she had risked her neck to leave for them.

She had made her move earlier that day, when her captors had stopped to change horses and to complete their proscribed daily prayers. She had been sitting in the carriage across from Alexa, much as they had been the night of the ambush.

With the men distracted, she had quickly opened Alexa's valise and taken out a long, brightly colored scarf, along with Alexa's tiny pot of rouge. Dabbing the red cosmetic onto her finger, Sophia had written a coded message on the scarf. Her men would know what it meant.

Peeking out the carriage window, she had waited for her opportunity. Moving quickly, she had laid the scarf out flat atop the carriage roof.

When the men returned from their prayers, they got back into the carriage and drove on. The breeze from their quickening pace blew the scarf silently off the carriage roof so it flew out behind them and landed, unnoticed, in the road.

That, however, had been hours and many miles ago. With the day waning, her captors turned off the sleepy country highway and headed up into the stark, gray mountains to find shelter for the night.

The already tired horses labored to climb the steep switchback road. For her part, Sophia was exhausted merely from riding all day in the bone-jarring vehicle. Its poor springs rattling over rough country roads had left her whole body sore.

She was glad they were stopping for the

night, even if it was only to shelter in one of the large hollow caves so common in the Dordogne Valley, with all of its bizarre, sculpted rock formations in the ancient limestone.

She could certainly use the rest, but more important, any halt on their part gave Gabriel and her men a better chance of catching up.

This turn off the main road up into the mountains worried her, however. How were her friends to know they had changed course?

If she did not find some way to leave another clue for them, Gabriel might never realize that Kemal and his men had veered off the main highway. They could go riding right past the turn and end up ahead of them.

She racked her brain all the way up the long, slow drive through thick pine forest to the mountain's crest and the cave that the men finally chose for their shelter.

How on earth was Gabriel to find her up here?

Her captors seemed very familiar with their wilderness hiding place and she realized that they'd used it before. Sophia could have despaired — except that Gabriel had spent most of his career fighting on rugged Indian frontiers full of mountains and forests. He might not know *this* ground, but he knew how to operate in this type of setting.

She kept both hope and fear under wraps as she slid out of the carriage and looked around, stretching her back with a wince of pain.

Alexa was staring dazedly at nothing, but the men had begun carrying their supplies into the wide, yawning mouth of the cave where they had stopped. When she told her captors in haughty tones that she had to use the necessary, the Tunisian gestured at one of his underlings.

"Take her into the woods."

The woods? Sophia curled her lip, but in this wilderness, even a royal princess had little choice.

Her armed, swarthy captor made her walk ahead of him across the dirt road from the caves into the pine forest.

"You'd better not look."

"If you try to escape, I will shoot you."

"I'm not stupid," she retorted.

"Be quick about it."

Still stewing with anger to find herself in the power of these fiends, she walked farther into the woods, her footfalls muffled by the deep bed of soft pine needles. Lord, it was much too cold for this. She kept looking for some way to signal Gabriel. All she saw was barren branches, sharp evergreen underbrush with red berries, probably poisonous.

"Hurry up!" her warden called.

"I'm trying!" she belted back. As she walked on deeper into the woods, she saw a sharp drop-off a few yards ahead.

"That's far enough!"

"I'm still here, don't look!"

She tiptoed toward the high ledge to try to gain a better sense of her location from atop that vantage point. When she reached the edge, she looked down and saw the winding, switchback road below.

Escape would have been nice, but it was too high to jump. On the other hand, if Gabriel was being watchful, he should be able to look up from the main road below and spot another clue from down there. What could she leave for him this time to signal where she was? She had nothing but the clothes on her back at this point. *Well* . . .

With a quick glance over her shoulder at her captor, who was pacing as he waited for her to return, she quickly slipped off her bright white petticoat from underneath her walking dress, and threw the whole white fluffy mass of fabric over the rocky ledge, holding her breath until it landed on the mountain road below.

There.

Hopefully he'd see it when he came along.

She was going to be very cold tonight without the extra layer of clothing, but any clues she could send her rescuers was of greater value to her now. She just hoped they managed to spot it before it got much darker out.

"You must be done! Get back here or I'm coming after you now!"

"I'm coming!" When she strode back to her captor, he glared at her for making him wait.

Holding his rifle diagonally across his body, he gestured at her to go ahead of him again.

Sophia did so, measuring out a small exhalation of relief once her back was to him. She crossed the road again, but as they neared the cave, she heard a commotion from inside.

Then Alexa screamed.

Immediately, Sophia rushed toward the cave. She could not see her friend — the laughing men had Alexa on the ground and were clustered around her — but she could hear her and she could feel her terror.

"Stop it! Leave me alone! Help!"

Sophia did not know what came over her

in that instant. Pure, blind rage.

The man who had escorted her into the woods was right behind her. Sensing trouble, his hand clamped down on her shoulder. Without warning, Sophia spun around and smashed the heel of her fist upward into his nose, jamming his head back and throwing him off balance.

She yanked the rifle out of his hands and ran into the cave to her fellow female's rescue.

"Leave her alone!"

The cretins cursed and scattered; she knew not how she put herself between them and her sobbing childhood playmate, but the next thing she knew, she was in a standoff with herself and one rifle against six heavily armed Janissary warriors.

Why she was not dead in the next instant, she did not know. But for reasons known only to them, they left her alive. They all just looked at her, an ugly light gleaming in their eyes.

They exchanged uneasy glances.

"You will not touch her," she ground out, her teeth clenched. "Stay behind me, Alexa."

Their leader, Kemal the Tunisian, walked into the cave just then with a map in his hand. Sophia supposed he had been taking the lay of the land, but he cursed when he saw their standoff and stalked over into their midst.

"What is going on here?"

His men glanced at him sheepishly and then at each other.

"Your men were considering breaking their Janissary vows, monsieur. Or are you all mere hypocrites? This wrong you would do my friend offends Islam, does it not?"

The Tunisian pushed one of his men roughly out of the way and rebuked him in his native tongue. Then he turned to her and put out his hand. "Give me the gun, Your Highness. You cannot win here."

"Back up unless you want a hole in your shirt!"

"It is not wise of you to threaten me. Why would you protect her when she betrayed you, anyway?"

"You wouldn't understand. You aren't human."

"Threats and insults, too? Are you brave, or mad, or merely foolish, Princess?" Their onyx-eyed leader stepped forward. "I have a threat for you. No — a promise," he corrected himself. "You pull that trigger, and by Allah, you will both regret it. We do not need you alive; we merely prefer it that way. But if you provoke us, what happens to you will be your own fault."

Sophia looked him in the eyes. "I am not afraid of you," she whispered with her finger on the trigger.

"Give me the gun."

"Give me your oath that you will not let your men lay a hand on us. Swear it on your Book."

Alexa was crying behind her. They were either both going to die very soon or they would get through this together. But neither of them would be raped.

The Tunisian stared at Sophia for a long moment. "Very well, little lioness. I will not permit my men to touch you or your stupid friend. They need me to remind them of their Janissary oath." He cast an angry glance around at his men. "Besides, I'm sure Ali Pasha would prefer you intact, anyway."

"Ali Pasha?" she breathed.

"Now give me the rifle. Come. Do we have a deal?"

Sophia stared at him, at a loss. Promises to infidels didn't count, but she realized if she did not give up the weapon, they would kill her and Alexa in a trice.

Ali Pasha?

Good God, was that where they were taking her? Delivering her to the Terrible Turk himself? How she wished in that moment that her suspicions about him had been wrong all along.

"The rifle, Your Highness," Kemal urged her. "What's it going to be? You've got one bullet. Squeeze the trigger, and you're the one who'll end up full of holes. Or you can live."

Though it took all of her strength and self-control, she turned the rifle sideways and handed it over.

He gave her a polite smirk as he accepted it. "Stay over there. Both of you." He jerked a nod toward the cave wall. "I will remind my men of their manners." With that, he walked away and unleashed a rapid, incomprehensible tirade on his men. They looked ashamed.

And so did Alexa. "Thank you. Oh, thank you, Sophia," the girl whispered, trembling.

"We'll see if he keeps his word," she replied as both women huddled by the cave wall.

Having heard the news about their destination, Sophia was now quite as terrified as Alexa was. But she did her best to hide it.

"Sophia — I'm so sorry!" The sob from her traitorous lady-in-waiting tore at her heart.

She looked over at her traumatized companion, feeling reluctantly merciful. It was a little late for apologies, but she did not have the heart to say so.

Instead, she touched Alexa's shoulder in a token of forgiveness. "It'll be all right," she murmured. "Don't worry. Colonel Knight and the others will find us."

"They'll save you, maybe. But they're going to leave me to die. I know they will — after that!"

"They will not leave you to die," she answered wearily. "You know them better than that."

Alexa kept crying while Sophia inhaled a shaky breath and braced herself upright against the rough stone wall behind her. *Hurry, Gabriel.*

She sent out the very whisper of her heart to him to save them. In this, her hour of greatest need, it was not in her bodyguards that she placed her faith, nor in the prince of Denmark. She knew her true mate was coming to find her.

Her guardian angel.

Her knight.

Her message on the silk scarf, written in ladies' cosmetics, had given them several pieces of valuable information. It read: + + *11 E.*

As Timo had explained, it meant that both she and Alexa were there, that they were both all right, they were not hurt. There were eleven enemy fighters, and they were heading due east.

The news that Sophia was still unharmed came as a blessing to all of them and buoyed up their strength for what was sure to be another long night. Pounding doggedly down the main road through the beautiful French countryside, they kept their eyes open for any fresh sign from Sophia.

In the fading light of evening, they almost missed the distant bit of white fluff lying in the middle of a steep road that wound up into the mountains. But Gabriel spotted it through his telescope as he rode on, constantly scanning the landscape through his lens. At once, he held up his gloved fist to signal the men to a halt.

"What is it, Colonel?"

"Did you see something?"

"There. Some white object in the road." Reining in his blowing mount, he looked again through the telescope and found the object once more through the lens.

It had been hard to make out while his horse had been in motion, and even now, as they came to a stop, he still could not tell for certain what it was. The distance was too great.

"Markos, what do you make of it?"

The eagle-eyed sharpshooter urged his horse up beside Gabriel's and stared for a moment through his own spyglass.

"Can you tell what it is?"

Markos lowered the telescope slowly from his eye and turned to him with a grim expression. "I think it might be a body."

"A body?" Demetrius echoed.

Markos eyed them uneasily. "It looks like something in a gown."

"They wouldn't," Timo whispered. "He must be wrong. Why would they kill her?"

"They tried before."

"But it could be nothing!"

"We have to make sure," Gabriel said.

Niko was shaking his head. "It doesn't look like anything to me, and riding up there to investigate is going to cost us precious time. We've got to stay on their tails!"

Gabriel searched the landscape. *Sophia . . . where are you?* He could feel her somewhere near. He knew she was still alive. She was waiting for him. *Hold on, my love. I'm coming for you.*

The men were arguing, tense and worn out, in need of rest and a decent meal.

"What if you're wrong? It could be somebody's laundry blown away — or a dead bird or something, or nothing at all!"

"The horses are already near exhausted."

"So am I," Yannis muttered.

"If we spend what strength they have left on a wild-goose chase, then we are fools!"

"And if she's somewhere up there and we go riding past, we're even bigger fools," Gabriel countered. "What if they've gone up there into the woods to take shelter for the night? It's what I would do if I were them. I wouldn't want to risk being seen at any inn along the way. Whatever that white thing is, it could be another clue that she's left for us. We know they want to throw us off their trail."

"I agree," Timo said stoutly. "Let's go check it out."

Gabriel nodded and urged his horse back into motion. The others followed, some reluctantly. About a quarter mile down the road, they took the turn onto a smaller, rockier country lane that led up into the rugged limestone hills.

They pressed on in taut silence, each man wrestling privately with his dread that they were about to find either Sophia or Alexa dead in the middle of the road — murdered and dumped by the abductors like so much refuse.

If that fear were not enough for them,

there was its alternative: that the white object in the road was nothing, and they had wasted valuable time investigating it.

But then, still some distance off, they examined it through their telescopes again and exhaustion fell away as they realized that it had to be a clue. They were sure it wasn't a body. It seemed to be a dress.

Through his telescope, Gabriel scrutinized the ledge above the place in the road where the garment lay. If that was the clue from Sophia that he believed it to be, then she had clearly passed through here and might still be in the area. That, he decided, was where they would begin their search.

But he ordered the men to hang back and keep a distance for now. If the enemy was somewhere nearby, then stealth and silence would be their best weapons, especially since the kidnappers already owned the double advantage of good cover and high ground.

They would have to approach with great care to avoid being seen or heard. As much as possible, he wanted to control the element of surprise.

"Yes," he murmured as he looked around, "she's here on this mountain somewhere. I can feel it."

"They must have stopped for the night

like you said," Timo agreed. "We've got to track them down and find them before they're on the move again."

"But how? God, we've got thousands of acres of wilderness ahead of us. Caves, gullies, ravines," Demetrius said. "How are we going to find her?"

"We're going to use our heads. And we're not coming down until we've got her." Gabriel glanced around at them. "Take a break, boys. I'm going to go retrieve that bit of clothing she left us and do a bit of scouting around the area."

"Shall we come with you?" Yannis offered.

"No. I want you all to get a bit of rest for what's to come," Gabriel said. "And I want silence, understand? Sound will travel right up this mountainside, and they're sure to have sentries posted. Let's keep the element of surprise for as long as we can."

"Yes, Colonel."

"Aye, sir."

In grim quiet, the men led their horses into the woods on the side of the road, taking cover among the trees. They found a stream and let the horses drink while they stretched a bit, took a few swigs from their canteens, and began checking their weapons and getting themselves ready for battle.

Meanwhile, Gabriel sneaked farther up

the mountain on foot to get that blasted petticoat out of the road before it drew the Scorpions' attention the same way it had drawn theirs. As twilight deepened to dark, crisp night, he arrived at the place where Sophia had thrown the garment. He rejoiced to touch it, knowing she was near. Quickly sweeping up the white cloth and concealing it under his black coat, he spent a good hour scouting out the terrain. Then he selected a small cave away from the road where he could bring Sophia once he had her safely in his care. He stocked it with firewood and supplies and made sure she would have all she needed.

God, keep her safe.

Before going back to his men, he paused outside the cave to survey the surrounding area one last time. The air was thinner at this elevation. He took note, for it would cause the men to tire faster. He was a little more used to it himself because of his battles in India.

Countless memories of those days prepared him well for what lay ahead tonight.

Dark impulses, long dormant, had begun stirring to life inside him, a savagery he had thought, or hoped, that he would never need to use again.

But he needed it now, and he realized it

had never truly left him. He closed his eyes and felt the fury fill him. He let it come, rushing into his veins, a dark ecstasy. Aye, he welcomed it. The time to kill had come again. If he was damned for this, for saving Sophia, then he wanted no part of redemption.

The men seemed to notice the strange look in his eyes when he stalked back through the woods and rejoined them.

Having come back down the mountain, he laid out his battle plan, describing his plan for how and where they would start their search of the woods above that ledge where they had found Sophia's signal.

"Once we've found the enemy camp, here's how it all will go. First, Timo, you're supposed to be the best tracker."

"That's right," he said.

"Good. I've got a job for you. We know Sophia wounded one of these bastards during the ambush."

"Yes. One of them reached into the carriage to try to get her, and she slashed his right arm open."

"It's too soon for it to be fully healed yet. So, we know that one of these men is already wounded. If anyone's going to tend to back down from a fight, it'll be him — especially if he can't use his sword arm properly."

"What does that have to do with me?"

"We're going to let him run. The rest you can kill at your leisure, but if you see a man with his right arm bandaged, try to let him go. We'll have you track him, Timo, and eventually he should lead you to wherever the Order of Scorpion has its headquarters. We need this information. Can you do this?"

"Yes, of course."

"Good. You can take one man with you, but I want no more than two of you going. You don't want to attract undue attention. And keep your distance. Do not allow yourself to be captured as you near their base of operations. We need you to stay alive and to report back to us what you find.

"For the rest of you, if anyone should become separated from the rest of us for whatever reason, make your way to Kavros as quickly as you can. We will rendezvous at the naval base. Right, then. Who's the best marksman?"

They all pointed at Markos. He lifted his rifle with a wry smile.

"When we close in on the camp, you'll take a position where you can give cover. I don't care if you have to get up in one of these trees. Other than our bandaged friend, feel free to pick the bastards off as you find the opportunity."

"Will do."

"They'll want to move Sophia as soon as they know we've found them," Gabriel continued. "Getting her out of there is going to be their top priority. To prevent their escape, we're going to want to find their horses first and set them loose before we attack. The horses will likely be under guard. No noise dispatching the sentries, all right? Cut their throats. That way, when the others come out to try to spirit Her Highness away, they're going to look for their horses, but what they're going to find instead is me.

"The rest of you will launch the main assault. I'll be in position to intercept Sophia and get her to safety. I'm not sending her off by herself like Leon did. Not now."

"Agreed," they said grimly.

"Any questions?"

"What about Alexa?"

"Well, we're not going to leave her to them," Gabriel replied. "She's not their main priority, or ours, frankly, after what she's done. Just look out for her as best you can."

They discussed a few more details, then Gabriel looked around grimly at them. "If any of us don't come back tonight, it's been, ah, interesting working with you all. It's been an honor," he added in a more sincere tone.

"And you, sir."

The men returned his salute. Then with fierce looks they rose and took to their horses to find their princess and bring her safely home.

CHAPTER EIGHTEEN

Having her wrists tied with hard, chafing ropes complicated the task of finding a comfortable sleeping position, Sophia was learning, especially when her bed was a meager blanket over cold stone.

With her fastened arms resting atop her bent knees, she had managed to doze off, sitting with her back against the clammy wall of the cave.

She hadn't dared lie down. Merely resting her head against her arm felt vulnerable enough with all these hostile men around her.

They had not bothered her or Alexa again, thank God. But presently, their low-toned exchange from somewhere nearby summoned Sophia from her light slumber. In the eerie, dripping stillness of the cave, the taut echo of the foreign words escaped her comprehension, but the tone of agitation in

their voices was universal enough to understand.

Something was afoot.

She did not even lift her head, only opening her eyes slowly, drawing no attention to
herself. She went on listening as she scanned
the cave with all of its strange, glittering
dragon's teeth of stone hanging down from
the ceiling and jutting up from the floor.
Her gaze came to a small cluster of men
over by the cave's mouth.

She saw that one of the sentries had come
back. The man was pointing angrily toward
the woods, and if she read his gesticulations
correctly, he seemed to be trying to convince
the others that he had seen something — or
someone — out there in the darkness.

Gabriel . . .

At that moment, the harsh cry of a night-
jar broke the windy silence of the autumn
night beyond the large cave's mouth. She
held her breath, recognizing the familiar
signal from her Greek bodyguards.

It meant they were coming. They were
very near, but they had not yet managed to
home in on her exact location.

It asked her to give them some sort of
signal to lead them to her, if she was able.

Her heart began to pound. She glanced
around in need of a signal her men could

not miss. As soon as she made her position known to them, their attack was sure to follow.

There was only one direction for them to approach from: the cave's mouth. Perhaps she could give them a signal that would not only confirm her whereabouts, but would also distract her captors from the direction of the attack.

She noticed the dimly glowing lantern that someone had set on the flattened top of a stalagmite. One of the men's bedrolls was below it. That should burn well, she thought. Nudging Alexa awake, she silenced her questions with a warning look, and then inched her way toward the lantern.

The sentry was still trying to explain his worries to the others. The mood inside the cave was still quiet, but a couple more of the men who had not yet fallen asleep got up and went forward to join the others. Up by the wide, arched mouth of the cave, they conferred about what was going on and what action should be taken.

She knew she had to act before they all retrieved their guns. Moving toward the natural stone pedestal where the lantern sat, she swept the cave with another wary glance, making sure no one was watching her, then she suddenly batted the lantern off the rock with her bound hands. It flew, crashing down onto the empty bedroll; the glass around the flame broke on impact; the whale oil spilled; flame erupted; and the Arab's bedroll, with its thin coating of human hair and body oils absorbed into the fabric, caught fire in the blink of an eye and became an instant torch.

Sophia let out a girlish shriek, feigning innocence as the blaze flared. "Fire! Help!"

But she climbed to her feet and got ready to run, for she knew the flash of orange light would be bright enough for her men to see exactly where the kidnappers were keeping her.

Pandemonium broke out. Amid yells and curses, some of the Janissaries rushed to put out the flames.

Others saw her trick for what it was and ran to grab their weapons.

But they were too late.

She knew her men were coming as two of the Janissaries rushed to beat out the flames.

"How did this happen?" one demanded angrily, coughing as the cave filled with smoke.

"I don't know!" Sophia cried, backing up against the wall. "The wind must have blown it! We were sleeping!"

"Sit down! Nobody gave you leave to

stand up!"

"Get us out of here!" she demanded. "We can't even breathe!"

"Too bad," he retorted.

"Highness, what's going on?" Alexa whimpered, cowering beside her.

"Just . . . hold on," she murmured barely audibly. "Steady . . . when I give you the word, be ready to run."

"Run where?" she squeaked in terror as the smoke thickened, pouring toward the cave's mouth.

"Wait . . ."

Then the attack was upon them.

Black-clad shapes in the smoke materialized into men. They rushed in with a roar, a full frontal assault at the mouth of the cave. Shots flew, bullets ricocheting off the rock face. When one sparked off the stone above Sophia, she crouched down and covered her head with her arms, holding her ears, but she pulled Alexa's arm. "Come on. Let's go."

Alexa blanched at the prospect of having to face again all the men she had betrayed, but Sophia was not heartless enough to leave her behind, not after seeing how these filthy hypocrites would have used her. The girls began creeping slowly toward the cave's mouth, Sophia praying all the while that they could get closer to her bodyguards before the Janissaries noticed their progress along the cave's wall.

Blades flashed by firelight up ahead, near the cave's mouth. She saw two of her captors die, and then gasped in horror as Demetrius was mowed down.

Alexa screamed, and of course, Kemal noticed them.

When the girls saw him coming with a look of death darkening his face, Alexa screamed again and bolted before Sophia could stop her.

"Alexa, no!"

The frenzied girl made a run for the exit, overtaken by her fear. Surely she would be killed in the cross fire, for the battle was raging all around the cave's mouth. She knew Alexa had cause for terror; while the Janissaries seemed to need Sophia alive, they had no such concerns about her lady-in-waiting. They had only been keeping her alive so far for added leverage over Sophia — and their own sport.

Sophia held her breath, watching in disbelief as Alexa miraculously escaped the whirling blades and flying bullets, tearing out into the dark woods alone like a horse spooked by a thunderstorm.

With a scream trapped in her throat, she

saw Niko, fighting with two swords, criss-cross them through the innards of one of the Janissaries.

His opponent crumpled.

"Princess!" he called to her. "To us!"

"Behind you!" she shrieked in answer.

Niko whirled around and took on the next opponent as Kemal reached for her.

"You little fool. I will kill you myself before I'll let them take you," he said. Then he barked an unintelligible order at two of his brethren.

They immediately retreated from the battle at the cave's mouth and came for Sophia.

With his sword, Kemal pointed deeper into the cave as he gave them some instructions. Listening to their swift exchange, Sophia fought back panic, wondering if her end was upon her.

While Kemal stalked forward to do battle with her guards, the other two swarthy Janissaries grabbed her by her arms and began dragging her back deeper into the cave.

"Let go! Where are you taking me?"

"Shut up! You're more trouble than you're worth, infidel witch."

"If it was up to me, we'd cut your throat and be done with it," the taller one muttered. She believed he was called Zacarias.

"Help! I'm here! Timo! Gabriel!"

"Not another word, or we cut your tongue out, understand?" the shorter man, bearded and thick-bodied, threatened her in French. She had heard the others call him Osman.

When Osman gave her a warning look and showed her his curved dagger, exactly like the one they had found at the scene of the ambush, Sophia clamped her mouth shut.

"Ali Pasha will probably like her better if we mute her, anyway," Zacarias opined as they half-dragged, half-carried her farther into the cave. "I know I would."

With Kemal now having joined the fight at the mouth of the cave, her men were having a harder time of it. Still, she did not see Gabriel.

Had she been wrong all along? Had he not come? Had he washed his hands of her after she had dismissed him from this post?

Maybe she had misjudged him as completely as she had misjudged Alexa.

God, if she was so naïve that she could not tell her friends from her enemies, what business did she have ruling a country, anyway? Lord Griffith had been wise to doubt her.

In the din of battle, nobody seemed to notice that she was being smuggled away. The floor of the cave tilted downward into the mountain. The darkness deepened to the claustrophobic black of the tomb, and all three of them moved carefully.

"This way," Zacarias muttered, feeling his way along a left-hand turn in the slope.

Inching through the lightless void, she realized after a time that she could feel a draft of air coming in, trailing against her face. After another twenty blind steps or so, they reached a fissure in the rocks where a little rivulet no more than three feet wide trickled out of the mountainside.

The water escaped by an opening in the rock just big enough for a person to slip through; this, Sophia and her captors now did, first treading carefully over a couple of big, flat stones above the water's flow, and then climbing out silently into the thick pine woods.

As Sophia stepped out into the world again, free of the pitch-black cavern, new hope rushed into her. Now, if she could just get away from these two thugs, she could escape like Alexa had. She stole a quick glance around to get her bearings.

To her right, a steep, pebbled path led down the slope, hugging the rocky dome. Uphill, to her left, she saw they were not too distant from the cave's mouth, where the battle still raged.

She had to let her men know that her captors were trying to move her again, or their attempt to rescue her would fail — and she doubted they would get another chance.

Nobody's taking me to Ali Pasha. Shrugging off their threats of cutting out her tongue, she rallied herself with a fresh surge of fight, and began thrashing, trying to pull free of them as soon as she had stepped down from the stony fissure in the rock. "Help! I'm here! Let go of me!" she shouted, but almost at once, Zacarias grabbed her and clapped his hand over her mouth, stilling her struggles with a violent jerk.

"Not another word from you!" Osman whispered in her face with a greasy sneer. "You walk properly, or we will cut your feet off and drag you."

Her bound hands balled into fists, but the moment Zacarias let go of her mouth, she spat off the taste of his hand. "Is that all you know how to do, threaten people?" she asked fiercely.

"No," Osman replied. "I also know how to kill them. Do you wish me to demonstrate, Princess?"

She subsided into mutinous silence and gave up on fighting them for now, lest she provoke them into carrying out one of their bloodthirsty threats.

"Come on," Zacarias muttered. "Let's get to the horses."

As they started down the precarious angle of the rocky path in single file with Sophia between them, she was still bold enough to steal one last angry glance over her shoulder toward the cave.

And it was then that she caught a fleeting glimpse of a large, black silhouette outlined before the flames.

Watching her.

Gabriel.

Astonishment made her stumble over a rock as she continued their descent.

"Watch where you're going!" Zacarias snapped when she knocked into his back before quickly catching her balance.

"Sorry," she muttered.

"Hold onto her or she'll send us all falling down the cliffside, clumsy wench."

Osman did as he was told, clutching her arm with a grip that hurt.

"Ow," she complained, but as she looked over her shoulder again, pretending that her only purpose was to scowl at him, she saw that the man-shaped shadow had vanished again, as if it had been no more than a trick of the smoke. *Was he truly here?* Had Gabriel come for her, or was her mind merely playing tricks on her now?

Zacarias led the way with his rifle at the ready, hurrying them down toward the pine grove where the horses and carriage had been concealed among the trees.

The noise of the battle by the cave's mouth grew muffled in the distance, the shouts and guns' reports blunted by the soft mass of pine needles, yet the rock faces here and there did strange things with the sound. Intangible echoes seemed to reverberate from the wrong direction. Above, the indigo sky glistened with stars and a sharp crescent moon.

"Where are the horses?" Zacarias blurted out, peering into the shadows ahead.

"By the Prophet, I do not know! A little farther on! Keep going. It's hard to tell in the dark."

"Wait." Ahead, Zacarias halted.

Sophia nearly stumbled into him again, but Osman yanked her to a rough halt. "What is it?" he demanded.

"I thought I saw something ahead."

"The horses!" Osman said impatiently.

"No," he clipped out. "Is your weapon drawn?"

"Of course. Would you move? We have to keep going! If we fail, Kemal will kill us."

With a mutter, Zacarias pressed on, but

now Sophia could feel it, too. A presence in the darkness.

They were not alone.

They were being watched.

She held her breath, her pulse a wild staccato.

Gabriel.

She knew now that it was he, as though her heart could see in the darkness where her eyes could not.

She could feel his presence. She knew him too well to be mistaken. No, he was here. He was very close.

And she could almost smell the doom that overhung these two unsuspecting fellows.

Any moment now, he was going to strike. She told herself to be ready . . .

"Move, girl!" Osman's curt order cut into her thoughts.

"I tell you, there is something out here," Zacarias mumbled as they pressed on.

"Or someone," Osman corrected him uneasily. "Hurry up, then."

"Man or beast? Or both?" Sophia whispered, taunting them to keep them off balance. "Maybe it's a bear. Or a big . . . hungry . . . mountain lion."

"She could be right," Osman said uneasily, glancing around into the trees. "A catamount could have smelled the horses and come hunting."

Zacarias stopped abruptly, holding up his hand and staring forward. "Did you hear that?"

"Hear wh—" Osman started impatiently, but behind her, his words broke off with a strange gurgle.

Sophia did not even turn to look. She ducked down, dropping to her knees to clear the route for Gabriel's dagger. It flew through the air above her head like a lightning bolt, striking Zacarias in the base of his throat the second he spun around to see what was happening.

He crumpled and rolled a little farther down the rocky path.

The next thing Sophia knew, she was lifted, scooped up into Gabriel's arms. Without a word, he hoisted her over his shoulder.

As she quickly held onto him, she caught a glimpse of portly Osman behind her, his eyes wide open in surprise. A bayonet was sticking all the way through his thick neck, the tip poking out beneath his ear.

Zacarias had hastened his own death by a few minutes, instinctively pulling the knife out with his last seconds of strength. Now a river of blood, black in the darkness, poured out of the hole at the base of his throat where he lay. It trickled down the stones like a tiny mountain rill.

Sophia could only stare at the carnage in shocked disbelief at how fast it had happened. Gabriel did not say a word, but secured her over his left shoulder as though she weighed nothing. Rounding the dying man, he began racing down the narrow path, his body angled to the side; leading with his right foot, he kept his left arm clamped across her backside, while using his right arm for balance, his big, black carbine cocked and loaded in his hand.

Sophia was no wilting flower, but she was a bit in shock. She held onto his waist for dear life, saying not a word, and trying not to move too much so as not to upset his balance. She did not bother asking why he didn't let her just walk for herself — she was not about to question anything that he saw fit to do — but instead, she kept a weather eye out for anyone who might be coming down the path behind them.

The progress he made with his mountain-goat agility carried them down swiftly to the pine grove where only one horse waited: his. The rest were gone, the sentry assigned to guard the animals facedown in the pine mulch.

Gabriel didn't even set her on her feet,

but put her right on the horse. "Sit astride."

She did, swinging her leg over the saddle.

"Are you hurt?"

"No."

"Give me your wrists." She turned to him but could not help cowering slightly from the deadly creature as he slid yet another knife out of a compact sheath against his ribs and quickly cut the ropes.

He noted her momentary fear of him with a grim glance. Sophia tried to hide it as she threw the loosened ropes aside and rubbed her chafed wrists. But she could not help staring at him, rather wide-eyed.

A fleeting memory of her first meeting with him sailed through her mind. That morning in the old barn, she had pulled her knife on him with no inkling of how she had been taking her life in her hands by threatening him.

"Are you all right?" he clipped out as he passed a hard, assessing glance over her face.

Sophia nodded, but suddenly, from her vantage point astride the horse, she saw motion farther up the path.

"Gabriel, they're coming!" she whispered, pointing.

He sent a piercing glance over his shoulder, then turned to her with a cold, silvery gleam in his eyes that was downright terrifying. "I'll take care of them."

"Can't we just go?" she breathed, touching his hand.

"No. I don't want them following us. Move deeper into the trees," he ordered in a low, hard tone. "Wait for me. I won't have you going off by yourself. If I should fall, then ride. Right here is a knife and a pair of loaded pistols, should you need them." He showed her the additional weapons strapped to the horse's gear. "Hopefully it won't come to that, but if it does, you'll need to ride hard to get down the mountain. Take the road — these hillsides are too treacherous. Ride as fast as you can go. As soon as you've crossed the little bridge across the stream, turn west off the road. A hundred yards up the next slope into the woods, you'll find a cave with supplies. Have you got that?"

"Yes." She knew she could not stop him. Her hand atop his tightened. "Gabriel — be careful. Please. I need you."

He captured her fingers lightly and gazed at her for a second. Then he closed his eyes with an impassioned look and pressed her knuckles to his lips. "Princess," he breathed against her skin. When he released her hand, she touched his face ever so briefly, but he pulled away and grabbed hold of the horse's reins, starting the animal in the right direction. "Out of sight, now. Hide," he ordered, glancing quickly over his shoulder.

Farther up the path, there was activity but very little sound. It seemed that the other Janissaries had just discovered their dead comrades.

Gabriel looked at Sophia again, his jaw tightening. By the moon's glow she could see the sheen of sweat on his face. "Do not come out under any circumstances."

"But —"

"I am just one man, Sophia. You must think of your people."

"You're more than that to me. You're everything . . ."

"Go," he whispered fiercely.

With one last, searing look, she obeyed, urging her horse deeper into the thicket while he prowled off with stealthy speed to get into position for whatever dreadful fate he had planned for the new arrivals.

She guided the horse quickly down a little slope, but she could still see into the clearing where Gabriel now lay in wait for the enemy.

Now it was *his* turn to ambush them.

Prayers surged through her mind as she scanned the darkness, trying to pick him out. *Please, God, keep him safe. Make him win. Don't take him from me . . .*

Where did he go?

Once more he had dissolved into the darkness. Then she caught a glimpse of movement across the grove. He had turned back into a terrible figment, a shadow. As she watched, wide-eyed in the darkness, she saw the shape of him separate from the trunk of a tree and then jump up onto a lower branch, climbing with easy agility.

He disappeared up into one of the great pine trees.

Sophia petted the horse with one hand to keep the animal calm, but the other she pressed to her mouth to silence herself as Kemal and two of his men came prowling down from the path. Barely making a sound, they stole into the grove, their muskets at the ready.

Sophia waited as they crossed some twenty yards away from her, moving in a triangular formation, Kemal ahead and in the center.

She held her breath. Her heart pounded so loud in sheer terror that she feared they would hear it. Her horse stood in uneasy silence, his ears swiveling toward the smallest sounds the men made.

Her nerves stretched thin, she squeezed her eyes shut for a second, unable to bear it as Gabriel waited for them to come closer, to come right to him.

With barely a snapping twig under their feet, the Janissaries progressed through the grove, their heads turning as they scanned the woods in all directions while still moving forward.

The only way they did not look was . . . up.

Even if they had looked, she doubted they'd have seen Gabriel. For such a large man, he had an uncanny ability to make himself all but invisible.

Shoot them! her mind screamed to him as Kemal stalked under the very tree where he waited, but still nothing happened.

Two steps, three . . .

He waited until the two men flanking Kemal were right underneath the tree. A flare of orange exploded up among the branches as he fired his carbine downward, killing one man instantly; almost simultaneously, he dropped to the ground and knifed the second man before the latter was quite sure what was going on.

At once, Kemal spun around and brought up his rifle, but Gabriel stopped the second man from falling, and used his meaty body for a shield.

The man let out a garbled cry as Gabriel tossed him aside and went toward Kemal, drawing his cavalry saber, the one that she had found back at the farmhouse, notched with its wicked tally of deaths.

No mercy.

Kemal answered in kind. With no time to reload, he slid his curved Turkish scimitar out of its sheath and brandished it as he retreated a few steps, getting into position.

The terrible, arced swords that both men wielded were made for slashing. The points were sharp, but the cruel curve of both terrible blades was really designed for severing limbs and heads from bodies.

Sophia was rather glad of the darkness and the branches shielding from her a full view of the proceedings. How she kept from screaming, she simply did not know.

The two were still for a moment, sizing each other up.

Sophia felt sick to her stomach, knowing that this would be a duel to the death, and chilled, as well, to realize that the sounds of the distant fight up by the cave's mouth had subsided. *Were they the only ones left alive?*

She stared, her heart in her throat.

Without warning, the battle erupted.

She heard the clash and ring of metal, saw the whirl of furious motion through the trees as they slashed and swung and flew at each other, their swords like a churning metal wheel.

They parted, circled, lunged again, trying to hack each other apart with brutal speed and force in every blow. Metallic clangs reverberated through the pines. She could feel each man's intense concentration.

Time seemed to have stopped.

They fought their way out into the clearing from among the trees. Gabriel was giving ground; Sophia watched with her heart in her throat. Seeing him back up like that terrified her. Was he weakening, pained by his scar — or was he simply moving the fight to more open terrain?

He ducked with lightning agility as Kemal's blade swooped in a vicious arc above his head, then Gabriel struck back from below, delivering a backhanded blow that slammed the edge of his blade deep into Kemal's right ribs.

It went into the center of him, only stopped by his spine.

Sophia jumped and stifled a cry as the Tunisian staggered backward, hunching over what was surely a terrible wound.

But her violent flinch startled her horse, in turn, which moved just a little, causing a few twigs to crackle.

Clutching his side, Kemal looked straight over at where Sophia was hurrying to steady the horse. Seeing her outline through the underbrush, he reached inside his vest and pulled out a pistol, aiming it at her.

Before he could pull the trigger, Gabriel let out a roar and brought down his saber with such force that the hand holding the pistol fell to the ground separately from its owner.

Kemal screamed and toppled to earth, writhing briefly; Gabriel loomed over him, keeping the tip of his sword against the Tunisian's throat until he was certain the man was dead.

Sophia knew the moment this occurred because Gabriel's entire posture changed.

His massive shoulders slowly loosened, he lowered his head, his chin dropped toward his heaving chest, and he placed his left hand vaguely on his scar.

She watched him in welling tenderness, part of her wanting to jump off the horse and run to him. But another part, instinctively, didn't dare.

He would come to her when he was ready.

Having steadied the horse again from its skittishness, she sat in the saddle, barely able to wrap her mind around all that had just occurred. With a shudder, she closed her eyes and thanked God for keeping Gabriel safe.

Just then, from across the grove, a familiar voice called hesitantly to Gabriel. "Colonel?"

Yannis.

Sophia opened her eyes and turned to look. It was he!

"Yannis!" She leapt off the horse and grabbed the reins, pulling the animal toward the men.

"Sophia?" Gabriel barked, sounding slightly shaken.

"I'm all right!" she assured him, pulling the horse out into the clearing. "I'm here. Gabriel. Yannis!"

Gabriel turned around with an air of weariness as her easygoing bodyguard came running toward them. "Your Highness!"

She held her arms out to him, and though he had long been in her employment, like all the rest, she considered him closer to family in her heart. She hugged her old friend like a brother while Gabriel took a moment to collect himself.

"Thank God you're safe." When Yannis pulled back and looked at her, there were tears in his eyes.

"What of the others?" she whispered.

"I'm sorry — Demetrius is dead."

Sophia squeezed her eyes shut, but she had already known this. She had seen it.

"The rest?"

"All alive."

Her eyes widened. "Really?"

"Nobody's hurt too badly except Markos. Damned fool broke his leg falling out of the tree where Colonel Knight posted him for a sniper."

"Let me go and check on him," she said.

"No," Gabriel murmured, joining them. "I don't want you going up there."

Sophia looked at him in dismay, but when he shook his head with grim finality, she knew he only wished to spare her from the sight of all the bloodshed.

Perhaps she'd had enough of that for now, in truth.

"Don't worry, Your Highness. I've already seen to Markos," Yannis assured her. "But he'll be traveling slowly. You two are going to have to go ahead of us. I will stay behind to help him. And I will bury Demetrius. And Alexa," he added with a glance at Gabriel.

"Alexa is dead?" Sophia breathed. "I thought she escaped! The last I saw her, she had just cleared the cave. Was she struck by a bullet? What happened?"

Yannis dropped his gaze. "I'm sorry to have to tell you this. Markos saw her pass from his vantage up in the tree. She bolted straight on through the woods and in the darkness, must not have seen the ledge in front of her until it was too late. When Markos told me what happened, I ran down to see if she survived the fall, but she was dead. Her neck was broken."

"Oh, God," Sophia whispered, lowering her head.

Gabriel glanced at Yannis. "Did the injured man among them flee as we expected?"

"Yes, sir. Timo and Niko went after him, just as you commanded."

"Excellent. You all fought well."

Coming from him, this was quite a compliment, Sophia thought, but she eyed each man dubiously. "You all are getting along now?"

Both men favored her with jaded smiles.

"I think we've learned our lesson," Yannis admitted.

"And that, not a moment too soon," Gabriel agreed. "Come, Gypsy girl. Let's get you out of here."

"Gypsy girl?" Yannis murmured.

"Don't listen to him," Sophia answered with a blush.

She gave Yannis another hug with words of praise and comfort to pass along to Markos.

Then she and Gabriel both got on the horse and started down the mountain.

CHAPTER NINETEEN

They rode the few miles down the mountain in silence, then crossed the little bridge over the cold swift stream, and turned off the road. They plunged into the dark forest again, but with Gabriel riding behind her, his big, warm body so solid at her back, Sophia was no longer afraid.

He urged the horse onward through the dense trees, but when they came to a quiet meander of the stream, he reined in, took a quick, wary glance behind them and in all directions, and then dismounted.

She watched him in silence as he walked over to the bubbling creek and crouched down beside it. Sophia's expression turned somber as she realized he was washing the blood off his hands from the vicious battle.

His words from that night at the farm-house haunted her. *"I could not possibly kill another human being again . . . I'm quite sure it would cost me my immortal soul."*

Now he had had to do so for her. Was this brooding silence of his . . . anger? Anger at her?

Did he believe that he had damned his soul for her? The thought made her tremble. Warily, Sophia got down off the horse and left the animal there, joining Gabriel quietly by the water's edge.

Upstream of him, she knelt down and lowered her fingertips into the cold current.

He finished cleaning his hands. Staring straight ahead, he took a deep breath and let it out.

She eyed him askance, worried by his silence.

"You all right?" he asked her evenly, aware of her watching him, even as he avoided her gaze.

"Yes," Sophia murmured. "You?"

"Hm." The short, vague syllable was neither confirmation nor denial, but it was all he offered for the moment, scooping water up into his cupped hands and splashing his face. "That's cold," he said.

"Yes." She shivered a bit as he pushed up to a stand once more, set his hands wearily on his waist, and walked off to get the horse.

They went up toward the cave he had prepared earlier for her, but first, he led the horse to its hiding place among the trees.

Sophia followed on foot, stepping carefully over the uneven ground.

"Our shelter's right there." He pointed toward a small cave a few yards away through the pines. "Should be warm in there. You can go and make yourself comfortable."

She shook her head. "I'll wait for you." After the events of this evening, she was not about to wander off from her protector. All too happy to stay close to him, she leaned against a tree while he unsaddled the horse.

When he was finished, they walked up to the cave together. He assisted her over the boulders while an owl hooted in the distance.

Ahead, silver moonlight illumined the rock face with the cave's pitch-black opening. Behind them, the wind whispered through the pines. Gabriel moved ahead, bending under the cave's arched mouth as he went in. Right behind him, Sophia did not have to bend down at all; she kept her hand on his back in the darkness, but then he reached ahead and brushed aside a large, black blanket that he had hung previously like a curtain to conceal their camp.

Behind the curtain, the little cave was downright cozy, dimly lit by a pair of lanterns, warmed by glowing coals in a circle of rocks, with waiting bedrolls and a few fur throws, water and food, basic medical supplies, and more weapons leaning here and there around the walls if he should need them. He held the curtain back, letting her go in first, and as she stepped inside, Sophia's heart lifted, for this small, primal shelter seemed more welcoming and safe than any palace she had ever lived in.

"My knapsack!" she suddenly exclaimed, pointing across the cave in recognition. She turned to Gabriel with an adoring look of gratitude.

The trace of a smile softened his granite countenance.

"Wouldn't forget that."

"Did you bring my knife?" she asked eagerly.

"See for yourself."

As if he had promised to give her a handful of diamonds, she rushed across the back of the cave and crouched down to open the old canvas knapsack that Leon had always kept ready for her, the one she had escaped with on the night of the ambush. She peered inside and found that, indeed, all of her survival things were there. Including her knife.

She sent Gabriel a smile from ear to ear. The threat was over, but she strapped her favorite weapon to her thigh immediately. It instantly made her feel a good deal better.

He shook his head to himself in amusement, then took a long swig from his canteen.

Sophia slowly sat down on one of the fur throws beside the fire and stared into space. Images of all that had happened were flashing through her mind in the most rapid and disturbing fashion. She barely realized she was still shivering.

Gabriel frowned as he watched her, then he crossed to add fuel to the fire. This done, he went to the stash of supplies and picked up a small bottle of brandy and took the cork out. Pouring a large splash of it into a tin dipper, he brought it over and offered it to her.

"Take a few swallows of this," he ordered.

She stared blankly at the bottle. "Are you sure it's not drugged? That's how all of this started."

"Hey. Look at me."

She trembled again as she lifted her gaze to his. His cobalt eyes searched hers with probing depth.

"You're safe now. Drink this, Soph—Your Highness. You're as white as a ghost. Go on. It will help."

Hearing him address her as "Your Highness" once again was not an encouraging sign. He was keeping his distance, she realized.

But after what she had put him through, not even her royal self possessed the audacity to object. Taking the dipper from him without argument, she lowered her gaze and did as she was told.

"Just sit there and relax for a while," he said in his terse, no-nonsense way, still in commander mode it seemed. "You'll feel better in a bit."

Sophia was not about to argue. Sipping the fiery liquor, she grimaced at how strong it was, while Gabriel took the bottle and walked toward the hanging blanket.

"I'll give you some time alone. I'm sure you could use it. Be right out here," he muttered, then ducked out again.

Sophia frowned. It seemed as if he was the one who needed some time alone. All things considered, she couldn't blame him. She took another sip of brandy and tried to relax. Drawing her knees up to her chest where she sat, she closed her eyes for a moment and said a prayer for both Alexa and Demetrius.

As tears threatened, she sat up straight again, banishing them. If she allowed herself to start crying, she wasn't sure she'd be able to stop. She turned her thoughts toward Gabriel and wondered uneasily if he was all right.

Shaking her head at the vivid memory of the savagery he had unleashed on those quite deserving barbarians, she found herself decidedly intimidated by him in a way she had not been before. She had to admit that this side of Gabriel left her a little afraid.

She dared not let him notice her newfound trepidation. After all he had just risked for her sake, she did not think he would appreciate her cowering from him as though he were some sort of wild beast.

After she had finished the brandy, she decided to go and check on him. She rose and went outside, and found him sitting on a boulder at the edge of the cave.

He was just sitting there in the darkness, staring off into the woods and the dark, starry horizon above them, a million miles away. *Where are you right now?* she wondered. *Come back to me.*

He took a large swig from the bottle. She frowned in concern and reached out to lay her hand on his shoulder as she approached, but when she saw him tremble once with the lingering aftermath of violence, she thought better of it. She did not dare risk startling him.

With a certain degree of caution, she joined him, uninvited. Going over to his side, she crouched down slowly, resting one knee on the stony ground. She studied him with an upward gaze, but he kept his head down, shutting her out, as deep in his brooding as he had been that first night she had spied him from the hayloft, lighting candles in the little ruined church.

Candles for the men he had slain.

He had a strange look about him. It worried her. He seemed so remote, she did not know if he would permit her to reach him.

When she laid her hand on his knee in silent, comforting inquiry, he still did not look at her, but after a long moment, he slowly turned his palm upward where his hand rested on his thigh.

A tremor of gratitude swept through her at his silent, stoic invitation. Sophia gazed at him with her heart in her eyes as she rested her hand in his.

His fingers closed around hers with a gentleness that shook her after his ferocity up on the mountain.

"Are you . . . all right?" she murmured, dismayed by how weak the words were in expressing the fullness of her concern for him. How much she cared.

He nodded.

"Does your scar plague you?" she whispered.

He shrugged, still avoiding her searching gaze. "A little sore."

"Gabriel." When she bent her head and kissed his hand, he looked at her slowly, at last. His blue eyes focused on her as if from a great distance. "Thank you," she choked out.

She laid her head down on his thigh. Gradually, he let his hand come to rest on her hair. "Don't thank me," he said in a hollow tone. "It was my fault you had to go through all that in the first place."

"No, it's my fault *you* had to kill again. I dismissed you from your post and walked right into Alexa's trap. She knew me well enough to play upon my jealousy."

"Mine, too."

"Yours?" She lifted her head from his lap and gazed at him.

He shrugged self-consciously. "When she told me you had kissed the prince, I —"

"Kissed the prince?" she echoed. "But I didn't!"

He suddenly frowned at her. "You didn't?"

"No."

"Oh, for God's sake," he muttered, pausing with a look of extreme vexation with himself. "Well, that is what she told me, and I fell for it. And I thought that meant . . ." His words trailed off. He tried again. "I was hoping that I could forget you . . . with her. Obviously that was never going to work."

"It's over now. Please, don't be angry at yourself. It was her purpose to divide us so she could carry out her plan."

"I never would've thought she had it in her."

"Of course you didn't," Sophia said fondly. "Your chivalry causes you to look upon women tenderly. It's one of the things I find dearest about you." She gripped his hand more tightly. "We all were duped, Gabriel. Even those of us who knew her best — or thought we did. But if it's any consolation, she did not do it willingly. They threatened to kill her if she did not cooperate, poor creature."

"That I can believe," he assented. "But why didn't she come to us, and trust us with this threat?"

"She might have, if she had known how good you are. She had no way of knowing the extent of your abilities. Even Yannis looked to be in awe of you back there. You were truly magnificent tonight."

"Well, I am glad you think so," he said grimly, "but I would not blame you if you never spoke to me again."

"Nonsense, you saved my life. Gabriel, they were going to take me to Ali Pasha."

He nodded. "You said so all along, didn't you? That it was Ali Pasha behind it. You were right about that. You were right about a lot of things." He placed his hand on her shoulder and gave a tender squeeze as he gazed into her eyes. "You're safe now. That's all that matters. I'm not letting you out of my sight again. I will protect you. Always. I won't leave you, even if you've decided to marry the prince. That, Sophia, is my destiny."

She stared at him then lifted her arms around his neck and hugged him for a long moment. It felt wonderful to have him in her arms.

"I could never marry him," she whispered as Gabriel's hands alighted on her waist with a tentative touch. She did not let go, but kissed his cheek. "Even if the alliance could help Kavros, he would force the two of us apart, and I can't have that. I can't do without you, Gabriel. I need you too much."

He closed his eyes with a soulful look and laid his head down on her shoulder as she held him.

"I knew you'd come for me. I knew you would do whatever it took, even though I had fired you from your post."

"I did not come as your bodyguard," he whispered.

"I know." She hugged him a little more tightly and squeezed her eyes shut. "Oh, darling, I'm so sorry that you had to break your vow. I so did not want for you to have to do that."

"For you, gladly."

"I was trying to protect you," she confessed in a strangled voice. "Every day that's passed, I've felt a deeper bond with you. And yet everything's turning more dangerous, and you're my first line of defense. I couldn't bear to lose you, like I'd lost my father and brothers and Leon. I care for you too much. I know I'm a fool. First, I dragged you into this and then I started to realize that I wanted you out of it for fear of anything happening to you. But I knew if I told you so, you would never back down and never quit."

She sniffled, tears in her eyes. Gabriel set her back a little and searched her face.

"When I saw you with Alexa, I seized my opportunity to send you away," she confessed. "Otherwise I might not have had the strength to let you go. That's why I would not listen to your apologies, and why I would not give you a second chance. Oh, darling, I *know* you, and I know what Alexa is — was," she corrected herself, flinching. "I know she was up to her old tricks and that it wasn't your doing. But what choice did I have? Or so I thought. It seemed the only way to protect you. All this, the assassins, it's my problem, not yours. The more I care for you, the more I know that you deserve to live in peace. You deserve to be happy. That's all I wanted."

"Sophia." He said her name barely audibly as he let out a slow exhalation. "Don't you understand?" He took her face between his hands with a stare full of fierce tenderness. "Being near you makes me happy. That's all I want. I can't believe you thought you were protecting me."

"You must think it rather amusing, in hindsight," she said with a somber smile. "Obviously, you can take care of yourself. I didn't know what you were capable of — I've never seen anything like that."

"I hope you never do again. Sophia. My sweet girl." He hugged her gently. "Don't worry about protecting me. That's my job, all right?"

She returned his embrace with fresh tears in her eyes. "Please don't say you feel damned for my sake."

"No. I see it differently now."

"You do?"

He nodded and pulled her onto his lap. "It started while we were tracking you. Thanks for all of your excellent clues, by the way, you brilliant creature." He kissed her temple. "At any rate, it all came clear to me on the way up this mountain."

"What came clear?"

"It wasn't the act of killing itself that had me destined for a fiery place," he murmured in a musing tone, his gaze turning faraway. "It was the way I used to think about it and treat it, in my mind. Almost like a sport," he admitted grimly. "Not that I ever enjoyed killing. But I took a certain pride in my skill and I desired to be the best."

"What's wrong with that? Of course you want to win, especially when your life is at stake — and those of your men."

"Well, all I know is that there is a greater purpose in it for me now. What the hell do I care how much of India England controls on any given day?" He sent her a wry glance with his grim admission, but did not retract his words. Instead, he shook his head. "But saving you?" He paused. "Back at the farmhouse, I was trying to escape the past and change what I was, but tonight, I am glad of every single one of my abilities, even if I should be damned for it. Because here you are, alive and safe, and that is all I care about."

She cupped his face. "You could never be damned, Gabriel, not if there is any justice in this world or the next, and if you were, then I would go there with you and we would have a grand old time. Roasting chestnuts on the flames. As long as we were together, how bad could it be?"

He smiled at her for a long moment, his gaze moving wistfully over her face.

"What?" she murmured.

"You're adorable." He caressed her cheek, his smile fading. His touch trailed along her jaw. "All I know is that I won't deny what I am anymore. Or how I feel about you."

Butterflies danced in her belly at his words.

"You," he went on, "now, you are a cause, my beautiful friend, that I can fight for without the slightest compunction."

"Am I a cause?"

"You are," he whispered. "You know you are, one that any man would be eager to follow. So beautiful and smart. So brave, with your willingness to stand up to these bastards and to fight for something larger than yourself. You inspire me," he said haltingly. "I want to help you however I can. Not merely because the mission is just, but because of how much the whole thing means to you . . . and how much you mean to me."

His words melted her. "I thought you said a bodyguard can't do his job if there are . . . emotional entanglements."

"Yes, well, that is one school of thought on the matter."

"There's another?"

"To my mind, there is." He took her hand and kissed it. "When a man cares intensely, that can also be a formidable weapon."

"Is that what I saw tonight?"

He nodded, a steely hardness flickering in his eyes with the recollection of the violence he had wreaked on the enemy. Then he shook his head, lowering his gaze. "God, I have been trying so hard to keep you at arm's length."

"Why?"

"Because you are a royal princess! You will be a queen —"

"So? I am also a woman."

"Believe me, I know."

"I have yearned to be closer to you."

"And I you. Sophia, I've never felt this way before about anyone — but if an alliance with Denmark is going to be what's best for Kavros —"

"I am what's best for Kavros," she whis-

487

pered emphatically. "And you're what's best for me — and I'm what's best for you. I know I am." She lifted his chin with her fingertips, forcing him to meet her gaze. She searched his eyes, unable to hold back her heart any longer. "I love you. Oh, Gabriel, I've loved you ever since your first conversation with that silly kitten."

Staring at her intensely, he lifted his hand to caress her face with the lightest touch. He looked overwhelmed by her words, and shook his head. "I will always be yours." He shuddered. "I thought I'd lost you."

"No. You saved me. Just like I knew you would. We belong together, Gabriel. Tell me you know it, too."

"I love you, Sophia. I am so caught up in you I could die for want of you."

"Don't die. You've already done that," she teased in a low tone. "You came back to live for me, live *with* me. As my husband, and my mate."

"How can I be your husband?" he asked barely audibly, his expression guarded but his soulful eyes so full of longing.

"Darling," she chided, "you think too much. Kiss me."

He did. As his lips pressed hers, she could feel his trembling restraint. It maddened her. Why was he still holding back even now? It would not do.

She gripped his shoulders and deepened the kiss, parting his lips with a hungry stroke of her tongue. He moaned as she invaded his delicious mouth. She cupped his face so he could not turn away from her in all his blasted chivalry.

"You're still holding back?" she whispered after a long moment, her heart pounding after that passionate kiss.

Finally, he blurted out what was bothering him. "I just can't believe you'd still want me after what you saw me do up on that mountain."

She lifted her eyebrows. "Is that what's wrong?" Then she frowned, realizing that he felt exposed. "Surely you are not ashamed of it."

"Not ashamed." He shrugged, looking away. "But it is a bad business, and I wish you had not seen it. That's all."

"Gabriel, Leon prepared me for this, and so have all the losses I've known. These were evil men. They deserved what they got," she answered in a hard tone. "And for my part, I shall never be too cowardly to look and see and know what you and all those like you sacrifice for people like me and for the greater good."

He eyed her intently as he listened.

"What you make yourselves become may be dark and terrible, but it is beautiful at the same time, you know. Your selflessness, your courage. You are what the poets call sublime, my love. You see? I understand . . . you. And there is no part of you that I cannot love. I want all of you. Even your ferocity. Yes, I want that, too," she whispered. "Let me taste it. I know you'd never hurt me."

"Never," he echoed hoarsely.

"I want to belong to you," she murmured as she held him. "No matter what may lie ahead. I need you, Gabriel." She paused for a long moment, staring into his eyes. "Make love to me." She saw him hesitate one last time, but she clutched at his black jacket, pulling him closer. "Don't push me away! Not even for honor's sake. I know you will say I'm a princess, but I am still a human being — I'm a woman, and you are the man I love. My royal blood does not make me some divinity, above the needs that others feel. By God, if you can't see past the crown, I will throw it away and go back to your farm with you, or India, or anywhere —"

"Don't talk like that."

"I don't care," she whispered in trembling defiance. "There is no point in anything if

490

we are not together."

"Then we shall be." He drew her hands to him and placed one on his chest while he kissed the other in burning hunger. "Sophia, I want you so much."

"Do you?"

"Love you," he breathed against her fingertips.

"Yes. Take me to you, my wolf, my warrior. Lay me down."

He raised her off his lap without another word and rose, leading her back into the cave.

The moment she followed him into the dimly lit intimacy of their shelter, he pulled her to him and swept her into his arms. As his mouth swooped down on hers, both of them were already on fire. Sophia moaned under his ravishing kiss while he dragged her clothes off her slowly and laid her down on the mound of furs.

She tore his jacket off his shoulders, but first he had to remove an assortment of holsters, sheaths, and his ammunition belt. When he had fought his way free of his personal arsenal, he ripped off his jacket and threw it against the wall. Sophia helped him with his black shirt. He peeled it off over his head and when he gathered her to him again, she whimpered with desire at the feel of his hot, bare skin against hers. The taut, supple power of his hard muscled chest against the yielding softness of her breasts seemed to entrance them both.

Sophia was so aroused she almost felt that she might faint. She relaxed more deeply into their primal bed while Gabriel kissed his way down her neck and made a feast of her body, on his hands and knees above her.

Her chest heaved and her skin tingled as his lips traveled down her chest, her waist, her hips and thighs, skimming every curve. She cried out in pleasure, arching under him as he claimed her swollen nipple; his hot, wet mouth kissed and sucked it firmly before moving to its twin. Mere moments had passed and he already had her writhing. She had not realized how much her body had hungered for him and savored the memory of his hands, or how well she had remembered the skills and sensations he had begun teaching her that night at the farmhouse. She was so ready for more.

She raked her fingers through his hair, letting him slide more deeply between her legs. His hand grazed expertly down her side. Somehow she was naked now except for the knife strapped to her thigh, but never breaking his kiss, his clever fingers unbuckled the strap and took her last defenses away. After setting her weapon aside, his hand returned to her thigh. Her heart slammed in her chest as his smooth touch ran up the inside of her leg. Gabriel all but sobbed with need as he found her core drenched with anticipation.

Kissing her with fierce, impassioned depth, he reached down and quickly unfastened his black leather riding breeches. Sophia helped him, caressing his waist; her hand glided downward over his taut, quivering abdomen, glorying in every chiseled ridge and steely contour. He reached back for the nearest blanket, pulling it up over them, while Sophia groaned as her wandering hand came to the thick base of his cock, sprung up huge and hard from amid the thatch of coarse hair at his groin.

Her hand closed around his shaft. He shuddered violently as she stroked upward. The length of him seemed never-ending, inch by inch, and she wanted it in her.

He let her play for a moment longer, but then, with an air of thrilling command, he captured her hands and gripped them gently above her head on the luxurious furs. He kissed her neck as he entered her slowly.

Her body accepted him with a hero's welcome. He was burning and tense, as hard and as smooth as forged steel as he claimed her. She watched him helplessly, panting; the glance he gave her brimmed with so much pent-up need and emotion.

"Love you," he breathed again as he lowered his head and glided his lips atop hers with a sweet, nuzzling kiss.

Sophia was dying for him. She knew that she had been made for this moment, this man.

His silken lips still lingering against hers, he paused when his luscious incursion reached her maidenhead.

But if Gabriel feared she was going to stop him, he was badly mistaken. He waited only long enough to afford her a brief chance to change her mind.

Her fingers splayed down his broad back and clutching at his burning shoulders gave him her answer, assuring him that she had no such intention. His chest heaved against hers; he lunged; she let out a small, fierce cry against his mouth, welcoming the pain of being joined to him at last.

He kissed her with slow, tender deliberation while she trembled beneath him, overwhelmed by the mix of pleasure, pain, and the heady knowledge that her mate had claimed her as his own. She had marked him with her virgin blood.

There was no turning back for them now.

He remained with her, still and gentle,

holding her in the glorious safety of his arms. "I adore you," he breathed.

She could not say why his tender whisper brought tears to her eyes, as if her heart was breaking. Or maybe it was finally being healed from so many losses, so many years of isolation. She could only pet him and hold him, too choked by the lump of emotion in her throat to utter more than his beloved name. *"Gabriel."*

"I'll always belong to you, sweet. Does it hurt?"

"Doesn't matter. I love you."

He closed his eyes and kissed her brow, holding back his desire with a will until she was ready.

It didn't take long. She shrugged off the pain despite his enormous size. He had waited so long — they both had. She did not want to put either of them through another minute's torment. All she wanted was to give herself to him completely.

Again, she let her body tell him when she was prepared for more. He was toying with her hair, which she was sure must look thoroughly untamed after two days without a brush. She kissed his cheek and then nibbled his iron jaw, where a dark scruff had begun to form, rather like the one he had worn at the farmhouse.

"More, please," she growled in pleasure.

He flashed a roguish half smile at her quick recovery.

"My girl," he murmured in fond pride. He settled down onto his elbows, planting them on either side of her head as he went on stroking her hair. "You're a fighter, too, Sophia. That's why we belong together." His lazy smile turned sober. "I'm so lucky to have found you. Of all the farmhouses I could have leased."

"Darling, it was fate," she said, then drew him down to kiss her anew.

He began to love her with a slow, tender rocking. She draped her arms around his neck, her lips lingering against his jaw. His taut panting by her ear as he caressed her made her realize that he was still holding himself back.

That was the last thing she wanted.

She wrapped her legs around him, offering all she had to give to slake his starved needs. A groan whispered from his lips. He turned his head and captured her mouth in a wild kiss, rising up on his hands above her, his disciplined restraint eroding.

Yes. Sophia welcomed his deepening strokes, his quickening pace, arching with him in fearless union.

She gritted her teeth as the pleasure-pain

intensified. Her eager acquiescence gave him full permission to let go completely. He did.

He took her by storm, on the verge of hurting her but never crossing that line. Sophia dragged her trembling fingers down his iron chest, nearly sobbing with his beauty as he ravished her.

Forces, instincts as deep and ancient as the earth, surged through them as their bodies joined in this desperate, needy coupling that they both had craved for so long. She braved the full brunt of his warrior power, absorbing his aggression into her love, turning it to pleasure, to release, all the while knowing he would keep her safe no matter what.

All the terror and pain of the last two days was forgotten as they reveled in each other, affirming their survival, grasping life and lust and their love for each other with both hands.

A thrilling notion trailed through her mind. She hoped he made her pregnant. Together they would restart her family line after it had been nearly obliterated.

The thought aroused her so deeply that it heightened her pleasure still more. Her senses rose to the climax he had taught her to understand that night at the farmhouse.

She could feel her hunger building.

"Gabriel."

His ragged whisper by her ear guided her closer. "Come to me, angel. Surrender."

She gasped with bliss and looked into his eyes in innocent astonishment as pleasure crested through her; her lashes drifted downward, her body undulated slowly beneath him. The spectacular wave crashed over every inch of her body. He slammed her like the earthquakes she remembered from her childhood in Greece, the same brief, bewildering powerlessness as his passion overcame him almost simultaneously. He climaxed with a lion's roar, arching above her in triumph as he flooded her with his seed.

Her breath heaving, Sophia gazed at him in awe.

The soul-deep delight etched upon his face in the next moment would remain imprinted on her mind forever. Oh, the pride that welled in her to know that she had won him, this marvelous beast.

The pleasure seemed to drip from him, every sound from his lips, every flinch of delight, the flicker of total release in his eyes, until he was emptied.

"Come here," she murmured, pulling him down atop her and holding him, while he struggled to retrieve his wits after the explosion of pleasure.

"Oh, God," he said breathlessly after the fact.

Sophia let out a dazzled, weary laugh. "I love you."

"Love you. I'm sorry if I was too rough," he panted. "It's been — a long time."

"I adored it. I adore you."

"You all right?"

"I'm in heaven. Get some rest, Colonel."

He let out a growly sort of sigh full of satisfaction and dragged one last caress down her hair to her shoulder. Then he closed his eyes and obeyed her order.

With his slackening arousal still nestled peacefully inside of her, she held him, slowly caressing his bare back, running her fingers through his black hair. His lips rested softly against her neck, the fierce panting gradually turning to slow, steady breaths.

At last, her warrior was in a state of deep and very long-needed relaxation. For her part, she was too happy to sleep.

"I love you," she whispered again. She couldn't stop saying it now that she was allowed to.

"Mm," he answered in a deep purr, just enough of a reply to let her know that he was still slightly awake, enough to spring to her defense again if need be, she thought with a tender smile.

His big body lay atop her as though he were made of lead, but she did not mind at all. They were together now as they should have been from the start, she thought, and finally, the world made sense again.

As she lifted her gaze, watching the shadows from their low fire play over the rock formations, she spied some of the ancient cave paintings that were said to exist all throughout the Dordogne.

Nobody really knew who had made them or just how old they were, but as she peered up at the childlike drawing of a bull and other animals running across the top of the cave and disappearing into the shadows and the memory of time, their message echoed to her over the innumerable ages. They hailed back to a time long before anyone had dreamed up the divine right of kings or notions of empire. In that age so shortly after Eden, kings were not decided by bloodlines, she mused, but by who was the strongest, who was the bravest, who was the smartest, and the best leader.

People would have happily followed whoever had the greatest chances of keeping the whole group alive.

Dawning recognition stole over Sophia's

face as she held Gabriel tenderly and pressed another soft kiss to his looming shoulder. Her mind reeled and her heart soared, for she understood better than he did in that moment why he had been spared, sent back from the brink of death. What his true destiny had been all along.

My king.

CHAPTER TWENTY

Princess Sophia of Kavros.

Her Royal Highness.

HRH

Too beautiful for words, and Gabriel could not believe he had deflowered her. Still wonderstruck, he watched her sleep in tender silence as the new day dawned.

Making love to her had been the most sacred and glorious thing he had ever done — and possibly the most depraved.

After all of her losses, it was mad of him, perhaps even cruel to risk getting so much closer when he still had the outcast Janissary army to vanquish and might well not survive. Deep down, ever since he had nearly lost his life, he had sensed that a fate like this was probably waiting for him not far down the line.

If death claimed him in the coming battle, then Gabriel had to face the fact that he, who loved her best, would have ended up wounding Sophia worse than the enemy could ever hope to do. Bereaving her just when she most needed to be strong for her people.

Ah, but she would never have forgiven him if he had denied her last night. Nor *could* he. Even he wasn't that strong. He could no longer fight his feelings for her, the sheer overwhelming love. His heart welled even now as he gazed at her in sweet repose. Her silky midnight spiral curls fanned out around her while she slept trustfully beside him, her hand curled into a loose fist beneath her chin.

With a lump in his throat at how dear she was to him and how close he had come to losing her to those fiendish bastards, he could not bring himself to believe that their blessed act of love last night had been wrong.

But whether it had been sin or pure redemption, it was what they both had wanted. Today, he was still reeling with such a strange blend of happiness and ferocity over the lingering threat to her. Watching her here with him, safe and sound, still dazed by the poetry of her body beneath his last night, Gabriel made up his mind to shelter her from any additional ugliness until they reached the coast.

There was no need to tell her yet about the full scope of the threat from the Order of the Scorpion. She had already been through enough for now and would need a few days to recover before he told her just how bad it was.

He only hoped that the Royal Marines stationed on Kavros would be ready for action by the time his scouts returned with the location of the Janissaries' hideaway.

When Sophia began to stir, he thrust his ominous thoughts out of his head and focused his mind on his plans for the lady. It wouldn't take long to reach the Mediterranean, but he fully intended to spend the next two days attending to her every pleasure.

God knew, just watching her was quite the delight of his life. Her eyelashes fluttered with waking; Gabriel looked on in soft joy, waiting to say good morning.

Her dark eyes suddenly flicked open, not fully focused yet. "Oh, God, was I snoring?" she blurted out with a start.

He flashed a smile at the unexpected greeting and lied, "Like a drunken sailor."

"Oh — I'm so embarrassed!"

"I'm teasing you," he chided, laughing as he grabbed her and rolled her playfully atop him. "Princesses don't snore, Highness.

Everybody knows that."

"Well, I'm not a princess today. Good morning, my love." She rumpled his hair with a reproachful pout for his jest and then hugged him back; he wrapped his arms around her. The way she snuggled her head into the crook of his neck simply turned him inside out. "Oh, I was so afraid to wake up and find this had all been naught but a beautiful dream. Is it real?"

"It's whatever you want it to be," he whispered, caressing her naked waist. For a long moment, he shut his eyes and reveled in the feel of her slim, lovely body atop him.

He was still ready to protect her with every fiber of his being, yet he found himself — most unusually — wanting to shirk his duty and explore this love unlike any he had ever known. Escape their normal roles, as they had at the farmhouse, and spend time together simply as a man and a woman. It would probably be their last chance.

And with her soft, lithe loveliness on top of him, once again, Gabriel found himself getting hard.

Damn, but the sense of death breathing down his neck seemed to make him uncontrollably horny. As if he must grab onto life at its very core while he still could.

Oh, give Sophia a break, he ordered his

libido, doing his best mentally to hold himself in check, as he had done for so long with her. But he loved her so much.

Whatever she wanted . . .

With his elbow resting on the bedroll, he silently put his hand up; she mirrored it, touching his palm. Their fingers linked, then he pressed a gentle kiss to her forehead. "Hungry?" he asked, distracting himself from those warm, silken thighs around him.

"Starved. What supplies did you bring for us, Colonel? Hardtack?"

"Hardtack? Mademoiselle, you're in France. No hardtack for you. Let's go and find some proper food."

She lifted her head and frowned at him. "Are you so eager to leave our little cave already?"

"Well, it is a cave," he said. "They have hotels."

"I love our cave. It's very special to me."

"Yes, but la belle France awaits, chérie." He kissed her precious hand. "It is the one true country of all lovers, don't you know."

She arched an eyebrow at him. "My stern soldier, are you going to turn out to be a romantic after all this time?"

"You'll have to wait and see," he whispered sweetly.

"I'm not sure how I feel about that," she

said archly. "I have never approved of those wild-eyed poetic types."

He laughed.

She wrapped her arms around him and wouldn't let go. Nor would she let him get up. He could not pry her off him to get the day started. Not that he tried very hard.

"Gabriel?" she mumbled, her voice muffled against his neck as she held him.

He furrowed his brow at the note of anxiety in her voice. "What's the matter, darling?"

"What if we get to Kavros and my people decide they don't like me? What if no one will listen to me? I'm only a girl. Honestly, would you tell me if you thought I had bitten off more than I could chew?"

"You'd be a fool if you weren't scared," he whispered tenderly. "But don't worry. They will fall in love with you, believe me."

She lifted her head and favored him a grateful smile. "You are so kind to me."

"I love you," he explained.

Her smile grew, beaming like the sun. "Enough of my gloom! I don't want to talk about anything serious today!"

"No, it is forbidden," he assented.

"Gabriel?" she called his name after a moment in a bewitching little singsong.

He arched a brow at the flirtatious sparkle

in her eyes. "What is it, sweet?"

When she crooked her finger at him, he quivered.

The pretty smile she gave him said it all.

He let her pull him back down gently into their bed of furs with a randy laugh and made love to her until mid-morning.

Her first time had been an experience of fierce and all-consuming passion, but her second was playful, joyous, and exploratory. Gabriel, her patient teacher, made her giddy with the lesson. Her third time — and fourth — came later that afternoon after they had strolled into the livery hotel at the next quaint little medieval *bastide* town they came to.

Arriving mainly to change horses, they ended up getting a room for the night.

Gabriel looked at her wryly when she gave their names to the landlord as Mr. and Mrs. King.

The French country inn was a cozy haven full of charm and made them welcome. While servants filled the bathing tub in their room, Sophia ordered supper for them from the kitchens. She could hardly wait to see what delicacies of the Perigord might appear when their meal was ready. Gabriel, meanwhile, sent a message to Lord Griffith that she was safe, then spoke to the innkeeper's wife about the horses they'd need from the livery on the morrow, and also where they could procure some fresh clothes.

Sophia could understand him wanting to be rid of the bloodstained black clothes he had worn on the mountain. She, too, was eager to leave behind the reminders of her abduction.

The landlady sent her eldest daughter off to see what ready-made pieces could be had from the local shops. "My firstborn," she declared, "has an eye for the mode of fashion."

The young woman came back a long while later with an armful of smart French clothes for them both, new underthings and three muslin day gowns for Sophia to choose from. For Gabriel, she had found a gentlemanly ensemble, a linen shirt of creamy white, tan trousers, and a plum-colored morning coat of fine wool.

The fit was rather tight, large as he was, but he decided to take it. The French girl looked love-struck by the dashing Englishman and offered to alter it for him by morning. He told her to do as she pleased.

"Are you sending the bill to the Foreign Office?" Sophia murmured as Gabriel wrote out a draught for the items.

"No, I am sending it on to my brother," he informed her.

"To Derek? Why?"

"Didn't I tell you? I signed over my whole inheritance to him some time ago. I might have been very rich if I hadn't."

"You did?" she echoed, amazed. "Why?"

"I was feeling generous," he said dryly.

Laughing, she put her arms around him dotingly as they walked toward the stairs leading up to the upper floors where the guest rooms awaited. "You are so wonderfully strange," she teased, recalling how she had found him out in the middle of nowhere living like some wild, brooding hermit.

At any rate, the farm was long behind them now. Upstairs, they stepped into their room, a soft-toned and cheerful retreat with a view of the garden. Under a simple brass chandelier with all four candles shining, thick plaster walls glowed a golden cream hue, with muted red-and-white toile draping the windows and the four-post bed. An oil painting hung above the waist-high chest of drawers, where glasses and a few bottles of the superb local libations had already been sent up. A cozy armchair was set against the wall. Beyond the bed, a folded wooden screen stood in the distant corner; behind it, the bathing tub awaited, filled and steaming, towels and soaps on hand. All of their needs had been anticipated.

Sophia found the place enchanting. But with their new clothes paid for, they had no intention of putting them on. Instead, they shut the door to their room and undressed, bathing together, washing each other with the fine soap scented with homegrown lavender. They made a holiday of it, hands sliding over wet, sudsy skin as they scrubbed each other clean with a slip and splash, tickle and taste, each damp caress leading to some new delightful discovery, new territory to claim, arms, legs, back, belly.

They were completely entranced with each other. Gabriel nuzzled her bent knee while she trailed her finger down the center of his face, down his handsome nose, over his lips, and down his angular chin. He captured her foot under the water, cleaned it carefully, rinsed it thoroughly, then lifted it, dripping. He kissed it several times. She watched with her temperature rising.

She knew he was up to something when he made her turn around. At first, he soaped her back for her, but his true, wicked intentions soon became clear as his hands began roaming lower. Before long, he had pushed her up onto her knees and bent her slightly over the edge of the tub, kneeling behind her as he took her, water sloshing everywhere.

Sophia groaned with pleasure; he lost patience with the cramped quarters of the tub and ordered her over to the bed. Shaking, she obeyed. Both of them still damp and slippery, he stood between her legs at the side of the bed and had his lecherous way with her, cupping the cheeks of her backside in his hands. Sophia lay back in delirious pleasure, basking in his deep penetration.

When she dragged her eyes open and gazed at his towering physique, his hard face taut with passion, she was sure there was no one like him in all the world.

He cupped her legs to his waist as he leaned down and kissed her like he would devour her. She hooked her heels behind his muscled buttocks and let him carry them both away to a new floodtide of bliss.

As they lay panting afterward, temporarily spent, they laughed to find that he had moved the bed several feet across the floor with his exertions. Sophia could barely move, enervated by pure pleasure.

Fortunately, having ordered a feast from the kitchens, their late supper arrived and now, donning the robes the hotelier had given them, they ate to keep up their strength in between bouts of making love.

They had already opened a bottle of the famed Armagnac brandy for an aperitif to sip during their bath, but when the waiter arrived, wheeling in his little cart, Sophia poured the superb Bergerac wine that had been left to breathe in anticipation of their meal. Gabriel accepted the hotel's bill of fare, tipped the waiter, and then locked their chamber door, turning to her with a devilish smile. "*Now* we'll eat."

Sophia oohed and ahhed over the hors d'oeuvre, a pâté de foie gras on fresh white toast. The foie gras made both of them moan, it was so rich and buttery-smooth, delicately flavored with the local black truffles. The entrée was a warming rabbit stew with wild mushrooms, green beans, carrots, and pearl onions from the nearby market.

The sweet course brought a cinnamon apple and walnut tart with a touch of honey, the flaky crust crumbling and light. They opened a bottle of Monbazillac for the dessert wine and brought it with them back to bed. Gabriel opted for the brandy to accompany the final course, a few bites of smoked brie on a slice of the heavenly bread, along with a clutch of green grapes.

Sophia eyed *him* hungrily, not quite sated

yet. If the last time had been his turn to do whatever he liked to her, this time, she seized the initiative and used him as she pleased. She pushed him down onto the mattress and straddled him, holding him down — not that he fought her.

He stared at her in lust; the feeling was mutual. She caressed him possessively, relishing the feel of so much muscle and brawn and pure male power between her legs, under her control. She kissed him in flagrant seduction, letting her breasts caress his chest, teasing him with her body until he was breathless, his blue eyes begging for her. She gripped his mighty erection, all virginal shyness left behind, and angled it into her waiting passage. Her most delicate flesh was admittedly tender from all of his rough exercise, but she didn't care. She wanted him again.

Needed him.

He watched her in unadulterated hunger as she rode him, seated upright while he lay on his back against the mound of pillows. When she released his hands, he placed them on her hips. His flexing arms guided her movements, until once more they both were panting and straining in the throes of passion. She collapsed on him with a small, wild scream of release. He cupped her head to muffle her cries in the pillow as ecstasy blazed through her. Before her climax had ceased, his arrived; she watched his face and held his gaze as he came to her.

By the candlelight, the flicker of sweet anguish in the depths of his eyes unlocked her heart completely. She kissed him, touching his face with trembling hands, telling him over and over that she loved him as he surrendered.

Later that night, however, she wasn't sure why — she cried. The tears came unbidden in the middle of the night when she could not sleep. Thoughts of Alexa and Demetrius, and the terror of those two days were still with her, as were all her fears about her royal destiny ahead . . . and a foreboding awareness that the danger was not over yet.

Gabriel heard her sniffles and awoke; he gathered her to him and held her as she wept. He tucked the sheets more snugly around her and dried her eyes with a dinner napkin for a handkerchief. She put her arms around him and shed her tears against his chest. His steady presence helped to calm her, though he barely said a word. He understood better than anyone the strain she had been under.

Eventually, her tears subsided, but still he held her. Around two in the morning, he kissed her forehead tenderly and whispered, "Go to sleep."

At last, she did.

By the next morning, she felt better. They dressed in their smart new French fashions and hired a post chaise with a driver and postillion so they could ride together in the carriage for the remainder of their journey to the Mediterranean coast.

Traveling under the pretense of being newlyweds, they set out early and admired the picturesque French countryside as it went on about its day. They spotted a little boy driving a flock of big gray geese that waddled across the lazy meandering road ahead. Some nuns were readying their convent garden for the winter. Now and then the road humped up gently over an ancient Roman bridge across a stream; the occasional flatboat passed at a leisurely pace, taking its goods to Bordeaux or some other port town.

It was easy to while away the hours in this rural idyll, but her insatiable lover had his own ideas about how to pass the time. Gabriel drew her onto his lap with a wicked half smile that she was coming to know all too well.

There was a particular manly dimple that appeared in his left cheek when he was feeling roguish and about to misbehave.

"Oh, darling, we really shouldn't," she protested unconvincingly as he caressed her with obvious intent.

Blast, but she could not resist the man.

"Give me one good reason why," he whispered as he nibbled her shoulder and discreetly lifted her skirts. "I want you."

She closed her eyes, melting against him. Facing forward while sitting on his lap, she laid her head back on his shoulder. He reached inconspicuously under the billowy mass of her gown and petticoat, and freed his rigid manhood from his trousers. No one was the wiser as Sophia draped her knees apart; beneath her skirts, cloaking their true activities, she soon could feel her bare backside against his now exposed loins. Her heart raced as he slid his throbbing hardness into her already wet passage.

He rocked her with slow, leisurely enjoyment as the carriage rolled along. His arms around her waist, his kisses at her neck, his member sheathed inside her, all filled her with the most exquisite sensations.

Unfortunately, neither of them realized they were coming up to another little country town right in the middle of market day. The weekly vendors thronged the main road through the town. There were no blinds on the carriage windows, though the glass panes were closed. Sophia panicked. People could see right into the windows! Her skirts concealed the fact that his hardness was thrust deep inside her, but — nevertheless!

"What should I do?" she whispered frantically.

"Just enjoy the ride," he drawled in a breathless tone. "I know I will."

"Gabriel Knight!"

"It's France. Who's going to care?"

"I am the Princess Royal of Kavros —"

"No, you're my pretty plaything at the moment."

She groaned, loving the sound of that.

"God, don't stop."

"Oh — there's a priest! I hope he doesn't see us."

"Just act natural."

"This is indecent."

"Relax," he whispered, laughing, but he would not let her up off his lap. He held her impaled upon his shaft.

Her pulse galloped while the carriage wound slowly through the town. The vendors came up to the window as they rolled by, trying to sell them their goods.

"N-no, thank you. Merci, non!" Sophia declined with an air of desperation. Her cheeks were bright red, filled with a hectic blush.

"You're doing great," he taunted.

"I'm going to strangle you for this."

"That could be fun. There, darling. Buy some nice French bread from this chap. I'll bet you like the shape."

"You're a demon," she answered under her breath as the fellow from the baker's shop pressed in to sell them a long, hard baguette. When Sophia handed over a few sous with trembling hands, the baker's man frowned.

"Is your lady ill, monsieur?"

She could not speak, he was so deep.

"Fever," Gabriel forced out.

"Eh, there is a physician in the town."

"Non, non," he said, "I will tend her myself."

Sophia bit back a moan.

"Ahh," the man said with a sudden, hearty laugh and a knowing wink as understanding dawned. "Excusez-moi, monsieur. Merci beaucoup. So sorry to interrupt."

"You didn't," he muttered. "Oh, God, drive on!" he yelled at the coachman, sounding rather out of breath.

"Let them pass! Let the lovers pass!" the baker's man announced, waving them through the crowd with a grin from ear to ear.

Cheeky French humor. Laughter abounded as the people cheered and got out of the way.

As soon as they had cleared the town, Sophia held onto the leather hand-loop above the carriage window, supporting herself as Gabriel finished the deed.

"Oh, God — are you trying to get me pregnant?" she asked, out of breath and resting against him after their enthusiasm.

"That would be nice."

"Mmm, it would." She turned and pressed her lips to his in dreamy rapture.

Ending the kiss, he gazed tenderly into her eyes, and in that moment, Sophia felt as if her life was now complete.

When they reached the Mediterranean, neither of them was very happy to see it.

Their mood changed from romantic euphoria to one of more somber intimacy as they each contemplated what still lay ahead. They walked the beach at sunset, hand in hand, and barely spoke. Beside them rolled the jade expanse, its crop of lazy sailboats bobbing gently on the waves.

Gabriel was trying to figure out how to broach the subject of the threat from the

Order of the Scorpion when Sophia turned to him abruptly, her cheeks pink with the breeze.

"I want to thank you for saving my life," she said earnestly.

He kissed her hand and smiled. "Thank you for loving me," he answered.

She gazed wistfully at him and brushed her blowing hair out of her face. "It's easy."

"You make me so happy," he whispered, assisting. He tucked the curl behind her ear for her.

At once, it blew free again. That mane of hers had a mind of its own, like the rest of the strong-willed lady, he thought in amusement.

"Gabriel?" She clasped his hand in hers and moved closer. "There's something that I need to ask you."

"Such serious eyes," he murmured, furrowing his brow with a tender look as he studied her. "What is it, love?"

She stared back at him, her velvety brown eyes huge and earnest. "Do you plan to marry me?"

He blinked. "Of course! What do you take me for, darling? None of this would have been happening if that were not my intention."

I'm just not sure if Fate is going to cooper-ate.

Before he could qualify his statement, relief burst across her face. Blushing, she laughed at herself almost nervously. "I'm sorry. It's not that I doubted you, it's just that you never mentioned it — oh, Gabriel, let's go and do it right now!"

"Now?"

"That way no one can stop us! Oh, I so want to be your wife. What have you done to me?" she asked as she clung to him in doting affection. "I used to be too terrified even to think of sharing my position with a man before you. But I trust you so much. I know you would never betray me. I want to rule equally with you by my side, equal in every way."

He gazed at her for a long moment. "Are you sure that's how you see me? As your equal?"

"Yes, of course!"

"What about divine right and all that?"

"Oh, that's nonsense! Our quality is proved by what we do. And you have done marvelous things," she said with a sigh.

"What about Kavros?"

"My people will only benefit from the two of us being together. With your strengths and my strengths combined, think of it! We will make the country whole again in no time."

Moved by her faith in him, he captured her chin on his fingertips and tilted her head back to press a soft kiss to her lips. She smiled as his kiss ended and he slowly straightened up again.

"So, what do you think?" she murmured. She squeezed his hands with an eager little laugh. "Shall we go get married? There must be twenty churches in this town. Where are we, anyway?"

"Perpignan. Sophia," he said in a cautious tone, "I think we'd better wait a bit."

"But why?"

"Darling, with all that is at stake, we both must think practically. The Foreign Office as well as the local powers on Kavros could challenge the marriage if it's not done out in the open, in front of everyone. You know I am yours. Don't scowl, it happened to Prinny. Remember?"

She lowered her head.

"The world found out that he had married his Catholic mistress when he was only, what, twenty-one? It was a great scandal and in the end, they forced him to put her away — and he's a man. With you as the royal personage, being a woman, I cannot even think what they would do if they didn't like our match. They'd say I had swindled you for wealth and power — and even worse, you'd be deemed an easy virtue! Your loss of credibility and authority, in turn, means that Kavros would suffer."

She turned away.

"You could lose the throne if we are too hasty, and I won't let that happen to you. Your people need you, and I think you need them."

She sent him a soulful glance over her shoulder.

He moved closer. "I adore you for wanting me so much, but you already have me. And protecting you also means forcing you to think things through," he added in a soft tone, brushing her hair behind her shoulder with an intimate touch.

"Well, when you put it like that . . . I suppose I can be patient," she conceded with a glum look.

"Good. Because —" Gabriel hesitated, then braced himself and took a deep breath. "There is another aspect to all this that I haven't yet told you about."

He briefly related the information that he had shaken out of the Turkish ambassador after she went missing. He told her what they knew about the Order of the Scorpion and how he had purposely ordered her

Greek bodyguards to leave the one wounded Janissary alive so that they could track him to the villains' headquarters.

"I gave that mission to Timo. He took Niko with him and they're to report back to me as soon as they are able. When we find these devils," he said in a hard tone, "we are going after them."

"I see." She absorbed this in silence. "You plan to be a part of the attack?"

"Hell, yes."

"But I don't want you to risk —"

"Darling," he interrupted firmly. "You know me better than that." He paused. "Think of it as my way of trying to show your people I am worthy of you."

"But you *are* worthy of me! You don't need to prove it to anyone! You could be killed! No, I forbid you from taking part —"

He silenced her with a finger over her lips. "Need I remind you what happened the last time you tried to protect me? All hell broke loose, as I recall."

She jerked away from him. "I'm not going to let you die! Do you hear?"

"Sophia, you'll be a queen, but you are not God. If I am called, then I must go. When it's over, I will do whatever you want. As soon as this threat is put down. In our hearts, we already belong to each other, but if I were to fall, then you must marry someone else. And quickly. For the sake of any . . . child we might have created," he forced out with a pang. "Even — the prince of Denmark — if you must."

"Have you lost your wits?" she cried. "Denmark? After what he did to his wife?"

"Yes, well, I'm confident that you are smarter than he is."

"I cannot believe we are even discussing this!"

"I'm sorry, Sophia." He shook his head stubbornly, refusing to budge. "I could not resist you anymore. I need you too much. Nor would I take it back for all the world, loving you. But now I have to see this through. You are in danger, and by God, I will tear them apart before I let them hurt you. But if I marry you now, and then I die, the fact that your dead husband was your bodyguard is hardly going to win you any suitors."

"Gabriel!"

"Better that you should lie about us than face public censure and disgrace."

"Do you think I want to live if these bastards kill you?" she whispered. He could see her shaking.

"You have to. Especially if there's a babe."

"I think you want to die," she accused him. "You want to go back to your precious Light, your angels. You don't want to promise anything because you don't want to get dragged down onto this miserable earth once more! I'm not a fool! That's why you gave your brother your money, isn't it? That's why you swore never to kill again, why you fought me so hard. Don't you love me enough to want to stay alive?"

"Of course I love you, and of course I don't want to die! Don't be absurd! But I should despise myself entirely if I ever cowered behind you."

"Still your warrior pride takes precedence."

"My love for you is everything," he ground out fiercely, glaring at her.

"Love? How could you be so cruel to me? Making me love you so much I could die without you? How could you do this to me?"

"You didn't give me much choice." The more she eroded his certainty, the more he hardened his resolve. "Sophia, I will handle this threat, I assure you. But you're going to have to be strong. Whatever happens to me, you need to stand for your people. Everyone is threatened by these monsters."

"But I want you to stay with me. I don't understand why you think you must go!

There are plenty of other soldiers —"

"No. Don't even travel down that road, my love. It will lead you nowhere. It's not just you, my darling love, whose life is at stake," he whispered, forcing himself to take a gentler tone. "It's more than even Kavros."

She looked at him in question, teary-eyed.

He shook his head. "Why do you think the Order of the Scorpion wants your island chain? The same reason Napoleon did, and the Russians, and the Austrians, and us."

Her face turned pale as she absorbed his words. "Are you saying that these men have designs on all of Europe?"

"Not for their own power-lust, of course, but for Allah," he answered dryly. "Now you understand the true threat we are dealing with."

"Oh, God," she breathed, looking away.

"Be brave," he ordered her. "We both have our roles to play in this. You didn't want a lapdog, and I expect more from you than some carefree Gypsy girl."

"The Iron Major," she murmured in a bitter tone, then sent him an accusing glance. "No mercy?"

He looked her in the eyes, and in that moment, Sophia knew it was as useless to try to dissuade him from his duty as it would have been to try to talk her out of claiming her destiny.

"None," he answered.

God, she loved him, even as he dashed her hopes upon the rocks. She closed her eyes and lowered her head, fighting tears.

A thought of Leon trailed through her mind, her hardheaded old mentor taking her sternly in hand at their fencing practice. *"Come! I'm not going to baby you. Your enemies won't! Now try again."*

"Sophia?" Gabriel murmured, watching her. "It was not my intention to hurt you."

"You never wanted to kill anyone again," she reminded him in angry reproach.

"Yes." He did not flinch. "Until they came after you."

It was pointless. He was stone. She shook her head, at a loss, and walked away.

Gabriel let her go; he seemed to understand her need to be alone right now, and in truth, he probably fared no better than she behind his stoic façade.

All she knew was that the time had come to be a princess. And if this was what it was going to be like, then maybe she should have opted for the lounging life of exiled royalty.

They hadn't even reached Kavros yet, and the crown was already proving to be so much heavier to bear than she had ever expected. But it was too late now. The Iron Major could have worn it without bending, but now she did not know if he would even be by her side in a month or so.

If her duty took her love from her, if she must sacrifice even her mate for Kavros, then, at least, God willing, she would have his babe.

She went into their hotel room alone, folded her arms across her belly, and wept like an orphaned child — which, in fact, she had been, not so many years ago.

CHAPTER
TWENTY-ONE

Gabriel hated himself for having to be so hard.

When he had come into their hotel room at Perpignan and found her with her eyes red and puffy, his leaden heart had sunk further, but she would not share her tears with him as she had the previous night at the country inn.

What could he do but let her treat him however she needed to? This whole ordeal was going to be difficult enough for her. He didn't want to make it any worse. His calm, respectful manner in the following two days showed, he hoped, that he was there for her if she wanted him. But he kept a safe distance in case she did not.

God, he wished he had never had to say those things, advising her to marry someone else if he fell in the coming battle. He hated the thought of his woman with anyone else. And if he let himself dwell on the possibility of her giving birth to their child nine months hence, he became dismayed by the idea of not being there to raise his son or daughter.

But he told himself to calm down. To take it one step at a time. There was no reason for his ominous intimations of death. He quite knew how to handle a sword, after all. And besides, there was no point in distracting his mind with such a monumental question when it was still too soon to know if she was with child. *But what the hell, then?*

What the hell was he going to do? The mere notion of absentee fatherhood offended every atom of his being. It violated his sense of duty as a protector and turned his precious cavalry honor to ashes in his mouth.

He almost wished that he had never touched her. But he would not have traded the past couple of days with her for the rule of Heaven itself. Sophia owned him now in body and soul. He had never known such happiness as he had tasted in those brief hours, nor had he loved like this in all his life.

Whether he'd live to enjoy it for years, or if those most capricious hags of Greek myth, the Fates, had nearly finished weaving his little thread of the great tapestry — that remained to be seen.

In the meantime, he got them onto a good, seaworthy fishing boat and paid for their passage to Kavros, still traveling incognito as newlyweds.

Presently, the island chain his little "bride" would rule unfurled ahead.

Stark and dramatic crags of earth-brown rock climbed from surrounding waters of brilliant blue intensity. The sharp white of the hilltop town spilled down the shoulder of the main island like the curl of the white breakers smashing into the island's rugged approaches.

Great chunks of stone made it treacherous going for boats unfamiliar with these waters. The British Navy had stationed its base over in the deepwater harbor, where the way was clear, but elsewhere — all around, among, between the various size islands of Kavros — these giant useless boulders loomed, tossed at random, as if Cyclops had had a temper tantrum.

With the sails billowing overhead, Gabriel ignored the rowdy fishermen trying to capture a shark that had glided by, making a pass at their bulging nets, and continued to study this country he might either move to or die for.

Kavros Town was an irregular collection of bleached white boxes — houses and shops — all piled and jumbled together along the angle of the hill. Dominating all was the smoothly rounded blue dome of the cathedral with its gleaming cross on top.

Clusters of deep green olive trees skirted the town and the hills here and there, giving the scrambling goats a little shade. He spotted the ruins of an ancient something or other — only the outline of the sand-strewn foundations and a few marble columns were left standing.

As they came closer, he spotted an impressive hilltop palace above a beach of glorious white sands. Sophia had mentioned the sprawling Mediterranean royal villa where she had grown up. To the best of his knowledge, it had been sealed up tightly ever since the royal family's exile. On the beach below it, a collection of lazy fishing boats bobbed here and there, the sun-browned men done with the bulk of their work by midday.

With any number of questions he wanted to ask her, Gabriel glanced at Sophia to read her reaction to this first sight of her homeland after all these years.

But when he saw her face, his friendly questions withered on his tongue.

Her expression was muted, her stare faraway. Her taut, serious expression was more foreboding than happy, or even sentimental. He supposed he should not be surprised. Still, he was worried about her. "Are you all right?" he murmured cautiously.

She just looked at him.

She hadn't had much to say to him since their argument on the beach at Perpignan. She hadn't turned hostile at all, only cool and distant and withdrawn. He almost would have rather had her angry at him. Her temper was something he could deal with. This distance . . . she was shutting him out and he didn't know how to respond.

She stared forward again.

Frustration surged through his veins. Eyeing her beside him, Gabriel abandoned his attempt at conversation and decided to keep his mind fixed on his task — getting her safely to shore.

Their first destination was the naval base, and as they approached, Gabriel saw it was much like the ones in India and Africa and the Caribbean and all the other spots around the world where Britain ruled the waves.

With the Union Jack flying above it, the base's cannons bristled from the thick stone ramparts. He did not see as many Navy vessels in the harbor as he had expected and realized the big warships must be out on patrol.

The sheer power and force that the first-rates represented with all their bristling gun-decks were a major factor in keeping order throughout the Mediterranean. They held the Barbary pirates away from the merchant ships trundling past, kept petty rivals in the region from sneaking into each other's back gardens, and generally made sure that everyone played nice together, Gabriel mused. He rested his hands on the rails, waiting as the fishing boat drifted to a halt, and watching patiently as the Navy cutter scuttled forth to intercept them.

Nobody got much closer than this to the base without first speaking to the lads in charge of the harbor. And if they didn't like your answers, you were politely invited to leave.

When the cutter pulled up alongside the fishing boat, Gabriel gave the officers his name, but not Sophia's, and asked permission for him and his "wife" to come aboard.

She flinched a little at the words; he could not bear to look at her.

"Commander Blake has been expecting us for some time," he informed them. "We are his cousins from Nottinghamshire."

"Nottinghamshire?" the young lieutenant

exclaimed with a grin at the mention of that familiar place. "Welcome, sir." Seeing that he was English, they let him and his missus aboard.

Gabriel thanked the fisherman, who looked on with nosy and suspicious curiosity while Sophia climbed down the ladder into the cutter. The sailors helped her into the boat, and when she was secure, Gabriel followed her down.

Once aboard the cutter, Gabriel produced the Foreign Office papers informing the crew who she really was.

The sailors' eyes turned as round as English teacups, and the usual bowing and scraping began. It seemed to pain Sophia, this return to her Royal status, but she accepted their homage with her usual grace.

He supposed she had good reason to be upset. This was not how the princess royal was to have arrived to accept her throne. There was to have been great pomp and ceremony, celebrations, music, flower petals, speeches, and an army of attendants disembarking from the treasure ship scheduled to bring her people all the supplies they had been missing.

Instead, thanks to the action of her enemies, she had arrived in secret with nothing but the clothes on her back and one scoundrel of a bodyguard, he thought, who had some gall to show his face here, considering he was delivering the luscious beauty back to her nation, sans virtue.

Rather than announcing her royal presence, they kept up their pretense as ordinary visitors from England all the way into the base, where out in the commons, the sergeants were drilling their troops. Hearing the rhythmic bellows of their commands, Gabriel felt a twinge of nostalgia for his regiment; Sophia faltered, meanwhile, when she first stepped on Kavros soil. He reached out to steady her, but then she appeared to remind herself that the base was officially a little piece of England transplanted here. She nodded her thanks to him and then walked on.

"Sir!" the lieutenant exclaimed upon delivering them to Commander Blake. "Your *cousins* from *Nottinghamshire* are here!"

Wink.

Why, the precious boy seemed to think this was some mysterious code rather than just a quick lie that Gabriel had made up on the spot. Gabriel smiled wryly and explained himself to the sunburned Scot in charge of the Adriatic base. Commander Blake made them welcome, but even he gazed at Sophia in awe as he offered the lady a chair.

"Would you please send for the Archbishop Nectarios, Commander?" Sophia asked when the three of them were closeted in Blake's private office. "He counseled my father and baptized me and my brothers when we were babes. I shall be counting on him to make the introductions between me and my people."

"At once, Your Highness," Commander Blake replied with a gallant bow. He opened the door to his office and ordered his clerk to send a carriage for the old holy man and bring him here, posthaste.

"I hope the manner of our arrival does not cause undue inconvenience," Sophia said with dignified reserve.

"Not at all, Your Highness. All of Kavros has been anxiously awaiting you."

"I did not deem it prudent to notify you ahead of time about when, where, and how we would arrive in case the message were intercepted," Gabriel said sternly. "We have been traveling incognito, as you can see." Then he took a few moments to explain how Sophia had been kidnapped by the Janissaries, along with the still looming threat from the Order of the Scorpion.

Sophia had asked him previously not to

reveal Alexa's role in the abduction, so Gabriel left that part out. Because Alexa's ancestors had been loyal for generations, Sophia had generously decided that the girl's whole family did not deserve to be disgraced due to the treachery of one.

Commander Blake was still looking at him in amazement when he finished his account and folded his arms across his chest. "This might be a good time to ask how many men you have under your command," Gabriel added in a dry tone.

"Normally, two hundred," Blake replied, "but right now, I'm afraid I'm down to only fifty." He glanced guardedly at Sophia, as though unsure if it was acceptable to discuss such unpleasant matters in front of a lady. "There have been earthquakes lately throughout the area —"

"Bad?" she interrupted anxiously.

"A little stronger than the usual rumblings, Your Highness, but thankfully, there have only been a handful of fatalities. The aftershocks continue. I'm sure you'll feel them. I dispatched a goodly number of my Marines to help sort out the towns that were hardest hit."

"Thank you for lending assistance," Sophia murmured. "I'm sure with so many of our buildings already damaged by war, one good shake could bring down more of these structures than might appear at first to be at risk."

"Just so. Fortunately, on the whole, you Greeks have a talent for building to withstand the test of time," Blake said with a respectful smile.

Sophia gave him a grateful look.

"Well, considering that Ali Pasha seems to be the one behind all this," Gabriel resumed in a businesslike tone, "it might be a fine time to parade the first-rates along his coastline for a show of strength. That should help remind the Terrible Turk to keep to his side of the water."

"Capital idea," Blake agreed, looking outraged on Sophia's behalf. "I will send a summons to them at once. They should be able to get here within a few days. In the meantime, we've got about ten second- and third-rates on hand in case of any unpleasantness."

"Excellent," Gabriel murmured, nodding.

"Are we sure the big gunships can make it through the narrows?" Sophia asked in a more cautious tone.

Commander Blake seemed impressed by her sensible question. "They'll not have much room to maneuver, Your Highness, but there is a deep, narrow channel they can sail through without running aground. With all my heart, ma'am, I hope you were not harmed in your ordeal."

"Colonel Knight executed a magnificent rescue," she murmured with a pensive smile.

"The princess is too modest. She handled herself with superb self-possession," Gabriel countered, returning the compliment. "Her Highness has been well trained from childhood to protect herself. Marksmanship, knife combat. Trust me," he added with a proud half smile, "they'll not get the best of this one."

Commander Blake raised a brow and glanced discreetly from one to the other. "I see."

Something in his tone made Gabriel drop his gaze and suddenly wonder if he had said too much.

Sophia cleared her throat in a delicate fashion and quickly changed the subject. "What is the disposition of my people at this time, sir?"

Blake hesitated politely. "I daresay that all are very eager to see you."

"Hm," she replied, folding her arms across her chest with a wry smile. "Please, Commander, feel free to speak as plainly to me as you would to a man. Have they been very unruly for you?"

"Well, Your Highness —"

"A simple ma'am will do, Commander."

He nodded. "To tell you the truth, ma'am, lately, they've been at each other's throats. Setting fire to each other's farms, blowing up each other's fishing boats, insulting each other's ancestors, and generally causing a riot, here, there, and everywhere. As soon as I send off my men to go and calm things down in one quarter, some wild disruption breaks out on the opposite end of the island. And then, as often as not, when my lads arrive, they are greeted with thrown rocks and curses."

"Oh dear, oh dear," Sophia said with a sigh. "It seems I have my work cut out for me."

"Indeed."

"This can't all be coming from them," Gabriel said with a frown. "No, I fear our friends are doing their best to stir things up. Divide and conquer. It couldn't be more plain. It's what I'd do if I were them."

"Well, it isn't going to work," Sophia said in a hard tone. She rose from her chair. "Their dirty tricks will never intimidate me. Nor will I let them intimidate my people. I'll want a tour of my realm at the first opportunity. I want to see my countrymen face to face. I am sure they still doubt me, being that I am . . . not one of my brothers. But when they look in my eyes, they will know that I will fight for them as hard as Giorgios or Kristos would have done. Or even Father himself."

"A tour?" While Gabriel admired her spirit, he did not like the sound of that one bit. "There are people trying to kill you."

"We all have our burdens to bear. You will do your job and I will do mine, oui?"

He flinched as though she had slapped him and turned away from her cool stare.

"I, er, can understand the colonel's position, ma'am," Blake said gingerly. "Taking you out to meet your people at a time like this does seem as though it would pose a great risk to your security."

"Especially since we don't yet know where the Order of the Scorpion is lurking," Gabriel added through gritted teeth.

"No matter," she answered in a polite tone of ice. "I have full confidence that you clever English gentlemen will know how to protect me. My people need me, and this is my will."

She walked out and left her two "clever Englishmen" standing there, exchanging a glance of chagrin.

"Just so I know — is she always like this?" Blake asked barely audibly.

"Just be glad she didn't take out her knife," he muttered.

Meanwhile, in the next room, Sophia had just been reunited with His Beatitude, Father Nectarios, the Archbishop of Kavros. As Gabriel and Commander Blake joined the pair, they found the old man teary-eyed before her, lowering himself down onto one stiff knee to kiss her ring.

That was the first moment that it all became truly real to Gabriel. She really was a princess, soon to be a queen. And he was still a commoner. How could he have ever thought . . . ?

He lowered his head in pain, but it was not his solar plexus that hurt anymore. The ache was a little higher now, right around the region of his heart.

While Sophia reminisced with her family's spiritual adviser, giving *him* the cold shoulder, Blake dispatched a few fast boats to find and bear messages to three of the formidable first-rates, summoning them back to Kavros with orders to travel through the straits.

Then, since her Greek bodyguards were scattered on their diverse missions, Blake assembled a company of Marines to escort Her Highness up to the hilltop villa that had once been home to the royal family.

Father Nectarios got into the carriage to lend her a little moral support for the abandoned, empty home she had to face. Gabriel reminded Blake to keep a weather eye out for any of her Greek bodyguards returning, especially Timo and Niko, who would be coming soon, God willing, with information on the whereabouts of Sheik Suleiman and his throng of followers. If their location was in Albania, then there was a chance they would never see their two brave scouts alive again. The Terrible Turk did terrible things to spies who were caught in his country.

God keep them, Gabriel thought.

Then they left the naval base for the drive up to the palace, and everywhere they passed, people stopped and looked and pointed in amazement. Word of her arrival traveled like wildfire over the dry Greek hills.

At length, they arrived at the palace, which had been locked up tight for many years. Gabriel ached for Sophia as he watched her glancing around at the lonely rooms with their rounded arches, broken windows, and empty marble floors. He longed to go to her and take her into his arms, but then again, every Marine watching over her probably felt the same. He scowled in their direction, but damn it, this instinctual possessiveness had no point. How could she ever really be his?

As Sophia walked ahead into the once grand, now empty throne room, Gabriel could hear a growing, chanting clamor coming from somewhere outside.

Father Nectarios followed her as she grasped the pair of double doors at the end of the room and slowly opened them. She paused. Staring, Gabriel drifted after her. Then Sophia stepped out cautiously through the doors onto an ornate balcony overlooking some open space below, a square or something. Gabriel could not see it too well, for he hung back at the doorway, remembering his place — a few steps behind her at best.

"I think that's where King Constantine used to address the people," Blake whispered.

As she walked out ahead toward the railing with its chipped gilding, Gabriel saw her hesitate, glancing down at her clothes with a flicker of worry that her beige French traveling gown was quite ordinary. No royal robes or jewels adorned her yet. But then, in profile, he saw her lovely face harden, and his heart clenched as she seemed to remind herself that it was not the outer trappings that had ever made a queen.

No, it was something in the eyes, something in the way she moved. And Sophia had it. By God, she did.

He held his breath as she advanced out to the balcony and claimed it for her own, resting her hands on the dusty railing and surveying the crowd with a look of determination. It veiled whatever fear she might have felt.

He felt tears of sheer love for her fill his eyes. He blinked them away before anyone saw. After all, he was just the bodyguard. But watching her from a few steps behind, his heart in his throat, he had no idea what she was going to say. He doubted she knew.

Only one thing was clear: The moment of her destiny had come, and now he, right along with the disorderly crowd that had gathered to see her, waited on tenterhooks to hear her very first address.

"People of Kavros!" she yelled more fiercely than even she seemed to have expected. "I am Sophia, daughter of Constantine!"

They fell silent at her introduction, waiting to hear what she had to say.

"Many years ago, we were parted. You have suffered — I know the pains that have been visited upon you. I suffered with you from a distance as a child. You know the losses I have endured, as I know yours.

"Our enemies cut down my father, your king. They cut down his firstborn, Prince Giorgios. And when my brother, Prince Kristos, would have taken their place, they killed him, too." Her somber words carried out over the crowd as she swept them with her gaze. "When I prevailed upon our British friends to give the throne to me so that I could serve you, our enemies also tried to destroy me. But they have *failed!*" she roared.

The throng surged, screaming back at her, cheering her ferocity.

Gabriel felt chills run down his spine.

The people stared up at her, quieting when she held up her hand. They seemed awed by some indefinable note in her voice as she continued.

"They are trying to tear us apart," she explained in a strong tone, pushing her blowing hair out of her face. "To tear *you* apart. My people, don't let them. We are one nation. I beg you —" she started, then stopped. "No," she said as if to herself, "I *command* you as your rightful queen to keep the peace, obey the law, and stop attacking each other. Justice will be done."

Skeptical murmurs now buzzed through

the crowd.

"You must be patient," she continued. "Have a little faith. Now that we are together once again, our country can begin to heal. Help is coming. Many new resources are on their way from those who have pledged their help. All I ask is the chance to prove to you that you can trust me to keep my word. And with your prayers, after all you have endured, we shall prevail!" she promised in a stern shout.

When she came back inside amid a cloud of cheers rising from the balcony beyond, she was trembling and pale.

Gabriel stared at her in wonder.

Father Nectarios had the presence of mind to pull a chair over for her to sit on. Clearly shaken, she mumbled her thanks.

"Magnificent, my dear. Simply splendid," the old man murmured. "Neither of your brothers could have done better."

She rested her left elbow on the chair's arm and bowed her head, her forehead leaning on her fingertips. She dismissed them all with an agitated wave of her hand. "Leave me."

They did, reverently obeying. A whole entourage had somehow accrued between their exit from the base to their arrival at the palace. Gabriel barely knew, himself, where all these people had come from. Priests, soldiers, advisers, and courtiers all retreated from the grand saloon, but for his part, he hesitated, certain that she was suffering in her heart.

"Even me?" he asked softly, so proud of her that he could burst and eager to lend her his comfort and strength.

But she looked at him coldly. "Especially you."

A country could not die. It could be maimed, partitioned, sold off, invaded, but few countries ever truly perished, Sophia thought. That was why she had once decided to give her heart only to Kavros. That neat safety had once been her whole philosophy of love.

Now she had met her new "lover." She had addressed her people today. She hoped she had made a good first impression. Tomorrow, she would have her tour.

Unfortunately, she now knew that this love would never be enough to satisfy her. Only Gabriel Knight knew how to do that. As she lay awake that night in her royal chamber, listening to the muffled roar of the distant surf hitting the rocks, everything in her yearned to go to him.

Wanted to go to him.

Refused to go to him.

Going anywhere near him would only make the pain worse when he deserted her to carry out his destiny.

Alas, as big a fool as Cleopatra for her handsome soldier, in the end, Sophia could not stop herself.

Not when any day with him could be her last.

Gabriel was in bed when she appeared in the doorway dressed in a white chemise. She came to him in silence with her dark hair spilling all around her shoulders.

He moved over a few inches to make room for her and pulled back the covers for her to join him. But instead of sliding in beside him, she climbed on top of him and without so much as a greeting, claimed his mouth in a deep, aggressive kiss.

This was no ordinary seduction. She was as angry as hell at him, and still they could not stay away from each other. He felt they should probably talk, but it was clear that was not why she had come. He tried to stop her, grasping her arm gently, even as his blood caught fire with her smell, her softness. She ignored his subtle signal, driving her open mouth against his.

She was trembling. Whether from passion

or fury, he could not say, but his body responded to her nearness with helpless want, even as his heart sensed her churning, conflicted emotions. He shared them. He, too, had been lying awake with nothing but her on his mind. All he knew as he ran his hands down the cool, silky skin of her arms was that he was hers for the taking.

And take she did.

She grasped his already rigid cock like she knew that it belonged to her and simply claimed him, guiding him inside of her, straddling him as she had that night in the hotel. Gabriel's chest heaved as she had her way with him. He could not tear his lust-soaked stare off her. When he was deep inside her, she tipped her head back, staring up toward the ceiling, and gradually, as she savored him, all the anger seemed to leave her. He heard her sob.

Sorrow flooded him in answer.

He pulled her down into his embrace and held her in his arms.

"I can't —" she wrenched out.

"Shh," he whispered. He sought her mouth again and gave her the most exquisite kiss that he was capable of, a kiss he hoped could in some small part communicate all of his love for her, all of his yearning and devotion, for when it came to words, he did not possess the silver tongue to tell it all.

Sophia wrapped her arms around his neck and let him roll her gently onto her back. Then he made love to her slowly, sweetly, taking all the tender care with her that he should have on that savage night when she had given him her virginity.

She wept in his arms, tears spilling from her eyes as she reached her climax, arching under him. Gabriel kissed her throat again and again, his own eyes not entirely dry.

"I love you," he breathed.

She clutched him more tightly. "I'll always love you," she choked out in a trembling whisper.

But she did not stay the night. Having got what she came for, she left his bed, gliding away as silently as a ghost in her gown of white.

He reclined on his elbows, watching her, his body sated but still needing her near, his heart and mind a tangle of battling emotions.

She paused in the doorway and looked back at him over her shoulder, and for a long moment, just stood there, as though memorizing him.

Then she slipped out and pulled the door shut behind her.

He fell onto his back with a low exhalation, covered his eyes with his arm, and tried to quiet the thunderous pounding of his half broken heart.

He had a feeling, this time, she would not be back.

CHAPTER
TWENTY-TWO

The next day, Sophia went out to tour the country that she was to rule. A bevy of her father's loyal advisers accompanied her, including Archbishop Nectarios, and a wall of heavily armed Royal Marines conducted her from place to place. Gabriel was there, scanning the crowd continuously; she knew that he took note of a few suspicious-looking faces in the crowd, strangers skulking along the background of the throngs that gathered wherever she went. But she ignored her lurking enemies and let him deal with that.

Her sole mission was to extend her love and service to her people, meeting them face to face with a familiarity that her father would never have dreamed of; listening respectfully as they aired their grievances and giving them the reassurance they had so long craved, that help for their plight was on the way. She walked among them, shaking hands with the elderly, receiving flowers from the children, surveying the damage from wars and from the latest round of minor earthquakes. Indeed the ground shook a little while they were traveling in between towns. By the evening, as her whole contingent returned to the palace, she was beyond exhausted. It was a wonderful, scary, exhausting day.

Maybe it was the sun that had made her so tired, she thought. Maybe the strain of it all. Or maybe she was carrying Gabriel's child.

Back at the palace, she walked in wondering if there would be time for a nap before dinner, but to her amazement, Timo and Niko were there waiting for her.

She hugged them tightly, moved to see her friends and longtime guards again. But despite their thanks to God to find each other safe and their warm congratulations on her accession to power, both men were grim and all business, eager to meet with Gabriel, for they had brought the information he had been waiting for.

The three of them withdrew into the adjoining room and conferred for a moment, but Sophia did not intend to be left out. She went in, bringing Father Nectarios with her.

Gabriel likewise beckoned in Commander Blake, who had been invited to dinner. He shut the door and turned to Timo with a dark look. "What did you learn?"

"The audacious bastards are right under our noses — er, sorry, Father."

The priest gestured forgivingly.

"They're hiding up in the old medieval fort at Agnos."

"Agnos! But it's practically a ruin," Sophia said.

"What's Agnos?" Gabriel clipped out.

"One of our smallest islands out on the fringe of the chain," Sophia replied. "It's barely inhabitable, but there's an ancient fort there originally built for keeping out the Turks."

"How fitting."

"No doubt the location has helped them to go unnoticed by my ships," Commander Blake said with a scowl. "I feel terrible about this."

"Don't worry, Commander. You could not have known. These men know exactly what they're doing. They are not common fighters, but the trained former bodyguards of the Ottoman Sultan himself."

"Bodyguards who betrayed him," Gabriel specified.

"Well, listen to this," Timo said with a

grim smile. "Sheik Suleiman himself is there. Their leader."

"You saw him?"

"I saw an imam preaching to his followers," Niko affirmed. "Bloody religious zealots — er, no offense, Father."

Archbishop Nectarios frowned.

"If we could grab Sheik Suleiman," Gabriel said, "we could use him for a bargaining chip. Offer to hand him over to Sultan Mahmud in exchange for him taking stringent action to rein in Ali Pasha."

"By stringent action, do you mean cutting off his head?" Timo asked pleasantly.

"That is what I would recommend," Niko agreed.

"No doubt Mahmud will be tempted to do just that when he hears that Ali Pasha has been teaming up with the bleeders who betrayed him," Gabriel murmured.

"How many of them are there?" Commander Blake inquired.

"By our count, some two hundred."

"Two hundred?" Sophia breathed. "How are fifty Marines and you three going to overcome two hundred Janissary warriors?"

"By stealth, my dear, and a great many explosives," Gabriel said. "How are your powder stores, Commander?"

"Well stocked with whatever you could

want, Colonel."

"Black powder?"

"Now you're talking," Niko said with a grin.

"Fifty barrels, easily. Crates of mines, as well."

"That should do the trick."

"Gabriel, what exactly do you mean to do?" Sophia asked, barely noticing how she had slipped and used his first name in front of the others.

"Blow the place up with the lot of them inside it, I should think."

"Capital notion," Blake joined in.

"That fort will not be easy to approach," Timo warned. "It's on a steep rock hilltop with very little cover going up. No matter what we do, they're going to see us coming."

"Well, the first-rates aren't here yet, but our smaller ships can give us cover."

"Good, but tell them to hang back," Gabriel replied. "They've got the numbers and the high ground. The element of surprise may be our only advantage when we spring the attack."

"When will that be?" Sophia breathed, her heart pounding.

"Soon. We've got to hit them hard before they even know it's coming."

"We're ready," Timo said eagerly.

"Commander, do you think it can be organized to launch the attack before dawn?" Gabriel asked.

"I don't see why not."

"Maybe you should wait until the first-rates come," Sophia said with the feeling that she was swimming against the tide in this. "There'll be more guns and many more men on those ships to help you fight."

"No," Gabriel said gently, though his eyes were flinty-hard. "Now that you've come, they're going to be expecting something. By the time the first-rates get here, our best opportunity will have already passed."

She dropped her gaze; Father Nectarios noticed her hurt look and glanced at her in concern.

"Well, then, gentlemen, Godspeed," she murmured. "If you will excuse me."

They bowed as she took leave of them and withdrew to her chamber — as if she could escape the parting that was about to descend on her like the hounds of hell.

But it was inescapable.

Trembling, she sat on the edge of her bed and waited for Gabriel to come, with a sense of impending doom.

All too soon, he slipped into her chamber, closing the door behind him with barely a sound. She rose and drew in her breath when she saw him all dressed in black for his mission like he had been that night on the mountain, armed to the teeth once more.

She wanted to back away from him when he came toward her, as if her refusal to tell him good-bye could stop him from going. Her heart pounded and her stomach tied itself up in knots as he rested his hands on her shoulders and gazed tenderly into her eyes.

No words came.

Sophia threw her arms around him, ignoring various holsters and sheaths, and hugged him with all her might. Squeezing her eyes shut, she fought back tears and the horrifying awareness of the violence ahead and the very stark fact that she might never see her man again.

But if this was good-bye, then her parting gift to him would be her courage. If she never saw him again, the last image of her that she wanted him to take away was one of strength. She refused to cry.

She had given her heart to a warrior and now the moment had come to prove herself worthy of his sacrifice and his gallantry.

Gabriel would not flinch before his duty, after all; to honor him, she would do the same, even if the soul in her was dying. A wave of pain swept through her as she held him, like a cruel and blasphemous inversion of the pleasure they had shared.

She touched his hair, his shoulders, his arms. She lifted his hand to her lips and kissed it lovingly, then looked into his blue, blue eyes with the threat of tears in her own. She willed them back and cupped his hard, beautiful face for a moment.

"I will always love you," she whispered calmly. "Always. And if there's a child, I will tell him — everything about you."

"Princess." He crushed her to him and claimed her mouth. His kiss seared her very soul with his fiery passion. When he ended it, he lowered himself slowly to his knees and kissed her belly for a long moment, his eyes closed.

Sophia caressed his raven hair.

He rose again and took her gently into his arms, grazing his lips along her forehead with a low, burning vow. "I will come back to you."

She trembled. *God, please.* But though it took every drop of royal blood in her veins to do so, she held on to her composure.

"I will be here," she replied with her chin held high.

"You are so beautiful," he whispered with

complete understanding of her gift glimmering in his eyes.

"Thank you, my darling, for what you're about to do," she said calmly, and then she did the hardest thing she had ever done in her twenty-one years.

She let him go.

As she stepped back, he bowed his head and brought both of her hands to his lips. He kissed them, looked one last time into her eyes, and then let her hands slide free of his light hold.

His cobalt stare burned into her heart forever.

Neither of them could speak, for the only word to be said, the one that neither could bear to say, was good-bye.

He took a deep breath, pivoted, and marched out with the grim, bristling air of a man on a mission.

A man with no fear of death.

That was what scared her. He should fear it. He should be careful. But he never would.

The moment the door had closed, Sophia crumbled.

Sinking to the floor, she put her head in her hands and wept.

Hours later, in absolute silence the long-boats cut through the waves approaching the fortress island of Agnos, ten heavily armed men and several barrels of black powder to a boat. Navigating each light, fast craft were some of Kavros's ablest seamen.

Stealth was key.

Approaching the island from different directions like the five points of a star, they were setting up a coordinated attack. As soon as they landed, each jumped lightly out of the boats into the knee-deep water. Hefting the barrels on their backs, they sped the powder into place, rolling out the long fuse cords.

No doubt sentries were posted. They worked in total darkness to avoid being seen. The jagged outline of the fort loomed against the indigo sky.

With the explosives in place, they took up their positions for the second phase of their attack. Boulders on the beachhead would make fine cover for the rifle attack. Lastly, they would charge the fort itself and kill anyone who hadn't been shot or blown up already.

As for the sheik himself, they wanted him alive.

Gabriel waited for his men to signal they were ready. He glanced over his shoulder toward the sea, his mood keyed up. Though it was too dark to spy the smaller ships that

Commander Blake had ordered to give them cover, he knew they were there. *Good man, Blake.*

Gabriel had also decided to leave Timo back at the palace to guard Sophia. Of course, the hairy fellow had been disappointed to miss out on the fun, but if things went wrong, Gabriel had wanted to leave her with at least one man she knew she could trust completely. Whatever happened, he knew Timo would look after her.

Hang it all, but these Greeks had grown on him, he thought. Then the long-awaited signal came.

Everyone was ready.

He nodded to his team and then struck the flint.

The spark he used to light the fuse cord was the first warning the Janissaries even had that they were there.

Gabriel smiled darkly as the flame caught and began to race along the wire toward the stacked barrels of explosives.

"Morning, boys," he murmured.

Then the men covered their ears and looked away as the first fiery crash tore through the night.

Sophia had tried to stay up waiting for news of the battle, but worn out from grief and from sheer exhaustion after the day's tour among her people, she had fallen asleep in her clothes a couple of hours before dawn.

Now, however, deep reverberations in the distance found their way into her sleep and shook her awake. Not thunder, not the deep rumble of an earthquake, but the sounds of battle.

It was happening. It had begun.

She opened her eyes and lifted her head from her pillow. How many hours had passed? she wondered, but she did not wait to find out. The new day was only at first light as she jumped out of bed, rushed across the room to the balcony, grabbing her trusty knapsack along the way.

With shaking hands, she took out her folding telescope and tried to locate Agnos from her balcony. She struggled to hold the spyglass steady despite her frightened trembling and searched the predawn sky until she saw black smoke rising in the distance. She gasped when an orange explosion flared out, so small with the miles between.

Oh, Gabriel.

Her heart thumping, she scanned the horizon for further clues about what was happening around Agnos. Blast, it was too far to make out much. Slowly sweeping the whole area with her telescope, she stopped in astonishment, suddenly spotting the first-rates.

Good God, they must've gotten the message faster than Commander Blake had realized. They were already sailing toward the strait in a massive line like lumbering Leviathans. Before long, they would enter the narrow channel and pass by Ali Pasha's coast, reminding him, as ordered, of their protection of Kavros.

At first, Sophia was heartened to see them. With Gabriel's attack already under way, this was most felicitous timing. Their arrival was not too soon to tip off the enemy that something was afoot, and indeed, at this point, Gabriel's lesser forces, for all their courage, surely needed whatever fresh help they could get.

But then — studying the scene before her, a bit of movement on one of the rocky outcroppings caught her eye.

Puzzled, she focused the telescope on the tall, jagged clump of rock and suddenly gasped to spot a dark-skinned man in position there — with a carronade!

Bewildered, she trained her spyglass on another of the seemingly uninhabited rocks. And again, she saw another turbaned foreigner lying in wait with a fat-barreled, short-range artillery piece.

And another, stationed on yet another cluster of rocks. As the sun made its first foray over the horizon, it glimmered over the mighty masts of the approaching British first-rates, and illumined several more of the enemy's unobtrusive positions.

Chills ran down Sophia's spine, and as she lowered her spyglass from her, it all came clear.

It's a trap.

This is exactly what they want us to do. They're going to destroy the ships.

The fiends were lying in wait with their portable cannons, positioned to blast the mighty first-rates in the one spot where every ship was most vulnerable: its unprotected stern.

Any attack from the side was useless and would be met with a devastating broadside from the vessel's full arsenal of guns; the bow, too, was well protected. But the stern was every ship's Achilles' heel.

All they had to do was time it right, let the ships pass to the fore and then hit them from behind.

With the first-rates crippled, foundered in the strait, Kavros's defenses would be severely compromised.

Then the Order of the Scorpion could

take the island.

Gabriel's dire warning of the greater threat echoed in her ears. Not just Kavros was in danger. Those first-rates kept the peace throughout the Mediterranean.

Oh, God. Her heart in her throat, she realized she had to keep those warships out of the strait! They had to be warned to stay back immediately. But how?

On the beach below the palace, the fishermen were already out and stirring, readying their boats for the morning's catch. Her eyes narrowed as her gaze homed in on them. Why, if that was the only navy that Kavros could boast of its own, then it was hers to lead.

The next thing she knew, she was running out of her room.

"Timo, wake up! Come with me!" Her trusty guard was seated on a chair outside her chamber door. She shook him back to wakefulness but did not wait for him, dashing off and rushing through the palace with a few sleepy attendants scrambling after her.

He leapt up, still groggy, and came bounding after her. "What's going on?"

"The first-rates have come! We've got to keep those ships out of the narrows! Hurry up!" Tearing out of the palace, she went barreling down to the water.

The atmosphere was tense down on the slowly lightening beach. The fishermen could hear the distant cannon-fire coming from the direction of Agnos and did not know what to make of it.

When Sophia came tearing down into their midst, calling to them, they turned and looked at her suspiciously, unaware of who she was.

"Fishermen of Kavros! To your boats! Your country needs you!"

They turned and looked at her in question, not quite sure who this young woman yelling at them was.

Timo came rushing after her.

"Will you take me aboard?" she cried, racing over to the shaggy captain of the largest boat. She stared eagerly at him, out of breath.

"Your Highness!" Timo exclaimed, but he could not stop her as she zipped up the ladder and jumped onto the boat.

"Highness?" the men murmured. "It's the princess?"

"Indeed, it is!" she cried, grabbing hold of a line and jumping up onto the rails. She addressed them at the top of her lungs. "And I implore your service now! We must into the straits at once!"

"Princess — what is going on?" the captain exclaimed.

"The British ships are coming into the narrows, and if they advance much farther, they'll be destroyed! We can't let that happen! They are our allies, and if they're destroyed, they can't protect our country. It's a trap! Don't you see? Oh, there's no time to explain! Are you with me or not?"

They hesitated, probably unsure if she was a madwoman.

"Don't you hear the guns?" she cried with an angry, sweeping gesture toward the sea.

"Is it really the princess?" someone yelled.

"Can't you tell?" Timo retorted loudly.

"Hurry, for the sake of your country!" Sophia shouted. "Get this boat moving! Please!"

"Your Highness, what do you want us to do?" asked the captain of the boat that she had commandeered.

"Follow me!" she shouted, pointing passionately toward the straits.

And to her sublime amazement . . . they did.

The men flooded into their boats with a hearty cheer.

Moments later, they were yanking up anchors, letting out sails, speeding their vessels into the current.

Sophia's fishing-boat captain led the way.

The long-familiar crews were shouting back and forth to each other as they fanned out across the strait, a ragtag flotilla forming a little line across the narrows, and advancing bravely toward the mighty first-rates.

Hurry, she thought, desperate to ward the ships off. She only prayed the first-rates would not interpret their approach as threatening and blow them all out of the water.

Meanwhile, in the distance, the guns still roared.

Her heart pounded as they neared the hidden enemy positions. The fishermen realized that something was afoot, of course, but had not noticed the concealed men on the rocks.

Sophia knew that the warships were the enemy's prime targets, not them. Still, she hoped these Scorpion blackguards did not change their minds about that. She knew she was playing roulette with the fishermen's lives, but Leon had taught her to know that, sometimes, that's what a leader had to do. Decisions made for the fate of many were not easy.

She prayed that the Janissaries waiting with their artillery would think nothing of the approaching fishing boats. Every day, after all, the Greek sailors went out to make their living from the sea, just as they had done for thousands of years.

It was a tense sail out into the wind, but tension turned to heart-thumping dread as they neared the massive gunships, closer and closer, neither side backing down.

Stopping those big ships would be a test of nerves, but she had to do it to save them. As they neared, British voices shouted to them to move out of the way, but she yelled back, "Come no farther!"

"Stand!" she yelled at the fishermen when some of them started to shout that they were going to have a collision.

More cries from the towering deck of the first gunship in the row of three echoed through the dawn. Her heart pounded, but not until the gunships loomed over them did she quite believe they had managed to slow their pace to a crawl.

Furious heads peered over the side of the rails at them. "What is the meaning of this? We'll give you fifteen minutes to get out of the way, and if you don't move —"

"Wait! You don't understand! We are trying to help you!" Holding her ground on the fishing-boat's prow, she threw her head back and answered them. "You must not come into the straits! A trap has been laid for you there! Commander Blake did not know it! Come no farther or your ships will be destroyed!"

"Who are you?" the officer demanded.

"I am Princess Sophia of Kavros!"

A pause followed. She winced, fearing they'd think she was mad to claim such a thing. But the answer surprised her.

"Well, dash my wig, yes, you are."

She furrowed her brow, staring up at the silhouetted officer. All she could see was the outline of a head. "Do I know you, sir?" she yelled up, noting the sudden alteration in his tone of voice.

"No, but I saw you once, Highness, at a ball in London. Wanted to ask you to dance, but I didn't dare." He laughed modestly. "At your service, Madam. I am the first mate of this vessel."

"Well, first mate of this vessel, I will certainly owe you a dance if you aim your guns at those rocks there, where our enemies have set up an ambush for you."

"Have they, indeed?"

"See for yourself!"

In the brightening light of morning, she could see the first mate pull out his folding telescope and train its lens upon the boulders where those blackguards were hiding.

"Well," he said with a very British determination. "Very decent of you to warn us, Princess."

"Fire at will, sir, as soon as we're out of your way."

"No worries, we'll fire over your heads."

"They'll scare away all the fish," her boat's captain grumbled.

Sophia frowned at him, then looked back at the first mate. "Please dispatch whatever men you can spare to reinforce the Marines at Agnos. That is where the fighting is under way even as we speak."

"With pleasure, Highness. Do you care to come aboard?"

"No, sir. I am headed to Agnos now myself."

"You are?" the fishing captain exclaimed indignantly.

She turned to him and gently teased him into complying. "Why, yes! You're not afraid, are you? I'm not, and I'm just a girl."

"Well, if you put it that way," the fishing captain muttered while some of his crew laughed. "Make sail for Agnos!"

The first-rates did the same.

Sophia flashed a dangerous smile and moved toward the bow, eager to see how Gabriel's battle was progressing.

Covered in sweat, flecked with blood, and streaked with the grime of black powder, Gabriel had fought his way into the fortress and now, with the Marines engaging the Jan-issaries who were left, he was hunting Sheik Suleiman with his trusty carbine.

Panting with exertion, he searched the shattered stone rooms inside the ancient fort, pivoting past one blown-out stone doorway after another. *Where the hell had he gone?*

Just a moment ago, he had had the tall, lanky Arab in his sights, but had lost him in the fray. The imam had disappeared amid the clouds of drifting smoke. He seemed to have some firm destination in mind.

Gabriel was fairly sure the wily blackguard was trying to make an escape, never mind the fact he'd be leaving his embattled followers in the dust.

If he could not catch him, Gabriel was prepared to kill him. They could not afford to let him get away merely to corrupt more men with his festering hatred, spawn more enemies who cared only for power disguised as jihad.

Maneuvering around another corner, he stepped into what remained of a medieval corridor and spotted the sheik across the open gallery.

"Suleiman!"

The sheik whirled around and brought up his rifle, firing at Gabriel. He threw himself back against the wall, narrowly darting out of the bullet's path, but a split second later, he returned fire with his carbine, hitting Suleiman in the leg as he tried to run away.

The sheik let out a yell and clutched his bleeding leg. Limping fast, he disappeared out the stone doorway. Gabriel didn't waste time reloading but whipped out his cavalry saber and raced after him.

When he reached the hollow doorway, he saw that it dropped away into a steep flight of exterior stairs with no rail; they were carved right into the limestone, weathered smooth. The stairs hugged the fortress wall as they descended sharply, but with no hand-rail on the right they fell away in a drop-off into the bright jade water. At the bottom of the stairs, a simple one-man craft was waiting.

"Damn you," Gabriel growled. *You're not getting away.*

Sheik Suleiman hobbled in rapid motion down the flight of stairs, one hand braced against the fortress wall, the other clutching his hurt leg.

Gabriel started down after him immediately, determined to see the bastard brought to justice. These stairs were treacherous, but in a few seconds, he would have him cornered.

He was closing in on him when the quake struck.

The earth began shaking.

Damn it! Gabriel fell back against the wall, steadying himself. Lower down the stairs, the sheik did the same.

Then a horrible cracking noise rent the air. He looked up in horror as a chunk of the old fortress wall high above them sagged, teetered, broke off, and came crashing down.

Gabriel flattened himself back against the part of the wall that still held. The broken section fell before his eyes, plunging into the water with a tremendous splash that rose so high, the water sprayed him in the face.

The largest piece was gone, but more of the wall was still crumbling away in the tremors. Smaller pieces. Dust.

This is not good.

Heart pounding, Gabriel held out his hand and lowered his center of gravity, trying to balance himself on that precipice as the shaking continued. It was almost as if the island were trying deliberately to buck him off into the sea.

He heard a garbled shout from below as Suleiman suddenly slipped and tumbled off the side of the stairs. He hung there for a moment by his hands.

The bearded man sent Gabriel a wild look, but before he could think to do anything in response, a slab of rock about the size of a tombstone came crashing down and smashed into the sheik, ripping him away from the wall.

Gabriel glanced down in shock as the sheik disappeared under the water's surface, the boulder on top of him. He breathed an expletive and looked up again at the wall.

It was a split decision, but that wall was still deteriorating, and with the violent shaking still causing it to crumble, he knew that he had to jump clear of it all before the rest came down.

Sliding his back up the wall so that he was standing at his full height once more, he glanced out desperately at the water.

Some fishing boats approaching caught his eye. Kavros locals no doubt, come to crane their necks at the battle.

Bloody hell.

"Stay back!" he yelled at them, but the clamor of falling rock was too loud.

When another chunk of stone plunged down past him, Gabriel knew his time was running out. He gathered himself, still clutching his cavalry saber; then he pushed out away from the wall with a sudden heave, taking as much of a running step as possible and leaping out as far into the blue as he could launch his body.

Down and down he plunged, his arms up over his head. Feet first, he was nearly at the water when a fist of rock about the size of a grapefruit hit him in the back of the head and knocked him cold.

Sophia screamed when she saw him fall.

Timo shouted, too, standing at the rails with her.

With a wild look around, her quick-thinking bodyguard jumped into one of the jollyboats and gestured frantically to the crew to lower him down.

When Sophia climbed into the boat with him, Timo gave her a startled look. He started to protest, but when she stared fiercely into his eyes, understanding dawned. He nodded. "Very well. Let's go get him," he murmured grimly as the boat descended on its clattering chains down to the water.

They each unhooked their end as soon as the rocking rowboat was set down among the waves. Then they both grabbed a pair of oars and worked together to get to Gabriel before it was too late.

■ ■ ■ ■

Gabriel was falling, floating down through the water, flung into another realm, the mystic blue. Light rays penetrated deep into the azure waves as he went sinking slowly, weighted down by all of the weapons he carried.

His body's instincts maintained enough dim awareness to preserve his breath, but his mind had been knocked into a twilight state.

His cavalry saber, lost from his grip, went falling and falling down into the deep.

Bubbles rose up past him, sparkling like tiny pearls. Peaceful silence filtered through the waving seaweed after all the deafening noise and strife of battle, the screams, the guns' report.

Fish of every shape and color went shimmering past him about their business. Farther below, columns of lost temples stood at the bottom of the sea; a marble Athena wore corals for a crown.

Still floating, his whole body gone limp, Gabriel dreamed that he opened his eyes and saw a light. He knew this light. He stared at it serenely, so soft and pure and white. He only knew that in its presence, everything was fine.

Where am I? he whispered.

You know this place, it replied.

Am I dead? But I can't be. He panicked, struggling. *I need to go back!*

Last time, you wanted to stay, it reminded him gently.

No, it's all changed now. Please — let me go back. Is my debt not paid?

Gabriel. The soundless voice drew him nearer. *There never was a debt, my son. There is only Love.*

That's why I must go back. For love's sake. Please, she needs me.

Behind the light, a little angel shape went flitting past, light as air.

She's not the only one, the voice replied. He could feel it smiling.

Gabriel stared in astonishment, trying to see the bubbly little spirit. *You mean — ?*

Your destiny isn't fulfilled yet. Go back, my boy. Your life is waiting. We won't be seeing you here for a very long time . . .

He felt a pull on his arms but did not yet have command of his body. The falling sensation was being reversed. This time he was going up.

"Please wake up, come back to me! God, do not take him from me!" As if from a distance, he could hear Sophia screaming, sobbing "Timo — do something! Gabriel, please don't leave me, darling. Please, I can't do this without you!"

Sophia shook him vehemently, pumping on his chest; he came slamming back to the world of the living with a violent cough.

His throat choked for air while his lungs seized up in protest at the large amount of salt water he had swallowed.

"Turn him over! Cough it out, Colonel. That's right, breathe!"

Timo was dripping wet like him, and now rolled him onto his side in the jollyboat. Gabriel was not sure where he was or what was going on, but his head hurt, and his lungs were on fire. He writhed as his body convulsed, ejecting the seawater from his chest. He coughed it up, his body racked with the effort.

Then he hung his head, wearily gasping for air.

Sophia sobbed.

"Am I dead?" he whispered, still a bit confused from the blow to his head.

"No, my love, you're safe now and very much alive." She gathered him into her arms, crying as she rocked him. He laid his head on her lap in exhaustion, then he noticed Timo looking on anxiously.

Feeling as weak as a newborn, Gabriel

summoned up the strength to speak. "Did you just save my life?"

"Something like that," Timo said. "I had help." He nodded at Sophia.

Gabriel followed his glance and stared at her as though seeing her for the first time.

Perhaps, in truth, he was. And she was a wonder to behold. The morning light glimmered in her hair, her skin glowed, and the bright spangles of pure heaven shone in her eyes.

He realized then that it was already here, all around them, the light, a million glistening pieces, like the sun's brilliance dancing on the water. Beautiful, inescapable. It always had been, and it always would be.

All you had to do was look.

"You silly man," Sophia whispered in a shaky voice, tugging him back to the mortal realm. "Don't you ever scare me like that again, do you understand?"

She was so wonderfully real, so solid and vibrant and warm. He found the strength to lift his arm, and reached up wearily to touch her face. "I love you," he replied, still in a bit of a daze. "Thanks . . . for saving me."

"Oh, Gabriel — I'm happy to return the favor," she choked out. Then she hugged him to her with tender protectiveness, cradling his head against her bosom.

It was the best place on earth for him. He was right where he belonged — fully alive at last in her arms, his destiny still waiting to be born.

EPILOGUE

The whole Knight family had arrived in Kavros for the week-long feast that began with Sophia's coronation and proceeded on to the royal wedding. Since winter had now descended on England, nearly three months having passed, no one was in a particular hurry to get back home.

They had waited just long enough to send word to Gabriel's favorite cousin, Lord Jack Knight and his wife, Eden, to arrive from the West Indies, but considering Sophia's pregnancy, it would not have been prudent to wait much longer than that.

Now they were married, the wedding bells having rung all over Kavros to celebrate their union. When the fishermen of Kavros had spread the word of Gabriel's heroism in leading the fight against the Order of the Scorpion — and how their tenacious princess had wept in despair, thinking she had lost him — the people of Kavros had embraced the Englishman as one of their own.

He had converted to the Greek Orthodox church, as required, and accepted the title of Prince Consort to Sophia's Queen.

This, of course, raised eyebrows all over Europe — so much for Gabriel's distinction as the one nonscandalous member of the Knight family. Perhaps some people thought that he was an adventurer on the make, and that she had been duped by a schemer, but neither of them cared what anyone thought, for they were happy. Their future and that of Kavros was wonderfully bright.

The Order of the Scorpion had been destroyed. Their leader, Sheik Suleiman, was dead, his bones pinned to the sea floor under a huge hunk of stone from the old fort that had crumbled away in the earthquake.

Though Ali Pasha had denied any involvement in the rebel Janissaries' scheme to overthrow Kavros, his overlord, Sultan Mahmud, was deeply displeased with the Terrible Turk and would be keeping a close eye on him for the foreseeable future.

Once the tide had turned, the changes needed on Kavros took place with startling speed. The money and resources promised by generous Britons at Sophia's Grecian Gala had arrived. Repairs were underway throughout the island chain.

With a great deal of patience and a little advice from Lord Griffith, Sophia managed to broker a truce between the warring factions who had been at each other's throats in recent years. She also held a joint meeting with the women from the feuding families to remind them of the important role they played in the home, and encouraged them to use their power to preserve peace among all parties for the good of their husbands and sons.

One of the first things she did as queen was to knight her loyal bodyguards — Timo, Yannis, Niko, Markos, and Kosta. It was her way of thanking them for their years of staunch service. For their part, the men had new concerns now that they had come home to Kavros. With a private nod from Sophia, they lent their support to the quietly growing efforts of patriots all over occupied Greece to begin to rise up against Ottoman rule. Again, Great Britain proved its friendship to her countrymen when the notorious English poet, Lord Byron, made the freedom of the Greeks a cause celebre and spoke of personally entering the fray.

Closer to home, the various members of the Knight family, while visiting Kavros, took an active part in improving life for the local citizens. Georgiana's wedding gift to Gabriel and Sophia was to found an English-style academy for girls. Lizzie and her husband, Lord Strathmore, wanted to help by having all the antiquities catalogued and protected for posterity as best they could. Between the earthquakes and damages inflicted by the war, many of the remnants of ancient Greece on Kavros were in jeopardy. Strathmore arranged to have a crew of classical scholars and antiquities experts brought in.

Indeed, these were exciting times for Kavros. The marriage of such a glamorous couple made it a place where all of European high society suddenly wanted to go.

Lord Alec Knight remarked in a rather offhand way, that it was a pity there was nowhere for the tourists to stay, and with a cavalier stroke of genius, he tossed out the notion that a Grand Hotel with a fine casino ought to be built so that visitors could sojourn in style; they could come for entertainment as well as to enjoy the fine climate. Hearing this, second-born Knight brother, Lord Jack, instantly seized upon the idea as an excellent investment opportunity, and began making arrangements at once to rent a stretch of beachfront land from the government. He and Robert went in on the project together — two brothers who once did not even speak to each other.

As for Gabriel's own brother, Derek's reaction to the outcome of all this was a sly sort of knowing amusement.

"That you should end up a prince, brother, does not surprise me at all," he had drawled, clapping Gabriel on his now royal back. "Hang me, you gave up all your money and rank and somehow ended up with a crown and country."

"Yes, but more important, I ended up with her," he had replied, nodding in Sophia's direction.

Derek had grinned at him. "Now you know."

As for Sophia, her new role as queen did not intimidate her half as much as she had feared it would, now that she had Gabriel to steady her and counsel her when she needed it. Life was so much nicer now that she did not worry anymore about people trying to kill her. No one seemed inclined to try these days, and with her husband on hand to protect her, those worries were long gone.

She noticed that his near-drowning that day at Agnos had affected him in a rather peculiar way. Ever since he had come back from his second brush with death, he wore a mysterious, knowing, little smile that both intrigued and perplexed her. He seemed to know something she did not.

The cobalt sparkle that she had glimpsed only occasionally in his eyes before that day was now there all the time. He seemed settled and at peace now, but of course, Gabriel was a man who needed to be needed. He found such fulfillment in his new life on Kavros because it wasn't just Sophia, but her people, who looked to him for wisdom and protection. She was not surprised at how easily he glided into his new role as her co-ruler.

A born leader, he had no trouble taking charge whenever he was needed, but he never made her feel as though he would encroach upon her authority as queen.

Each day, they went about their royal duties, but every evening without fail, they got away from it all by taking a slow, private stroll along the beach, much as they had at Perpignan, when Sophia had attempted to propose to him. This simple shared ritual gave them time to be just a man and a woman together, like they had been at the beginning, in Gabriel's farmhouse.

That was what she needed more than anything. These simple moments, serenaded by the lulling surf with her love by her side, kept her grounded and true to herself. Gabriel was her rock, and she, well, she kept his life interesting.

Barefoot in the sand, they walked off down the beach, hand in hand in the glowing light of sunset, soaking in the enchantment of each other's company, and laughing as they argued over what to name their child. . . .

The employees of Thorndike Press hope you have enjoyed this Large Print book. All our Thorndike and Wheeler Large Print titles are designed for easy reading, and all our books are made to last. Other Thorndike Press Large Print books are available at your library, through selected bookstores, or directly from us.

For information about titles, please call:
(800) 223-1244

or visit our Web site at:
http://gale.cengage.com/thorndike

To share your comments, please write:
Publisher
Thorndike Press
295 Kennedy Memorial Drive
Waterville, ME 04901